LIAR LI

Sarah Flint

About *Liar Liar*

A faithful dog lies wounded beside the mutilated
body of its owner.

A woman is discovered bound and gagged, dead in
her own bed.

Both are police officers.

Both have a red rose at their side… worryingly more
will follow…

Lies and accusations abound but who is behind the murders and why are the victims being targeted?

Charlie, Hunter and the team must find the killer targeting their own before another body is found.

To PC Keith Palmer and the many victims affected
by the
Westminster Bridge terror attack. I walked out from
the tube station
into the carnage on 22nd March 2017 and will
always remember the
courage of the wounded and the bravery of the
emergency services
who attended the scene.

You will not be forgotten.

Prologue

September 1969

The door slammed shut and heavy boots thumped slowly across the wooden floorboards. The woman started, her eyes dull with weary acceptance, her arms thrown up, indicating in panic that the child should run. But it was too late. His voice rang out, a low whistle at first, rising with each footfall to a crescendo, loud and spiteful, every word designed to incite terror.

'Ring a ring o' roses, a pocket full of posies, Atishoo, Atishoo.'

He stopped singing as he entered the room and gripped the woman tightly by her arms, forcing grubby nails deep into her skin, pulling her to her feet.

'Sing me the last line,' he demanded.

She shrank from his grasp, recoiling from the stench of beer on his breath, her body shaking uncontrollably. She despised every inch of him for what he was doing to her and their child. 'Please, not again. Please don't make me.'

The back of his hand slammed into her face, a stream of red springing immediately from her bloodied nose. 'I said, sing me the last line, bitch.' He raised his arm above her again and laughed. 'Now!'

The woman shrank even further, her eyes closed tight against what she knew was to follow. It happened every week. Her voice trembled with fear. '*We all fall down.*'

She dropped to the floor as his fist took the breath from her body and lay curled tightly in a ball on the boards, blood pooling under her face.

At the sound of his voice singing the words over again, her eyes shot open, fearfully scanning the room, resting finally on the small child hiding behind the armchair. Her eyes beseeched the child to stay hidden as the voice grew louder.

'*Ring a ring o' roses, a pocket full of posies.* Daddy's looking for you. Where are you, you little brat?' He lifted his leg and kicked the chair to one side, sneering with pleasure as the child started to whimper and sob. '*Atishoo, Atishoo.*' He raised his foot again, the heavy black boot underneath dark serge trousers poised above the child's trembling form. He started to laugh maniacally now, before throwing all his weight into the strike.

'*We all fall down.*'

Chapter 1

It was surprising how easy it had been to get in. He'd expected the security to be better; but then it was summer and people left windows unlocked and insecure, didn't they? Complacency was his accomplice every time. Just because the bungalow was remote it didn't mean it couldn't be accessed… and he'd rarely, if ever, failed. Leaving a window open just made his job easier.

As he reached through the small window with gloved hands and turned the handle of the larger window below, a waft of air freshener hit his nostrils. The aroma was fruity, citrus-scented, possibly orange. He wasn't very good at discerning nice smells. His senses recognised only the stench of decay or the disinfected corridors of medical or penal establishments.

Carefully he pulled the curtain back and peered in. The room was dark. A small, red fluorescent light pulsed out from a digital clock on a cabinet in the corner. It showed 03.32. Its tiny glow reflected against the screen of a large curved TV, the glint refracted at oblique angles across the pastel wall opposite.

In the past he would have taken the TV and anything else of value, but today he had a job to do, rules to follow.

He switched on a small torch and flashed it across the room, before climbing through the window and lowering himself down on to a thick dark, shag pile carpet, perfect for cushioning the sound of his trainers.

The room was decorated exquisitely, almost luxuriously. Every gadget was the latest, every ornament exclusive, every photo framed in gilt. No expense had been spared. The bitch who lived here was clearly on a good salary. The clock clicked on to 03.33, all the threes. Bingo! He heard her stir in the next room, the sound of a body turning on a mattress, a small cough, a sigh, then silence again, save for her slow, rhythmic breathing. He held his breath. The air was hot and heavy. Sweat dripped down his back.

Soon her breathing would get even slower, weaker. Soon it would stop all together, but not yet. She owed it to society. She was a taker. Now she would pay the price.

He saw the suitcases stacked neatly in the hallway as he made his way towards her. A rucksack sat on the floor, a passport and documents spread out across the table by the door, a set of keys lying to the side. Everything was ready for a vacation in the sun, but today she would be going nowhere. The taxi would turn up and leave without its fare, the phone would ring but would remain unanswered and the front door would stay shut. Sleeping Beauty would lie ready to be awakened, but this time there would be no handsome prince. He loved the plan.

He pulled a scarf from his bag and tiptoed across the hallway to her bedroom. Her door was open. He could see her shape under the sheet, curled into a crescent, her back towards him, an arm hanging lazily above her head, her hair cascading in ringlets around her shoulders. A thin raft of light from the moon filtered in through a gap in the curtains, directly against the pillow on which her head was resting. Its beam lit up her face; her button nose casting a shadow across her cheek and the upper edges of her mouth. Her lips were thin, parted slightly in sleep, her breath louder, more constant now as he approached. Her eyes remained tightly shut, twitching slightly as she dreamed, unaware of his presence.

A few more steps and he was on top of her, his gloved hand across her mouth to stifle any scream. He rolled her on to her back, his weight pushing her further into the mattress. She couldn't move. Only her eyes darted around now, wild and wide, trying to make sense of what was happening. Roughly he tied the scarf around her mouth and pulled her flailing arms up in front of her, securing her wrists in metal restraints. Her hands balled into fists, but they were impotent within the handcuffs. Her voice came out in staccato gasps, any words muffled within the material of the scarf. She tried to buck, but he was too heavy for her. He pulled the sheet off her, strapping her legs tightly to each other before binding her whole body to the bed, each limb held in place by electrical cable.

She lay trussed and immobile, her thin cotton pyjamas tight against the curves of her body, the scarf exchanged for paper wadding, held in place by duct tape wound round and round her head. The job was nearly done. He bent down over her, his face close, squinting through the eyeholes of the balaclava that he wore, his eyes exploring her body. Her physique was good for her age; she had obviously spent time working out in the gym, but she held no sexual attraction to him. She was staring directly at his face, trying, no doubt, to focus on his features. His mouth curled into a sneer. It wasn't in his instructions, but it would be an amusing addition. He lifted the balaclava up and grinned down at her desperate attempts at concentration, before pulling it back into position. She would not live to give a description, but he liked to think she'd try.

What he did, needed to be done. He felt no guilt. He hated her and her kind. How he wished he could kill her now, to revel in how she dealt with the sort of intimidation, humiliation and agony that he himself had suffered.

But he had his orders.

And, before the clock in the lounge clicked on to 03.59 he'd slipped silently out of the front door, having followed every single one of them.

Chapter 2

For PC Brian Ashton it had been a normal Monday late shift. Normal in as much as he'd dealt with two adult shoplifters, a violent robbery and a severely disturbed woman threatening to commit suicide. At just gone 10.15 p.m. it had all kicked off. It was the same every evening shift; too early to leave the call for night duty, too late to be able to deal with it properly and still finish punctually at eleven.

It had taken almost an hour to talk the half-demented woman off Waterloo Bridge, but eventually she had agreed to climb into the back of a police van to be taken for an assessment at the Maudsley psychiatric unit. The malevolent eddies of the River Thames had gone on their way hungry, having had their latest tasty morsel removed from the menu. The hordes of curious bystanders had dissolved back into the crowded footways of the South Bank and the river police, so recently circulating the dark waters underneath the bridge in their patrol boats, had moored up and changed crew. PC Brian Ashton was left to write up the paperwork.

It was just gone 00.30 when he parked up in the yard at Southwark police station and signed the van over to the night-duty crew. There had been little of the usual waiting at the hospital. The woman had been received into the bosom of the inpatients facility without a hitch. Things were looking up.

Brian undid the heavy, stab-proof vest that he wore, hooking it over his arm along with his equipment belt as he jogged lightly down the stairs into the basement. The men's locker room was empty, night shift having long since gone out on patrol. The usual mix of men's odours, both pungent and perfumed, assaulted his nostrils. He breathed in the different scents, realising the back of his shirt and underarms were wet with sweat. It had been touch and go at one stage whether she would jump. They had all felt the pressure. He pulled off his shirt, balled it up and squashed it into the bottom of his rucksack. Tina would deal with that in the morning.

A few minutes later he'd replaced his work trousers for jeans, his boots for trainers and thrown on a thin cotton T-shirt with the words 'World's Best Dad' emblazoned on the front. It had been presented toothily to him for Father's Day by four-year-old Emily and six-year-old Bobby, Tina's children from her first marriage. It meant the world to him, especially as he didn't get to see Max, his own son from his first marriage, that often. The police service and the marriage service were no better partners than he and his ex-wife, Lorna, had been.

He slammed the door to the locker shut and turned the key. Police officers could be thieving bastards sometimes; especially if there was some spare uniform on display. It was only borrowing; they just forgot to give it back. He swallowed hard as his conscience pricked. Everything he did, he did for his family. He shrugged the thought away guiltily and headed for the door, slinging his rucksack over his shoulder.

His car was parked, as usual, fifteen minutes away in the multi-storey at the rear of Guy's Hospital, close to The Shard. London Bridge and Borough Market, both scenes of a recent terror attack came into view, Borough Market having only reopened to the public six days previously. He'd been at home when the terrorists had struck but had rushed in to assist when the news broke. Now, despite his proximity to the recent incident he walked the route without thinking, ignoring the regular warnings to vary routines thrown out by senior officers. It was easier said than done. Even though the threat level to police was heightened, no other parking facilities were provided. You parked where you could... and nothing was ever going to happen to him anyway.

A single lamp flickered forlornly in the entrance to the multi-storey, most of the lights having been vandalised so regularly that the council no longer had the money, or the inclination, to replace them. He walked through the entrance noticing that the last of the damaged CCTV cameras had also been removed. Skirting past the lifts, he headed towards the stairs, holding his breath to avoid the overpowering stench of urine. Even the foul smell of the stairwells was preferable to getting stuck in one of those stinking sweat-boxes. By the time he got to the dimly lit sixth floor his heart was pumping and he was glad to see his car still parked where he'd left it. Several other vehicles stood dark and empty on the same floor, their shapes casting shadows across the concrete.

He clicked the key fob and the headlights pulsed on and off the usual two times. Although he wasn't overly nervous in the multi-storey at night, he was still glad to hear the reassuring clunk of the door locks securing him inside. There were too many crazies around these days, and he'd arrested a good percentage of them. Officers returning to their cars late at night were easy meat.

Settling down into the arms of his trusty old BMW, he selected the ignition key before firing up the engine. The headlights came on and the car park was at once bathed in illumination. The shadows receded and he relaxed, fatigue seeping through his bones. It wouldn't take long before he was home, twenty minutes at most. A quick beer while walking the dog and then he could slip into bed next to Tina. He wound the window down, letting some of the stuffiness out of the interior. It was a balmy night; he'd enjoy taking Casper, his Labrador, round their normal route.

As he pulled slowly away he didn't notice the slight movement of the man crouched behind the old white van in the corner of the car park or the twitch of his arm as he lifted his hand to check the time on his watch.

*

The countdown had started and now he needed to go. So far so good. Timing was the key to his success. It had been tempting to take the bastard out on his way to the car, but he had to wait, the cop was twitchy here, ready to defend himself; he could see it in the way his eyes had darted all around, small pinpricks of white against the darkness, the way he held his shoulders, poised ready for action.

The strategy was correct again. He needed to strike when the cop was unprepared, unguarded, at his most relaxed. He checked his watch once more. Within the hour, that time would come.

*

The house smelt of pizza and soap. Tina had ensured the downstairs windows were closed, so the smells were trapped in the lounge, as was Casper, who bounded towards him, his tail wagging his whole rear end when he opened the door. Brian bent down to greet his ageing black Lab, stroking the soft fur on the top of his head and rubbing his belly when he flipped on to his back. The dog had been with him longer than either of his two wives and there was no question that Casper, unlike his wives, knew who was boss. He smiled to himself at the analogy and then tiptoed up the stairs to check on Tina and the kids.

Emily and Bobby were fast asleep, each in corresponding pink and blue bedrooms, with girls' toys and boys' toys surrounding them. Tina was very traditional. Girls should be girlie girls and boys should be fearsome boys. It was not surprising, given this attitude, that she now liked policemen. Her previous husband had been a prize prick. She was not going to make that mistake again. He blew a kiss to each of them and moved on.

Tina stirred as he entered the bedroom, lifting a silky white arm from under the thin sheet and turning towards him. Her eyes remained closed but he heard his name murmured sleepily.

'Bri, is that you?'

He bent down and kissed her lightly on the forehead. The room was muggy and he had the sudden urge to mop her brow with a cool flannel. She was heavily pregnant with their first baby and recent antenatal classes had taught him that this was the thing the man was expected to do. He hadn't gone to classes the first time round with Lorna, his ex. He'd been young and impetuous then. Tina was a calming influence. She grounded him. She also spent his wages – every penny of them. Tina, the new baby, her existing children and the maintenance he paid monthly for Max ensured that every penny of his meagre wages was accounted for, even before they hit his bank account. He didn't mind though, even if it was a struggle sometimes. His family was his life. Everything he did was for them, good or bad.

'Yes babe, it's me. I'll just take Casper for a quick walk and then I'll join you. Go back to sleep.'

He squeezed her hand, pulling the sheet carefully over her, before returning downstairs, grabbing a can of beer from the fridge and heading for the door. Casper had his lead in his mouth ready to go. He knew the routine. Out of the house, left, right, left again, along past the parade of shops and on to Tooting Bec Common; then through the footpath that ran across the centre and off on to the right-hand trail to skirt around the small lake under the railway bridge. This end of the common was deserted; any illicit activities occurring around the car parks and toilets on the other side. Brian couldn't remember the last time he'd seen anyone on this particular track, in fact he chose it for this reason. It was his time to be on his own; just him, Casper and nature, or at least as close to it as he could get in a London borough.

As he walked, he felt all the tensions from the day drain away. Casper ran to and fro, stopping to sniff at each tree, bench, item of interest, before catching up again, his tail wagging in excitement as if seeing Brian for the first time, over and over. Although into his senior years, what Casper lacked in speed he more than made up for in enthusiasm. Creaking joints and the usual aches and pains of age were not going to prevent the dog's enjoyment of each and every walk.

It was dark by the railway bridge; a row of trees having been planted to shield the common from the noise and sight of the intercity trains that trundled up and down the line at regular intervals throughout the day and into the night. The trains had stopped for a few hours now and the only sounds were the rustle of the summer leaves and Casper's panting as he scampered about. Brian lifted the can to his mouth and took another gulp of beer, stopping briefly to wait for Casper to catch up. It was all quiet. He waited for a few seconds, expecting to hear the thud of the dog's paws on the footpath running towards him. Nothing. He called out his name. Still nothing. The dog had obviously found something of interest under the railway bridge.

He heard a slight whimper. Retracing his route, he saw a shape on the pathway, lying in the feeble light of an ancient street lamp. It hadn't been there a few seconds before. He blinked as he recognised the shape as Casper. The dog lay still. Brian called his name as he ran towards his pet, noticing now a dark pool spreading out from underneath his body.

It was only as he was bending down that he noticed the other shape standing to one side, but by then it was too late. A jet of foul-smelling liquid hit him in the eyes and the pain shot straight through his head, as his corneas and the skin on his face began to burn and sizzle. He opened his mouth to scream, but as he inhaled the burning fluid, the fumes caught in his throat, taking the breath from his lungs and the cry from his larynx.

He lurched forward blinded and mute, falling down on to the pathway next to Casper, his arms spread out in front of him to cushion the impact, the palms of his hands, now covered in his pet's warm blood, scraping the stony ground. For the briefest of seconds, he visualised a tiny new baby, each finger and toe curling and stretching freely, its perfectly formed face locked on to his own… and a wave of pure regret ran through him. As the screams in his head dulled into silence and his mind became blank, the last thing he heard was the sound of his own bones splintering as the axe came down on his wrist.

Chapter 3

It was getting towards 04.00, the time of the morning when DC Charlie Stafford started to relax. The frenzy of the first few hours had petered out; prisoners were bedded down, and with only a couple of hours left before they were due to finish, it was time to write up the night duty occurrence book. Tonight was her last night shift.

She started to type the date and time when their duty had commenced, on to the screen in front of her. They always finished their week on a Monday night; the new team starting on the Tuesday, that way their bodies had time to acclimatise to being awake all night and asleep all day before the weekend spike in crime.

It had been a long, tiring week of duty, but Charlie always relished her nights. Every three months every detective in each London borough had to complete a set of nights, whether based in the main CID office, the Community Support Unit, intelligence units or any of the myriad departments that dealt with serious crime. While others moaned, for her and her boss, Detective Inspector Geoffrey

Hunter, their week couldn't come round quick enough. Nights were their favourite shift, the time when they got to deal with crime as it actually happened, rather than hours later as it appeared on the computer screen. She and Hunter would cruise the streets of South London in an unmarked police car, searching for the robbers and drug dealers who terrorised their communities and initiating the start of investigations into the various pub fights, rapes, GBHs and shootings so prevalent in the inner suburbs of the capital.

Her bread-and-butter work was in the Community Support Unit, at Lambeth HQ, dealing with every kind of hate crime, whether domestically or racially motivated, or relating to faith, sexual orientation or disability. She loved the thrill of getting a racist, homophobic or domestic thug incarcerated for a long time, but for Charlie, the streets were where her heart was. While the CSU provided the usual platter of crimes, the streets provided the à la carte menu.

As she typed, Charlie felt a slight sense of anticlimax. Although it had been a busy week, nothing particularly memorable had occurred and while she realised this was good for the borough, it had provided no real challenge to sink her teeth into. She glanced down at the keyboard as she wrote, her eyes focussing on the small red scar on the finger of her left hand. It was fading now, but the case it had resulted from had been memorable for many reasons. She would be dealing with the mental and physical fallout from it for some time to come.

A loud snore brought her back from her reverie. One of the other detectives seconded to the night shift had fallen asleep, his head lolling backwards in his chair. The noise was accompanied by a shout as his mate threw a pen at him, chuckling at his confusion when he woke, trying sleepily to place where he was. Charlie grinned to herself, refocusing on the report. Her night shift colleagues had been a laugh, but she was looking forward to returning to her usual team in the CSU. They were a close, loyal group and they'd been through a lot together. She couldn't wait to hear Bet's report on the workload of new cases, as well as the up-to-date précis of Paul's, Naz's and Sabira's ongoing social escapades.

A phone rang in the adjoining room. It was picked up immediately. Hunter never slept... nor did he ever, seemingly, want to retire. At fifty-eight years old he was a seasoned professional, much to his wife's dismay. Charlie, 28 years his junior didn't know how he did it as his age, but she hoped to follow in his footsteps. Even in the quietest, deadest hour of the night he would be alert. Where others much younger than he were flagging, Hunter would be full of energy… and expected everyone else to be the same.

She heard his voice, low and authoritative, followed by the sound of his chair scraping as he pulled himself to his feet. She glanced at her watch again as he strode through to the main office, his expression alive with anticipation.

'A body's just been found, believed suspicious.'

With only two hours left before they were due to head to their beds, it didn't take a detective to realise that night duty would roll into day shift and the memorable case for which Charlie yearned was now a distinct possibility.

*

'All I know so far is it's a male, found by an old drunk who stumbled across the scene on his way back from a mate's house. It sounds pretty brutal. Uniform are starting to cordon off the area as we speak and have the informant with them.'

Charlie nodded at Hunter. She'd heard as much herself from the radio and was keeping half an ear on what was going on as she drove.

The crime scene was not too far off. It was situated on Tooting Bec Common, on the borders of Wandsworth and Lambeth boroughs. The common was well known, the southerly end having historically been used by prostitutes and rent boys to ply their trade. It was bordered by Ambleside Avenue, at the Streatham side, the street made famous by Cynthia Payne, aka Madame Cyn, the brothel keeper who sold sex for luncheon vouchers in the 1970s and 80s. Various purges on the area by the local councils over the last few decades had failed to solve the problem, just serving to move it from the Bedford Hill side on to the residential streets. More latterly the sex workers had been shifted up on to the High Road and were now spreading out towards Brixton.

The area where the body had been found was further north, towards the Balham and Clapham end, and was set in a part of the common that was mainly woodland, crisscrossed by railway lines. It was the remotest part, but still, at this time of the year with the temperature remaining balmy and the hours of darkness short, the killer would have to have acted swiftly. No time to hang around. Kill and be gone.

Little over ten minutes later they arrived to a sea of blue lights. All Lambeth's uniform teams were scattered about the common, along with officers from Wandsworth; blue and white cordon tape being wound around trees in ever-expanding circles. It was a large area and it was already plain to see how difficult it would be to contain the scene adequately. A crime scene log was being started and the uniformed Duty Officer was briefing a constable on what was required.

Hunter strode straight across to join her, closely followed by Charlie.

'Morning, Glenys. Just when we were about to finish our week of nights… What have we got then?'

Inspector Glenys Chapel turned towards the voice, smiling broadly as she recognised its owner. She had almost as many years in the job as he and also, like Hunter, had never slowed her pace. She remained sharp, smart and quick-witted. Any young constable who presumed she might be happy to coast into middle age and turn a blind eye to laziness would find their backside kicked straight out on to the streets with a list of competencies to achieve. Inspector Glenys Chapel led by example and even now, in the wee small hours, was smart to the point of looking almost ceremonial.

'Ah, good morning, Hunter.' She held out her hand and he shook it warmly. 'You're lucky to be nearly finished. I'm covering for someone's annual leave, so it's my first night and I was just beginning to look forward to my bed. I knew I was tempting fate thinking of the B word with a few hours still to go.'

Charlie watched the pair of them. It always amused her that everyone within the job called Hunter by his surname. He and Inspector Chapel had been friends for years, having worked on and off together on various squads and different stations, both reaching the rank of inspector before staying put... yet still Inspector Chapel didn't call him Geoffrey. Hunter was just Hunter to everyone.

Inspector Chapel instructed the scene loggist to note down their names and indicated to them both to follow her, walking straight along a designated pathway across the grass towards a wooded area and the railway line. She nodded towards Charlie as they started.

'Charlie, nice to see you too. Right, all we know so far is the body is a male. It was found by a Mr Eddie Pritchard, our informant who is a little worse for wear and who is waiting in the back of one of our cars for you. He wasn't a witness to what happened though. He just called it in. It appears the victim has had some sort of acid thrown into his eyes and face. His features are so badly burnt it'll be impossible to get a facial identification. He's also been mutilated and, with the amount of blood around, my guess is he probably died from blood loss. Or shock. Curiously, a red rose was left by the body.'

She pursed her lips at the words, continuing to walk.

'Because of the presence of the acid, no one has touched the body other than to check for signs of life. The first officer on scene assessed that there was no pulse and it appears that our victim may have been there for a while as the body was cool. A paramedic has confirmed this too.

'On first appearance it looks like he was probably out for a late night dog walk as there was a black Labrador lying next to him and a lead on the ground. The dog was attacked too with what appears to be the same sharp implement, but amazingly is still alive, just. He's been taken to an emergency vet. Luckily for us the dog was wearing a collar with his name, Casper, and a phone number. I've got the control room running checks on the number now and we'll get a subscriber's check done ASAP. Hopefully it'll come up on our system. If not, we're going to ask the vet to check him for a microchip to see who he's registered to. As he's got a collar, the chances are he has a responsible owner who has had him chipped.'

Hunter nodded. 'Good stuff. With any luck we'll have a provisional ID pretty quickly.'

'Other than that, we have nothing. No known witnesses and no suspects as yet.'

They continued to walk, falling into silence as they neared the woods. Sunrise wasn't due for half an hour but the night seemed lighter than usual; the moon and stars shining brightly in the cloudless skies. The air was warm and a soft wind stirred the tops of the long grass at the edge of the trees, sending a flurry of spores up into the atmosphere.

They weaved their way through a small thicket of trees, their footsteps disturbing a family of coots who plunged, panic-stricken, into the safety of a small pond, making its surface rear up, sending a tsunami of ripples to its opposite bank. The sounds of the fleeing birds and the splashing of the water relieved the tension of the moment.

'We're nearly there. It's not a pretty sight,' Inspector Chapel commented, turning towards a path under a red-brick railway bridge.

An inner cordon had been set up. Inspector Chapel ushered Hunter and Charlie through and within a few yards they were there. The scene was as grisly as any Charlie had seen before. The thin light of an ancient lamp post lit up the footpath leading to the bridge. The whole area was splattered with blood, with several scrape marks highlighting the path where the victim's body had been dragged. The dead man was now propped up in a sitting position against the wall of the bridge, his legs splayed out in a V-shape, his head lolling back against the brickwork. His arms had been positioned to lie towards each other, across the front of his torso and his hands had been severed. They lay neatly placed between his legs in a large crimson pool of blood that had clearly flowed out from the jagged stumps at his wrists and down the slope of the pathway under the bridge. A single red rose lay between his legs, diagonally across his detached hands.

'Shit,' Charlie couldn't help herself. The sight of the rose on top of the two severed hands was gruesomely captivating. 'He must have lost a good few pints.'

She forced her eyes up towards his face, but there was little left of it. Where his nose, cheeks and eyes should have been, all that remained of his skin was a yellowy-red mass of tissue with the odd remnant of hair from a beard or moustache sticking out in small wispy clumps. His lips were blistered and burnt, along with any part of his hair and scalp that had come into contact with the caustic liquid. What she was looking at was unrecognisable as a face.

Without features it was hard to determine his age. His hairstyle looked modern, dark and clipped short, his physique toned but with a slight paunch and the skin on his arms brown, not lined with age or smooth as with youth. His clothing too looked up-to-date, jeans, trainers and a T-shirt with wording that struck Charlie to the core – 'World's Best Dad'. One child at least, would now be fatherless, but who knew how many more would have their lives irrevocably changed forever?

She tore her gaze away from the man's body and scanned the immediate area. There was little more to see other than a dog's lead lying desolately halfway across the path, an empty can of beer on its side with its contents glistening around it and another pool of dried blood circling a dry spot where the dog had obviously lain. Looking at the brutality meted out on the man, it was amazing the dog had survived.

As if on cue Hunter's phone started to buzz. He answered it immediately, his expression becoming yet more serious as he pressed the handset to his ear and listened.

Glenys Chapel was staring directly at him as he thanked the caller and sombrely ended the call.

'What's up?' she queried, asking the question that was on Charlie's lips.

Hunter grimaced before he spoke, taking a handkerchief out from his pocket and wiping it across his forehead.

'That was the control room. They've got the results on the enquiries you asked for. The dog's owner is registered as a Brian Ashton, living just around the corner in Havering Road. His name rang a bell with one of the female staff members and she checked his details against Book 1.'

Charlie felt the colour draining from her face as he spoke. Book 1 was where the personal details of all Metropolitan police officers were kept.

'She made a few more phone calls to confirm what she thought before she said anything, but she was right. Brian Ashton is one of ours. He's a police officer who works at Southwark police station on team. He only finished his late shift a few hours ago, talking down a suicidal woman from Waterloo Bridge. He has a young family, but the worst thing is his wife is due to give birth imminently. In a fortnight's time she's going to have a baby that will never now know the World's Best Dad.'

*

Number 8 Havering Road, SW12, was just a regular house, in a regular street. It was nestled into the middle of a row of terraces, all uniform heights, with uniform frontages and uniform gardens. The cars parked outside on the road were mainly family cars, with child seats strapped into the rear and finger marks smeared across the windows. The families who lived in these houses were 'just about managing'; parents struggling to earn enough money to pay the mortgage and going without themselves to ensure their child was fed and clothed and not singled out as the poor kid. They led day-to-day existences; nursery and school runs, TV evenings, trips to the local shops and sorties out to the nearby common to wear the children out before bedtime. People who lived in these houses had unextraordinary lives.

Yet as Charlie and Hunter walked along Havering Road, they knew that the news they were about to impart would catapult the family of number 8 into the headlines, a whole new world of pain, publicity and exposure. Their comfortable existence would be gone and the spotlight would fall on every nuance of their relationships, work life and family life. Never again would they moan about the dullness of the daily routine, wishing instead that each day would return to what they'd always known.

The sun had risen by the time they opened the gate and paced forward the dozen steps to stand before the front door, but it was still early. A few houses they'd passed showed the beginnings of movement, a TV flickering, lights peeping out from the curtains of the baby's nursery, but in the main, the houses and their occupants were still sleeping.

Charlie took a deep breath before rapping quietly on the door with her knuckle. A family liaison officer would be appointed later that morning, but for now, imparting the worst possible news would be her job. If she could speak to the wife first, without the little ones becoming distressed, then so much the better. The house remained silent, so she knocked again, her breath catching in her throat as she heard the slight sound of movement from within.

*

Tina Ashton woke confused. She thought she'd heard a knocking noise but wasn't sure where it was coming from. It was still dark in her room, but behind the curtains she could see the first shafts of daylight shining. She reached across to rouse Brian, but he wasn't there. Maybe he was the one who was making the noise? Maybe he was making her an early morning cup of tea. It must be Bri, otherwise Casper would be barking. She remembered him briefly kissing her last night when he'd come in. He was a love.

She closed her eyes again, rolling over into her favourite foetal position, her hands automatically moving down to hug her extended belly. She felt their baby move within her and thought of it mirroring her position, its tiny legs and arms reaching out in a morning stretch, before tucking back into position. She smiled inwardly at the thought, yawning as she drifted off again.

She heard the same knock repeated, quiet and persistent, not forceful enough to wake Emily and Bobby, but loud enough to disturb her. It must be Brian. He knew she was a light sleeper. He must have got up early and sneaked out without waking her to take Casper for an early morning walk. That's why Casper was quiet too. Maybe he'd forgotten his key, the silly idiot.

She swung her legs over the side of the bed and heaved her body upright, stretching her spine and shoulders out as she did so. She'd be glad when this baby arrived, looking after two young children and carrying this extra weight was playing havoc with her lower back. Two weeks couldn't come fast enough. She pulled her summer dressing gown on over her nightdress, tying the cord up over the top of her bump, and carefully descended the short flight of stairs. Casper's lead was missing from its usual place on the hall table. So Brian must have taken him out.

The front door was solid wood, so she couldn't see through it, but it would be him. He was always forgetting his keys, but this time she'd make him pay for getting her out of bed so early. This time he'd be making her tea in bed every morning for a whole month. She pulled the door open, ready to say the words on her lips when she saw the man and woman standing on the step. She knew immediately that they were police, even without seeing the warrant cards held in their hands. It was the knock on the door she had always feared.

Her mind spun back to the last time she'd heard her husband, the gentle kiss, the murmur that he'd be back soon, but had he returned? She suddenly couldn't remember the feel of him slipping into bed beside her, the touch of his cool fingers, the breath against her neck as he nuzzled in close like he always did. No, he hadn't returned. Something awful must have happened to him.

She looked into the female officer's eyes and saw her discomfiture, the way her face was creased in a mix of worry and sympathy, and she knew exactly what words to expect. The voice she heard was far away, the question indistinct and fuzzy. Was she Tina Ashton? She nodded speechlessly. In that case could they come in? They needed to speak to her about Brian, her husband. She nodded again, her mind numbing. As strong arms reached towards her, a pain shot through her abdomen and everything went blank.

Chapter 4

It was just after midday by the time Charlie and Hunter returned to Lambeth HQ. The journey back had been quiet, each mulling over what they'd seen and what they now needed to do. The sun was bright, the sky a vivid blue and daily life was continuing all around them. Tourists thronged the streets and bridges of the River Thames, cameras in hand, selfie sticks projected at all angles as they smiled and pouted, with the Houses of Parliament and Big Ben as spectacular backdrops. Office workers were just beginning to emerge from their glass prisons to look for the nearest vendor selling the latest foreign cuisine trending in street food. Everybody in the outside world was going about their normal business, oblivious to what Charlie and Hunter had been witness to this morning.

In contrast, the atmosphere in their own building was sombre, even the security guard, normally effusive on seeing Charlie, was unusually subdued. News of a murder on your patch spread fast. News of a dead police officer travelled even faster, especially one from a neighbouring borough. Everybody either knew the victim or knew someone else who did.

They waited for the lift, stepping into it as a couple of Police Community Support Officers exited, one dabbing at her eyes with a tissue. Charlie's own eyes were sore and gritty. She was mentally and physically exhausted, having now been up almost twenty-four hours, but if she needed to be up for another twenty-four to catch the person who had mutilated their colleague she would be. They all would.

The rest of the team were scattered about the office when they entered, each with their heads burrowed deep into their computer screens. As one body, they all turned and rose when they saw Hunter and Charlie. Paul headed for the kettle, Naz and Sabira hovered above their work stations and Bet came straight towards them, throwing an arm around Charlie's shoulder and giving her a little hug.

'You OK?'

Charlie nodded for both of them.

'How's Tina, the wife. We heard what's happened.'

'She's gone into early labour, but she's in good hands now,' Charlie replied. 'Her sister is with her at St George's maternity unit and her parents are looking after Bobby and Emily, her two kids from her previous marriage. She pretty much passed out at the sight of us. I'd barely had a chance to even introduce myself or check I was speaking to the right person.'

'That's the problem with being married to a cop.' Hunter spread his arms. 'Mrs H worries about getting that knock on the door. It's always at the back of her mind when I'm working. That's why I try not to tell her what we're up to these days. It's better that she doesn't know.' He turned and looked pointedly towards Charlie. 'She knows the dangers though. She'd guess in exactly the same way as Tina did if two coppers turned up on our doorstep.'

'Dave's the same,' Bet agreed. 'We forget that to us it's just a job, but it must be hard for our families on the outside. How awful for Tina. Finding out that your husband's been murdered, then having to give birth without him. And the poor kid will never even get to meet its father.'

'Their son or daughter won't be the only child who's never met their father,' Naz walked across to help Paul, bristling slightly, before taking a deep breath and shaking her head. 'To be fair though, Brian Ashton sounds like he was a good father. At least *he* was paying maintenance for his first kid.' Paul gave her a wink and she smiled weakly in return. Everyone knew the ongoing trouble Naz was having, trying to track down her younger son's father. She'd almost given up a few times, but then her sense of injustice had kicked in. Nathaniel's father would rue the day he tried to shirk his responsibilities. 'Sorry, guys. Bad weekend. Not half as bad as yours by the sound of it though.' She shrugged and frowned apologetically towards Charlie and Hunter, before brightening, 'Did you realise Sab knew Brian Ashton a few years ago, boss?'

Hunter spun round towards Sabira. 'Really? How long ago?'

Sabira looked startled at the sudden attention but quickly composed herself. She perched on the edge of her desk and pushed her hair back over her ears. Being the least extrovert member of the team, she didn't usually like being in the limelight, but in the last year she had steadily grown in confidence, recently having purple highlights put into her silky, black hair. They were still a source of mild concern to her, but she was gradually embracing her new look and revelling in her effort to become more assertive.

'It was before I became a detective, about three to four years ago, boss, when I moved over to South London, from my parents' house in Hounslow. I requested a transfer to a station a little closer to my new address and I was sent to Southwark. Brian was on a different team, but we both did a stint on a crime squad for a while. He seemed like a nice guy; happy-go-lucky, popular with his team, always up for doing overtime.

'We were posted together a few times and I remember him saying he'd recently got divorced and it was costing him a fortune. That's why he was eager to do the extra hours, but then he met Tina and got all loved up. They were hoping to marry at some time, so he was saving for that too, but her ex-husband was being a bit of a twat about custody of their kids. I did hear that he got married a couple of years ago, but I don't really know what happened to him after I came here.'

Hunter inclined his head. 'So it sounds likely there could be a few domestic issues that will require our assistance. As we've already taken the lead, I'm sure my bosses will be happy to second you all on to the Murder Investigation Team... and they know how invaluable you've been in the past. Have you been able to do much this morning? Anything yet on possible suspects?'

Paul shook his head. 'We've made a start, but there's not much to go on. We've mainly been liaising with different units re trying to get a positive ID, CCTV, scene logs and any possible witnesses or officers who might be able to help. We've got other officers putting feelers out for any snouts who might know the word on the street about what's happened. I also sent off for Brian Ashton's full personal file to see if there's anything in his family history that might be of interest. Naz and Sabira are going to work on his relationships, seeing as Sab already knows a little, but they need to speak with Tina first, so they'll have to wait for her to give birth. We also need to make sure Brian's first wife, Lorna, and their son, Max, are informed and spoken to, although I believe that's in hand with family liaison.'

Bet joined in. 'DCI O'Connor has also been asking whether there is anything further to indicate whether our killer knew Brian personally. Or that he was a police officer. He's briefing the Superintendent in Counterterrorism. They're obviously worried there might be CT implications, what with the increased terrorist threat to police and the armed forces.'

Hunter frowned immediately. Everybody knew how much he hated dealing with top brass, and the more political the incident, the more uncomfortable he became.

'It seems too covert to me,' he rubbed his hands over his head. 'Terrorists like publicity. No one has claimed responsibility and usually there is no shortage of big, bold statements telling the world what they've done and why. So far, there are no known witnesses, no CCTV in the immediate vicinity and no footage coming to light. We had a quick chat with the caller, Eddie Pritchard, before we went to Tina's. He hadn't seen or heard anything or anyone, although he did admit to being pretty drunk when he found the body. By the time we spoke though, he'd well and truly sobered up.'

'From what I hear, that sight would have sobered anyone up!' Paul came over and sat down on a nearby desk. 'Any theories from the scene? From what we hear there was a red rose left by the body. Sounds a bit sinister. Bet's done some research on the significance of roses in the past.'

Hunter turned to Bet. 'Go on. What did you find?'

Bet scratched her head. 'Well, as we all know red roses are full of symbolism. They're most commonly associated with love and romance, but I did some reading once when I had a dozen left by a particularly unloving, unromantic, controlling ex of mine and they can also be symbolic of courage, or power, as in the War of the Roses. I think in my ex's case it was a power thing.'

'Interesting,' Hunter nodded. 'Dare I ask who won your particular war?'

'Who do you think?' Bet laughed. 'I snipped the flower heads off each bloom and threw the thorny stems straight back in his face. Never saw him again.'

'Nice one, Bet,' Naz smiled appreciatively. 'Show 'em who's boss. Talking about throwing things in faces. Why the acid?'

Charlie tilted her head to one side thoughtfully. 'To disable his victim immediately? Or prevent any description of his attacker? Or could there be more to it? There didn't appear to be any sign of a fight, so it's fair to assume our attacker used the acid first. What do you think, Sab? You're the expert on acid attack cases.'

Sabira took a deep breath, before exhaling noisily. With acid attacks historically being most prevalent in the Bangladeshi and Asian communities she, as an Asian officer, had dealt with the most. More recently, however, the use of acid had risen, particularly in gang-related assaults and with hospital admissions doubling in the last ten years, she was now using her knowledge to update the team.

'Well, it's a bit of an excessive method just to disable a victim or stop him giving a description. Why not cover your own face, with a balaclava say, or use something a little less drastic, like pepper spray or CS? Both are relatively easy to buy on the internet these days; even a good squirt of hairspray direct in the eyes works just as well. It's much more likely to have been used for a specific reason.'

Paul pursed his lips. 'Was anything stolen from Brian?'

'Not that we know of,' Charlie replied. 'But he couldn't be searched properly because of contact with the acid.'

'So… it doesn't sound like a robbery, although you can never completely rule out a random psycho.'

Sabira walked across to the kettle and claimed her mug, spooning in three teaspoons of sugar before stirring it thoughtfully. 'You can't rule out a stranger attack completely, but I agree Paul. It sounds to me more like our attacker knew Brian Ashton personally and wanted to blind or disfigure him deliberately; maybe to teach him a lesson for something he's done or make him unattractive to the opposite sex, like in honour attacks.'

Paul nodded. 'That's all well and good but why blind or disfigure him if you then kill him? What about the severed hands then? What the fuck is that all about?'

'To stop him touching what is not his?' Naz threw the cloth down that she'd been using to mop up some spilt milk. 'If we're thinking the acid might be a symbol, to stop him looking attractive to other women, or looking *at* other women, maybe removing his hands is also symbolic, to stop him touching them? Maybe our Brian is not quite as squeaky clean as we thought?'

Sabira took up the thread.

'Or as some kind of barbaric punishment, like they do in some extremist Islamic countries. Even now flogging and stoning is prevalent and, in some areas, courts still order thieves to have their hands severed. The Qur'an sanctions the removal of a person's hands for theft, but obviously most moderate Muslims would never actually do this. Extremists take the passages out of context and use sharia law to justify their actions. You've only got to look at the rise of ISIS to see that. They're mad.'

Sabira shook her head sadly. She had a working knowledge of Islam, being a Muslim herself, although these days more in name than practice. Her sexuality was not recognised by the religion, but ironically she still felt criticism of the faith keenly.

'Don't worry, Sabira, they're not the only ones,' Bet consoled. 'Christianity is just as brutal. In medieval and biblical times, they believed in an eye for an eye. If you stole or coveted your neighbour's property, including their wives or daughters, the punishment was designed to fit the crime. There are many cases from the Middle Ages onwards in this country where thieves were flogged or had their hands or ears cut off. Some thieves were even hanged. Thankfully we've got more sense these days and can see how barbaric and OTT these punishments are, but there are still some hardliners about. The debate about the return of the death penalty and corporal punishment still rears its ugly head regularly, doesn't it? In the last few days, I heard a news item talking about bringing back the death penalty for child murderers.'

'Now, that wouldn't be a bad idea.' Hunter stopped abruptly on saying the words, having realised the implications. The office went quiet. It was a little too close to home for everyone.

The silence was broken by a knock at the door, but before anyone could shout out, a man opened it and popped his head round, his smile turning to alarm at the sight of six mute faces all turned towards him. He had a boyish face with startlingly blue eyes, bleached blond hair, cut into a short, classy style, designer stubble and a pair of Ray-Ban sunglasses propped on the top of his head.

'Oops. Sorry. Have I come at a bad time?' He manoeuvred a large cardboard box between him and the frame and pushed the door open fully, stepping confidently into the room. His physique was in harmony with his face; six feet two inches of slim, toned torso on top of long, muscular legs, all encased in ripped Levi jeans and a Superdry T-shirt. He looked as if he'd be more at home on Bondi Beach than in the staid environment of Lambeth police headquarters. 'Maybe these will help?'

He pulled the lid up. Charlie immediately tore her eyes away from the delivery man to focus instead on the delivery; a dozen Krispy Kreme doughnuts, in an assortment of shapes, colours and decorations.

'You've timed it well. Come in. I'm certain they will help.' Hunter was clearly glad to have the subject changed, although Charlie noticed he couldn't hide a hint of displeasure as his gaze swept over the man's casual attire. 'Team, this is our new member, DC Nick Arrowsmith. He's come from Croydon CID and will be working with us from now on. Have a quick chat and bring him up to speed with what's been happening. I believe it's his birthday today.'

'The big three zero,' Nick grimaced. 'Not the best day for a celebration and not the best day to be starting here, I have to say. I heard what happened this morning. Sickening! I presume the pressure will be on to work long hours?' He placed the box down on the nearest desk and beckoned them all over. 'Help yourselves.'

They didn't need to be told twice. Naz and Paul clustered around him, introducing themselves and chatting animatedly. Charlie chose a doughnut to eat now and one to eat later and stood close to Bet and Sabira as they spoke further about the murder and the possible motives. Her eyes were stinging with fatigue but the conversation was enthralling. Could Brian Ashton have been killed and maimed for something he'd done in his private life? Was it totally random? Or did just being a police officer merit the dreadful injuries inflicted on him by the killer. To her mind it seemed far too planned and personal to just be the job, but they'd have to wait and see.

She noticed Hunter standing to one side watching them all. It was as if he was taking stock of the team and its new addition. He often stood quietly observing, before coming to a decision and she wished she could do the same. Too often she engaged mouth before mind. She heard him speaking eventually. The Scenes of Crime Officer and forensic examiners would be doing their bit first; until then nothing further would come from the scene. Bet, Paul, Naz, Nick and Sabira were to continue enquiries, find out everything they could about Brian Ashton, his loves, his hates, his work life; anyone that might bear a grudge. Charlie was to get some kip before starting afresh the following morning, as was he, but before he left, could he have a quick word with Nick in his office.

A wave of tiredness washed over her and she tried to stifle a yawn. As she pulled on her old trainers and running gear, Charlie wondered briefly what the word would be about. Hunter had not looked particularly enamoured with their new addition. Nick Arrowsmith had talked the talk, but would he walk the walk? If not, he would be out. Hunter didn't suffer fools gladly... but only time would tell.

A few reporters were starting to gather outside the front of Lambeth HQ as she pushed through the revolving doors and squinted into the sun. She felt bad at the thought of her team continuing to work on the murder of a colleague while she slept in her bed, but for now there was nothing she could do. She started to jog wearily towards her flat in Clapham, feeling the fatigue take hold. In a few hours' time she would be up again, driving to her family home in Lingfield for dinner with her mum and sisters, as she did nearly every Tuesday evening. Then tomorrow it would be Wednesday, and Wednesdays were always special. St Thomas's Hospital came into view, its windows reflecting intense rays of sunlight across the shimmering water of the Thames. For once, even Charlie thought the river looked bright and alive.

Her thoughts returned to Tina Ashton, tipped into early labour by the trauma of their news, lying in pain in another hospital in London, without her husband and without hope… and with a tiny new life that was soon to be born.

She thought of her own mother. Her life had not been easy, but Meg had survived; they had all survived. Tina Ashton's relatives would rally round; she and her children would be drawn into the wider family of the police; they would be supported and sustained. First though, they needed to find her husband's murderer and Charlie for one would be doing everything in her power to do just that.

Chapter 5

Charlie rose at the same time as the sun the next morning. It wasn't yet 5 a.m. but she felt refreshed and raring to go, having crashed out at her mum's house after an early dinner. The house was silent. Her half-sisters, Lucy and Beth, had joined them for the meal but with their exams now finished they'd gone out with friends afterwards, not returning until late. Charlie had been glad to catch up, but equally as glad to have some peace and quiet. She'd said little to Meg of the latest case, the conversation with the team weighing heavily on her mind. Meg had seen plenty enough to know the dangers of Charlie's job, she didn't need to be worried any further.

A bag of freshly laundered clothes was waiting by the front door as she tiptoed out. Her mother always made time to ensure Charlie had them, whether it meant staying up until the early hours or not. Meg would never fail her on a practical level, but it was a source of constant pain that she couldn't share her innermost thoughts and fears with her daughter. There was a note pinned to the top item today. Charlie bent down and read it, catching a waft of her mother's favourite fabric conditioner as she did so. It was the smell of her childhood, the scent of family togetherness, the smell of before.

The note, in her mother's handwriting of beautifully formed lettering, as neatly controlled as her emotions, read: 'Thinking of you'; short, succinct and to the point. She knew her mother would be thinking of her; she was probably lying in bed now listening to her leaving, knowing where she would be headed. Freshly washed clothes and thoughts of love were all well and good, but they would never beat the physical presence of her mother by her side on a Wednesday, sharing her grief on her weekly visit. Nothing would.

She picked up the bag, sighing heavily. One day maybe.

Charlie's destination was the churchyard where her little brother Jamie was buried. Every single week she walked the same path to his grave. Every single week she stood alone. Every single week her mind ran over and over the events of that first Wednesday when Jamie had drowned, at the age of ten, in a dilapidated boat whilst out in a storm. They should never have been out on the sea, but any chance of receiving justice had died along with the captain that day. Charlie had lived, remaining determined to fight for any other person treated unfairly. Her guilt at survival had also remained and it was this that motivated her to return every week.

The graveyard was close to the family house in Lingfield and was half the reason for her overnight stay with her family each week. After a recent case had ended with Charlie being abducted, brought to the site and threatened by the killer she was tracking, the place had taken on a more sinister feel, a slight sense of evil pervading the location, but this was gradually decreasing and Charlie was finding solace in her memories of Jamie again.

She didn't stay long. She didn't need to. Sometimes it was enough just to come.

She was driving back up to London now, her planned rest day having been cancelled. There was no time to waste. Her first port of call, even before starting work was to Anna Christophe, Ben's new counsellor. Ben Jacobs was her best friend and Charlie accompanied him each week to see Anna, in his bid to beat the debilitating Post-Traumatic Stress Disorder that had resulted from his previous military career. She'd first met him begging for money in the nearby park a couple of years earlier but it was not until he was robbed at knifepoint by a group of thugs that their friendship was cemented.

Until recently he'd pushed for more than friendship, but she'd been too scared to commit. Now it was probably too late. All his early progress had been negated by what he'd witnessed at the graveyard with her, and he was well and truly back to square one, possibly worse.

Charlie loved the bones of the man… but it wasn't his bones that were the problem. It was his brain. Physically he was strong. Mentally he was a mess, but she was determined not to give up on him, for as long as he was prepared to try. He just had to keep trying… she couldn't do it for him.

*

Anna Christophe had kindly agreed to come in early to see Ben. Her office was on the first floor of a maisonette, overlooking the most westerly part of Tooting Bec Common and was within sight of the previous day's crime scene, therefore it hadn't been difficult for her to guess which case had caused the cancellation of Charlie's rest day. Gossip was rife in the local shops and news of what had occurred had already elicited strong reactions from the community. No one could quite believe that it had happened on their doorstep. Anna had offered the early appointment without even being asked to do so. She just knew what had to be done and did it without question.

The table lamp was on in the office when Charlie arrived and as she parked she saw the silhouette of

Anna against the light, pushing the window open as far as was possible. Summer helped psychologists, so Anna had explained at their last meeting. It brought with it warmth, hope and new life and was a direct contrast to the dark depression of winter and the cold harsh realities people faced. It was no coincidence more suicides occurred in the winter months. Anna advocated allowing fresh air to circulate as often as possible for that very reason. The sounds of life outside the wood-panelled walls brought what was said within the stuffiness and introversion of the office into perspective. It was harder for the person on the couch to sink into a quagmire of pain with the laughter of children and bustle of everyday life going on outside.

As Charlie watched, Anna beckoned her up. She checked the clock on the dashboard. There was still another ten minutes until Ben was due. Dammit. She should have parked around the corner. Anna was lovely, but she had a disconcerting way of slipping a comment that demanded a meaningful answer into a previously harmless conversation, after which she'd remain silent, without any outward discomfiture, until Charlie capitulated to end the awkwardness. Charlie always found herself talking, even when she'd determined to stay silent. The guilt surrounding Jamie's death and her ongoing inability to mend her relationship with her mother were both subjects that were firmly off limits. Although Anna had managed to worm a few details out of her, the majority of her life had stayed safely compartmentalised, and needed to remain so for her own mental stability. She could wheedle any amount of information out of a suspect during an interview, but she could never cope with having the tables turned.

She waved back and headed slowly up the stairs, having the sudden sense of foreboding that she imagined a person sentenced to the gallows might have. She would need to keep the conversation focussed on Ben.

Anna answered the door before she'd even knocked, ushering her through to her office.

'Glad you were still able to come. How are you, Charlie?' The words were directed straight at her.

Charlie found herself mesmerised immediately by Anna Christophe's unblinking gaze. The psychologist had opaque brown eyes that were difficult to disengage from, once fixed. She was a small woman, barely five feet two inches tall, with narrow shoulders, a wasp-like waist and slim hips, but what she lacked in stature, she made up for in intensity. The concentration in Anna's eyes held Charlie enthralled and the temptation to tell the woman everything was almost overwhelming... but she needed to get to work. Work took her away from her problems. It also took her away from having to watch

Ben crucify himself day after day, knowing that, in part, his regression had been because of her. If only he had not witnessed the climax to her last case. If only the sights and sounds of that night had not triggered a recurrence of his nightmares. Things had just started to become clearer before then, but now everything was messed up. Ben needed her but couldn't bear to be with her. She had started to overcome her previous reservations and reached out, only to be pushed away.

'I'm fine,' she said eventually. 'Ben's not really improving as yet though, is he?' Charlie tried to throw the question back to the psychologist, but it didn't work. She was an open book and Anna had the pages in her hands.

'He'll get there in time... because *he* wants to.'

Charlie picked up the inference immediately. 'It's not that I don't want to. It's more complicated, Anna. I do want to, but you're right in one way. I haven't got time.'

She glanced down at her watch, feeling irritated at the implied criticism. She wasn't here for herself and she was suddenly annoyed at being put on the defensive. She knew Anna only wanted to help, but she also understood that she needed to want it and, for now, she didn't. It was safer to stay as she was. Unleashing her fears was not an option.

Ben should have arrived by now. He was late. She keyed his name into her phone and waited while the ringtone sounded, ringing and ringing until it switched to answerphone.

'Sorry, Anna, but Ben's not answering. I'd better go and check he's OK. We'll make another appointment as soon as we can.'

Charlie turned and headed down the stairs, glad to have been given the unexpected reprieve. She usually had a lot of time for Anna... but today she had none.

*

The curtains were closed when Charlie pulled up outside Ben's flat in Brixton and she immediately knew what to expect. The knowledge was heightened when the door wasn't answered. She pulled out the spare key he'd given her for just this eventuality and opened the door. It was the smell that hit her first, pungent and stale, much as she'd anticipated.

The flat was bathed in a dingy half-light, with dirty plates and crockery left to fester and empty beer cans littering the floor. She picked her way to the bay window and pulled the curtains open, lifting the sash window to dispel some of the staleness.

Ben was asleep on his favourite armchair, his legs and body twisted tightly into the foetal position. He stirred at the slight breeze, his eyes squinting into the brightness, before closing them again in dismissal of the day.

'Where were you, Ben?'

The words were spoken calmly and quietly, so as not to surprise him. She'd witnessed before what could happen if he woke with a start.

He blinked again, this time narrowing his eyes as he peered towards the direction of her voice. Carefully he unfolded his legs, stretching them out as he did so.

'What's the time?'

'Half seven. You were supposed to be at Anna's half an hour ago. She opened up an hour early especially to see us.'

'I'm sorry, Charlie. I had a bad night.'

His voice crackled with emotion and she suddenly felt bad for having scolded him. He looked so helpless. Gone was the confidence that had been growing so steadily, replaced instead by the haunted, hollow stare of the ex-soldier; the stubble, the dishevelment, the stale smell of beer on his breath. She bent towards him, her hands placed gently on his knees, and kissed him lightly on top of his head, sighing inwardly as she felt him stiffen at her touch.

'So I see.' She said the words this time with no hint of criticism. 'Right, let's get you sorted.'

Standing up, she accidentally nudged an empty beer can with her foot, sending it scudding noisily across the wooden floor, before bending to scoop it into a rubbish sack.

Within half an hour, the flat was back to normal; the furniture set straight, empty bottles and cans cleared and a line of clean cutlery and crockery drying on the side of the sink.

Ben sat with a pint of water, his expression more animated.

'I have to go,' she said. 'I'm late already and Hunter will be on my case.'

'He's a good bloke and a good boss.'

'I'll tell him you said that. He was asking after you the other day, by the way. Your name might be the only thing that'll get me out of a bollocking for being late.' She smiled towards him, knowing that actually Hunter held Ben in high regard and would indeed let her off if she told him where she'd been. He was as concerned for Ben as she was.

Ben nodded, looking suddenly forlorn.

'What would I do without you?' he said, as she left.

She smiled sadly at the words. Things had changed so much. It hadn't been that long ago that she had said exactly the same words to him.

Chapter 6

Hunter said nothing when Charlie walked into the office at 08.30, but she could see he wasn't pleased. The rest of the team, with the exception of Nick, who was conspicuous by his absence, were seated around him, propped up on desks in a semicircle.

'Sorry I'm late,' she tried to placate him without saying where she'd been. With everybody there she really didn't feel like answering the questions that would no doubt follow her mentioning Ben's name. She would take it on the chin now and explain later.

'Right, we were just beginning to talk through the events of yesterday, but before we start, Tina Ashton had a baby girl in the early hours of this morning. She's called her Bryony, after Brian. Mother and baby are doing well. Hopefully Naz and Sabira will be heading off to the hospital shortly to have a chat.

'Paul and Bet went through some of Brian Ashton's recent arrests and court cases yesterday afternoon. There are a few names that have cropped up that are worth a look at, several where they made threats against him. One is in prison now, but that doesn't mean he couldn't have got something arranged from inside. We all know how easy it is for inmates to get phones in and keep their drugs lines running.'

'It's a dirty job,' Paul chirped up. 'Last year I was in custody when Bill Morley was searching a prisoner. He saw some cable sticking out of this guy's arse and made him pull it out. Turns out as well as the cable and mobile phone, the guy also had the charger up there too, complete with the three-pinned plug.'

Naz winced. 'Ow, brings a new meaning to the phrase "talking out of your arse", though that's what most of my dates do. Maybe I'll have to check how they walk and sit before going out with them in future.'

Charlie pulled a face and Hunter shook his head. 'Right! Let's get on. Paul and Bet, carry on with your enquiries on possible revenge attacks and start looking at any CCTV that comes in. I've got others speaking with Ashton's colleagues. He was shown booking off duty on CARMS at 00.30 hours and leaving around the same time to collect his car, which was parked in the Snowfields multi-storey car park round the corner. There's no CCTV inside the car park but there is some on the main roads nearby. See if we can get any registration numbers of cars that might have been coming from that direction.'

Paul nodded. 'I'll give you the notes we've made so far on possible suspects, Charlie. One of them in particular is well worth a closer look. His name is Dennis Walters. He's got loads of previous convictions for violence, including one under the new Harassment Act for stalking one of his victims.'

'I've heard his name a few times. I'll take a look at him straightaway.'

Hunter turned towards Naz and Sabira. 'You two, check with St George's and see if Tina Ashton is up to having a visit yet. I want to know about anyone that might have had a personal issue with Brian, be it exes, partners of exes, new love rivals, friends or family even. Let's hope it's someone with a motive. They're so much easier to work with than a random attacker.' He stood up, watching as Naz and Sabira gathered together their things, their faces bright. 'Oh and don't go getting all maternal on me at the sight of a brand new baby. We're far too busy for you to have time off producing any of your own.'

Before either could answer, Nick burst through the door. 'Sorry I'm late. I had a bit of a late birthday bash.' His hair was fluffy and un-gelled and his cheeks looked white and pasty. 'My timing's always shit.'

Hunter glared towards him. 'Yes it is. Not great on your first proper day.' He looked Nick up and down. He was wearing smart trousers, a pale blue shirt and navy paisley tie. 'But at least you look better presented. Right, I need someone to go to the post-mortem, and seeing as you're the last one in, consider yourself chosen. Ashton's body is at St George's mortuary. You can go with Naz and Sabira; they're going to speak to Tina in the maternity unit.'

Nick looked crestfallen. Charlie smiled sympathetically towards him. She knew what it was like to be on the wrong side of Hunter's wrath, though her bollockings were more bark than bite. Everyone knew he had a soft spot for Charlie; she was a hard-worker. Nick had got off to a bad start; he had better start pulling his weight.

*

It didn't take long for Charlie to pull up Walters' record. He was shown as a PPO, or persistent and prolific offender, as Paul had indicated. The most regular conviction in his offending history was burglary and, even now at the age of fifty-four, he was still regularly being arrested for it.

The details made grim reading. As a child, Dennis Walters had been used by his father, Arthur Walters, as an accomplice, climbing through small gaps and railings to effect an entry for him. It was like reading something from the pages of Dickens.

Dennis had first been taken into police protection at the age of eight, at the scene of a burglary at a factory; where he had been hoisted up to squeeze through the tiny window of a toilet block before letting his father in. Both Arthur and Dennis had been apprehended as they went through the petty-cash box in the office. Dennis was too young to be arrested; he was under the age of criminal responsibility and so was returned straight to his mother… but he was not too immature to remember his father's training. He followed his instructions exactly, kept his mouth zipped and made the police do all the work. From that moment onwards, when Arthur was out of prison they worked together, but when his father was inside, the young Dennis Walters branched out on his own.

His life's path was set. His trade was learnt. He was a career burglar. Relationships started and ended, children were fathered and abandoned, all ties lost each time he was sent inside. He knew no different and the short terms of imprisonment he was regularly given just served to reinforce his behaviour, as well as providing useful tips on how to better avoid arrest and cheat the justice system. Prison was a hazard of the job but one that provided a warm, well-fed interlude from the business of crime. As he was only caught, on average, once in every fifty burglaries, it was a risk worth taking.

Over the years, drugs had addled his brain and he had branched out into other crimes, the crack cocaine fuelling his growing violence and rendering him impotent to control a temper that was prone to erupt on being faced with the merest provocation. Victims would be identified, followed and attacked when cash was required. Anyone daring to fight back would be battered to within an inch of their life and anyone daring to take to the stand in court would be stalked and terrorised until they dropped the case. Dennis Walters had a habit of finding out the details of where his victims lived. He also appeared, more recently, to have used Justin Latchmere's crooked law firm.

As Charlie read through his antecedents, she wondered whether those two details were connected. Justin Latchmere had been a renowned barrister before falling from grace after an ill-fated affair with a murder victim. During the investigation his professional and personal lives had unravelled, becoming a suspect for the murder himself, through his own lies and deceit. Although the case against him was eventually discontinued, he blamed the police for the loss of his reputation and now fed his hatred for them by working as a duty solicitor and doing everything in his power to make their lives difficult. Could Dennis Walters now have the means, through Latchmere, to secure the details of witnesses, in particular, police officers? Did his drug-addled brain now crave revenge on those he deemed responsible for leaving him to fend for himself and for repeatedly putting him behind bars? It wouldn't be too hard, even without the services of Justin Latchmere. Officers had to tell open court their names and the stations they worked from. How hard would it be to follow one at the end of their shift? Police men and women were used to being engaged in pursuits, but put the boot on the other foot; how many would ever imagine they could be tailed?

She scrolled down to Walters' last few arrests. Brian Ashton was shown as the arresting officer in two of them and witnessing officer in a third. He would know Walters' previous convictions and probably stopped and searched him on sight. He was known to be a proactive police officer; hadn't Sabira said as much?

Charlie found one of Brian Ashton's witness statements and scanned through it. She was right. He had recognised Walters acting suspiciously, involved in some sort of transaction in the street. He had watched before stepping in and searching him, establishing that the iPad Walters was attempting to sell had been stolen in a recent burglary, matching the circumstances of the other two arrests. Walters denied committing any of the burglaries, instead saying he had found the items in the street, and the Crown Prosecution Service believed him, or at least weren't willing to try to prove otherwise in two of the three cases. Walters was charged only with handling stolen goods, not burglary, in one case, and released with no further action in the other two, leaving PC Ashton open to the unfounded accusation that he was deliberately targeting and harassing Walters.

Charlie had to smile. How could a police officer be harassing someone if they found them in possession of stolen goods on all three of the occasions they were stopped? PC Ashton had been doing his job; and doing it well. Criminals needed to know they would be disrupted or arrested if they committed crime.

Hunter sauntered across and peered over her shoulder. She switched to the latest custody image of Dennis Walters, date of birth 03/09/1962, arrested on suspicion of burglary by PC Brian Ashton. His face stared out at them, with the eyes of an ageing drug addict, dark-rimmed, devoid of hope, slightly paranoid. His skin was pockmarked, with its brown pigmentation patchy in places, covered in part by a bushy, unkempt beard attached to a full head of thick wiry hair, forming an unbroken frame around his face. All the hair on his head was speckled grey, with the exception of the wisps of beard around his mouth which were stained a deep yellowy-brown with nicotine.

'I've seen him before on various briefings. Is he worth a visit do you think?' Hunter squinted at the screen as Charlie switched back to the last intelligence report, on which the circumstances of Walters' last court case were detailed. The intelligence report had a border which flashed on and off with the words 'Officer Safety' highlighted in bright red. They read the details in silence, focussing on the last two sentences which stated, 'Dennis Walters has made threats to kill or seriously injure PC Brian Ashton or any police officer who has dealings with him in public or who he feels is harassing him. It is believed that with Walters' violent history and mental instability this threat should be taken seriously when considering any engagement with him.'

Charlie opened her drawer and pulled out her safety equipment, clicking the ratchet of her handcuffs so they were in the ready position. She switched the screen off, noting down Walters' address as she did so.

'I don't think we have a choice. Do we, guv?'

Chapter 7

Dennis Walters lived in a fourth-floor flat in a block that was situated just to the rear of the Elephant and Castle shopping centre in South London. Southwark Council had started a major refurbishment of the area recently but it still had a long way to go and the whole area was therefore littered with roadworks, cranes and other heavy lifting equipment. His block was encased in scaffolding, complete with blue plastic tarpaulins which flailed and flapped in the light breeze, like the sails of a yacht. Charlie and Hunter made their way up the stairs, the exertion causing Hunter to suck the air into his lungs more noisily at each new level.

The door to his flat bore the scars of previous police raids. It was held together by a variety of oddly matched planks nailed across an area of splintered wood with a large metal padlock swinging between two metal brackets. If closed, it meant nobody was in, having locked the door in place on leaving. If open, as it now was, it hung from one bracket, allowing access to one and all.

Charlie pushed the door gently, but it remained firmly shut. Walters clearly had some way of securing it from the inside. She had to admit she was quite pleased. They were there only on a fact-finding mission, to get an idea of what made the man tick, and the thought of disturbing him on his own territory, thereby incurring his wrath, didn't particularly appeal. She was therefore happy for him to open up on his own terms.

Hunter knocked on the door. The plan had been for just the two of them to go to the flat, so as not to antagonise Walters more than necessary, but they had no idea who or what they were likely to find, so back-up was waiting just around the corner, a small contingent of officers that could arrive within seconds if necessary. They were banking on his assertion that he didn't want to be bothered in *public*; maybe if they kept things *private* he would stay calm. It was risky though; they were treading on dangerous ground and a few seconds would feel like hours if their plan failed. Once inside, Walters would have the upper hand and he would know this. Hunter and Charlie needed to show strength, while at the same time allowing Walters to feel in control.

There was no immediate answer to Hunter's knock, a fact that only served to heighten Charlie's trepidation. How much easier if they had evidence of his actual involvement in Brian Ashton's death. Going in with force was far less dangerous than going in softly, but as yet they only had threatening words, and although the assessment was that he was capable of carrying out his threats, there was nothing whatsoever to suggest he had.

Hunter knocked again and this time Charlie heard someone approaching.

'Who is it?' The voice was gruff.

'It's the police. I'm DC Charlotte Stafford. We need to speak to you,' Charlie answered. They were hoping that he would respond better to a female voice.

'Well you can piss right off, DC Stafford. I don't want to speak to you.'

'We need to ask you a few questions, Dennis,' she tried again.

'Who's we? How many are there of you?'

'Just two of us. Me and my colleague, DI Geoffrey Hunter. We don't want any trouble. We just want a few words.'

'And if I say no.'

'Then we'll come back another time, but next time we won't be so accommodating,' Hunter interrupted loudly. 'It's your choice.'

Charlie listened as the man's voice grew louder, gruffer still. 'I thought as much. You pigs are all the same. Trying to sweet-talk me into opening up when I don't have a bloody choice.' The door rattled ominously before it was half opened and Dennis Walters stood, his body filling the gap, a length of wood gripped tightly in his hand.

'Dennis, put that down,' Charlie indicated the wood but made no step forward. She held her hands out as if in a request. Again, she was playing his aggression down. 'We only want a few words. We won't keep you long.'

It worked. The door opened fully and Dennis Walters stepped to one side, balancing the length of wood against the wall.' You'd better come in then, but be prepared to piss off when I've had enough. You understand?'

Charlie nodded, smiling inwardly as she saw Hunter's grimace. He wasn't used to being spoken to like this, but sometimes they had no choice. Diplomacy was the only option if there was no lawful power. Still it wasn't easy. They stepped into the hallway, watching as Walters shut the door behind them and jammed the wooden bar between the wall and the door. She waited for him to move past them, before shifting it out of its position. There was no way she was going to remain in his flat without their back-up having access. She had seen Brian Ashton's body.

Walters led the way to his lounge, easing himself down on to a single armchair. He walked with a slight limp, dragging his foot across the creases in the carpet, before stretching his leg out in front of him as he sat surveying them. They stood, rather uncomfortably, by the door, there being no other unbroken seating. The flat was dirty, mired in years of neglect, as was Dennis Walters.

'So, what do you want to talk to me about?' he asked.

'You've made some threats against police in the past,' Charlie started, pulling out a notepad and pen and reading out the dates.

'Yeah, what of it? You lot don't leave me alone. Always giving me hassle in the streets. Always on to me, stopping me, nicking me, for nothing. Like now.'

'The last few times you had stolen property in your possession. I'd hardly call it giving you unwarranted hassle.' Hunter clearly couldn't resist.

Walters turned and stared at Hunter, his eyes burning. 'I was NFA'd on two of 'em, as well you know. The officer who nicked me is just a bastard. Every time he sees me he harasses me. I don't have to do nothin' for him to stop me. And he ain't polite neither. He talks to me like I'm shit.'

'I take it you're talking about PC Brian Ashton?' Charlie spoke up. 'I saw he'd been present in your last three arrests.'

'Yeah that's him, the bastard. One day he'll get what's coming to him.'

'And what exactly docs he have coming to him?'

Walters squinted towards her, his face screwing up in anger. 'With any luck, a long, lingering death. I hope he rots in Hell.'

'What were you doing the night before last?' Charlie changed the subject.

'Not much. The usual in fact. Eating, sleeping, scoring, scavenging around to get the money to buy more gear. I ain't got no one to help me out and I ain't got nothin' to call my own. You lot have taken everything off me.'

'Were you with anyone else?'

'Here and there. No one in particular. Why d'you wanna know?'

'PC Ashton was murdered yesterday.'

She watched Walters closely. His expression didn't give anything away. He stared back at her. It was as if he too was watching her reaction. All of a sudden he started to laugh.

'Ah, so that's why you're here. You want to pin his death on me. Well fire away. I'd be only too happy to have done it. In fact, someone's done me a right good favour. I guess I'm not the only one he's pissed off then?' He threw his head back and continued to laugh, his face becoming at one moment full of hate; the next twisted in delight. It was hard to watch.

'So, is there anyone who can verify your movements yesterday?' Charlie was struggling to control her emotions. Although she'd never known Brian Ashton, the circumstances of his death and his wife's situation were firmly imprinted in her memory. 'Anyone who can vouch for where you were?'

Walters stopped laughing and stared towards them both before hoisting himself to his feet. He leant over and picked up a broken chair leg, which had been lying on the carpet, before taking a step towards them.

'There ain't no one who can vouch for where I was, so I suppose that makes me a suspect. Well I'm happy to be one. I would quite happily have killed the bastard. In fact, I would quite happily kill the fuckin' lot of you if I had a chance.'

It was time to go. Hunter indicated for Charlie to follow him and turned to leave. It had been an interesting encounter. She snapped her notebook shut and smiled sweetly towards him. 'Well, thank you for your time, Mr Walters. We'll see ourselves out.'

Dennis Walters advanced towards them further, his mouth turned up into a snarl. 'You'd better come with a warrant next time, 'cause otherwise you ain't gettin' past my front door. Now piss off, both of yer, before I kick yer out. I hate all of you and your kind. The more fuckin' coppers who die, the better, as far as I'm concerned.'

After making it safely out of the flat, Charlie watched Walters as he slammed the door behind them. The whites of his eyes shone wild and intense, with a manic quality; as if the idea was taking form as he said the words.

Chapter 8

'DCI O'Connor phoned half an hour ago. He wants a word, guv. Says it's important. Something about an IPCC investigation.' Paul relayed the message as soon as they entered the office.

Hunter frowned. 'He'll have to wait then. It'll be their enquiry into our last case, because I called our armed response units in and they did what they're paid to do. If they hadn't taken that mad man out who knows what might have happened. It's just such a bloody waste of time. Anyway, I'd like to see some of their bosses make the sort of decisions that we have to make on a day-to-day basis.'

'There was no such thing as the IPCC when I joined.' Bet stood up, stretched, yawned and rubbed the base of her back. 'I know they have a job to do and they have to investigate serious incidents involving police, but it's just another layer of accountability. Police officers will be frightened to move soon.'

'Half of them already are.' Hunter was clearly irritated. The IPCC enquiry had obviously rattled him. He was about to disappear into his office when Naz and Sabira came in, chatting animatedly.

'Ah, ladies,' he turned towards the sound, relaxing visibly. 'How did you get on at the hospital.'

Naz dropped her bag on her desk. 'It was interesting, boss. Tina is recovering well. I think the new baby is taking her mind off things and keeping her busy. Bryony is beautiful and looks very much like the photos Tina has of Brian. We talked about him and his family and friends mostly. He didn't tell her much about his work, so she can't help us on that score.'

'She did say she wasn't aware of any problems with work colleagues though,' Sabira added.

'So, what was so interesting? Apart from the baby.' Hunter stuck the end of a biro in his mouth and chewed on it.

Naz smiled and sat down. 'Well, Tina was talking about her ex-husband mainly. It could be nothing, but she's got a thing in her head that he was somehow involved. There's certainly no love lost between them. He sees Brian as being the cause of their marriage breakup... and the reason he lost his children. He and Tina were teenage sweethearts apparently and although the relationship was always a bit on and off they had weathered the worst of the storm, had the two kids and stayed together for over fifteen years... until she met Brian.

'Her ex recently took her and Brian to court for sole custody of the kids, Bobby and Emily, but lost the case. God knows how he thought he would win it when he's on his own, in and out of work, and Tina is married and in a stable relationship. He isn't happy about it though, and to add to his woes he's been refused legal aid to appeal the decision. Tina and Brian fought the case on the grounds that he drinks and has been volatile in the past. They counter-claimed he is unsuitable to even have shared custody and argued that he should only have supervised access to the kids. Apparently, the ex blames Brian for ruining his life.'

'That is interesting. What's his name?'

'It's Carl Hookham. Tina was Tina Hookham before she married Brian. Bobby and Emily still have his surname, although she was saying she and Brian had been thinking recently of changing their names by deed poll to Ashton. She'd mentioned this to Carl too. She wanted her older kids to have the same surname as the new baby.'

'I can imagine he wasn't too enthused with that idea?' Hunter jotted down Carl's name. 'No father wants to have another man bring up his kids. Even less so if the one thing that marks them out as his is changed. There's something quite primordial about names. A man always wants a male heir to carry on the family name from one generation to the next. You only have to think of King Henry VIII to know that.'

'Really, guv? Do you think that's still relevant these days?' Charlie was incredulous.

'Who knows? Probably not so much as previously, but for some it's still important, particularly if the name reflects a tough time in someone's life. Your mum changed your name didn't she, when she married your stepfather?'

'Yes, she did,' Charlie shrugged. 'So we'd all have Harry's surname. Now I wish she hadn't. My stepfather turned out to be just as bad as my birth father. If it hadn't been for him taking us out on the boat…' She stopped talking. Even after all these years she found it hard to say Jamie's name and the fact that he was dead. 'Anyway, I would happily have stayed as Heath; that was her maiden name and the name she used for us before her marriage. Charlie Heath has a nice ring to it, but I suppose it's easier for Mum, Lucy, Beth and I to all be Stafford; makes us sound like a nice wholesome family unit… and it allows my mother to conveniently ignore the past.'

She laughed. She didn't know too much about her mother's history and Meg would never talk about her roots. All Charlie really knew was that Meg, Jamie and she had been born in Scotland but had moved down to London after her mother's relationship with their father broke down. Apart from the name Iain Frazer written on her birth certificate, she knew nothing more about her birth father and didn't really care to find out.

She picked a piece of paper up from her desk, screwed it up and aimed it at the bin, before concentrating back on the matter at hand. 'Does Carl Hookham have any other children from past or present relationships?'

'No, just Bobby and Emily,' Sabira confirmed. 'I suppose that's why he's reacted as he has. According to Tina, he's been getting increasingly unhappy with the situation; making threats about what he would do if they tried to change the kids' surname. It wasn't even that likely. Without his consent, they'd have had to apply to a judge for a court order and, given the children's ages and the fact that Carl still plays a role in their upbringing, their wish was unlikely to be granted. Still, it didn't stop them mentioning it and Carl fearing the worst.' Sabira paused and looked towards Hunter. 'None of the threats were reported officially though, guv. Brian didn't want his private life gossiped about by all and sundry. He wanted to deal with Carl himself.'

'Maybe Carl wanted to deal with Brian himself too,' Charlie piped up. 'Maybe he got there first, the jealous ex. Carl would fit the suspect profile; a loner who has lost his wife and kids to another man and wants them back. So, he takes away Brian's looks with acid and chops off his hands so he can't touch or have what he's had taken off him. Hey presto! His rival is taken out and his way back is clear. Job done.'

'It sounds as if our job is only just beginning.' Hunter looked round towards Naz and Sabira. 'Nice work, you two. Get going on researching Hookham's profile. When you're ready, we'll take a drive out and speak to him. Charlie, be prepared to come too.'

'Not so soon DI Hunter,' DCI Declan O'Connor charged through the doorway into the office. His expression was thunderous. 'I sent a message asking for you to come and speak to me as soon as you got back. That was three quarters of an hour ago.' He glared at Paul, before turning his attention back to Hunter. 'And now I come in to hear you planning to go back out again. Just when were you going to come and see me?'

Hunter put his hands up, as if in surrender. 'Sorry, boss, Paul did say. Something's just come in.'

'Don't tell me about what's just come in. I've spent all morning having to explain every single decision you made to a prize bitch from the IPCC.' DCI O'Connor closed his eyes and sighed heavily. 'I know you hate all the political stuff. Believe me so do I, but now it's your turn, and so help me God, if you do not come now she will have my full support to have you disciplined in any way she sees fit.'

The DCI opened his eyes again and Charlie couldn't help noticing the glint of good humour in his expression. She liked the man; he was untidy like her, but he dealt in actions, not words, like Hunter. Today, however, his usual shabby appearance was a hundred times worse, his thick, wavy locks hanging in untamed clumps against his scalp. He looked as if he had literally been trying to pull his hair out.

Hunter grinned. The two men had the same outlook on life; Declan O'Connor had risen to the next rank purely because he had marginally more patience than Hunter. Hunter's blood pressure always rose at the merest hint of a complaint, never mind disciplinary action or public enquiry, and today was no exception.

'OK, let's get this over with. You lot carry on profiling Carl Hookham and, Charlie, see how Nick is getting on at the post-mortem and do a bit more on Dennis Walters. Hopefully I won't be too long.'

*

Two hours later, it was Hunter's turn to slam through the door, ruddy-faced, frowning and with the vein on his forehead bulging ominously. He looked angrier than she'd ever seen him before.

'Ms Brenda "blood-sucking" Leach wants to meet you, Charlie. I've told her that she has five minutes maximum before we have to go out on murder enquiries. Anything more, just get up and leave. I'm not having her disrupting our investigation any longer.'

Charlie nodded and headed out, feeling suddenly nervous. The case being reviewed by the IPCC had concluded with their main suspect being shot by armed police. Hunter had led the enquiry and made the decisions, but she had been present throughout. The Met's own internal complaints unit, the DPS, or Directorate of Professional Standards, had attended the initial crime scene, investigating all police actions and decisions and it was their verdict which was now being reviewed by the Independent Police Complaints Commission. Although Charlie firmly believed that Hunter had not been in any way at fault, saying the wrong thing at the wrong time was something that came easily to her; and with someone who had as much political clout as this woman apparently did, it felt like she was about to be called into the witness box of Court 1 at the Old Bailey for cross-examination.

DCI O'Connor was waiting at the entrance to his office when she arrived. He ushered her in with his hand squarely on her back, propelling her forward towards a tall, slim, mixed-race woman, in her early fifties. She was dressed elegantly in a smart grey trouser suit, pink open-necked shirt and shiny black high-heeled shoes. Her hair was long, black and glossy framing an attractive face, with a liberal application of mascara accentuating the chestnut colouring of her irises. Her skin shone with a warm brown hue and a perfectly rounded mole under her left eye moved up and down as she blinked. Charlie found herself mesmerised by the mole, which appeared to her to be caught up in some kind of crazy Latin dance. Then she realised that the woman was holding her hand out towards her.

'You must be DC Charlotte Stafford? I am Ms Brenda Leach. I'm one of the commissioners who work for the Independent Police Complaints Commission. As our name suggests, the IPCC is a department, independent of any pressure groups, political parties and the government, designed to investigate police complaints in an unbiased, open and timely manner in order to increase the public confidence in the police and other law enforcement services.'

It sounded like a speech that was trotted out without thought at the start of every new meeting.

Charlie shook Ms Leach's hand, noting the way the woman barely made enough time for the greeting before releasing her grip.

'Yes, I'm DC Charlotte Stafford.'

'Well, take a seat, DC Stafford.' She dismissed the DCI with a flick of her hand and they both sat down, on either side of his desk, before Ms Leach cleared her throat. 'I'm in overall charge of the investigation into DI Hunter's actions in your last case. I've read the statements you have all made and I don't intend to go into any of the details with you. That has already been done, I see, by DS Hayley Boyle from the DPS. I take it you remember making your statement with her?'

'Yes, she was very pleasant, but I still took a federation rep with me.' Charlie kept her answer short, making a point she hoped would be noted. She would have preferred to have a fed rep with her now. Anything to do with complaints made her anxious, however innocent she was, and usually you were allowed to have a 'friend' present.

Brenda Leach continued, without comment. 'I've just had a long meeting with DI Hunter, as I'm sure you are aware. He gave me his opinions on what happened in the case and talked me through his decision-making processes. It was an informative and somewhat enlightening meeting. There are not many officers of his ilk around these days.'

Charlie watched her as she paused while choosing her last words carefully; debating whether they were said with her approval or censure. Ms Leach was difficult to read; smart, well-spoken and educated… and she was giving nothing away.

'I don't intend, as I say, going into the details, in fact I wasn't even going to speak with you, until after my last meeting.' She smiled towards Charlie, in a friendly manner, her head tilted to one side as if concentrating on every word she said. 'But seeing as we're both here I thought I would take the time to meet you. Your boss speaks very highly of you.' She glanced surreptitiously towards the scar on Charlie's left hand. 'I wondered if you would speak as highly of him. Obviously, with just the two of us present you are at total liberty to tell me exactly what you think, off the record.'

She blinked several times before flashing a smile at Charlie again. She seemed genuinely interested, but at the same time Charlie was suspicious of her intentions. Why not ask these questions in the presence of the DCI? Unless she was hoping for the answers to be more critical with just the two of them, in a way that she might appreciate. She wished she'd been able to assess the woman's feelings towards Hunter better.

Still, it didn't matter what Ms Leach thought. Charlie knew exactly how she felt and it was all good.

'I don't quite know what you are getting at, Ms Leach, but if you are asking me to tell you what I think of DI Hunter I'm more than happy to tell you exactly what I think; whether the DCI is present or not.' She stared straight at Ms Leach. 'In fact, I wish the DCI was here to listen to what I'll say.' Brenda Leach blanched slightly but her eyes didn't falter. 'DI Hunter is the best guvnor I've ever worked for. He is experienced, enthusiastic and knowledgeable and I would trust his judgement any day. Actually I would go as far as to say I would trust him with my life anytime, as I'm sure would every member of his team.'

She stood up, her chair snagging against the carpet and held her hand out towards Ms Leach. 'I do hope you weren't trying to cast doubt on DI Hunter's leadership.' Brenda Leach proffered her hand in return and Charlie gripped it strongly. 'Now, if that is all, I hope you'll excuse me but I am needed by DI Hunter to assist with a new investigation.'

Without waiting for an answer, she turned and walked out.

*

Nick was just struggling into the office on her return, carrying several large sacks of exhibit bags, containing assorted items of clothing, swabs and samples. His face looked even more pasty and white than it had earlier and there were large sweat marks under the armpits and on the back of his shirt.

As he emptied the first bag on to his desk, Hunter came out of his office. Gone was the ruddy complexion and anger of earlier, his expression now replaced by a look of tired defeat. He took one look at the bags of exhibits and shook his head.

'Right, that's made my mind up. Carl Hookham can wait until tomorrow morning. Let's all muck in and get these booked in together. By the looks of it, some will need to go into the exhibits freezers and fridges in the SOCO's office ASAP. Some we can book in to the property office downstairs. I presume you liaised with SOCO at the hospital as to what needs to go where?'

Nick nodded and pointed to the various bags. 'I've already split them into the relevant types, depending on how they need to be stored.'

They all crowded around, selecting a bag to deal with. Charlie indicated to Nick that she'd make a start on the freezer exhibits.

Hunter turned towards Nick. 'You've done a good job. While the others get started, you can fill us in on what Dr Crane said about Ashton's cause of death.' He gave him the merest of nods, but it was enough for Nick to brighten and he squared his shoulders and pulled out some notes. It didn't escape Charlie either. She flashed a smile as Nick looked up and gave her a little wink. The boss looked despondent, probably from the earlier interview, but at least he had cut their new team member some slack. It made the atmosphere less awkward.

'Right,' Nick started. 'Dr Crane will send a full report over as soon as it's completed, but in essence, as we suspected, the cause of death is shock; in principle as a result of the blood loss through the severed hands. The acid almost certainly added to this, as its reaction with the skin and eyes would have been extremely painful and the movement of plasma to the burn site would have contributed to the overall loss of blood and fluids to the major organs, causing the body to go into shock.'

Charlie winced at the thought. Even tiny burns are disproportionately sore; how painful must it be feeling your skin and eyes literally sizzling in acid.

'On the subject of the acid, the lab has already run tests on it and it is sulphuric acid. Dr Crane needed to know exactly what he was dealing with before he started the post-mortem. He showed me a clip on the internet where a professor shows the effect of sulphuric acid on a piece of sheep's skin. It's horrific.'

Paul picked up his phone and started to search.

Nick continued. 'The time of death was estimated to be between 01.30 and 03.30, but Dr Crane has yet to do further tests on the stomach contents which may pinpoint the exact time. He'll forward on his final report as soon as he can.'

Hunter nodded. More details always emerged after the initial examination.

'There were no defensive injuries that Dr Crane could find. It appears that Brian Ashton was taken by surprise. He barely had time to react. The burns are more severe to his scalp and the top of his face, rather than under his chin or neck. This would be consistent with the acid being thrown down towards him, i.e. Ashton was kneeling or bending at the time.'

'Probably to see what had happened to his dog.' Charlie said what she was thinking out loud.

'That's what we thought too. Anyway, his attention had clearly been diverted to something lower. There were no major burns to his hands, other than a few small blisters where the acid probably splashed, and no injuries that would show he had time to raise his hands to defend himself.' Nick stopped momentarily and paled even further. 'Dr Crane examined both hands independently. The right hand appears to have been severed in one action, probably from a heavy, sharp weapon, such as an axe or machete. The direction of the blade is consistent with it hitting the back of his wrist and it has then travelled straight through the skin and joint in one motion. There is gravel and dirt on the inside of the wrist where it has been pushed down into the ground. To do this, Dr Crane believes that the suspect would likely have been positioned to the right of his victim, so Brian would have had his hands out in front of him, as if he has fallen forward on to all fours.'

Charlie looked around the room. Everybody had stopped what they were doing and were listening in horrified silence to the report.

Nick continued. 'The left hand was severed from back to front too but not so cleanly, probably because the suspect was having to lean further across to get to it.'

Hunter sat down heavily on one of the desks. 'Hopefully by that stage Ashton was unconscious.'

Nick nodded in agreement. 'Or at least semiconscious. Certainly rendered defenceless. As soon as he's unconscious, the killer drags him to the wall, props him up and leaves him to bleed out completely, until he's dead. Apparently, it would have been pretty quick, but I still can't imagine what he must have gone through.'

Paul held up his phone towards them. 'This gives you an idea of what he went through.' They gathered around and Nick confirmed it was the recording that Dr Crane had showed him at the mortuary. They all watched in horror as a laboratory professor, in full protective clothing, held up a bottle of 96 per cent concentrated sulphuric acid, and stated that the liquid had been easily bought by him over the internet. He described how it reacted with water to become hotter and that, as the skin was made up of sixty percent water, the acid would cause horrific injuries to whichever part of the body it came into contact with.

He then held up a six-inch square piece of sheep's skin and poured a small amount of acid over it. Within seconds the sample started to swell, before contracting and shrinking. He explained that within a minute the temperature had risen to over 70°, but if more acid had been used, it would have reached boiling point.'

Charlie watched as the substance contorted into a shrunken mass, totally unrecognisable as skin, listening as the professor finished his demonstration off.

'So, an acid attack victim would at first feel a hot sensation on their face before suffering excruciating pain.'

The presentation was concluded but nobody in the room dared to move. The silence was palpable as they all continued to stare at the frozen image on Paul's phone. The professor had put into words quite candidly what every member of the team had been trying not to entertain. Their colleague, PC Brian Ashton would have died in agony.'

Chapter 9

Today was the longest day of the year, summer solstice June 21st. The sun was low in the sky, not yet ready to slip down over the horizon, as he reached his destination. There was a hint of mystery all around him as he surveyed the landscape; something strange and unfamiliar in the way the trees rustled gently in the balmy air. Maybe it was the thought of long-ago pagan rituals being performed that made his heart race or perhaps the anticipation of what he was to do again the next night.

The package was where the instruction had dictated, hidden behind a brick wall in the overgrown front garden of a derelict house; the middle one of a terrace of condemned properties. Nobody walked this way these days. The road led nowhere and if someone did happen to pass through and saw him, they'd think nothing of a scruffily dressed man, down on his luck, scavenging around for scraps. They'd more likely turn away from the sight, in case they invited his attention. He picked the bag up and started to head home, his curiosity ignited. This package was like the last, of similar weight, compact and neatly bound in brown paper. He peered into the black carrier bag in which it had been wrapped and wondered what would be expected of him this time.

All he knew at the moment was that it was happening tomorrow. Tomorrow he'd be going through it all again. Bang, bang, bang, three in a row. Three dead coppers. Three dead pigs. That's if the first one was dead yet. She should be by now. Three days to a week was as long as it normally took for dehydration to kill, but with their added extras, it should have taken far, far less. Four days had passed now. She should be starting to rot. He laughed, a deep, rasping laugh, tinged with bitterness. She deserved to die; all the officers in London's lauded Metropolitan Police Service did. They were a bunch of psychopaths in uniform. He hated them all.

He turned the parcel around in his hands, letting the malice roll over him, engulf him. Police officers had ruined his life, interfered, dictated and destroyed. Now, even his woman had left, taken from him… by the urgings of a copper. He didn't care what he did now. He never had. There was nothing left for him; nothing, except following the directions of the one person who had stood shoulder-to-shoulder with him all these years.

The timing was perfect and so the games had commenced. He had the perfect partner. One who believed the same as he. One with whom he had sparred over the years. One he had used, borrowed from, benefitted from… and the one who was now calling in the favour. He just had to play by the rules… and he had, almost. He just liked to add a few personal touches, embellish the instructions a tiny bit more, make the killings a little riskier, so each copper knew without doubt he meant it. So, he'd lifted his balaclava for the first cop, being mildly entertained as the bitch tried to remember his features while knowing she'd never live to speak of them. And he'd killed the dog, or nearly. What sweet retribution for the last few seconds of the bastard's life to be spent watching his beloved Labrador die.

He pulled a crumpled packet of cigarettes out from his jacket pocket as he walked, and thrust one into his mouth, drawing hard on the flame from his lighter as it flickered low. Expelling the smoke into the warm air, he watched as it floated away over the bushes before the last tiny white wisps dissipated into the evening sky. He strolled through some gates into a park, noticing the small groups of teenagers huddled smoking joints; the runners, jogging in time to the music on their headphones, the evening dog walkers standing, deep in conversation, as their dogs circled and sniffed.

A young couple sat on a bench, arms and legs entwined, turning to kiss every few seconds, as if unable to stay apart for any longer. An older pair ambled silently past, arm in arm, the strength of their

lifetime bond magnified in their closeness. He
stopped to watch as a third couple came into view,
their body language at odds with one another, the
way they walked a few feet apart, their arms
gesticulating, their voices loud. They didn't care who
heard their argument. It was happening; it would
happen again and just because they fought, it didn't
mean they couldn't be together.

The couple were almost out of view now. He
shifted uncomfortably from one foot to the other,
suddenly incensed by the sight. Why were they
allowed to stay together when he and his woman had
been prised apart?

He needed to get home. The package burned into
his thoughts, its contents poised to give him the
means to satisfy his anger.

The phone would be ringing at 22.00 exactly. It
was never early, never late; it was always on time and
he needed to be ready.

A few minutes later he opened his front door and
breathed in the familiarity of his flat, the earthy
aroma that came with the disarray and dirt, the fetid
smell of cigarettes, the overpowering air of
malcontent. Nothing had been cleaned, nothing
aired; the day-to-day clutter of living having built up.
Quickly he secured the door and headed inside,
placing the package on the table in the lounge, before
conducting an inspection of each room. There was

nothing there of consequence. He had followed his instructions well. Nothing was left to betray what he had been doing, all evidence from his earlier missions destroyed, even his clothing exchanged for replacements. If the cops came, they would find nothing incriminating in the flat.

He selected some new rubber gloves from a drawer in the kitchen and returned to the package, carefully taking out the brown paper parcel and positioning it on top of the plastic carrier bag. He pulled a balaclava over his head while he examined it, placing a tissue across the mouth hole so no saliva from his breath or spittle could land on the parcel's contents.

The first thing he found was a cheap Nokia mobile and a new pay-as-you-go SIM card which he inserted into the phone immediately, ready to receive his call at ten. The old SIM and phone would now be disposed of but a spare battery was charged up ready to go. He was well prepared.

Peeling the wrapping away, he looked down into the pack with growing pleasure. A single red rose lay across the top, its stem smooth, the thorns removed but laying nearby. He rubbed his finger along its length, staring at each additional item when his phone rang. He glanced at his watch. It was exactly 10 p.m. A new number was flashing on the screen. A wave of relief washed over him. He liked to maintain control his end and disliked the short amount of time before they each had their new numbers up and running. His first job after the conversation ended would be to save it into his phone so that he could make contact again, request advice or give a debrief; his own hotline if required.

A voice came across the speaker. It was a voice he recognised instantly, the voice that he had been waiting for, and it was always the same; calm, measured, reassuring and direct. He no longer recalled the identity of the voice, but he remembered the face to whom it belonged, how it reminded him of a person from his past.

It had told him that the world was full of weak people in positions of power and that he owed them nothing. It had told him that he was strong, but that they should work together because they would gain greater power in partnership. It was a voice that had urged patience, promised much and that had stayed with him. Now it asked for something in return. He grinned as he listened to the words.

'Hello,' the voice said. 'It's Ice. Are you ready to do exactly as I instruct?'

He pressed the receiver tightly to his ear, his head replaying the thrill of the chase and the sheer wanton pleasure of the kill. He couldn't say no. He didn't want to say no, but most of all, he was excited by what Ice offered.

*

Ice put the phone down and sighed with pleasure at the forthcoming execution. There could be no room for carelessness, no chance for the police to obtain DNA. Number One was good. He had no conscience, neither of them had... but Number One was also prone to stupidity and arrogance and that had to be taken into consideration. Any chance of Number One being identified had to be minimised.

Ice idly rearranged the thorns, sliding them about, moving them across the table until they were in a perfect circle. Ring a ring o' rose thorns. A single thorn stood out, the others swept from the table on to the floor. The barb was the longest, the sharpest, the deadliest. Ice picked it up, holding it to the light, admiring its lone threat.

Number One was alone. Ice too. They had nothing but each other, and a shared loathing of police... in the end though, that was all that was required.

Chapter 10

'Look, Charlie, Carl Hookham's phone was used in the same area as Brian Ashton's body was found, about an hour or so before he was discovered.'

The whole team had been punctual and had got straight to work, no one daring to provoke Hunter's temper after his previous day's mood. Nick looked smart and was busy checking through a printout of phone data he'd requested on the mobile number that Tina had for her ex. Charlie was helping him, though it was a job that she despised. She found it almost impossible to wade through the reams of call data and decipher anything of use. Give her a face or registration number and she was happy. Give her pages of codes, numbers and figures and it all looked gobbledygook to her. She leant over to look where he was pointing; squeezing his shoulders playfully.

'Hunter will be pleased with that little snippet.' She was beginning to warm to Nick, though she didn't know how long it would last. The cloud he'd arrived under was big, black and far-reaching and Paul had found out all the details from an ex-colleague of Nick's in Croydon the previous evening.

They'd all known that no CID officer would voluntarily transfer to a Community Support Unit on another borough under their own volition. Domestic crime, in particular, could often be gutty, unrewarding, and notoriously risky. Now they knew the reason for his arrival.

DC Nick Arrowsmith was on his final life, having been put on an action plan for failing to perform and given two previous written warnings. This was his last chance. Nick apparently loved the trappings of the job but disliked having to get his hands dirty. Give him the kudos, power and advantages of the office but don't ask him to work for it. He would do only what was absolutely necessary and was only interested, at best, in becoming a *Crimewatch* presenter or, at worst, promotion; the chance to get off the factory floor and into a supervisory role. In short, he was not a team player. He liked to give rather than receive orders and as a graduate entry he was adamant that he was destined for greatness. No wonder he had paled at the idea of the post-mortem.

Charlie had been disappointed to hear the news. To her, the best part of the job was at the coalface and she couldn't understand his lack of motivation, but for now she was willing to give him the benefit of the doubt. At least he appeared to be trying; maybe he'd turned over a new leaf with the transfer. He would have to be careful though. Hunter would be well briefed on the situation… and his motto was, 'you never get a second chance to make a first impression'. How it played out now was up to Nick. If he made the effort, he would be in, but if he didn't step up, he would be out. Hunter would bide his time… and then they'd all be forced to silently observe as Nick's future unfolded in front of them.

Charlie was still staring at the log of call data, deep in thought, when Hunter emerged from his office. They needn't have worried about his mood; he was back to his usual outlook, good-humoured, determined and ready to get on. The previous day's interview had evidently been forgotten and with nothing further coming through on Dennis Walters, today his mind was firmly set on Carl Hookham.

'So, what do we know about Carl Hookham, team? I can see you've all been in early and are keeping busy. It's much appreciated.'

Nick jumped in first, much to Charlie's amusement, clearly wanting to gain some ground with the boss. 'Well, I was just showing Charlie that Hookham's mobile phone number pinged up on a mast in the Tooting Bec area, about an hour before Brian's body was discovered. He must have been there at the same time as Brian was killed. I sent off for his call data yesterday. I'll carry on looking through it.'

'Good, Nick, thanks, keep it up. Naz, Sabira, tell me all about Hookham.'

Naz peered at a screen on her computer. 'I've been putting together a briefing document but basically Hookham is a thirty-five-year-old, white male, date of birth 19/04/1982. He is known to police mainly from his younger days when he was a Millwall supporter. There's no history of domestic offences and no assaults on women. The PNC shows his first conviction was at the age of seventeen when he was arrested for criminal damage, a brick through a shop window while on his way to a match. There are then about ten years of arrests and convictions for football-hooligan-type offences, drunkenness, fighting, threatening and abusive words and behaviour and similar, before eventually being banned from Millwall. Included in those offences are a couple of ABH assaults, nothing too spectacular, black eyes, broken noses that sort of thing.'

Hunter pursed his lips and frowned. 'So he is known for violence, although mostly just scrapping.'

Naz nodded. 'Enough to put him inside twice though. I think it was around the time the authorities were cracking down on football violence and making examples of anyone convicted. There is one more serious offence though.' She stared back at the screen. 'It happened in 2003, when he was twenty-one years old. Hookham was arrested for quite a nasty GBH but wasn't charged; the victim didn't want to pursue the allegation. Looking at the details, it appears that he was seen on CCTV outside a stadium bottling his victim across the face with a broken beer bottle, in retaliation for being hit with a fence post. Hookham had six stitches to his scalp; however, his victim, who was an Arsenal supporter, had twenty-five stitches to a large wound on his right cheek. They both dropped charges preferring to *sort it out themselves*.'

'Where have I heard that before?' Hunter grunted and pulled his handkerchief from his pocket. 'He likes a bit of overzealous retribution then?'

Naz leant back, still staring at her computer. 'He does have a temper. There's also another more recent case where he smashed a set of double-glazed doors at a builder's merchant after a dispute. He was given a suspended sentence and ordered to pay the full cost of the damage in compensation. He's still paying it back now.'

'Is he working currently?' Charlie remembered the comments about legal aid.

Sabira took over. 'Yes he is. His jobs have mainly been connected to cars, working in garages and for the AA. Over the last eight years or so, he'd finally settled down, probably since becoming a father, and got his qualifications as a driving instructor. However, since the split with Tina, he's reverted to form and come to notice a few times for drink-related offences. He also got himself disqualified for a year for driving with excess alcohol.'

'Tina said he was volatile and a drinker,' Hunter commented. 'So now he's got his licence back and returned to work? Hence being declined for legal aid. Any vehicle for him?'

'Yep,' Paul piped up. 'Bet and I have been checking his address for what vehicles are registered to it. He's confirmed on our systems at the address that Tina gave us and the PNC shows he has a red Vauxhall Corsa registered to him, a typical driving instructor's car.' He read out an index number. 'Bet and I are going to go back through what CCTV we have near the crime scene. If he's made calls from the area, we might also spot his vehicle in the vicinity.'

'Well hopefully we'll be able to hear straight from the horse's mouth shortly. Charlie, Paul, Naz and Sabira, get your stuff. Nick, carry on with the phone enquiries, as you seem to be a bit of an expert on it. Bet, let me know if you spot his car on CCTV.' Hunter spun round and headed for the coat stand, pulling a lightweight jacket off the peg and wrapping it over his arm.

'And his address is?'

'Norbury. He lives about two miles away from Tooting Bec, in a rented one-bedroom flat.' Paul gave the address. 'So he had no reason to be around the area of the crime scene, especially at that time of night.'

*

Carl Hookham saw the two Ford Mondeos parked outside his flat straightaway. They looked like police cars; the usual make and model, fit for purpose, not for recreation, a bit like his vehicle. The small gaggle of official-looking people waiting at the downstairs communal door reinforced his suspicion. Coppers always looked like coppers, even the female ones. They couldn't look normal if they tried.

He swung his car into the turning next to the railway station and headed for the car park, glad that as he did so, all their faces were tilted upwards towards the building. It hadn't been a surprise to see them there. Mutual acquaintances kept him informed of every aspect of Tina's day-to-day life, and with Brian being murdered, it was only a matter of time before his ex-wife bubbled him up. He balled his fists and drove them down on to the steering wheel, angry tears springing up at the corners of his eyes. Tina, his Tina. What had got into her these days? Her mind had been poisoned against him by that copper. Cursing loudly, he wiped the tears away with the back of his hand, his thoughts turning back to the last time he had seen Brian Ashton. That man was toxic. He was glad he was dead.

He checked his rear-view mirrors as he squeezed his little car into a gap at the end of the line, but no one was following. Hopefully none of the police officers had seen him appear in the road and disappear from view just as quickly. If they had, he would be in trouble. There was stuff in the back of his car that they would find very interesting.

He made a snap decision. It was time to get away. There was nothing to keep him here anymore. Tina had taken her new baby and his children to stay with her family, rather than set foot back in the house she'd shared with that man. He didn't even know where they were. She hadn't told him. She probably had no intention of talking to him either, but she'd evidently been more than happy to blab to the police about their ongoing conflict. That's why they were here now. They would keep coming to his address until they found him, and he couldn't chance being found. The courts would throw him into prison and he would never get to see Bobby and Emily then.

He switched the engine off, squashing everything from the car's interior into the dusty old rucksack that normally lived in the boot. The platforms of the station spread out in front of him, with a gate in the fence that led to the adjacent car park. There was no need to show his face in the road at all. For once, he was in luck. He swung his belongings up over his shoulder, flinching as a scab on his knuckle was knocked off in the process. It didn't hurt but it did start to bleed slightly, a drip weaving its way slowly down the back of his hand. He licked it away and pressed the remote control on his keys to lock the car doors, checking one last time that nothing had been missed. The tannoy system was announcing the imminent arrival of a train to Clapham Junction. From there he could choose whichever destination he wished.

The train was just trundling into sight as he dashed through the gate, offering his Oyster card to the card reader. It wouldn't do to get stopped without a ticket. There were a few other passengers waiting on the platform. They moved forward as the train slowed to a standstill, waiting for the doors to open. He paused behind an advert hoarding, glancing round for any sign of the coppers, until the doors were fully open; with the coast clear, he strode across the platform and into the carriage.

*

Charlie shook her head at Hunter from her vantage point on top of a wheelie bin she'd hauled up on to the flat roof of an outhouse, at the rear of Hookham's converted flat. The flat was on the first floor of an old house which had seen better days. Paint was blistered and peeling on the sills and a large crack ran down the exterior wall from the roof, almost to the top of the back door. The windows were closed and caked in several years' worth of dirt and grease, making the interior look gloomy, even in the June sunshine. An old sofa stood alone in the centre of the room, with a TV directly in front. The whole room looked tired and squalid, depressingly reminiscent of Hookham's present life.

She jumped down and went back to join the group, brushing some cobwebs from the bottom of her trousers.

'It doesn't look as if there's anyone in, although it does look occupied. Hookham must be out working. There're a few parking spaces around the back, but there's no sign of his Corsa.'

'Damn it. I was hoping to get him on our first visit.' Hunter exhaled noisily. He checked his watch and turned to leave. 'Give it a couple of hours and we'll try again.'

*

Brixton Road was buzzing with life as Paul drove Hunter and Charlie back towards Hookham's flat. Another acid attack had just been reported and Hunter had delegated Naz and Sabira to deal with it.

It appeared to be unrelated but Hunter wanted a confirmation as soon as possible. Assaults of this nature were still relatively unusual but if this was the beginning of a linked series, he needed to know.

The mid-morning drug dealers were out, positioned in their favourite spots. It was business as usual. A teenage dealer stepped out from a shop doorway, and whistled towards a youth on the other side of the road, pointing surreptitiously to a young boy emerging from an alleyway. Their target appeared unaware of the fact that both youths, now with hoods pulled tightly around their faces, were heading in his direction. Something was about to happen.

Charlie indicated the trio to Paul and jumped out as Paul slewed the car to a standstill. Within seconds he joined her, leaving Hunter to call for further assistance over the radio. The two youths grabbed hold of the boy, bundling him backwards into the alleyway. She saw the glint of metal as the first dealer pulled a knife out from the back of his trousers and flashed it towards the youngster. He was no more than twelve years old, young and cocky, the new boy on the block, and it was clear he had overstepped the mark and was about to be taught a lesson. The boy's face crumpled at the sight of the blade, his hands stretched out in front of him to try to fend off his attackers.

There was no time to wait for back-up to arrive. Charlie ran at them, shouting as she did so, with Paul in hot pursuit. The two aggressors turned towards the noise, before splitting at the sight of them and running off in different directions, the knifeman down the alleyway. Charlie concentrated on him as he disappeared around a bend in the path, watching as the knife clattered to the ground. She continued after him, panting with relief as a police car pulled up at the end, blocking his escape. He turned, rooted momentarily to the spot as she torpedoed into him, pushing him up against the wall and slamming him in handcuffs. She was joined within seconds by Paul, who had decided to assist her with the knifeman rather than risk both of them getting into danger in separate chases. Together they marched their suspect back towards the shops, stopping on their way to retrieve the knife from where it lay. It was all over; the whole scenario having lasted less than a minute from start to finish.

By the time they got to the main road the young boy had disappeared, melting into the background; his relief at being rescued on this occasion not transferring to gratitude. He would live to fight another day, but hopefully he had learnt a valuable lesson. A police van was waiting and a small group of onlookers had gathered on the nearby pavement. Hunter opened the van doors as they approached, taking possession of the knife while Paul searched their suspect.

'That's right, you bastards,' a woman screamed towards them. 'Stitching another poor young black boy up for nothing. Why can't you lot just leave 'em alone?' The woman broke away from the group and launched herself towards the van. She was short, white and middle-aged; a fiery, spitting ball of rage, with long bleached-blonde hair and huge hooped earrings. What she lacked in stature, she more than made up for in aggression. Charlie moved across, blocking her path with outstretched arms, but she needn't have worried. The woman stopped, sucking on her teeth and peered instead towards their detainee.

'You all right, Marlon?'

The youth turned his head towards them, narrowing his eyes. 'Yeah I'm all right, Shirley. Can you go to me house and tell me mum I've been nicked. Tell her to come to the station and bring my brief. Tell her I ain't done nothin' wrong.'

'I will do, son. Leave it wiv' me. I'll have you outta there before you know it.'

The youth nodded, pulling at his restraints in an arrogant show of strength. 'Thanks, Shirley. I know you will.' He continued to posture, showing off to the crowd.

Hunter stepped forward as Paul was concluding the search, taking hold of his other arm. 'Paul, get him away from here,' he said, as together they lifted the youth up into the van cage. 'We'll catch up with you later.'

*

Hunter stood at the front of the house while Charlie re-positioned the wheelie bin and clambered back up onto it. Hopefully, with several hours having elapsed Hookham might have returned. If so they'd call for more units. Nothing had changed though; everything being in exactly the same position as it had been earlier. She signalled with her hands, it was identical to their last visit and shook her head.

Hunter nodded his understanding, but she could see from where she was positioned that he wasn't happy. It was not what either of them wanted. She jumped down and headed towards him, watching as he answered his phone, his brow creasing further with the conversation.

'Damn it,' he repeated his earlier phrase as she joined him. 'That was Nick on the phone. He sent up for another cell-siting on Hookham's phone to see if we can get an up-to-date location and the result has just come back.'

'And? Anywhere we can head to now?' She knew the answer before he opened his mouth.

'It was last used in the Clapham Junction area about fifteen minutes after we were here before, knocking on his door. Since that time, nothing, and apart from late at night Nick says it's used a lot. He's worried the phone might have been switched off.' Hunter ran his hands up over his head. 'Do you think he could have seen us here earlier?'

'I don't know, but there's no way he could get to Clapham Junction that quickly from here, park up and disappear. It's at least thirty to forty-five minutes' drive at any time of the day in traffic.' She pulled the car door open, before glancing up and noticing the distinctive red-brick building of Norbury railway station and the line of minicabs queued up outside. A train horn sounded as she did so, the two-tone blast sending a warning to passengers that it was coming through. 'Unless,' she pointed towards the station, suddenly conscious of its proximity. 'He caught a train.'

Hunter grimaced and headed off, leaving her to secure the car. She slammed the door shut and started jogging to catch up. He was already halfway along the side passage, striding towards the parking area. 'If you're right, Charlie, we should turn a corner into the car park and see…'

'His little red Vauxhall Corsa.' She recognised the registration number instantly. 'Beautifully parked. Complete with learner plates and his name and number. Shit!' She started walking towards it, pulling a pair of gloves from her pocket. She tried the doors but they were locked, then she put the back of her hand on the bonnet, but the engine was cool, or at least as cool as the heat of the day would allow. It certainly hadn't been driven for a while.

'And no pay-and-display ticket. He's not bothered about his car being impounded.' She peered up at the sign on top of the roof. 'And if he's switched his phone off, he's risking his livelihood. Why would he do that?' She didn't need to say anything more.

The interior looked relatively tidy, nothing obviously incriminating left out on display. The front seats were clean, but the rear seat was dusty, with several patches of mud smeared across the material. A few burrs and leaves lay in the rear footwell. She strained her head closer to see if she recognised any of the same foliage that grew on Tooting Bec Common, when her eyes noticed two tiny splashes of red against the fabric, two dried drips of what appeared to be blood.

'Boss, look.' She pointed to the spots before moving forward and squinting at the driver's seat. 'And there's more here.' Hunter looked to where she was pointing, before shaking his head and staring skywards.

'For fuck's sake. How did we all miss seeing him drive in here earlier? The car stands out a mile. It's bright bloody red and has his name emblazoned all over it.'

Charlie was still staring at the scuffs of blood on the steering wheel. They weren't big but there were a few of them. 'Do you think its Brian's?' she asked quietly.

Hunter pulled his hankie out and wiped the face of his watch, squinting as he read the time. 'It would certainly explain why Carl wasn't keen to talk.' He pressed a number into his phone and barked some orders down the line. The Corsa had to be recovered to a secure pound to await an urgent forensic examination and another unit needed to get to them ASAP to sit with it until its removal. He had far more important things to do than stay here wasting his time with it any longer.

What he didn't say, but what he and Charlie both knew, was that each day about two thousand trains passed through the seventeen platforms of Clapham Junction railway station. It serviced the busy London stations of both Victoria and Waterloo with destinations all over the south of England and Wales and links to services running to the north of England and Scotland.

Carl Hookham could be on route to anywhere in the UK by now and they had no way of finding out where.

Chapter 11

It was to be another night to remember.

Detective Sergeant Leonard Cookson was to die. Vengeance would be sweet and brutal. Leonard Cookson deserved nothing less. He worked on Trident, the Met's answer to 'black on black' crime. It was common knowledge on the streets and behind bars that Trident officers were all bent, planting drugs and guns, taking backhanders, fitting innocent black kids up.

Trident officers thought they were special but they were nothing more than a bunch of lying bullies. None of them would stand a chance if they were on their own. How he'd love to see how they coped in prison. They wouldn't be such 'big men' then; they'd be the con's target, beaten up, spat at, shanked, or worse. They'd have to do their time on a special wing, no one to talk to except the screws or nonces. It would serve the fuckers right

Detective Sergeant Leonard Cookson was one of the worst. Prison was too good for the likes of him. He knew it… and Ice knew it too. All the stories circulating about him, all the images on display, just reinforced what people already believed about police.

Leonard Cookson was in charge of a team of the Trident lying scum, making up the rules as he went along, allowed to continue because he was one of them; none of his mates daring to stop him because they were all the same.

Tonight he would again be doing Ice's bidding, but he would also very much be doing his own. They were right to have picked this copper.

He hefted his kit up onto his shoulder and checked the time. The instructions were clear; researched, accurate and brutal, so fucking brutal. Now it was time to put them into practice. Around midnight, after the doors to the pub closed, the devil would claim his prize.

*

It was only a short walk home. Well to be more exact, it was only a short stagger. Leonard Cookson stood leaning against the gatepost of The Lonely Mole Public House, watching as some of his team crammed themselves into a single cab, one in the front and three bulky frames squashed together in the rear. He wanted to laugh at the minicab driver's expression. They both knew it would be a miracle if all four got home without one of them puking. God knows how many pints and shots they'd downed. Still, it wasn't his problem anymore. With a muffled shout from its passengers, the car was on its way, the chassis creaking noisily at the increased weight on the rear shock absorbers.

He turned to face the direction of his house. Now, all he had to do was to get there. Judging by his inability to walk in a straight line however, this was going to prove harder than he'd originally thought.

He lurched forward, allowing his momentum on the downhill gradient to carry him along. At each tree he steadied himself before moving onwards. The road bent to the right in a gentle curve before straightening again as it passed the entry to his local park. As he walked, his mind wandered back to the shenanigans of the evening. Coppers and alcohol were a bad combination. It had been a good night though, a double celebration; his forty-eighth birthday and the conviction of four teenagers responsible for shooting a young black lad in the torso, leaving him wheelchair-bound for the rest of his life.

The incident had taken place near the local skateboard park, the suspects together ambushing their rivals and firing towards the opposing gang arbitrarily, their faces covered, the violence meted out without thought to anyone who happened to be nearby. An innocent bystander, caught in the crossfire had ended up with a bullet lodged in her arm. The teen gunmen had all then melted into the nearby estate.

The shooting had been a tit-for-tat hit, in response to the stabbing of one of their own, but the tensions on the streets between the local gangs had escalated to such a point that it was only a matter of time before another kid from the neighbourhood was killed, or an innocent child, or parent, or pensioner. Bullets were indiscriminate. They didn't care whose flesh they tore apart or whose heart they stopped pumping.

How could he forget the look of fear in the expression of the sixteen-year-old boy, his spleen removed, his spine shattered, the skin of his torso held together with large black stitches, wired up to all manner of tubes, drips and monitors yet still trying so hard to look tough. The kid's eyes told the real story though; the way they flicked towards the door constantly, filled with terror each time it opened, in case a hooded-up enemy arrived to finish the job. Even the presence of an armed police officer couldn't negate his fear. Teenagers like him spent their lives looking behind them, waiting for their time to be up. They knew nothing better, their lives revolved around their gang families and the respect achieved by owning, or better still, using a 'piece'.

How could he also forget the confusion on the face of the petite Chinese lady lying on a stretcher in the same hospital, the bones in her right arm splintered by the stray bullet? A masseuse by trade, she would probably never be able to work again, her livelihood taken from her by fate, her life saved only by the fact she had lifted her arm to protect herself on hearing the first shot.

Something had to be done about it and DS Cookson's team were determined they would be the ones to do it. Kids couldn't keep killing kids. The guns and knives needed to be removed from the streets and local residents allowed to go about their business without fear. Trident played havoc with the gangs. It also played havoc with your home life, but if the cops on his team made a difference to just one person, then it was all worthwhile.

Photos pinned to the office wall showing their victims' injuries had kept the team spurred on at times when the investigation appeared to be stalled. He still had copies of them stored in his phone.

Pulling his phone out from his jacket pocket, he keyed in his passcode, missing the sequence twice before it finally started to load. He started to walk again slowly, wiping his brow to clear the continuous stream of sweat prickling on his body. Christ, he needed to lose weight. He could hardly do this pair of trousers up these days. Even the shirt was tight across his gut, wet with sweat at the base of his back. He breathed in, realising it had no effect whatsoever on the girth of his stomach. Too many hours worked, too little exercise. This job was slowly killing him.

The pictures came up and he scrolled through them, shaking his head at the memory of the investigation. There had been very little forensic evidence left at the scene and almost no witnesses willing to come forward. Mobile phones and social media had proved to be their saviour. Teenagers were teenagers. Their need to chat, both before and after the shooting, placed them all squarely at the right place, at the right time, and their thinly veiled bragging on Facebook and Instagram only served to accentuate their stupidity. They would be serving a total of fifty-two years between them; twenty-five for the main perpetrator armed with the gun and nine for each of his accomplices.

DS Leonard Cookson was justifiably proud of the outcome; in fact, he and his team had been commended by the judge. He threaded the phone back into his jacket pocket, next to his wallet which was now half the thickness it had been when he'd entered the pub. The team deserved to be rewarded for their efforts and he was happy to pick up the tab.

The entrance to the park was across the road on his left. His house, where his wife and family were sleeping soundly, a further two hundred metres on the right, but he needed a piss. Momentarily he weighed up the two options, before stepping down the pavement and staggering across the road towards the park. There was something almost obligatory about stopping for a piss behind a tree, or lamp post after a night out. These days he tried to be a little more discreet, but it still brought back a vague frisson of daring at the prospect.

The road was empty, his latest abode having been chosen for the quietness of its surroundings. Only the residents and the occasional carful of children destined for the park travelled along it by day and at this time of night all was silent. His wives, past and present, might not have appreciated the number of hours he worked but they'd certainly appreciated the salary.

He followed a trail of dried mud across the road towards the gates which were locked. The local council were in the process of tearing down the ancient cafe and unsanitary toilet block in readiness for a new cafe and sports pavilion. A few metres to the right of the main gates there was a break in the railings. It had been there for years, and even though the council had repaired the metal struts several times, the local teenagers had rarely left it more than a few days before creating a new access. It was where they hung out most evenings, but it was far too late for them now, thankfully. He could well imagine the local head-lines if he was caught proverbially, with his pants down.

He breathed in as he found the gap, pulling his gut in further with his hands. Even though two struts were missing, it was still a squeeze. His breath came out in a rush as he popped through the other side and he wiped the additional sweat from his forehead on the back of his sleeve. He needed to piss even more now, the pressure of the railings on his bladder increasing his desperation still further. He glanced up at the sky, just as a cloud moved slowly across the face of the moon, obliterating any last light from its pitted surface. He reached down over his belly and grabbed the fly of his trousers, pulling frantically at the waistband.

As his fingers took hold of the tiny zipper, Leonard Cookson sighed with relief before staggering forward into the darkness.

*

He couldn't believe his luck. The bastard copper was heading, of his own volition, towards the final destination selected by Ice. Ice always provided the end point and the means, but he was left to his own devices to work out the minutia of the execution and Leonard Cookson could have been difficult. He was a big man, albeit fat rather than muscular, but he was also drunk, and drunks could be pig-headed, loud and impetuous. Now, if he did manage to shout out, the noise would be muffled within the tree boughs and any scuffle would be hidden from prying eyes. It was fucking priceless.

He grinned with delight as he watched Cookson squeeze his fat body through the gap in the railings. The man was disgusting, every bit of him, lacking in both physical and mental self-control. He deserved everything he was about to get. Maybe it was karma. Fate had intervened and his job was now going to be far simpler.

The gag and hunting knife were grasped tightly in his hands, only a slight quiver betraying his anticipation. The handcuffs and cable were easily accessed in his pocket and the rest of his equipment packed carefully into his rucksack. He was ready.

Silently he skirted down the edge of the park, keeping to the darkest part of the pavement until he came to the hole in the railings. His heart pumped hard with the thrill of the chase, but his mind remained concentrated on what he had to do. He could hear the policeman's footfall in the undergrowth, the sound of heavy breathing at every movement. His fingers tightened against the metal grip of the knife and without a backwards glance he slipped through the gap.

Chapter 12

Friday 23rd June 2017

Charlie was running slightly late having fielded a call from Ben promising that he would try even harder to clean up his act. Maybe she would arrange for him to come with her next time she was visiting her mum at the family house. Meg, Lucy and Beth adored him and he was always the centre of attention when he was there. The so-called normality of her family seemed to calm him, focussing his attention away from his own worries onto the ups and downs of her half-sisters' lives. She made a mental note to invite him round soon.

She was still thinking about this when she literally bumped into Hunter coming along the corridor. She ran her hand through her hair self-consciously, realising she'd forgotten to brush it before she left home.

'Sorry I'm a little late, guv. Ben just phoned.'

Hunter's previously pinched expression softened immediately. 'How is he?'

'OK. Not great. We're working on it.'

Hunter nodded. 'Keep it up, Charlie. He's a good lad.' He paused as if about to add another comment before appearing to change his mind. Instead, he flapped a piece of paper towards her, on which he'd scribbled down a few notes. 'Get your stuff ready, there's been another body found. Another police officer. The call's just this second come in. I'm going to find out what's known and then we'll make our way. Tell Nick he can come too.'

Charlie felt the colour drain from her face. Another police officer dead. What was going on? She pushed through the door to find the others huddled around a screen, watching as the live call was updated with the newest information.

'What's the latest?' she joined them, straining to see over Paul's shoulder.

'Not much.' Paul shifted over. 'A body's been found by some workmen in a building they were renovating at the back of Streatham Common, partially burned. A warrant card was left by the body, but the name hasn't been aired as yet. They're still trying to confirm whether the body belongs to the person shown on it.' He glanced back at the screen and pursed his lips. 'Dammit, they've just protected the message, so we won't see the updates. We'll have to wait until Hunter returns.'

Bet, Naz and Sabira stayed rooted to the spot, staring at the still screen, deep in thought. Paul broke the silence eventually.

'I hear we missed Carl Hookham. Bet and I were going back through CCTV last thing yesterday and we have his Corsa now in Bedford Hill, a few streets away from where Brian Ashton was found. We spotted it twice within a couple of hours; the sightings match with the phone calls.'

'I've just circulated him as wanted,' Bet added. 'The boss asked me to get it done early this morning, as soon as he arrived, even before this latest call. He wants Hookham brought in for questioning ASAP.'

'At least we have his car.' Charlie turned towards Paul. 'Hopefully there'll be some forensics in it.'

'Yeah, hopefully. But unfortunately we don't have him.'

'Do you think he could be connected to this latest one?' Charlie hoped not. They felt bad enough about losing him yesterday. To think he might be responsible for the death of another colleague was mortifying.

'No idea as yet. Let's hope not. Or Dennis Walters. He's still about and hates us all.'

Charlie nodded. The memory of being hustled out of his front door was not lost on her. She could feel the frustration building already. She turned abruptly and went to her desk, pulling her equipment bag out, along with a rather hairy hairbrush that clattered onto the floor next to her baton and a spare pair of shoes. She picked it up, debating for a few seconds whether to try to clean it, before deciding against the idea.

Hunter strode back in as she was attempting to calm an unruly wave at the back of her head. He took one look at her before frowning.

'Right, let's go Charlie. We haven't got time for you to brush your hair. You should have done that before you got in, like everyone else.' He glanced around the office, his eyes skimming each workstation. 'Where's Nick?'

Charlie shrugged and threw the brush back into her drawer. She hoisted her bag on to her shoulder to indicate she at least was ready to go.

'Sorry, guv, I haven't seen him yet.'

Hunter stared around the others but they all shrugged too, the silence between them lengthening. Any progress Nick had made the previous day was well and truly lost.

'Waster,' he muttered under his breath and shook his head. Delving into his trouser pocket, he pulled out a piece of paper which he unfolded and slapped down on Naz's desk. 'Right, while we're out, Naz, Sabira, start doing some research on our latest victim. I need you to find out everything there is to know about his domestic situation which, by all accounts, sounds complicated. You did well with Brian Ashton's.' He turned to Paul and Bet. 'If and when Nick deigns to show his face, get him working on the phones of our latest victim and our other suspects. Paul, get in touch with Human Resources and make enquiries about getting his personal file pulled. We need to know any possible links between the two officers. Have they worked together at the same station, or on the same case? And Bet, likewise with Hookham and Walters, our two suspects. Is our new victim connected to either of them? Has he arrested them, stopped them or even dealt with them as victims. There must be some sort of link and we need to find it.'

*

Charlie swung the car out from Lambeth HQ and headed along the Albert Embankment. It was the end of rush hour but the traffic was still heavy, queuing up to turn across Lambeth Bridge towards Westminster. She was reminded that the Trooping the Colour had taken place the weekend before and all the roads heading towards Buckingham Palace had been closed for hours. For an instant, she wondered whether another event was in the offing, causing similar road closures.

She switched the blue light and sirens on and navigated the centre line, squinting momentarily towards Millbank and the Tate Britain on the opposite side of the river. The water of the Thames was tinged blue, reflecting the brightness of the sky and sparkling with refracted light, as each wave swirled seaward. A tingle of unease ran the length of her spine at the sight, so she concentrated back on the road ahead; luckily most of the tailbacks were in the opposite direction.

'The name that we have is Leonard Cookson. He was a DS on Operation Trident.' Hunter paused. 'I knew him many years ago when he was a PC and I was a sergeant. I did a spell at West End Central police station, uptown. I'd just been made up to a skipper and he had just joined. Even while he was still a probationer he was the sort who attracted work… and trouble. I'm not surprised he got out of uniform as quickly as he could. He wasn't a great lover of discipline, but he was a damn hard worker.' He stopped talking and looked down at his fingers. 'It must have been in the nineties. He's got to have had at least twenty-five years in.'

Charlie navigated past a stationary bus. 'He wouldn't have had long to go then.'

'No, only a few more years. Apparently, he worked most of his career in various CID offices around London, as well as serving postings with a few of the central squads. He'd been on Trident for the last four years and had a good reputation.' Hunter turned to look out of the window. 'He's probably dealt with hundreds, if not thousands, of people during his service.'

'And any one of them could have a grudge against him, for something he did or didn't do.'

'Or, like Dennis Walters, they might just hate police. Whatever their reason, it sounds like they went to town on him.' He paused. 'And they're doing it quickly. Two in a matter of days.'

They lapsed into silence until they reached Streatham Common.

The majority of the police units were gathering at the main entrance to the common in a car park by The Rookery, an area of landscaped gardens with a small cafe that was popular with local residents by day and the gay community at night. Most of the communal access to the common was from the main road at this side and more units were required there to assist with setting up cordons and keeping the area sterile.

The new pavilion was across the other side of the common in a far more secluded area, backed by a ring of trees, with a large grassy area in front of it that was to be converted into playing fields. The Duty Inspector and Scene of Crime Officers were meeting at this side and a designated route to the crime scene was already in place. Charlie made her way to join them.

'Leonard Cookson's house is only a couple of hundred metres further on from the access road into the common where his body was found,' Hunter said, as they turned into Ryecroft Road. 'There's no reply at his address at the moment. They've tried several times.'

'So he nearly made it home?' Charlie slowed the car as they swept down a slight hill and pulled up behind several police vehicles.

They climbed out of the car and Hunter stared in the direction of Cookson's house before shaking his head. 'Yes, nearly. He was certainly close,' he said, thoughtfully. 'But not close enough.' They donned protective clothing, gave their details to the loggist and headed towards the inner cordon, tucked inside the wooded area. A ring of blue and white tape encircled tall metal fencing, which in turn protected the buildings where the body had been found. Two gates that looked to provide access to the workforce had been opened and were slightly ajar, leaving a path visible through to the building site. A heavy-duty padlock lay on the grass nearby. Parts of the building had been pulled down to be replaced with an up-to-date changing area and viewing gallery, but other parts of the original building remained, awaiting modernisation. The frontage of the new building had been constructed from breeze blocks, rows of dull grey slabs, with the windows and doors marked out with metal frames. A carcass of steel struts showed where the new roof was to be fitted. The ground all around was rutted and dry, a cloud of dust being thrown up as they walked, making the possibility of finding any footprints from either the suspect or victim extremely unlikely.

Several people, clad in white suits, were huddled together to the side of the main building deep in conversation. Charlie recognised Inspector Glenys Chapel, the same Duty Officer who had been at Brian Ashton's crime scene, talking to a couple of forensic officers. She nodded towards them as they approached, but this time there were no words of greeting. The gravity of the situation weighed heavily on them all.

'Come through.' She indicated a path leading around the side of the main pavilion and they followed in silence. The path wound past the frontage of the building, skirting around what appeared to be a kitchen area and a new shower unit, towards the rear where an old brick toilet block stood, the roof of which was partially missing. A pungent smell emanated from the block, a mixture of charred wood and burnt clothing, together with the strong aroma of cooked meat. It was like nothing Charlie had ever smelt before at any scene of fire or arson and it was a smell that would stay with her.

Inspector Chapel pointed to the entrance. 'It's not pleasant,' she said, her face creasing into a frown. 'I'll tell you what we know once you've seen the body.'

Hunter nodded and stepped forward, Charlie following in his wake. She took a deep breath as she entered but still threw her hand up over her mouth and nose at the stench and the sight. The room was airless and windowless and a spotlight had been positioned by the SOCO to illuminate the crime scene. Leonard Cookson sat strapped to a chair in the centre of the space, his head lolling back and his mouth open. Blood covered his face and neck and was dried on to what was left of his clothing. His legs were bound to the front metal legs of the chair with a length of electrical cable and his arms were behind him, his hands held together with a pair of metal handcuffs looped through a metal crossover strut on the chair back. The seat of the chair had been burnt away and his pelvis and buttocks were wedged into the space that was left, his legs keeping him from slumping through the hole.

'Fucking hell,' Hunter muttered, bending down to stare at the ground underneath the chair. 'What did the poor bastard do to deserve this?' He pointed towards a small metal container standing upright under the body, containing the remainder of what appeared to be a firework. Ashes and burnt remnants of clothing and the wooden seat of the chair were scattered around it. 'Whoever did this lit some sort of fire underneath him which has burnt through the seat and set him alight. The poor guy's literally been burned alive.'

Charlie stared at the mess in front of her. She could hardly believe that a few hours previously it had been a living, breathing human being. It seemed that the fire had burnt strongly but only for a short time. There was little else in the building that appeared to be combustible. The murder had clearly been designed to send a message, leaving clues without obliterating the whole scene. She stepped to one side of the body and, as if on cue, her eyes were drawn to several items lying on the floor. The item she saw first and that drew her attention immediately was a rose, the redness of the flower a bright contrast against the black and grey of the ashes.

'Another red rose,' she bent towards it, staring at the delicate petals. Something about it looked odd. She stared at it for a few more moments before realising what was peculiar. 'It's had all the thorns removed. Look, the stem is smooth.'

'That's smart,' Hunter stared at where she was pointing. 'No risk of scratching themselves and leaving their DNA. I'll check with SOCO whether the rose at Ashton's scene was the same.'

Charlie shook her head, stunned, before her eyes strayed to the other items. 'Bloody hell boss, look at this too,' she said, straining to better see what was there. There were three other items laid together. 'Is that what I think it is?' She pointed in horror at a thin, pink sliver of roughened tissue, before putting her hand to her mouth subconsciously. 'Is it his tongue?'

Hunter took a step towards the body and peered at Leonard Cookson's mouth. 'I can't see properly, but it would certainly explain where the blood has come from.'

Charlie nodded, appalled, before staring towards the other two items. 'His warrant card is here too, but there's also a Bible and it's been left open.' She squinted at the writing on the page and saw it was opened at the Book of Exodus, chapter 20. 'Guv, it's the Ten Commandments. Thou shalt not murder, etc. Do you reckon he's being punished for disobeying one of the commandments?'

Hunter squatted down next to her and stared towards the open Bible, his expression serious. 'You could be right, Charlie. It's been left open at this page on purpose. The question is, with Leonard Cookson's rather chequered love life and career, which commandment is it that he's being punished for?'

*

Inspector Chapel filled them in on what was known as they walked back towards their car. There was no small talk, only business. With the news coming back that the rose left with Brian Ashton's body also had the thorns removed, they all knew that the murders were connected. And with a second, so hot on the heels of the first, this latest killing was unlikely to be the last. They couldn't afford to miss a single detail... or they'd have another dead police officer on their consciences.

The body had been found by one of the first builders to arrive on site just before 08.15, after they'd noticed the padlock had been forced. On checking the building, they'd smelt an unusual odour and, stepping in to the toilet block to investigate, had come across the body. They'd left immediately without touching a thing and dialled 999. They were now at Brixton police station, in a state of shock, waiting for a statement to be taken.

After careful scrutiny it had been agreed the photograph on the warrant card matched the body. Initial enquiries confirmed that Leonard Cookson joined the job in 1991, was a detective sergeant in the Trident South gang's unit and lived nearby. Officers had already attended his registered address but there had been no reply. His next of kin was shown as a wife, Maria, and it was believed they had two young children.

His date of birth was 22/06/1969; last night, therefore, having been his birthday. Discreet enquiries at his office, with the only member of his team thus far to have arrived, had revealed he had been out celebrating with many of them at his local pub and the last time he had been seen alive was at 23.45 when he had been left to walk the short distance home. Everyone present would be asked to recall the events, including any suspicious customers or occurrences... but as yet everything appeared normal.

The crime scene cordons had been put in place quickly and competently, allowing the forensic team to get started straight away. Once the initial scene was clear, Cookson's body would be removed for a full post-mortem and further forensic examination. It was difficult to imagine that much would be found to provide an identity for their suspect, bearing in mind the desolation of the scene and fire damage, but every possibility had to be explored. Cookson was one of their own. These murders struck at the core of their collective being.

There was not much else to pass on. DCI O'Connor, as the most senior officer on call, had been informed and was awaiting a full situation report from Hunter on his return. The senior management team were still jittery about Ashton's murder being linked to a terrorist network, either mainstream or one of the less well-known pockets of disaffection. How much more nervous would they be with a second killing? Charlie listened as Hunter and Glenys Chapel discussed the possibilities as they walked, but they both agreed it was unlikely. No one had claimed responsibility for either death and both had been effected far too clandestinely. With both murders having possible religious connotations, however, it couldn't so far be ruled out.

Their priority at this moment in time was informing the next of kin, Maria Cookson. They needed to tell her as carefully and sensitively as they could of her husband's death, before word got out. They were just agreeing to try the address again when a car screeched to a halt and a woman jumped out, running towards them before her vehicle had even stopped moving. Her face was tear-stained and large black smudges of mascara blotted her pale cheeks. She had long chestnut hair which lay across the top of her head, dragged into waves where her hands had pulled at it. Her eyes glistened with further unshed tears, large and wild; the dark brown irises fixed directly at them.

'Do you have my husband there?' she blurted out. 'The mums at the school were saying that a body had been found.' She threw her hands up to her face. 'And Leonard didn't come home last night.' She stumbled to one side, rubbing at her cheeks.

Charlie stepped forward and took her by the arm, steadying her.

The woman stared straight into her eyes. 'It's him, isn't it? I knew something was wrong when he didn't come home, but he's done it before, after a night drinking. I presumed he'd crashed out on someone's sofa. What's happened to him? Tell me what's happened.'

'What's your name?' Charlie said softly, though she didn't need to ask.

'It's Maria, Maria Cookson. My husband is, was, is Leonard Cookson. Is he dead? That's what they were saying.' A loud sob escaped from her lips and she threw her hand up over her mouth.

Charlie pulled the rear door to the police car open and guided Maria Cookson towards it. One careless word and the rumours had spread; a wave of destructive gossip that took no heed to the damage or pain tossed up in its momentum.

'I'm so sorry, Maria, but I'm afraid a body has been found, along with a warrant card in your husband's name. At this stage we can't confirm for definite it is your husband, but it would appear likely. Take a seat and we'll get you home.'

Maria Cookson took a deep breath, before slumping down onto the back seat, sobbing quietly. Her hair fell like a curtain in front of her face as she leant forward, her head in her hands.

An MPV pulled up across the road, an empty child-seat strapped into the rear. Another woman got out, her expression stiff with shock and regret. She headed towards Charlie.

'I'm so sorry. Everybody was talking about what was going on. We had no idea Leonard had not come home last night. Maria just ran off when she heard what people were saying.' She pointed towards Maria Cookson, her head still in her hands. 'She's my friend. Can I help?'

Charlie opened the other rear door, biting her lip to stop the words of retribution coming out. It wasn't this woman's fault. It was just pure bad luck, but how she wished they'd got to speak to Maria first, before her world was devastated so flippantly at the school gates.

Chapter 13

The mood in the office was even more sombre than after Brian Ashton's killing. Bet had been on the receiving end of several calls from colleagues of Leonard Cookson anxious to know what had happened to their friend, their voices breaking with emotion. It had been all she could do to keep her voice steady as she heard them speak of a big man with a big personality, who was not afraid to stand up and be counted. Leonard 'Cookie' Cookson evidently dealt with his allocated crimes in the same way as he dealt with life, he grabbed the cases by the balls and wouldn't let go until he had achieved what he wanted… and he wanted results. If the management didn't like his methods, it was tough. He knew a bad guy or girl when he saw one and he didn't rest until they were behind bars.

It was midday by the time they walked in, but as Charlie and Hunter entered the office, the team stopped what they were doing and turned towards them expectantly. Nick was there now, looking decidedly shame-faced. He opened his mouth as if to address their boss but shut it again rapidly on seeing Charlie shake her head surreptitiously towards him.

It was going to be one step forward with him and two steps back.

'Go through with the others what we know so far, Charlie,' Hunter said, indicating Bet, Paul, Naz and Sabira and studiously ignoring Nick. 'I'll go and brief the DCI. *I* don't want to get in *his* bad books twice in a week.'

'Fuck it, I've ballsed up again,' Nick said, as Hunter strode out. 'That'll be me off to the post-mortem for sure.' He tried to make light of it, but no one was in the mood.

'You'll be lucky to even be doing that, if you don't pull your socks up,' Bet muttered. 'It was bad enough with just one murder. Now we've got two, the pressure will be doubled... so I suggest you try not to piss the guvnor off anymore than you have to. He'll be expecting everyone, including you, to pull their weight.'

'That's the end of my sex life as I know it, then,' Nick grinned, trying to deflect the criticism again. He pulled at his tie, loosening the knot and unbuttoning the top of his shirt.

'What a shame,' Sabira frowned. 'But it's better than losing your actual life!'

Charlie stared as Nick ignored the comment, stretching and flexing his biceps. He seemed immune to Bet and Sabira's low opinion of him, preferring to concentrate on Paul and Naz who seemed more susceptible to his charm. She turned away from the sight of his muscular arms, embarrassed. She had yet to make up her mind.

'Right, I'll go through with you what we know so far before Hunter gets back. Then you can fill us in with what you've found.'

She sat down and her colleagues gathered round, listening in horror as she described the crime scene and recounted everything that had been discussed.

'We spoke briefly to Maria Cookson but she was obviously in no state to tell us much. Leonard worked long hours and was not what you'd call the model husband, but she was prepared to put up with his faults because he provided a happy, secure environment for her and their two daughters, China, who is eight years old, and Sophie, who is just six. She loved him for who he was, a hard-working, hard-living copper who loved his family but didn't always put them first.'

'That's similar to what I heard,' Bet added. 'DS Cookson was well respected and held in high regard. He liked a good bevvy and there was no side to him. You got what you saw. He would back his team to the hilt and expected total loyalty in return. I did get the impression that what happened at work, stayed at work. If you worked hard for him, you would be rewarded. If you didn't, you'd find yourself on a sideways move.' She paused, before turning to Nick. 'A bit like Hunter.'

'Maria said that he'd been married twice before,' Charlie continued. 'His first marriage was to his childhood sweetheart Mary. They'd been going out six years before they tied the knot but the marriage only lasted two years and they didn't have any children. Maria wasn't aware of any contact between them since the split.

'His second marriage was to Sheila and they had two kids, Lenny, now aged seventeen, and Helen who is fifteen. Maria says that Leonard did still see the kids sometimes but not as often as he probably should. The kids are typical teenagers who have better things to do than endure fortnightly visits to their father, and Leonard seemed content to share their lack of enthusiasm. He's happy when he sees them, but he's equally happy when he doesn't. It does all sound amicable though and he gets on well with Sheila's new husband, Glen. Maria thinks, in fact, that he's more than willing to allow Glen to deal with all the teenage angst as it's something he can't cope with. Leonard, like most men, with the exception of you, Paul,' she put her hands up to fend off the anticipated remonstration, 'couldn't deal with emotions or emotional people; he'd rather cut and run.'

Paul got up and headed for the kettle, smiling. 'So, he was an old-fashioned man's man? Not a metrosexual like me, in touch with their emotions and fully domesticated?'

'You could say that.' Charlie passed him her mug. 'There's a bit of domestic stuff to check. Are his ex-wives and their new husbands really OK with him? Could he have had any mistresses while working his long hours and, if so, could they or their husbands be out for revenge? Was he promising them the world? Or has he been boasting to friends or colleagues about his exploits? The killer cut his tongue off. Could that be to shut him up?'

The door flew open as she was speaking and Hunter strode in, swearing as he did so.

DCI O'Connor was right behind him and immediately turned towards Charlie.

'I know DI Hunter isn't impressed with what I've just had to tell him… and you have much more important things to do, but in case he tries to *forget* what I've just mentioned… DC Stafford, you and Hunter will both be required to make one final statement with regards to a few matters that the IPCC want covered in their review. It shouldn't take long. DS Hayley Boyle from the DPS will be contacting me again shortly to arrange a new date for your interviews. I'd like this over and done with

ASAP, so you must both co-operate as fully as possible so we can get the investigation concluded.'

'Yes, sir,' she said, dipping her head. DCI O'Connor was on their side... and anyway, he had no choice in the matter. He, like they, had to follow orders.

'Thank you, Charlie. I knew I could rely on you.' He turned on his heels and marched out.

'Bloody politics,' Hunter exploded, as soon as the door was shut. He paced across the room and stood by the window, his back towards them.

'Here, boss, ignore it.' Paul offered him a mug of tea. 'You know as well as we do that it's the job of DPS and the IPCC to be as stroppy and pedantic as they can, and to question every decision any police officer makes... on the spur of the moment... when faced with the imminent threat of death.' They all voiced their agreement. Both departments were disliked by rank and file officers, the IPCC in particular being viewed as having no experience of the actual practicalities and stresses of policing.

Hunter took the mug and sighed heavily. 'Thanks, Paul,' he blew hard at the steaming mug. 'Best I don't argue with the fact you've given me tea and I really fancied a coffee then.' He grinned, his expression relaxing. 'Give me a murdering scumbag, armed with a gun or machete any day, rather than dealing with any more do-gooders and their bureaucratic red tape. They'll be the death of me, I swear.'

The moment had passed. Hunter was back to normal, though Charlie knew that he meant every word he said.

'Right, now I've calmed down, let's get on with what's really important.' Hunter stood up. 'I've briefed the DCI.' He stopped. 'Naz, Sabira, are you sure your acid attack case isn't connected?'

Sabira nodded. 'As sure as we can be, guv. It's a classic honour-related attack. A young Punjabi girl who disagreed with the arranged marriage her parents had planned for her. We're just trying to establish which relative threw the acid, but no one's talking, as usual. It's definitely not connected to our murders.'

Hunter nodded his understanding. 'Good. That's what I told the DCI and he also agrees there doesn't appear to be anything to suggest the killings are terror-related. They're far too covert and personal, but I will be liaising regularly with Counterterrorism to keep them updated. So… in the absence of any forensic evidence so far, what do we have to link the two cases?'

'Well, the red rose left at each scene, for a start, with the thorns removed,' Charlie began. 'It's far too much of a coincidence for them to have been left by different killers.'

'I agree, and that detail wasn't made public. So, if we have the same killer, what links him to our two victims?'

'Well, firstly I looked on social media but they don't appear as "friends" or connected in any way, but...' Paul brightened as he looked towards Hunter. 'Brian Ashton and Leonard Cookson were both based on Lambeth Borough for about eighteen months around 2004. Ashton only had a few years in and was uniform, whereas Cookson had around thirteen years' service and was CID, so they weren't in the same branch but they could well have worked on some cases together. I'm checking now, but trying to search on every investigation or incident each officer was involved in over all that time is pretty impossible. There could be hundreds, and that's if they are even reported.'

'If it does go back that far then our killer has been bearing a grudge for a long time. Can you check if Cookson has had any dealings with Dennis Walters or Carl Hookham?'

'Bet's been doing that, guv,' Paul nodded towards Bet.

'Nothing yet, boss. I've started going back through their previous convictions to try and find arresting and investigating officers, but like Paul says, Cookson could have assisted without it ever being written down.'

Charlie pursed her lips. Bet and Paul were both right. While there were clear links for Walters and Hookham with Brian Ashton, they might never find if Cookson had dealt with either. Only one officer ever completed a stop-and-search slip, even though others may have been present. And only one officer was shown as arresting on the custody sheet, even though several may have been present or just hanging around the custody office dealing with a different prisoner. Any number could have assisted the investigating officers with witness interviews, exhibits or searches of premises. Or Cookson could have come across them while covering for an officer on leave, on a totally different case. It would be easy to miss, and it only took one oversight and the harm would be done... and that was if it was even recorded.

Police officers came into contact with members of the public dozens of times daily for all manner of reasons without pen ever being put to paper. A chance encounter might have sown the seed, allowed their murderer time for their hatred to fester until now... but why now?

She walked over to the window and stared out towards the skyscrapers of Canary Wharf, letting a thought take shape.

'Boss, can we just think of Cookson first. Why the Bible? The Ten Commandments must be the clue.'

Hunter raised his hands, open palmed. 'Fire away with your thoughts, Charlie.'

'Can someone look up the Bible verses? Exodus, chapter 20.'

Paul nodded and pulled out his phone.

'It's the whole business of his tongue being cut off.' She took a deep breath and continued, 'Several of the commandments relate to what a person says.'

Paul held his phone up, staring at the screen as the words appeared. 'Right, here we are. Exodus, Chapter 20. "And God spoke these words. I am the Lord your God, who brought you out of Egypt, out of the land of slavery."' Paul glanced up at Charlie. 'I'll try and precis the commandments. OK, here goes. You shall have no other Gods but me. You shall not make for yourself an image of anything in Heaven or on Earth and bow down to worship it. You shall not misuse the name of the Lord your God. Remember to keep the Sabbath holy. Honour your father and mother. You shall not murder. You shall not commit adultery. You shall not steal. You shall not give false testimony against your neighbour. You shall not covet your neighbour's house, or his wife, or his male or female servant, or his ox or donkey or anything that belongs to him.' Paul stopped speaking and looked up. 'Well, by the sounds of it, Cookson could have disobeyed almost all of them... except maybe murder or coveting his neighbour's ox or donkey.'

Charlie smiled, before closing her eyes briefly, thinking hard. 'But if we're concentrating on the tongue, then there are only two commandments that are relevant and they are; you shall not misuse the name of the Lord your God, i.e. by swearing and cursing; but that probably applies to most coppers in the Met, in fact the majority of the general public. So that just leaves one. You shall not give false testimony against your neighbour, i.e. you mustn't lie.'

'So what's he been saying? To who? And about whom?' Hunter rubbed his hands up over his head. He started to pace around the room. 'And why set fire to him?' As he was speaking his phone rang. Charlie watched him as he pulled it out of his pocket and answered it abruptly, before his expression changed from confusion to comprehension. When he finished he threw the phone on the table in front of him and breathed out heavily.

'Well?' Charlie couldn't wait to hear what Hunter had just been told.

'Well… that was the SOCO.' His expression was still animated. 'He said that he had run some quick tests on Leonard Cookson's lower clothing. He wasn't happy that the clothing should catch fire and burn quite so easily, because these days most garments are made with fire-resistant or retardant material. Anyway, suffice to say, he was right. The reason the killer was able to start the fire was because he found traces of an accelerant on the seat of his trousers. Charlie might just be spot on with her thoughts about Cookson telling lies.' He stopped pacing and lowered himself on to the edge of a desk. 'And if she's right, I have to say our killer has a somewhat sick sense of humour. Have you heard the phrase, "Liar, liar" …'?

'Pants on fire,' Bet joined in. 'Bloody hell,' she opened a drawer and pulled out Leonard Cookson's personal file, turning to a folder labelled 'Form 163s'. 'I was looking at his complaints record earlier. He's got quite a few, though just as many commendations for bravery and outstanding work, I have to say. He was quite a formidable officer. Anyway, I noticed that he still has two that are ongoing. One is for assault, pretty much par for the course when dealing with the sort of prisoners he deals with, but the other is a little rarer. It's for perjury, which might also explain why a Bible, commonly used in court, has specifically been left at the scene. He's alleged to have fitted up a gang nominal with possession of a firearm a couple of years ago and then further lied on oath in the box, when it eventually got to court.'

'Shit!' Paul bent down and unlocked one of his drawers, pulling out Brian Ashton's personal file. He leafed through the various sections until he came to a similar file labelled 'Form 163s' and opened the last page. 'I noticed this when I was looking through Brian's complaint history, particularly after Sabira and Bet had been talking about religious fundamentalists chopping thieves' hands off. With all the domestic issues taking precedence though, I put it to one side. I was going to come back to it. Look.' He pointed to the writing on the page. 'This is a complaint from the neighbour of an elderly lady who died alone at home, with no next of kin. It alleges that she had told the neighbour she had 10K in cash hidden in a chest of drawers, but after police had attended the scene and taken her valuables into police possession, there was only 9K recorded, £1,000 was missing.'

Paul paled as he read out the final sentence. 'PC Ashton was the officer who booked in the property and it is therefore alleged that, if indeed there was 10K initially, it was he who stole the cash.'

'That's it. It fits perfectly.' Charlie murmured out loud. 'Thou shalt not steal,'

*

It was midnight by the time Charlie stepped out from the revolving doors of Lambeth HQ and breathed in a lungful of London air. Her head was throbbing from the hours spent staring at her computer screen, her fingertips raw from pounding the keyboard and her throat dry from inhaling the air conditioning.

However hard they tried, none of them had been able to find a specific link between either suspect, either victim or between any of the persons named on either complaint. As the afternoon had turned to evening and the evening had turned to night, the others had drifted off, one by one, their heads hung low, heavy with disappointment, their initial enthusiasm crushed. The next day was Saturday, their day off. No doubt they would all be in, the unspoken expectation at the beginning of a murder enquiry being to continue the immediate work. The early days were usually the ones that provided the best leads and they needed a result for this case, fast. To that end, she and Hunter would be attending Leonard Cookson's post-mortem early the next day. He felt he owed it to his former colleague to be present.

Hunter himself had stayed late, his body hunched over his computer, the reading glasses he so hated, stuck to the end of his nose. Only several increasingly irritated calls from Mrs H eventually forced him home to socialise with her visiting parents. He led by example, his dedication to each new case second to none.

Nick disappeared shortly after Hunter but not because he was dedicated; it was Friday night and he was determined to make the most of belated birthday celebrations with his mates in Soho. It suited him to leave later and at the same time score a few brownie points with the boss. He'd teased Charlie gently for suggesting he might come up with a solution to the case when he was least expecting it. *He* didn't get paid enough to worry about work when he was out at play, even if the victims were police officers. Tonight he was out on the pull. His hair had been freshly gelled, his clothing carefully chosen and a liberal spray of aftershave completed the groundwork.

Charlie had left last, finding his words strangely disquieting, antagonising even. She took a deep breath as she left the HQ and started to jog, her scruffy trainers guiding her away from her usual route past the colourful graffiti-clad walls of the skateboard park on the South Bank, the scene of Ben's robbery. Her mind emptied itself of everything and everyone as she ran, glorying in the freedom of unlimited space, liberated from the confines of four walls. An image of Ben, alone and bleeding on the concrete floor of the park, came to her and she railed against the memory. She didn't want to deal with any more pressure tonight.

She turned instead over Westminster Bridge, past wilted flowers tied to the brick ramparts in memory of the innocent victims of March's terrorist attack. On towards Big Ben and the Houses of Parliament, their facades lit up yellow against the sky, with armed police equipped with MP5 firearms now standing guard along their perimeters. The brutal killing of a lone, unarmed police officer protecting the rule of democracy had shocked the nation. PC Keith Palmer would not be forgotten.

She dipped her head at his memory, before continuing on along Whitehall, past Downing Street, bristling with its own permanent armed police presence until she got to Trafalgar Square. Through the centre she jogged, her breath relaxing into a rhythm, her feet keeping time with the drumming in her head as she glanced up at the statue of Admiral Lord Nelson atop his column keeping watch over the capital's visitors.

The roads were still busy, black cabs vying for trade with the riders of four-wheeled rickshaws, night buses looming over their rivals, all competing for the night-time economy. She turned into Charing Cross Road, heading towards Leicester Square and Chinatown, the area of Soho where the streets never slept and the clubs never shut their doors. Music pumped out from bars and the pavements filled as she approached, gaggles of partygoers stumbling through the narrow criss-cross lanes of Frith Street, Dean Street, Wardour Street, Soho Square. Nick was up here somewhere enjoying himself.

She stopped running and stood stock-still as the air filled with the sound of sirens. Two police officers, one male and one female, ran around the corner, just as half a dozen drunken revellers burst out from the doorway of a bar, brawling with each other, on the opposite side of the street. A couple of the drunken fighters saw the two uniforms, turning towards them instead, their aggression aimed now at the officers.

'Come on then, you fucking pricks,' one screamed at them, gesticulating wildly.

Charlie started to run to assist, her warrant card ready, just as a police carrier screeched into the roadway and half a dozen coppers spilled out, manhandling the drunks away from the officers, bringing order back from the chaos.

The situation was under control, there had been enough police officers to deal with the fight without her assistance being required. She turned, about to start retracing her footsteps, when the final prisoner reared up, hatred etched into every word.

'Why don't you all go fuck yourselves?' he spat out, before being bundled into the rear of the van.

She checked her watch as the display turned to 00.28 and started to sprint back towards Lambeth HQ, where she intended sleeping for the night. In just a few hours' time she and Hunter would be watching Leonard Cookson's broken body, carved up still further.

As she ran, she thought of the man's vitriol, each word of hate becoming irrelevant, her mind reconnecting with the events of the day. Did their killer really hate all police, or just ones with complaints? Most hard-working officers received complaints; it was the nature of the job.

Whether restraining drunks, seizing firearms, dealing with the deaths of old people, or fending off armed terrorists on Westminster Bridge, it was abundantly clear to Charlie that all police officers were human. Sometimes they might err, sometimes they might be falsely accused, but they didn't deserve to die... and any one of her colleagues or the officers she'd just witnessed dealing with the fight could be next.

Chapter 14

By 7 a.m. the reek of the mortuary was all Charlie could smell.

Hunter had been on the phone the whole journey to the hospital, deep in discussion with the SOCO, so all her thoughts from the previous evening had been put to one side. Dennis Walters had not come to light for anything, nor had Carl Hookham been arrested. Both appeared to be lying low.

Dr Reggie Crane, the forensic pathologist, greeted them as they entered, shaking hands with Hunter formally and smiling enthusiastically at Charlie. He was dressed casually in comfortable slacks and polo shirt, with his dark hair let loose from a theatre hat and visible morning stubble. He seemed much younger and far less stuffy, but Charlie found his appearance a little disconcerting, given her previous assumption that he was very much older than she. As if reading Charlie's thoughts, he rubbed the back of his hand across his chin.

'Please excuse my appearance. I'm not usually called on to do PMs on Saturdays.' He grinned at Charlie's obvious confusion. 'Are you doing the exhibits this time?'

Charlie nodded. 'Yes, the whole lot.'

'In that case, let's get through the formalities and then we can get going properly.' After fifteen years doing the same job, Dr Crane never tired of pinpointing the cause of death and explaining his reasoning. Murders were a particular challenge as he liked to get the full sequence of events. Nothing was too trivial to be mentioned and nothing too important to take precedence.

They all gowned up before entering the lab to see Leonard Cookson's body laid out still fully clothed. It looked even more grotesque than it had at the crime scene. Somehow, seeing it now under the fluorescent strip lights of the mortuary heightened every sense.

Dr Crane grimaced. 'Right, let's get going. I'll start with what's left of his clothing and any personal possessions and then I'll move on to the cause of death.'

Carefully he began to remove each item piece by piece. It was a painstaking job, most of the remaining fabric of his trousers, around his buttocks and torso, having melted into his flesh. Dr Crane removed the material carefully with scalpel and tweezers, before placing it directly into exhibit tubes and handing them to Charlie, who logged and sealed each item.

Cookson's jacket was burnt away completely at its lower edges and halfway up the body, but the upper part of the chest and shoulders were, on the whole, intact, albeit singed and blackened with smoke. A lump in the material on the left-hand side of his chest indicated the presence of an item in the inside breast pocket.

Dr Crane reached inside, pulling out a brown leather wallet and a mobile phone. Both items were smoke-damaged, with the outer surfaces blistered and puckered from the heat of the fire. The screen of the phone was partially melted. He placed the phone and wallet into separate bags and handed them to Charlie, turning to Hunter as he did so. 'Both safe and sound in his pocket. It doesn't appear our victim was robbed… or that he had time to make a call.'

Hunter nodded his agreement. 'I'm told he was pretty inebriated. We'll get the phone analysed if we can, but I'll be surprised to find anything of relevance on it after he left the pub.'

Dr Crane nodded. 'And I'll get the samples off for a tox report as soon as I can too. Then we'll be able to tell just how much alcohol he'd consumed.'

Hunter turned towards Charlie who was spreading out the contents of the wallet on a plastic sheet, before starting to bag each item up separately.

'His credit cards are still here, but he's got no cash, other than a few coins.'

'That'll be his team,' Hunter commented, with a shake of his head. 'They'd just had a good result at court and it's tradition that the skipper buys the beers afterwards.'

They continued in silence, until Leonard Cookson's body was completely naked, his distended stomach taking up a good percentage of the stainless-steel slab.

Without clothing, the wounds he had sustained were even more horrific. As well as the dried blood and injuries to his mouth they had noticed at the crime scene, there were also various other contusions and grazes to his upper body and scalp and restraint marks to his wrists.

Dr Crane pointed out a few of the wounds. 'He's been cut with a knife and has various blunt-force traumas to his body, as if hit with various objects. The poor guy wasn't coming out of this alive.'

Hunter pursed his lips. 'That's what our SOCO said too. I had a long conversation with him on our way here.' He took a step towards Cookson's body, shaking his head at the pathologist before pointing at the worst of the burns on the buttocks and hip area. 'The SOCO established that an accelerant was used on Cookson's clothing but initial analysis showed it wasn't petrol, which is the most common accelerant used in arsons.

'Once his body was removed, they were able to check the remnants of debris that had been left under the chair. There was a partially melted plastic container lying on its side, which has now been examined in detail and has been confirmed as the remains of a bottle of nail varnish remover. The main component is acetone, which, I'm reliably informed, is extremely volatile and flammable.' Hunter shifted his weight to his other foot and continued. 'There was also a partially burned item that looked like a firework, with a small piece of misshapen red plastic stuck against it. The article was cylindrical and the bottom half was dark blue in colour, with small pink and white shell-like prints all around the circumference. The word "Kimbolton" was printed across it. The SOCO researched the name and is pretty sure the item relates to a static ground flare, made in England by Kimbolton Fireworks and easily available on the internet. It is advertised as low noise and burns intensely for sixty seconds.'

'So,' Charlie mulled over the facts. 'Our killer has soaked the seat and groin area of Cookson's trousers in nail varnish remover, before setting light to the flare underneath him. Once the old wood in the chair has started to heat up, the acetone has caught light, causing the seat of his trousers to catch fire. The flames would have been intense but short-lived; as soon as the flare was finished and the acetone had evaporated, there was nothing really to keep the fire burning. Hence, pants on fire!'

'Am I missing something?' Dr Crane was looking at them quizzically.

'Leonard Cookson was being investigated for perjury,' Hunter turned towards the pathologist.

'Ah, I understand. In that case the amputation of the tongue would also fit.' Dr Crane turned away from the body and bent down over a stainless-steel dish containing the pink tongue tissue. 'So what you need me to tell you now is what came first: the fire or the tongue removal? And which of those two actions actually killed him?'

There was a loud knock on the door to the laboratory before Hunter could agree. A rather red-faced lab technician clicked the door open before peering round the edge towards the pathologist.

'I'm sorry to disturb you but there's a police officer here who says he needs to speak to DI Geoffrey Hunter urgently.' He shrugged apologetically. 'I've tried to put him off but...'

The door was pushed open wide and Paul squeezed between the frame and the lab technician, his cheeks paling instantly at the sight before him. 'DCI O'Connor has sent me to take over, boss.' His eyes flicked towards Leonard Cookson's dead body before returning to face Hunter and Charlie. 'There's been another murder.'

Chapter 15

Declan O'Connor's voice was clipped, even through the hands-free speakers.

'She's an inspector in the Met but she lives in Surrey, and Surrey Constabulary have called us in. If there was any slight initial doubt about whether it is linked to ours, there isn't now. A red rose was left at this scene too, also with the thorns removed from its stem. They were aware of the previous two murdered police officers in the Met, but they didn't know about the rose until now, because that detail had been restricted. Now this link has been confirmed, they are happy for us to lead the investigation. Hunter, we need results. That's all I have to say.'

The phone clicked off and Hunter sighed heavily. 'You're telling me, we need results!'

*

Inspector Philippa McGovern inhabited a tiny bungalow, set on its own at the end of a cul-de-sac at the back of Box Hill in Surrey. The last time Charlie had been to Box Hill was as part of a crowd of cheering onlookers at the 2012 London Olympic Games when it had featured in a hill section of the cycling course. It was vastly different now. The bungalow was the last building before the road was swallowed up by woodland. The tarmac petered out as they drove along it, leaving the end more of a rough track, with nothing other than a turning circle and several parking bays. A bright green Hyundai was positioned in the last bay, leaving the rest of the area populated with police vehicles.

'It couldn't get much more remote,' Hunter muttered as their unmarked police car crunched over the bumps.

'Still, at least what neighbours there are might be more aware of any strange noises,' countered Charlie.

The bungalow itself had a postage-stamp front garden, ringed with an old stone wall on which ivy had taken root. A rose with perfect pink blossoms clung to a wooden arch at its entrance and a row of silver birches stood resolutely on either side of the archway, meaning that the house was barely visible from the track.

Charlie parked halfway onto the verge at the opposite side of the lane and squeezed out past a hawthorn bush. There was a foul odour in the air, not the usual earthy mix of compost and manure that signalled the more rural areas, but rather a stench that she was by now able to recognise only too well: death.

Hunter was already marching towards a uniformed Surrey officer standing at the gate, his warrant card held aloft. She pushed a sense of trepidation to the back of her mind and joined them.

A narrow stone path led to the front door, which was slightly ajar. It was made from solid, dark oak, the only embellishments being a weighty brass knocker set centrally above a matching brass letter box and heavy-duty black ornamental hinges. The same path branched off around the side of the house, through a wooden side gate towards the rear.

A quick call on the constable's radio brought an older, more serious-looking man heading around the corner of the building towards them. His hair was jet-black and slick, with a slight dye-line around the front of his ears and his parting. He was clean-shaven and clean-cut. Even the forensic suit he was wearing fitted him perfectly.

The man held out flawlessly manicured fingers towards Hunter, shaking his hand firmly. 'Detective Chief Inspector Richard Meaden. Thank you for coming so quickly.

'DI Geoffrey Hunter,' Hunter returned the greeting before indicating Charlie. 'And DC Charlie Stafford. Thank you for calling us in. We're not always welcomed so promptly by other constabularies.'

'Well, after we found out about the rose there was no hesitation. It's got to be connected to the two you've already had... and it's a Metropolitan police inspector. We were duty-bound.' He pulled a clipboard out from under his arm and referred to some notes. 'The body has been ID'd as Philippa McGovern. She was found by her sister, Fiona Priestley, at approximately 10.30 a.m. when she came round to bring some groceries for her, on Philippa's return from holiday. It appears, however, that Philippa never actually got away on her break. It looks likely that her attacker broke in just before she was due to go. She was found tied to her bed, unable to move or raise the alarm. Her bags are still in the hallway. I'll show you where we think the intruder entered first.'

He waited while the constable handed Charlie and Hunter some protective clothing to don. Hunter took a suit, struggling to thread his feet through the leg-holes, never mind pull it up over his outer clothing. There was no way a forensic suit on Hunter would ever be described as anything other than ill-fitting. Charlie's was not much better.

They followed DCI Meaden around the corner of the bungalow, pausing at a wooden, shoulder-high gate set into another stone wall.

'This gate was locked when we got here. We've opened it to allow easier access. The point of entry is around the back of the premises, into the lounge. It appears that the attacker probably climbed over this gate or wall to gain access to the rear. It's not that hard.'

Charlie had to agree. There were enough footholds on the gate and the adjoining wall that she herself would have had no trouble scaling it. The back garden was a good size, being mainly laid to lawn. It ran down a slight slope and the view from the end was of woodland, with the aspect of the South Downs looming up behind it. Trees were spaced along either side, affording almost total privacy. A patio ran across its width next to the building and a glass and wicker table and chair set was positioned under a large black parasol. Charlie wondered how likely it would be for the attacker to have come in through the woods. As if reading her thoughts, the DCI swept his hand out towards the trees.

'I've had dogs scour the garden for any possible entry points or dens through the woods, but they found nothing. No scents, no patches of trodden ground. Although the scene is a week old now, the dog handler is as sure as he can be that the intruder didn't scope out the house or enter from the garden.'

Charlie nodded her understanding and sniffed. Ominously, the smell she had initially noticed was stronger here.

'As you can probably gather, Philippa McGovern liked her privacy. By all accounts, she kept herself to herself both professionally and personally; even her family do not really know how she conducted her life. She was not on any form of social media and rarely spoke about her life or loves. She liked to go on holiday fairly regularly but didn't send photos or updates or anything. She'd texted her sister the night before she was due to go away, at about 22.15, confirming what date and time she was due back, and they'd arranged for Fiona to bring milk, bread and a few other bits in for when she arrived. Presumably she might have texted a few other friends or family similar messages, but none of them would have expected to hear anything from her while she was gone.'

'Hence why she wasn't found.' Hunter pulled his handkerchief out from the sleeve of his suit. 'What about any neighbours? Were any of them due to check the house?'

'No. We've spoken to them. Philippa maintains a friendly relationship with the nearest neighbours but has never asked them to do anything for her while she's away. And they don't ask her for favours in return. They did, however, confirm seeing a minicab arrive and leave last Saturday morning. They assumed that Philippa was in the car when it left and she wouldn't be back for a while.'

'Do we know what time?' Hunter wiped his forehead. It was getting hotter with every hour.

DCI Meaden glanced down at his notes again. 'As far as we know, she was due to fly from Gatwick on Saturday 17th June at 10.20 to Lanzarote. She had boarding passes printed out for Monarch Airlines, which are in the documents by the door. Her green Hyundai is still parked up outside, but there was a business card for a local minicab firm. She would have had to be at the airport by 08.20 and had a cab booked for 07.15. We've contacted the company, U-cabs, already and they've confirmed that their driver turned up on schedule, rang several times, but eventually left when there was no reply, assuming she'd made other arrangements.'

'And they didn't knock at any of the neighbours?'

'No, they thought it was too early. Anyway, I doubt it would have made a difference, knowing what we now know about Philippa.'

'What about kids?' Charlie knew Meg would often ask if she was available for airport runs.

'She had never married and didn't have any children. As far as her sister knew, she was going on holiday on her own.'

'Well I'm sure, had she been travelling with anyone else, we'd have heard as soon as she didn't turn up.' Hunter pursed his lips. 'So finding anything out about her personal life is going to be hard, or at least harder than usual.'

'According to her sister, she seemed to be well-liked, but even she doesn't really know the name of any of her friends, or anything much about her relationships.'

'Wow, that is private... and a bit weird.' Charlie's thoughts immediately flew to her family and the close friends she had in the office. Bet, Paul, Naz and Sabira especially looked after each other, and Hunter did too, although he was immune from a lot of the chat, being in his own office. A problem shared was a problem halved, her mother would say... though, unfortunately that didn't seem to apply to her.

'Everyone to their own, I suppose,' DCI Meaden was pointing to a set of windows into a lounge area, a small window immediately above a larger. Both windows were closed, as were the patio doors next to them. 'SOCO thinks this was the point of entry because there are slight scuff marks at the base of the larger one, as if the suspect has climbed through and partial footprints on the sill and across the carpet. He believes that the small window had been left ajar and the suspect has leant through to open the larger one to gain access. Both windows were closed, though, when the sister got here. It wasn't any of us that shut them.'

Hunter raised his eyebrows. 'It's unusual for a suspect to shut the windows once inside. They usually leave themselves an escape route in case they're disturbed. Any ideas why?'

Charlie turned her head towards the other side of the bungalow, to another set of identical patio doors and windows, both of which were wide open.

'And why those ones were left open?' she pointed towards them.

'Those were closed too. We opened them.' The DCI screwed his face up and frowned. 'Whoever did this wasn't after any property. Nothing obvious is missing and no cupboards were ransacked. We can pretty much rule out burglary or robbery. No, our suspect closed every window and door and pulled the curtains in the bedroom shut. When she was found by her sister, the heating was on full. The place was like a sauna. Philippa was tied to the bed, with no way of getting water or food, or raising the alarm. She was dead, probably from dehydration, and had clearly been dead for a good few days. There were quite a few flies.'

'Shit,' Charlie couldn't help herself.

DCI Meaden continued, 'We've had to open all the doors and windows at the back to let the heat and flies out. It was too hazardous for any of my officers or staff to be in there otherwise. You can imagine how bad it was. Poor woman.'

Charlie didn't have to imagine it. The smell of death still hung in the air, though it must have been a hundred times worse earlier. 'What a way to die… and what a way to find your sister.'

*

The bedroom was as bad as could be imagined. Philippa McGovern lay in her own excrement, still tied to the bed. The restraints employed looked to be identical to the ones used at Leonard Cookson's murder; metal handcuffs, like the ones used by police, and the same electrical cable looped around the bed and bedposts. In addition, her mouth was taped shut, filled with paper wadding, inhibiting her ability to breathe and soaking up any last saliva from her mouth and airway. She was not getting away and she was not calling for help.

DCI Meaden pointed towards a chest of drawers positioned against the wall at the end of the bed, directly in front of Philippa McGovern's body; it would have been in her full view. On top of it stood a drinking glass, next to a large jug, less than a quarter filled with what appeared to be water. A mark near to the top of the jug, showed where the water had reached before most had evaporated in the heat. A single red rose protruded from the rim, its stem devoid of thorns. An iPhone in a floral protective case was positioned next to the jug, standing on its base, its cover open to reveal the screen, blank now the battery had died.

The relevance of all the items was not lost on Charlie. Philippa McGovern's murder was linked to the others and just as cruel, possibly even more so. She could see the means to save her life, but she couldn't reach them. It was wicked.

The SOCO was already at work within the room, so they waited by the door, not wanting to disturb any miniscule particle that might assist the examination. This was an inside crime scene, unlike the others, so the possibility their killer might have left some tiny speck of DNA that hadn't been destroyed by the elements, or obliterated by acid or fire, was slightly more of a possibility.

Looking at the dead body in front of them now though, still alive with the movement of maggots, it was hard to see what could be retrieved, but they had to hope.

At the moment, apart from a wilting red rose, that was all they had.

Chapter 16

'Philippa McGovern is, or was, a Detective Inspector at Sutton police station, working in the Operations office,' Bet read from the personnel record in front of her. 'And before you ask, guv, she does have a complaint against her which is ongoing.'

Hunter sat down on the seat next to Bet, while Charlie hovered above them. It was now late afternoon and they'd only just got back to the office, having spent time with the DCI, SOCO, Fiona Priestley and several neighbours. Nothing more had come from the meetings, but it was always good to get a first-hand impression of the reactions and body language of family and friends. Naz and Sabira were ensconced at their work stations having kept themselves busy making further checks on their two suspects and sending off enquiries on the origin of the firework, the electrical cabling and Leonard Cookson's domestic arrangements. Nick had failed to show.

'What's it for?' Hunter looked tired.

'Dereliction of duty and falsifying the duty states. That's why she's in the Ops office now. So they can keep an eye on her.'

'Go on.'

'The complaint comes from when she was working in two community support units in the Met. She worked in our one at Lambeth some years ago, before moving to the CSU at Sutton.'

'I thought I recognised her name. I've seen it written on some of the older reports, signing off investigations. So what's she done? … Or not done?'

'She's alleged to have failed to supervise investigations and made incorrect decisions as to whether the cases should be further pursued, leading to a number of cases being NFA'd without adequate reason. Several suspects have gone on to commit further offences which might have been preventable had they been dealt with properly the first time around.' Bet turned the page and continued to read. 'She is also alleged to have falsely claimed to be on duty when she wasn't, either for full tours or just late in / early off type days.' She shut the file and looked up. 'She had less than two years to go before she retired.'

'So, in other words, she was acting as if she'd already retired… while still getting paid a full-time Inspector's salary, which is taking the piss.' He shook his head in annoyance.

Charlie had to agree. 'So, she was strapped to her bed and left to die because she was lazy.'

Hunter leant back in his chair and rolled his eyes. 'The punishment was designed to fit the crime again.

But, even so… it's totally disproportionate to the complaint… even without knowing whether there's any credence to it. Do we know who made it?'

'It was made by one of our own, anonymously through "Right Line". I've spoken to the DPS officer dealing with her case and he says there is evidence to substantiate the allegation, but we won't find out who made it.'

'Is it the same DPS officer as either of the other two?'

'No, they're all different.'

Hunter got up and walked slowly towards his office, running his hands over his head. 'I'll ask DCI O'Connor to sound out the Chief at DPS and see what he thinks of each investigation.' As he was about to disappear, Paul pushed the main door open and came in backwards, carrying a large bundle of paperwork.

'Just finished at the post-mortem.' Naz and Sabira went across to help him and he passed each of them some files.

Hunter turned back towards him. 'So, what's Dr Crane's verdict?'

'Cookson died of shock, brought on by a combination of blood loss from his severed tongue and the movement of fluids to the burn sites on his abdomen and lower torso. The injury to his scalp was sustained by being hit with a blunt instrument, severe enough to have caused concussion, and he had several contusions to his arms, consistent with having been gripped hard. That and the amount of alcohol he had consumed would probably have meant he was unable to fight, never mind stage any sort of decent defence.'

'Hopefully it would have dulled the pain too.' Charlie winced.

Paul shook his head, frowning. 'I doubt anything would have dulled that pain, and he wouldn't even have been able to shout for help. There were clear gag marks visible, so any screams would have been muffled. He then had his jaws forcefully prised open before his tongue was cut out, probably with sharp scissors.'

'How did Dr Crane work that out?' Hunter leant on the door frame.

'Because there are scrape marks around his teeth and an indented mark on the severed tongue that shows it was gripped by a hard metal object, possibly pliers or the like. Both sides of the tongue are evenly sliced. If a knife or blade had been used, the underside would have been jagged. Due to the amount of blood around the face, neck and shoulders, Dr Crane says the amputation would have been carried out before the fire, impairing any further chance to call for help, if he was still conscious.'

Hunter grimaced. 'And the rest is as we thought?'

'Yep.' Paul snapped the pile of paperwork down on his desk with a groan. 'Set on fire and left to burn until the flames died down. If he wasn't already dead by that stage, he was almost certainly dead shortly afterwards.'

The group lapsed into silence, before Hunter eventually spoke.

'Go home troops, there's nothing more we can do tonight. Tomorrow morning, come in fresh and we'll go through what we know. Or don't. We have two suspects, three bodies and, so far, not much evidence. And there'll be more; I can pretty much guarantee it. Our killer's on a roll… and we're spending our whole time playing catch-up.'

*

Ben was out when Charlie arrived at his flat half an hour later. There was no light burning within and no sign of him curled up on the sofa asleep. She was surprised, though she told herself she shouldn't be, it was Saturday evening and she'd turned up unannounced. Ben was quite capable of making his own arrangements… but it was still unusual.

She sat down on the wall outside, kicking her heels against the brickwork, suddenly restless. Something wasn't right, in fact everything was wrong. She needed to be with someone tonight and this was the last thing she'd expected.

A rich seam of frustration and anger was running through her head; even her limbs and muscles were twitchy. The ready ear and trusty shoulder on which she'd relied for so long was not there. It hadn't been for months... and she missed it. She missed Ben. She missed his ready smile and the way he could lift her spirits with a single wink or cheeky comment.

And Nick, for some reason, had stirred her up. She was annoyed at his absence today. Even though he was fully entitled to his day off, all the rest of the team had been there, prepared to go the extra mile.

But what if Nick was right? Maybe she should be cultivating a social life instead of concentrating only on work. Maybe she should switch off from the demands of the job and think about her own needs.

She stood up and stared along the road, willing Ben's tall physique to turn the corner and walk towards her, but the street was quiet.

On a whim, she pulled her phone out of her pocket and dialled her mother's number. Meg came on the line, a hint of concern in her voice.

'Hi Charlie. This is a pleasant surprise. Are you OK?'

'Yes I'm fine, Mum. Busy, but OK.' She took a deep breath. This was not going to be easy for either of them. 'Mum, you know when you were with

Harry and he was drinking, before you split. How many chances did you give him?'

There was a long pause, so long that only the absence of a click on the line reassured Charlie her mother was still there.

'Is this about Ben?' Meg asked eventually.

'Mum, how many?' She just needed to know.

'Too many, Charlie. If it hadn't been for him, Jamie might still…' Charlie heard her mother's voice catch, before she eventually continued. 'He'd been drinking heavily even before the accident and then, afterwards, well it was his excuse to get absolutely off his head. I gave him far too many chances.' She paused again. 'Ben's different though. He's witnessed so much and he only turned to drink to try to forget. I'm not saying it will be easy, but Ben wants to recover… and is willing to put the effort in. I know he had a relapse, but he is trying again now. Harry couldn't be bothered. He was happy to stay a drunkard.'

'But what if Ben doesn't want to go through it all again now? What if he never recovers from this latest setback? What if *he's* happy to stay a drunk? How long should I wait?' Or should I just give up. Maybe even Nick would be up for some fun? The thought kept repeating itself in her head.

'I can't answer that one for you, Charlie. I think you'll just know if he's worth the wait. He's a good lad.' Meg paused, and Charlie recalled Hunter saying exactly the same thing within the last few days. They both saw something in him that was worth fighting for. 'But, Charlie,' Meg sounded a note of caution, 'only you will be able to see if Ben truly wants to recover. If you really think he isn't bothered and is happy to stay a drunk… then don't waste your life waiting.'

Chapter 17

Parking up in the railway station car park, Charlie walked slowly towards Carl Hookham's flat. Something was telling her he was back. Unable to sleep, she'd finally given in to her hunch. The roads were quiet; Sunday morning saw only a few elderly dog-walkers out and the last few minicabs wending their way home after a busy night's work.

The flat looked the same from the front as the last time they'd visited, but still the niggle persisted. The rear also appeared unchanged, the same tired curtains hanging from identical positions at the window. This time though the wheelie bin was back in the bin shed. She needed to gain entry into the block.

The communal door was at the front of the building, with a box to the side containing letter boxes scrawled with the surname of each occupant. Hookham's letter box was empty.

Next to the frame was a chaotic array of doorbells, set askew and untidy, with a tradesmen button at the base of the barely legible labels. It buzzed her welcome at the press of her finger. Silently she climbed the stairs to the first floor, wincing at each creaky floorboard and squeaky stair.

The door to Hookham's room was shut and there was no sound coming from within, but a large gap at the base of the door gave her a partial view inside. Squeezing her head against the lino of the stairwell and squinting through one eye, she could just see the floor of his hallway. A pair of men's shoes was positioned to one side, appearing to have been kicked off and lying on their uppers where they'd landed. Charlie had no idea whether they had been like this on their last visit, but what her nose was telling her was that someone had been there recently. The smell of curry was unmistakeable and there was no doubt it was seeping through the gap under the door from within.

She checked her watch and groaned. If he was their killer, she couldn't risk losing him by attempting an arrest on her own, but, six-fifteen on a Sunday morning was not the best time to get help, with night duty about to knock off and early turn only just surfacing. Even Hunter and the team would not be in... and she didn't yet know whether Hookham had only visited or if indeed he was still in there.

Raking around in her pocket, she found the paper wrapper of a chewing gum and pulled it out, folding it carefully several times. At least this, placed carefully between the door and its frame, would prove whether anyone was coming and going. They could come back later and check for any movement and, if necessary, sit up and observe the place. It was unlikely Hookham would expect a visit on a Sunday.

Operation complete, she tiptoed down the stairs again and made her way back to her car. Just time for a quick visit to Ben's flat on her way into the office. She needed to know that he'd arrived home safely the previous night.

The curtains to his flat, unlike Hookham's, were drawn partially shut. He'd evidently returned at some point. She was about to leave when her curiosity got the better of her. What if she was waiting for him, but he wasn't waiting for her? What if her presence was just too hard for him to deal with and he'd found another girl? As Meg had cautioned, she didn't want to waste too much of her life on him, if he wasn't bothered with her.

A few steps later and she was at his window, telling herself she was just checking his welfare, after all he was quite capable of drinking himself unconscious. Peering in, she saw his shape curled up on the sofa, alone, where he preferred to rest when he knew his sleep was likely to be spasmodic. He was facing towards the window where she stood, his eyes closed, his chest rising and falling in time with his breathing. Every few seconds, his hand, hanging loose to his side, would twitch, the movement causing his whole arm to jerk towards the small coffee table at the centre of the room.

Her eyes followed the direction of his hand movement, to where several cards and a mug stood carefully placed in a row on the table, directly in his line of vision. As she did so, a wave of guilt washed over her at the realisation that the cards and mug contained messages of encouragement and reassurance she herself had sent him over the last few months.

*

By the time Charlie got to the office, everyone, with the exception of Nick, was in. She quickly described to Hunter what she'd found at Hookham's flat before he called everyone over. Bet had stuck photos of their three victims on a whiteboard, along with the names and images of their suspects. With two further victims, since Brian Ashton's death, there was no time to waste. As they settled themselves into a semicircle around him he started.

'Team, Charlie has been for a drive past Carl Hookham's flat this morning, and she believes he might be back.'

'Blimey, Charlie. Don't you ever sleep?' Paul stifled a yawn.

She shrugged. It was always the same mid-case. Her mind didn't stop working, even though her body had left the office.

Hunter turned towards the others. 'Naz, do we know yet if Hookham has any links to Leonard Cookson or Philippa McGovern?'

Naz shook her head. 'Sorry, boss, nothing at the moment, but I'm still working on it.'

'And we're still waiting for the results on the blood found in his vehicle.'

'I've found something on Dennis Walters though, boss.' Sabira straightened herself. 'Philippa McGovern was the Inspector in charge of Lambeth CSU between 2006 and 2014, before she moved to Sutton... and, as we know, Walters is a drug user, with a history of abusive relationships. I've been looking through every domestic report Walters was involved in during that time. McGovern is shown as supervising one of the reports. It's quite a nasty assault on a prostitute that he was believed to be pimping; according to the report, she was being given a roof over her head in exchange for sexual favours.'

'Nice,' Hunter leant forward in his chair, his brow creased. 'And the result?'

'The case was dropped after the prostitute; Angela Mousley, declined to substantiate the allegation.

There's nothing to suggest anyone tried to persuade her otherwise.'

'I thought there was a positive action policy on domestic assaults in place then?'

'Not, it seems, if the victim is a prostitute.'

'Or Philippa McGovern was supervising.' Hunter exhaled noisily. 'Can we contact the officer in the case or Angela Mousley herself and see if either of them remembers what happened with the report?'

Sabira nodded enthusiastically. 'I've done that already, boss. Angela Mousley moved to Nottingham a few months after the case. She was arrested for prostitution and drug offences several times afterwards, but from 2014 she is shown on her PNC record as deceased; found dead from an overdose.' She paused, glancing down at her notes. 'And the officer in the case is now working in the Child Exploitation Unit. She remembered Mousley and Walters because they were always coming to notice. She said DI McGovern told her to get rid of the case on to the local St Mungo's Team who deal with prostitutes and vulnerable women. She said it was a waste of their time prosecuting offences with prostitutes because the women would always go straight back to their violent pimps.'

'Probably because they're too broken to stand up for themselves.' Naz tutted loudly.

Sabira grimaced. 'Agreed, but on this occasion the St Mungo's Team were able to help. Mousley was relocated back to her home town.'

'Not that it helped her a great deal, judging by her death.' Hunter stood up and walked to the window, staring out across the roofs of the nearby estates. 'We never deal with the problems. We just displace them.'

'But at least it got her and her problems off DI McGovern's back.' Charlie snorted.

'So…' Hunter turned back towards Sabira. 'Did Dennis Walters know who made the decisions? He might have blamed police for Mousley leaving him. Maybe he blamed DI McGovern personally for the decision to refer his girl on. He'd be losing street credibility, as well as money.'

'Yes, I asked that, and the OIC was sure he did. Apparently, he made quite a nuisance of himself for some time afterwards, wanting to know where Mousley was. He demanded the names of all the officers in the case, including hers and the DI's. Bearing in mind what has happened to McGovern now, she's a bit worried for her own safety.'

'And rightly so.' Hunter jotted a note down on a piece of paper. 'I'll give her line manager a ring later and discuss any extra security she might need.' He folded the paper and put it in his pocket. 'In fact, I'll get a briefing put out for all officers, particularly those with complaints, to be extra mindful around their own security until this is over. Well done, Sab. That's enough to go after Dennis Walters. We'll get a drugs warrant initially to get in and have a look around, but while we're there we'll have a quick word with him about his relationship with Angela Mousley and DI McGovern and this time we'll be doing it on our terms. If he wants to play dirty, then we will too.' He checked his watch and clapped his hands. 'In the meantime, team, let's go and find Carl Hookham, before he disappears again.'

Chapter 18

'I think he's in there,' Charlie whispered down the radio, having pressed herself against the lino in the stairwell again. 'My marker's been dislodged and the shoes are in a different position. He's obviously been out but now he's back.'

'All units standby. Charlie, get ready to knock on the door,' Hunter's voice was clear. Charlie, Naz and Hunter were positioned at the door to the flat, Paul was deployed to the front of the house, checking the windows, and Sabira was watching the rear. Only Bet had remained in the office, fielding calls and continuing what research she could. Hunter had also purloined some uniform assistance in the shape of Charlie's mate, Bill Morley, and his partner off early turn to assist with the entry. 'If the door opens and it's Hookham, detain him. If any of you see him and he fails to answer, let me know immediately and the door will be put in.'

'All received,' Charlie nodded towards Bill who was positioned just to her side, holding on tightly to the enforcer. 'Right, I'm knocking now.'

She banged hard on the door twice, calling out Hookham's name, but there was no reply. She knocked again and heard a scraping sound from within, followed by Paul's voice bellowing on the radio. 'All units, he's trying to climb out of the front window.'

'Go, go, go,' Hunter shouted.

Bill Morley didn't need to be told twice. With a loud splintering of wood, the door frame buckled and the door was flung open, its lock shooting across the hallway and lodging against the wall opposite. Charlie roared into the front room and immediately saw Carl Hookham bending down at the window, one leg already across the sill. He appeared to freeze for a split second, giving her time to take the half a dozen steps across the room and grab hold of him. Naz was right behind her, taking hold of the back of his waistband, and together they dragged him backwards into the room. Thirty seconds later and their suspect was lying on the floor, his arms handcuffed behind him and his mouth curled up in anger.

'Where do you think you're going this time?' Hunter stood staring down at him. 'You don't think we'd let you get away a second time, do you?'

Hookham bit his bottom lip, before sneering at them. 'It was worth a try, especially after kissing you lot goodbye the first time as you all stood gawping up at my flat. That was fucking quality.' He turned towards Charlie as she bent down and took hold of him. 'I shouldn't have come back so soon, should I?'

'No, you shouldn't.' Charlie pulled him up to a kneeling position. 'But now you have, I'm arresting you on suspicion of the murder of Brian Ashton. You do not have to say anything. But it may harm your defence if you do not mention when questioned, something which you later rely on in court. Anything you do say may be given in evidence.'

'Murder?' Hookham eyed her with barely concealed malice. 'Tina is scraping the barrel if she's told you that.' He looked pointedly at a photo on top of the nearby sideboard showing Bobby and Emily on a beach, standing hand in hand, their smiling faces grubby with dirt. 'Someone's done me a right good favour though. God knows I'd like to have killed the snivelling bastard myself... but do you think I would do anything that would prevent me seeing those two?'

*

Charlie picked up the phone and dialled Tina Ashton's number. She answered the phone almost immediately but her voice sounded weary.

'Hi, Tina, it's DC Charlie Stafford from Lambeth police. How are you?'

Tina Ashton sighed heavily. 'Tired. I keep going over and over what Brian must have gone through, the pain he must have been in, and all alone.'

Charlie knew exactly what she meant.

'It will get better,' she lied. 'You might not think so now, but in time you will be able to concentrate on the good times and the pain will gradually fade.' She bit down hard on her lip to stop herself from saying what she wanted to say. How sometimes, late at night, when it's dark and you're on your own, it will hit you straight in the heart and the pain will be a thousand times worse.

'Anyway.' Tina brightened slightly. 'At least I have the kids to keep me busy.'

'And Casper. How is he recovering?'

'He's on the mend apparently. He lost a lot of blood and had a couple of broken ribs, but none of his vital organs were affected. I can't visit him though.' She stopped talking for what seemed like an age and when she started her voice was quiet. 'He was always Bri's dog. They were inseparable... but I can't help thinking that if it hadn't been for Casper, Brian wouldn't have been out walking on the common. He would still be here with me and his new baby. I know it's not the dog's fault, but every time I think about seeing him and the scar he'll be left with, I know it'll bring everything back.'

Charlie was shocked at the words. 'He might also bring you comfort... and good memories. See how it goes, Tina.'

'We'll see,' she sounded suddenly lost. 'Anyway, what can I do for you?'

'We've located Carl but I wanted to know if you'd heard anything from him this week.'

'Ah, that's good, but no, nothing, which is strange. He had been phoning me daily, sometimes several times a day before Brian... died.' Her voice faltered as she said the word. 'Hassling me about the name change and saying that he would never give consent, that sort of thing; but I haven't heard a word since. No calls, no texts, nothing. It's as if he thinks he doesn't have to, now that Brian's not here.' She paused. 'You know, it was my idea to change Bobby and Emily's name to Ashton, not Brian's. It was me that wanted us to be one big happy family.' She laughed bitterly. 'Maybe this wouldn't have happened if I'd kept my mouth shut. Right from the start, Carl was always jealous of what Brian and I had.'

Charlie waited for a few seconds before speaking. 'Tina, Carl has been arrested for Brian's murder.'

There was a sharp intake of breath, before Tina Ashton started to sob. 'Oh my God, Oh my God. Do *you* think he really did it? What's he saying?'

'Nothing so far. We've only just brought him in, but I just need to check something out with you first.' She waited for Tina to stop crying before she spoke again. 'We'll be carrying out a full search of

Carl's flat for any forensic evidence, but when we were there just now we took possession of several photos and an old rucksack.' She didn't mention the fact that, just like the car, the bag had what appeared to be specks of blood on it. 'The rucksack had Bobby and Emily's original birth certificates in it. Is there any reason that you know of, why he would be carrying these around with him?'

Tina exhaled noisily, before taking another deep breath. 'Oh my God!' she said again. 'Brian and I thought that we'd have to send the kids' birth certificates off, if we wanted their names changed... so Brian had been carrying them around in his wallet to get advice. During the custody battle, Brian and Carl argued. Brian stupidly pulled them out and pretended to score out Carl's surname and insert his own. I know it got to Carl. It turns out that the birth certificates don't get altered anyway, even in the unlikely event that we'd gone to court and got permission to apply to change their names. We'd pretty much given up on the idea anyway, but Carl didn't know that. He probably thought if he had them we wouldn't be able to go ahead.'

*

The atmosphere in the interview room was tense. Charlie had been hoping to get a few answers from

Carl Hookham but with Justin Latchmere acting as his solicitor he was having none of it. It was frustrating, though not unexpected. She decided to drop the bomb.

'So, tell me Carl. How come you have Bobby and Emily's birth certificates in your bag?'

'No comment.'

'Did you steal them out of Brian's wallet when you attacked him? You knew they were there didn't you, because you saw Brian with them after court.'

Carl Hookham sat up straight, looking panicked. 'No comment.'

'Did you take them so that he couldn't get your kids' surname changed?'

'No comment.'

'Because you were incensed that Brian was rubbing your nose in it. Because he wanted to take over from you as father to Bobby and Emily? He wanted to replace you and you didn't like it, did you?'

'No comment.'

'You wanted him out of the picture, didn't you?'

'No comment.'

'He'd stolen your kids off you, hadn't he? And you wanted to punish him?'

Hookham swallowed hard. 'No comment.'

'So that he could never see your kids, or touch them again?'

'No comment.'

'So you planned what to do. You waited until he was on his own in the area where you knew he walked his dog. You watched for him to come and you picked on the dog first, the one thing you knew would be guaranteed to take his mind off what was going on around him.'

'No comment.'

'And then you threw acid in his face, didn't you? So he couldn't fight back?'

'No comment.'

'Because he's bigger and stronger than you, isn't he? He's a big, strong cop and you wanted to take him out. Make him crawl on his hands and knees, maybe even beg for mercy?'

Hookham squared his shoulders. 'No comment.'

'Before you finished him off?'

'No comment.'

'That's why there's blood on your bag, Carl, and in your car, isn't it?'

'No comment.'

'So, tell me whose blood is it, Carl?'

Carl Hookham shot a look towards his legal rep who shook his head.

'No comment.'

Charlie leant back in her chair and sighed heavily. Hunter kept his gaze fixed on Hookham who was now squirming in his seat, every few seconds shifting position, his eyes darting from one to the other and then to his legal rep.

Justin Latchmere nodded towards him, a slight shake of his head indicating for Hookham to remain silent. She concentrated on Hookham, studiously ignoring his solicitor.

'So where were you in the early hours of Tuesday 20th June and the evening before? At work, at home, at a friend's house?'

'No comment.'

'OK, to be more specific then. What were you doing near to where Brian Ashton's body was found?'

'No comment.'

'You were in the area, weren't you?'

'No comment.'

'Your phone was used around 02.30 from the locality and your car was seen on CCTV nearby. So what were you doing?'

'No comment.'

'I don't understand why you won't answer my questions. It's quite simple. If you've done nothing wrong then tell me what you were doing so I can eliminate you from our enquiries.'

'Officer, you know as well as I do that it is my client's right in law to say nothing if he does not wish to. It is up to you, as agents for the prosecution, to prove my client has transgressed. It is not up to him to prove his innocence. His innocence is a given.'

Justin Latchmere slapped his clipboard down on the table in front of him and fixed Charlie with a stare.

Charlie stared straight back at him. 'Mr Latchmere, it is also my job to extend the opportunity to provide a defence at this stage, which can later be used at court if your client so wishes. Indeed, I have already cautioned him that failing to answer my questions now may actually harm his defence should the case get that far. I am sure you wouldn't want to give your client advice that may harm his prospects now, would you sir?'

Carl Hookham looked from one to the other, clearly confused.

Charlie smiled towards him. 'I think there's something that you want to tell me, that for some reason you're not explaining. You have been arrested for murder, Carl. That is the most serious offence on the statute book and if there's something you know that could assist you, or us, I'm giving you the opportunity to say now.'

Carl swung round wildly towards Justin Latchmere, his eyes wide. The solicitor frowned towards him and again shook his head.

'No comment,' Hookham repeated obediently before turning towards Charlie and Hunter. 'I can't say anything more because I don't want to lose my kids.'

The front doors to the veterinary surgery were closed by the time Charlie entered the car park but there was a light on towards the rear. On Hunter's instructions, she had bailed Hookham out to a suitable address to let him sweat, while his house was searched. He was clearly rattled but had held firm, refusing to explain just how he had got his hands on the birth certificates. So now it was their turn to sweat. They needed the results of the blood analysis from Hookham's car and rucksack and they needed answers. Suspicion was not enough; it was cold, hard evidence that was lacking.

But for now another issue was pressing on her mind.

She knocked initially, but when there was no reply, she rang the emergency out-of-hours number, watching as a young nurse came to the phone in the reception. A few minutes later Charlie was ushered inside.

She was escorted through an examination room, to the rear of the surgery, where a row of metal cages held half a dozen animals. The smell of disinfectant filled her nostrils, along with the assorted scents of dog, cat and rabbit, all blended headily together in a haze of dust and hair. Casper lay on a blanket in a metal cage at the end of the line, his tail waving automatically at the sight of the newest guest.

The fur had been shaved across the whole of his belly and a row of stitches zig-zagged across the pale skin on his underside. The fur on his head, body and tail was lank and dull, although its usual glossiness looked to be returning in places. A plastic cone around his neck hampered his easy movement, as well as preventing him chewing at the stitches. Various charts placed above the cage plotted his recovery from near death, to life, as well as prescribing the required medication, fluids and food.

He laboured to a stand at her entrance, pressing his nose against the metal bars of the cage, his tail continuing to move rhythmically from side to side.

Charlie bent down towards him, staring into his doleful eyes. His pleasure at the attention was not in doubt, but a sadness in his expression gave away his knowledge that something was wrong. Charlie was not his master… and his master had not visited.

She held out her fingers as Casper pressed his muzzle to the cage, stroking the dog's nose gently through the bars. It was cool and wet and alive, a living, breathing example of an animal's innate survival instinct. It wouldn't be long before he was fit enough to be released, and as Charlie whispered her farewell, she knew that whatever final decision Tina arrived at about the dog's future, Casper would not be forgotten.

*

The call came in at exactly 22.00 hours from Ice. The voice was, as always, calm and authoritative. The voice was, as always, persuasive and compelling. The voice, as always, asked to be obeyed. Be prepared for your next assignment in the morning it instructed, with no room for questioning or defiance.

He listened, smiling at his partner's barely concealed glee. Did Ice really think he would do as instructed unless he himself wanted to? But he did want to; in fact he couldn't wait... so he listened, feeling the adrenalin coursing through his body at the final instructions.

When I say the word, be ready to collect your equipment.

When I say the word, be ready to do exactly what is instructed.

When I say the word, be ready to kill.

Chapter 19

Monday morning was not going well. Pressure was mounting and DCI O'Connor was keen to pass it downwards. The murders were making headlines and they needed to start making their own. Within the first half an hour of their arrival, he had summoned both Hunter and Charlie to his office for an update on the case. Hunter had tried to exaggerate their progress but, after scrutiny, had to admit that apart from their two suspects, they were barely keeping their head above water.

Forensics were still pending on almost everything and without that they were left with the non-existent chance of Carl Hookham miraculously admitting to his part in Ashton's murder, or a search of Dennis Walters' flat turning up incriminating property.

At best, they were hoping for the blood samples on Hookham's bag and car to belong to Brian Ashton. At worst, the body count would continue to rise and they would be helpless to stop it.

Declan O'Connor was clearly tense. His hair was even more unkempt than usual and the creases in his trademark cream linen suit covered every inch of fabric, suggesting that he'd spent the weekend lying sleeplessly in it, worrying over the case. More resources were to be thrown into the investigation, which, on the face of it, was good news, but on the flip side only served to emphasise to all of them their failures so far.

The DCI agreed to press the lab for the results of the analysis of the blood spots to be prioritised, along with any other speck of evidence that might assist. What would the public and politicians think if further cops were killed and a speedier turnaround of the forensic examinations could have prevented further carnage?

In return, however, he expected them both to make themselves available for a quick interview with DS Hayley Boyle from DPS at 2 p.m. in the office adjacent to his, at the insistence of Ms Leach from the IPCC. There was to be no argument; DCI O'Connor wanted this done and dusted. It was becoming a thorn in his side.

'We'll see what happens when he makes the phone call to the lab,' Hunter muttered to Charlie on their way out, with a defiant glint in his eye. 'Or, if that's a negative, I'm sure we'll find ourselves far too tied up executing the warrant at Dennis Walters'.'

'I heard that Hunter,' the DCI spoke sharply. 'I have just granted you additional officers who can attend to the warrant and leave you free for your interviews. I need to do my job too, and that means getting this IPCC investigation concluded. So... unless you can bring me the name, address and inside leg measurement of our murderer, I shall expect to see you both outside my office at two. Consider it a lawful order. Is that clear, Inspector?'

'Yes, sir,' Hunter said the words slowly; he didn't often capitulate, but this time there was no point arguing further. As the door shut behind them, however, Charlie had to smile. It made a pleasant change for someone else to get the bollocking.

*

By mid-morning the office was buzzing. The warrant for Dennis Walters had now been granted by the magistrate's court and was in their hands, awaiting execution. Charlie had organised a briefing and the extra officers had arrived, injecting a fresh urgency into the investigation. Even Nick was pulling his weight. The atmosphere was electric. They all wanted a result.

Hunter was busy in his office, so she knocked on the door to update him, entering just as his phone sounded. He picked up the receiver and mouthed over to her that it was the lab, and indicated the chair opposite.

It was easy to follow the gist of the conversation just by watching Hunter's expressions and listening to his tone, at first gracious, then frowning in disappointment, his mouth pinched, his head shaking from side to side. He covered the mouthpiece and mouthed across to her. 'They've done the DNA on the blood spots. They're Carl Hookham's. It's his own blood.'

Charlie pursed her lips in dismay, although not overly surprised. He seemed too emotional and chaotic to have the ability to clinically carry out the murders, although they all knew from experience how easy it was to be fooled.

The conversation continued for a few moments longer before Hunter became animated and started to scrabble for a piece of paper and pen, gesturing for Charlie to help. She turned the page on her briefing notes and held her pen poised ready.

'Take this down, Charlie.' He repeated the details out loud slowly, his eyes checking she had written the details correctly. 'Samson Louis Powell. Date of birth 16/01/1974, PNCID 85/24968CM. Last known address, 23 Ribblesden Road, SW16.'

She read over the name in her head. Somehow it sounded familiar.

'Thank you so much for your help,' she heard Hunter saying down the phone before he banged the receiver down and stood up with a shout. 'At last!'

He raised his eyebrows and exhaled, before repeating the name on the page. 'Samson Powell, you murdering bastard. He very kindly left one of his hairs on the bedding of Philippa McGovern. The SOCO found it at the scene and asked for it to be checked as a matter of urgency… and DCI O'Connor's call obviously brought it into sharp focus. There's no reason it should be there.'

'Bloody hell! And if he's murdered McGovern, then he's in the frame for both the others.' A twinge of uncertainty caught Charlie off guard as she said the words, but she swept it to one side. She was not going to let the merest of hunches ruin their moment of glory. She ripped out the piece of paper with Powell's details and snapped her notebook shut. 'We'll get straight back to court for another warrant.'

'And I'll go and pass on the good news to DCI O'Connor.' He clapped Charlie on the shoulder. 'I trust he'll let us off bringing him Powell's inside leg measurement until the bastard's fitted for his prison uniform.'

Chapter 20

The phone rang and he breathed a sigh of relief. He'd been ready for Ice's word all morning, expecting his instructions earlier, the anticipation mounting with every minute that passed, unable to relax for fear that he'd drop off to sleep and miss the sound of the ringtone.

When at last the call came, it was gone midday. He listened as Ice ran through the instructions a second time. Was it his imagination or was there a note of irritation in the way the words were delivered. He listened extra carefully, committing each word to memory. He wasn't allowed to write notes, which could be found, and he certainly didn't want to fuck it up. The instructions were, as always, clear and precise. The last command was repeated a third time before the call was ended abruptly: 'Phone me as soon as you have the package in your possession.'

He shrugged and shoved the phone into his trouser pocket. Ice was clearly agitated. It must be difficult getting every tiny detail organised, while planning the next killing... and the next. He was looking forward to finding out what was required this time.

He went back over the orders in his mind. He couldn't get them wrong. Failure was not an option and, anyway, he enjoyed his responsibilities.

His light summer jacket was hanging over the back of a kitchen chair. He picked it up and slung it over his shoulder before heading towards the door. He was to leave home now and go immediately to the designated spot where he would find the package, wrapped in brown paper inside a black plastic carrier bag.

Once in his possession he must make the call that Ice was so insistent at receiving. There was no time to waste.

The latest death had been planned perfectly, designed to fit its recipient. Now the wheels needed to be set in motion.

*

'Samson Louis Powell is a forty-three-year-old, Afro-Caribbean male with a long criminal record and a history of violent offences. He comes from a dysfunctional background, having been taken into care as a four-year-old child after the death of his parents in a house fire, and he has lived a chaotic lifestyle ever since. He himself sustained burns to his limbs, neck and shoulders in the fire and has attempted to cover them up with a variety of tattoos down both arms and on his neck.'

Charlie looked out across the tightly packed office. Paul and Sabira had just returned from a second visit to the magistrate's court in a matter of hours and the paperwork was ready to go. Their number had swollen by at least a dozen extra Murder Investigation Team detectives and Nick was holding court with a group of them. The MIT officers stood in clusters, having been divided into smaller units already, designated to entry, search, arrest and exhibits, with a leader who had received an earlier briefing on what exactly was required by each group. The last to arrive had been a contingent of armed officers, resulting in the office now groaning under the strain of so many bodies and equipment squeezed into such a small amount of space.

The room had silenced as Charlie started, pointing to the front and side profiles of Powell projected on to the whiteboard at the front of the office, next to the photos of their victims and other suspects Bet had compiled earlier.

The image of Samson Powell was everything she'd imagined their murderer to be; a solidly built man, with a neck so short that his shaven head appeared to merge seamlessly into bulky shoulders. His forehead was lined; his eyes dark-rimmed and his nose looked to have been flattened across his face at some juncture in his colourful career of crime. His top lip was clean-shaven but he sported a full chinstrap beard of coarse black hair that disappeared down his neck until it was swallowed up into his chest hair. Two gold teeth, one on either side of his front upper incisors blinked out from the lazy smile he wore, and a large diamond stud hung from his left earlobe. A range of sordid tattoos appeared like a rash across the front and sides of his neck, the red and black inks used, hardly visible against the pigment of his skin.

'He has convictions for almost every offence you can name and has served various terms in prison. He has also been detained under the Mental Health Act on a compulsory detention order in Bethlem Psychiatric Hospital for four years after throwing a kettle of boiling water over his long-term partner, Lisa Forrester… though the term "partner" might be an over-exaggeration.'

The reason his name had sounded familiar had come to Charlie shortly after she'd heard it. Their address bordered Lambeth and Wandsworth borough, and although any disturbances were dealt with by the neighbouring Community Support Unit, both his and Lisa Forrester's photos had appeared quite regularly on their local briefings when one, or the other, or both, were shown as wanted.

'Several months ago, Lisa Forrester was taken into detox, with the help of social workers and officers from Wandsworth CSU, the unit that dealt with them regularly,' Charlie continued. 'She was adamant at the time that she did not want to see Samson again… *ever*. Whether she'll be able to give him up for good is another question, but it might have been the trigger for Samson starting this rampage.'

There was a murmur of agreement from some of the gathered officers. Relationships such as theirs rarely ended happily.

Charlie continued. 'He has come up on a DNA hit from a hair found at DI McGovern's murder scene. I don't need to say, that detail is not to be mentioned in his presence. We'll drop it in to conversation while in interview and see what he has to say.

'He currently lives at 23 Ribblesden Road, SW16, in a ground floor, converted flat. There's a floor plan for you all to peruse before we go. He is wanted for the murder of three police officers, so there can be no doubting that we will not be top of his favourites list. He has a full gamut of warning signals flashing up on his PNC record, including violent, mental, drugs, suicidal, weapons, escaper and alleges, so be prepared for anything. The armed unit will enter first in case he arms himself. He has used an axe or machete, as well as acid, in the linked murders and may well have them to hand in his premises. For that reason, we're going straight in as quickly as possible. He's to be neutralised before he has a chance to retaliate.'

She glanced across at Hunter, who was standing to her side, for confirmation and he nodded and stepped forward, taking over.

'Yes, that's right. We need our operation to be short, sharp and effective. Our intelligence is that he regularly deals drugs around the area at night, and therefore sleeps during the day. Hopefully that will be the case now. We don't want Powell given any warning that we're coming and no leeway when we're inside. You'll be briefed by your respective team leaders on your exact role before we go.'

He checked his watch. 'Be ready to move out at exactly 13.30 hours. I want Samson Powell in a cell and out of action as soon as possible.' He clapped his hands and the room shifted immediately. 'And remember, we'll have the eyes of the press on us this afternoon, so be on your best behaviour. More importantly, we'll have the hopes of every police officer in the Met on our success. Let's make sure we don't fail.'

*

The designated spot was less than a mile from his home. He was to leave his car parked on the road outside his address and walk. He slammed the gate to the front garden shut, as a wall of heat slapped him across the face, immediately wishing he was back inside, in the shade. It was sweltering. The heat of the midday sun beat down on his shoulders and within minutes a river of sweat was streaming down the small of his back. He wiped his forehead with the back of his hand, the roughened skin around his scarred forearms brushing against his cheek.

A neighbour scurried out of sight as he approached, no doubt fearing another confrontation. He stuck two fingers up at the man's retreating body, his gesture going unheeded, but it didn't matter if it hadn't been seen. It was satisfying just knowing his mere presence was enough to cause that reaction.

He came to the end of the road, waving towards the old drunk propped up against the bench outside the church and turned towards the shops, stopping briefly to buy some fags and a bottle of water, before greedily downing the contents. He crushed the bottle in one hand and slung it down on to the footway, stepping out across the main road between opposing rows of traffic with little regard to its speed and movement. Then onwards along several side roads and under the railway bridges into a maze of footpaths, one of which led out to the old Thames Water building, positioned on its own at the quiet end of Conery Road.

The building was half derelict but was still visited each morning and evening by a workforce of one or two employees, who turned up in their works van and walked once around the perimeter to check the padlocks were still intact and the cover in place over the well-shaft at the centre of the site. There were few residents of the local area who hadn't trespassed there at one time or another, to gaze across the thirty-foot span of the gaping hole, into its murky depths. His curiosity had also brought him to the grounds previously, the opportunity to appropriate some copper piping and old lead flashing from the roofs of several outhouses being too good to miss.

The road was quiet, most local residents having the sense to stay indoors to avoid the stifling heat. He ducked behind the only large tree in the street, glad of the cool umbrella of leaves, and checked the driveway. There was no sign of the van. A length of metal fencing ran from either side of the tree attached to the top of a brick wall, into which the tree was set. As its trunk had expanded over the years, part of the wall to one side had crumbled away and the fence was insecure. He pulled it back slightly and peered over the wall, seeing at once the black plastic carrier bag lodged behind a laurel bush.

Once again, the directions were accurate, so specific that he wanted to laugh with delight. What manner of death had been dreamt up this time? He couldn't wait to see the contents of the package but he remembered Ice's last instruction and how insistently it was delivered. *Phone me as soon as you have the package in your possession.*

There was still no one about. Peeling the broken fence back, he slid over into the site and retrieved the bag, sitting down in the shade of the tree with his back against the wall. Ice's number was the only one in the cheap Nokia. He'd left his personal phone at home as instructed. He dialled the number and waited for it to ring the usual three times before it was answered.

'I've got it,' he said breathlessly. 'What do you want me to do next?'

The voice that answered was Ice's. There was no doubt about it, but instead of its usual calm, soothing tones, it prickled with anger.

'I want you to use it now, every bit of it, where you found it. The contents of the parcel have been chosen specifically for you. You didn't follow my instructions as I demanded and right now the police are on their way to your home to arrest you. You fucked up, Samson, and I can't work with people who fuck up. From this moment, you are on your own. There is no one in the world for you now. You will never hear from me again. Ever. So, take my last piece of advice, Samson… and die.'

*

'Go, go, go', Hunter instructed clearly on the radio.

As if with one movement, every officer swept forward, the armed team crashing through the flimsy front door, screaming their demands, the back-up moving swiftly behind, waiting for the shout that any suspect inside had been detained. A small group of local residents appeared, as if by magic, on the street outside, watching from the opposite pavement, their phone cameras poised to record the moment when their rather sullen, aggressive neighbour would be brought out. They were used to the arrival of police at the address, but this time there were more than usual and they were armed.

'All clear,' shouted the sergeant in charge of the armed police. 'There's no one here.'

'Fuck it,' Hunter swore out loud. 'That's all we need. A madman who kills police officers and who will soon know that we're on to him, if he doesn't already. Even more reason to despatch a few more quickly.'

Charlie swallowed her frustration and said nothing. The vein on Hunter's forehead was standing out prominently. She watched as he pulled the officers back, sealing the empty flat off for a full forensic examination. Finding evidence would now be as vital as finding the man.

She saw the frowns on the faces of the team as they bunched together on the pavement outside and heard the guarded comments. They would all feel a little more vulnerable on the streets until Samson Powell was arrested.

*

Samson Powell looked out from behind a tree in the churchyard at the end of the road. His drunken mate was still sitting on the bench, swigging from a can of Stella, his head turned towards the police activity, every now and again muttering to himself. Samson unscrewed the cap on the top of the Smirnoff vodka bottle, one of the selected items left for him inside the black plastic bag, and took a slug from it. For a long moment, he thought about drinking it with his mate, but that could never happen.

The neat vodka hit the back of his throat and a wave of melancholy and anger swept through him. Ice was right. The pigs were on to him and there was nothing he could do to hold back the inevitable. His life would be fucked. He pulled the phone from his pocket and dialled Ice's number. An automated message told him the number was unavailable. He dialled it again, and again, and again, swigging more and more vodka with every repeat of the message and each time he heard it, the realisation that he'd been left to deal with this alone was hammered further into his head. *You fucked up, Samson, and I can't work with people who fuck up. From this moment, you are on your own. You will never hear from me again. Ever. So take my last piece of advice, Samson... and die.*

He wiped at the sweat on his brow angrily. He wanted to kill every single one of the police officers standing outside his door, rip each of them apart, tear out their hearts, beat them, maim them all. He hated them. They had tormented him throughout his life, but still, how could he have fucked up when he'd followed the instructions so carefully?

He started to retrace his footsteps, back across the road, along the side streets and under the railway bridges, his mind wandering to each killing; the axing of the dog, the lifting of his balaclava, the money; they were the only bits he'd added to personally. How could he have been identified from any of those? Still, Ice had blamed him and, deep down, he knew that Ice was right. *You fucked up, Samson.*

He was at the waterworks now. The road was still empty and there was no sign of the works van, but he wouldn't have cared had it been there. He knew what he had to do. He had only two choices... a lifetime in prison, or following Ice's final order. There was no other way.

Squeezing back through the gap in the fence, he pulled the black plastic bag out from under the bush and sunk down to his knees. The electrical cable spread out across the grass, strong and unbreakable, its end looped into a noose and tied tightly. He downed the remainder of the vodka and allowed the pure alcohol to wash through him, bringing with it a calmness and clarity.

The events of his life started to run through his brain, slowly at first but gathering pace. The flames and screams of his parents as they died in front of him, the pain of his own flesh sizzling in the heat, the separation, the foster homes, care homes, always moving, never staying in one place. And the agony, denial, rage and numbness, every part of him deadened in time so he could feel nothing. No emotion. No empathy. No responsibility for his actions. No guilt. Then the beatings, police stations, courts, prisons, wards, hospitals, inmates, disinfectant, more beatings. Words of love and words of abuse, love and abuse, never one without the other. Neither meaning anything. Lisa, loving him, hating him, leaving him, returning, going, going, gone. But he didn't care. He didn't give a fuck because that was his life, but now his life was over.

He hadn't known the policewoman, or the policeman with the dog, but he had known the fat one, the one he had set on fire, understanding the pain of charred skin only too well, the smell and memory of burning flesh returning him to his childhood. His hand moved subconsciously over the scar tissue on his arms and neck, his roughened, hairless skin lying in mounds where the flesh had withered and shrunk in the heat. The fat cop deserved it. They all deserved it. Ice had told him so and he had known it too. But now Ice was gone, fucked off and left him to deal with all their shit. He dialled the number, giving a wry smile as the answerphone kicked in again. *You will never hear from me again. Ever.* He wanted to laugh at the words. He'd been truly shafted, but deep down he knew it was his destiny. He and Ice had played a game. For years he'd thought he was the smartest, but now, because of his need to leave his own signature, to upstage Ice, he'd lost the game.

Throwing the empty bottle down on to the black bag, he stood and walked unsteadily towards the well-shaft, knowing instinctively what Ice had been thinking. A single magpie landed on the path before him, hopping back and forth, leading him forward, its beady black eye enticing him towards his grave. *One for sorrow...* He came to the side of the hole, pushing the cover across and staring through the metal railings into the abyss. The sunshine lit up the upper edges but no light permeated to its base, the furthest reaches of the watery pit rearing up towards him, a matt black hell. A metal ladder was attached to the rim, hanging fifteen feet from the railings. It led downwards but stopped mid-air, as if fearing to go any further.

Samson pulled the phone from his pocket and dialled the only saved number one last time before throwing it forward as the automated message sounded. He had no use for it now Ice had gone. He didn't care anymore as he listened to its eventual muted splash far down below. He never truly had. He climbed the railings, looping the noose around his neck, before descending the ladder and tying the free end to the bottom rung. For the first time ever, he would be following Ice's instructions to the letter. The irony was not lost on him. He thought about leaving a note, but to whom? There was no one left. *You are on your own.*

The very last words from his final ever conversation came to mind.

So take my last piece of advice… and die.

He took a deep breath and closed his eyes, smiling inwardly at the recognition that a tiny part of him would miss the voice and what it signified; a ghost from the past, dominated by the commands of the present. The Ice that had been his future had won the game, and as he flung his body out into the darkness, he knew without doubt that when news of his death was reported, Ice would be smiling too.

Chapter 21

Charlie knew exactly who the suicide at Thames Waterworks would be. The workmen conducting the late afternoon security check called it in, the tattooed, scarred dead body hanging grotesquely from the ladder, its neck stretched unnaturally, its mouth gaping open.

They had gone straight there, Charlie immediately recognising the corpse to be that of Samson Powell from the custody image. His body was still in situ, the same electrical cable as had been used on Leonard Cookson and Philippa McGovern gouged deep into the skin of his neck. His arms hung lifelessly by his sides, his shoulders slumped forward and his feet splayed outward. His midriff was bare, gravity having pulled the waistband of his trousers down over his elongated body as far as his knees, leaving only a scruffy pair of boxer shorts clinging around his groin to maintain any sort of dignity.

'Fuck it,' Hunter muttered as they peered over the railings. 'We missed our chance.'

Charlie said nothing, unable to tear her gaze away from Samson Powell's final statement, knowing that his last act of violence turned inwards had effectively robbed the relatives of his victims of any chance of closure. They would never see justice served and they would never breathe a sigh of relief at the knowledge that the killer of their loved ones was locked up for life. The police could fill in the gaps, the when's and the how's, they could come up with their own theories about his motivations, but they would never, ever, have the chance to really know why.

'At least he won't kill again,' she said, knowing that the words were admitting failure. It was *their* job to put an end to his activities, not his. Samson Powell had exercised total control over the situation from the beginning to the end and they had been powerless to stop him.

She broke away from the well-shaft and wandered towards a broken-down fence, noting immediately the empty bottle of vodka weighing down a black plastic carrier bag surrounded by scraps of brown paper. The cordons were being put in place now. The forensic examiners and lab technicians would have yet another crime scene to pore over. Divers would be sent down into the pit to scour for any further clues. The team would still have to search through hours of CCTV, compile lists of witness statements and check retrospectively over the last known movements of their named suspect. The investigation would continue, even though there would never be a satisfactory conclusion. The coroner would expect nothing less before the cause of death could be formally entered on the death certificates of their victims and confirmed in court.

Charlie knew, however, that in addition to the investigation into each murder, the life of their murderer would also require a full dissection. Samson Powell's background would have to be scrutinised and full factual reports compiled, before the myriad bloodhound journalists got going, intent on being the first to publish the diary of a serial killer or the biography of a psychopath.

She returned to where Hunter still stood by the well-shaft, listening as he sighed loudly and turned to leave. 'I just wish we could have got the bastard to Crown Court instead of just the Coroner's,' he said, as if reading her mind.

Charlie nodded, staring down at Powell's disfigured body one last time. His actions had been beyond comprehension, his chosen methods of murder both barbaric and heinous. He would justifiably be labelled one of the capital's worst ever police serial killers but, as she tore her eyes away from his dead face, Charlie registered silently that there was something desperately pathetic about how he now appeared; the obvious burns, his efforts at masking the scarring with ink, his eyelids closed as if in sleep.

His life had clearly been as violent as his death.

*

Ice turned the volume up on the TV, listening to every word of the headlines. Samson Powell's picture filled the screen, his stupid, fucked-up arrogant face dominating the news. The man was a loser, in life and in death; he deserved to die. They all deserved to die.

The vision of a woman lying dead at the foot of a flight of stairs came to mind, a young child crying by her crumpled form. A man in uniform stood over her lifeless body, his mouth curled up in a snarl, his foot held above the small child, daring the child to speak the truth. 'Accidental death' was recorded on the certificate, the stair carpet blamed for causing the fall, the woman's brutalised body buried, like the truth had been. The child had remained silent, but now the adult was being heard. Now was the time for retribution.

The file lay open on the cabinet, the details inside, concise and accurate. Samson Powell – Number One, was a violent brute of a man, broken from childhood, moulded by abuse, an uninhibited monster… and one that Ice had recognised as a kindred spirit, played with and ultimately defeated.

Ice pulled out a pen and scored through the page. Samson Powell had been strong but with a fatal flaw, one that he was unable to control and one that ultimately had led to his death, falling, falling, down, down through the air, his mind broken and his body destroyed. It was perfect.

The face of Number Two came into focus, already activated, already dedicated, already desperate. Number Two would continue where Number One had failed.

Ice paced the floor, staring in fury as the face disappeared from the news. More deaths would follow. For a short while, though, because of Number One's disobedience the plan had to wait; at least until it was safe again to proceed. The words of a song started to replay, quietly at first but growing, growing in strength until everything else was obliterated. The best was yet to come.

Ring a ring o' roses, a pocket full o' posies, atishoo, atishoo, we all fall down.

Chapter 22

Tina Ashton was waiting in the reception of Lambeth HQ when Charlie and Hunter returned. Baby Bryony was strapped to her bosom in a baby sling sleeping soundly, totally unaware of the passage of officers and visitors in and out of the building.

She stood as she saw Charlie enter through the revolving doors and searched her face curiously.

'Not a good day?' she pronounced uncertainly, reading Charlie's mind exactly. 'I wondered if I could speak to you in person if you have a minute.'

'Of course you can, Tina. Anytime.' Charlie pasted a smile on her face, waved Hunter off and indicated a small interview room to the side of the reception, peeping in towards Bryony as Tina stepped past. She reached out, stroking the baby's soft downy head gently. 'She's growing already. Come in. What can I do for you?'

Tina took a deep breath, and started to speak but stopped suddenly, her voice faltering at the first word. She looked close to tears.

Charlie guided her towards a chair and she slumped down into it.

'I'm really sorry but I think I might have inadvertently misled you when I said that Bri had the kids' birth certificates in his wallet when he was killed.' She swallowed hard. 'The day after I came out from hospital I collected as much as I could from home and took the kids to stay at my parents. I couldn't bear to stay at our house knowing that Brian was gone.' She glanced down at the baby, moving her hand without thinking to rearrange her tangled legs. 'Well after we spoke on the phone I decided I should go home and check everything out, just in case. I went back this morning, but when I arrived, I found the kitchen window had been smashed and I'd been burgled. Whoever had broken in had obviously cut themselves on the broken glass as there are blood spots around the kitchen.'

Tina stopped talking and looked stricken.

'Go on,' Charlie prompted, pursing her lips. For the second time in a matter of hours, she knew what was coming next.

'I haven't reported it yet because I think it might have been Carl. Hardly anything was stolen, certainly nothing that you would normally expect. In fact, it looked like the study was the only room that he'd gone in. There was a photograph of Bobby and Emily in their swimming costumes on a beach, on holiday a few years ago that was missing from the wall… and the filing cabinet was open right at the section where we kept the kids' documents; their passports, baptism certificates and school stuff, that sort of thing. The birth certificates weren't there.' Tina shook her head, her eyes cast downwards. 'Brian may well have returned the certificates to the filing cabinet. Carl must have got them when he broke into the house. He might not have had anything to do with Bri's death.'

Charlie smiled at the woman. She must have lain worrying that Carl had somehow been involved in Brian's murder. It couldn't be a particularly palatable thought suspecting that the father of your first two children had somehow despatched the father of your third.

'Tina, I don't think you need worry any further. We have yet to confirm all the details, but we are pretty sure we have just found Brian's murderer. Unfortunately for us, he killed himself before we could get to him, but all the signs are that he is responsible for all three deaths. That's where we've just returned from.'

Tina Ashton burst into tears, dropping her head into her hands. 'Oh thank God it's not Carl. I've been so worried that he was involved, especially after you said you'd arrested him yesterday.'

'What I didn't tell you was that we'd found blood spots in his car and on his bag. That's why we brought him in; to ask him about them. Not that he said anything.'

Tina wiped her eyes, her mouth gaping open in disbelief. 'And you thought they were Brian's?'

Charlie grimaced. 'We thought they might be, but we had it confirmed this morning by the lab, that the blood was indeed Carl's, and if your suspicions about him breaking into your house are correct, that would explain where they came from... and why he didn't want to talk to us.'

'The stupid man,' Tina suddenly blurted out, before shaking her head. 'He must have been more desperate than we thought.'

'Well that was pretty much all he said in his interview... that he didn't want to lose his kids. He is a fool though. He should have told us what he'd done, but I guess he knew that he'd be in trouble for breaking in and that we'd suspect him as soon as we heard about the burglary... but it could have been far worse for him. It's lucky for him that we know who the real murder suspect is.'

'Poor Carl. Will he get into trouble for breaking in?'

'That's totally your decision. It's up to you whether you want to report the matter and pursue it, or not. There's enough evidence already to have him charged with burglary and sent to court. With the recent domestic problems you'd been having, I'm guessing the courts wouldn't look too kindly on him. He may well even get a prison sentence.'

Tina stood up and turned away from Charlie, her hand gently cupping Bryony's tiny head.

'I don't know. Can I think about it?' she said. 'He should never have done what he did, but maybe I should have realised how much stress he was under and how much we were pushing him. He does adore the kids, even though he has a funny way of showing it sometimes. Maybe we can come to an amicable arrangement if he admits what he's done and pays for the damage.'

'Of course, Tina. You've got enough on your plate at the moment. Give me a ring when you've decided about Carl, and any other issues worrying you.' Charlie smiled warmly at Tina as she turned back round to face her. 'We'll wait for your decision before we make ours.'

Tina reached out towards Charlie and they shook hands, Tina's handshake stronger than Charlie was expecting. Their eyes held each other's for a moment and Charlie had the distinct impression that Tina had guessed exactly where she'd been the previous evening.

Chapter 23

Every day the list of emails got longer, report after report landing on Charlie's lap. Hunter had designated her as the main point of contact, so she was in charge of collating the evidence coming in on the three murders and the suicide of Samson Powell that would eventually be presented to the Coroner, the Commissioner and the IPCC. It would take some time to complete the full report, so initially they needed to prepare interim files.

The team were all assisting as best they could. Paul and Bet were tasked to look at any overarching evidence around all three crime scenes, such as CCTV, the presence of the roses and where they might have come from, liaison with the forensic services and the general call data on all three victims' phones, as well as what appeared to be a personal phone found at the home address of Samson Powell. As they retrieved information, they then screened it and passed it on to the relevant team members. Naz was in charge of the report on DI Philippa McGovern's murder, Sabira on PC Brian Ashton's and Nick was compiling the file on DS Leonard Cookson's death.

The additional officers, so recently drummed up by DCI O'Connor, had all returned to their respective units, their assistance on the investigation having lasted for less than half a day in total.

Charlie was also compiling the report on Samson Louis Powell, the choice having been given to her by Hunter who was in overall charge of the final draft. It would be interesting to discover what had made the man tick, as well as trying to establish the catalyst for the horror that had unfolded.

They were determined, as a unit, to produce a comprehensive, professional report for the sake of each murdered officer, but it still felt as if they were working towards an inevitable consequence; like swatting for an exam but knowing the result was destined to be failure.

Each morning they would sit together discussing what new evidence had come in. Powell's guilt was absolute. The presence of the red roses, the stems devoid of thorns at each murder scene connected them irrefutably. However, the significance of the roses remained unknown, and the only reason for the removal of the thorns appeared to be the avoidance of inadvertent DNA contamination. The team wanted more; they wanted to find every possible speck of evidence to link each case and show Powell's guilt. It was a matter of pride now.

Although he had clearly been careful in his flat, destroying or disposing of most of the articles and implements used in each crime, he had been unable to eradicate the tiny scraps of forensic material transferred from his clothing, shoes, property or body to his residence. Even without the rose connection, Powell had made errors and now they had him matched to the McGovern crime scene it was just a matter of time before further forensic evidence connected him conclusively to the others.

Sabira was the first to start getting her results coming through, Brian Ashton's murder being the initial scene to be examined. Powell had driven a battered old silver Toyota Avensis on an 04 plate and it was from this vehicle that the majority of the evidence was now being found.

The car had been parked on the road outside his flat when they'd turned up to arrest him. It was unregistered but had been linked to him on many occasions; a set of keys left on the table inside confirmed this. The car was immediately lifted on to the back of a low-loader, covered and taken for a full examination.

With a make, model and registration number of a vehicle now known, Paul and Bet had scoured the CCTV from Brian Ashton's place of work to his place of death. The Toyota had been spotted travelling along main roads in the vicinity of both areas with only one male occupant inside. The quality of the footage wasn't good enough to identify Powell facially whilst in motion, but the driver appeared to be a similar height and build and sported the same shaved head. In one clip, about two hours before Brian Ashton left work, a clearly identifiable Powell had been captured leaving the car on the forecourt of a petrol station in Waterloo and buying snacks. It was implausible that he had lent the vehicle out to another person fitting his description in the timescale that they had. Powell was therefore in the right place at the right time.

The forensic results, when they started returning were as conclusive as they had hoped and it was these that linked Powell directly to Ashton's murder and the other crime scenes. In the foot well and underneath the driver's seat of his Toyota was a miscellany of evidence, a jumble of fibres, fluids and flora mixed together in a potpourri of proof.

Three black hairs carefully removed with tweezers from this mixture was the clincher; three black hairs that had no doubt been stuck to the soles of the footwear worn by the killer. Three black hairs that, on closer examination, belonged to Casper, Brian Ashton's Labrador. The shoes were missing, but the remains of the shoe treads had provided everything they needed. The dog may have been the reason Brian Ashton was on the common that night, but the attack on Casper was also the reason they could prove the guilt of his master's murderer. Brian Ashton had clearly been targeted. If he hadn't died then, it was highly likely he would have been killed elsewhere. Charlie wondered whether this knowledge might now push Tina to accept the dog remaining with her.

Sabira's report was thorough and well presented; every shred of evidence, whether vital or insignificant, listed; the time, place, method and consequences clearly laid out in words, with photographs graphically illustrating the speed and ferocity of Powell's attack. Brian Ashton had not stood a chance.

Nick's report on Leonard Cookson's murder was just as comprehensive. Bet and Paul, whilst trawling through CCTV footage, had spotted Powell's Toyota in close proximity to the Lonely Mole, where Cookson had spent his birthday evening, within an hour of closing time. Although the CCTV cameras did not extend to the side roads at the rear of Streatham Common, it was deemed likely that the car would have been parked up nearby. A revisit of all the houses in Leonard Cookson's road was undertaken and threw up information from an elderly neighbour that she had noticed a strange car parked in a lay-by at the back of the common, its silvery hue manifest in the beams of an adjacent street light. Unfortunately, the witness had not scribbled down the registration number or seen an occupant, nor had she thought to phone it in, but there was no doubting that it was, in all probabilities Powell's silver Toyota.

Fragments of charred dirt and burnt fibres were also retrieved from the foot well of Powell's car adding to the mounting evidence, but Nick's pièce de résistance, of which he was justifiably proud, was the outcome of his enquiries into a quantity of cash found in Powell's flat. Witness statements from some of Cookson's team who had been out celebrating with him spoke of their skipper having a wallet full of cash, which he was happy to splash around. Nick had checked with his bank to find he had withdrawn three hundred pounds from the cashpoint closest to where he worked near Tower Bridge; but there were no notes left in his wallet at all when his body was found. Nick thought it unlikely he would have spent every penny. Added to that, three twenty-pound notes found in the cash in Powell's flat were newly printed and in numerical order. They had obviously come from the same batch. Could Powell have taken them from Leonard Cookson's wallet prior to killing him and if so could there be more? They would certainly be a temptation to a man like Samson Powell, with a liking for weed and alcohol.

Nick had phoned the Lonely Mole Pub and spoken to the manager. Luckily the week's takings were yet to be paid into the bank. They were still in the safe. Jumping into a police car immediately, Nick had gone straight to the pub, sifting through every single banknote until he found what he was looking for. Six shiny new twenty-pound notes, crisp and barely used and all with serial numbers within the same range as those at Powell's address. There could be little other explanation for why they were at Samson Powell's flat, other than him having stolen them from Cookson's wallet at the time of his murder. The odds of Powell having withdrawn money from the exact same cashpoint in Tower Bridge as Cookson, either immediately before or after him, were too fantastic to even try to contemplate.

Armed with that knowledge, all the notes at Powell's flat were sent off for analysis and the lab were able to confirm there were traces of acetone on them, along with the type of explosives found in fireworks. These facts, without doubt incriminated Samson Powell.

The final nail in the coffin was the length of electrical cable used to tie Cookson's body to the chair. This was found to be exactly the same type as

was used to secure Philippa McGovern to her bed...
and to provide the means for Powell to hang himself.
Forensic scientists had even been able to match one
end to another, each angle of the cut fitting with the
next. The sections used were all from the same length
of 2.5 mm electrical cable available from many
electrical or DIY stores.

Along with the roses, the cable was now the main
piece of evidence which irrefutably connected
Samson Powell with both Leonard Cookson and
Philippa McGovern and now they had additional
forensic material linking Brian Ashton's murder to
Powell the case was complete.

Naz was still hard at work, having to wait for the
final results coming from Philippa McGovern's
murder scene and post-mortem. Her cause of death
was recorded as organ failure as a direct result of
dehydration. Dr Crane had sent an explanation in his
email, detailing his findings. In it he said that with
water usually making up over two-thirds of a human
body, it was not difficult to see how vital it was to
keep the body hydrated. While some people had been
known to survive for up to seven or eight days
without water, the length of time could be drastically
decreased by outside forces, one of these being heat.
On a warm June week, lying between hot bedcovers,
with all the windows in the house closed and the
central heating turned up full, Philippa McGovern

would have lost moisture from her body at an alarming rate. Severe dehydration and death would have therefore occurred far sooner, with waste and toxins building up quickly, unable to be flushed away during digestion. The raised toxin levels would cause seizures, brain damage and eventual death, due to the internal organs shutting down.

Dr Crane estimated her time of death to be between 6 a.m. and 8 a.m. on Monday 19th June 2017, just two days after the night-time break-in, although it was likely she would have been unconscious for some time before death.

Charlie shivered subconsciously as Naz read out the email. It was a slow, agonising way to go, with cramps, seizures and pain, before being delivered mercifully into unconsciousness. She could only imagine the fear McGovern must have felt with her murderer leaning over her, close enough to leave a hair, alone in the dark, unable to move, gradually losing all hope with each minute that passed, her means to drink water or summon help frustratingly out of reach.

This then was the basis of the three reports. The case was to be closed when each file was complete. Samson Powell was without doubt the murderer and both Hunter and DCI O'Connor were pleased that he was now off the streets and unable to kill again.

The officers of the Metropolitan Police and Surrey Constabulary could breathe a collective sigh of relief.

Only Charlie was not convinced. A persistent niggle was turning into a hunch. There were too many unanswered questions and as she delved further into Powell's background more were coming to light. Her sixth sense was prickling with every new revelation but she had to admit the evidence against Samson was overwhelming. They knew the how's and where's, but what she really wanted to understand now was the why's.

In order to do this Charlie immediately contacted the various information governance departments for the social services to obtain his case history; the doctor to obtain his medical records and the NHS trusts for his mental health records, mindful of the protocols around data protection. The circumstances of the case would provide sufficient justification for the requests, added to which the Coroner would need to know all the facts to properly return a verdict.

As the details were returned she flipped the pages grimly. Powell's full history was starting to emerge and it made uncomfortable reading.

Samson Louis Powell was born in Peckham to Lionel and Delilah Powell, a West-Indian male and mixed-race female, and had been named Samson as a reference to the story of Samson, the strong man in the Bible and his love for a woman called Delilah. At the age of 4 years, he had been lucky to survive the night-time arson attack that killed both his parents. The police never caught the arsonist, though it was rumoured on the estate that it was a known racist thug who had fallen out with Lionel, his father.

Samson was then moved from one foster family to the next, each finding his increasingly erratic behaviour hard to manage. He was required to attend hospital regularly as he grew older for skin grafts on his growing limbs and, with each stay as an inpatient, he withdrew further into himself. Nobody could reach him and his behaviour became increasingly volatile, prone to bursts of uncontrollable temper or periods of withdrawal where he refused food or any communication. He was suspended from infant school and expelled twice from junior schools, finding himself eventually in a unit for delinquent children, as it was called in those days. His attitude worsened over time and, with his growing strength, came bouts of violence. He was labelled as 'emotionally bereft' and lacking in any form of guilt or moral compass.

As far as Charlie could see, he basically did what he wanted, when he wanted, and nobody could impose any control or structure on his life. The flames of the fire that damaged his body had also seemingly swept through his mind, searing him with an inability to understand or empathise with anybody, either socially, physically or mentally. He had no remaining family and found it almost impossible to form friendships.

With foster families no longer willing to risk taking him in, he was transferred from one care home to the next, each group of social workers becoming less effective in dealing with his increasingly antisocial personality traits.

At the age of eleven he started at a local senior school with the hope that he might see it as a chance to start again, but the damage was too profound by this stage. Within weeks of the new term beginning, he was suspended for fighting with another boy, battering him across the head and body with a hockey stick when the boy dared to tackle him. He was referred to a special school, spent the next few years in and out of education and began his life of crime, dabbling with cannabis and alcohol, before starting to sell the hard drugs that he would use to ensnare those he wished to control.

By sixteen he had been arrested a dozen times, attended Juvenile Court and been sent to a young person's Borstal. His offences ranged from minor drugs possession, to assaults and criminal damage, including the GBH on his fellow pupil. The social services paperwork included references to school report after school report, where he was almost always described as uninterested, lacking in any motivation or social skills and devoid of responsibility for his poor attendance and non-completion of homework.

Two reports, though, were highlighted and Charlie read these with interest, noting Samson's apparent ability to concentrate and follow instructions; skills lacking from the notes of all the other teachers. Both of the yearly accounts were written by the same female teacher at the special school he'd attended. Ms Saffron Bolt had taught Samson integrated science for just under two years, from the age of thirteen to fifteen. She described Samson as being attentive and willing to try, his efforts being rewarded with average results for the subject at the end of each year. This marked a huge improvement on every other subject, where his results were below average, bordering on negligible. Samson clearly enjoyed science or, perhaps, being taught by Ms Bolt. A separate page clipped to the two reports, written by the head teacher, speculated on why this could have happened. It mentioned that Samson had alluded to the teacher that she bore a striking resemblance to his own mother. This had been checked against records and found to be correct. Saffron Bolt was an attractive light-skinned black female, in her mid-twenties, slim and pretty, with her hair held in a ponytail. Samson's own mother, Delilah, looked remarkably similar, a dog-eared photo of her, singed at the corner being one of the boy's only possessions not destroyed in the fire.

Charlie, upon reading this, had checked the possessions found on Powell at the time of his suicide. The photo was listed as being contained in an old leather wallet in the back pocket of his trousers. It was a miracle the wallet hadn't fallen into the well shaft as his body jerked downwards. She dug it out and gazed at the image of the serene young woman, wearing a beige blouse with large collar and a brown and cream patterned skirt synonymous with the seventies. Had she not died, Charlie wondered whether her son's life might have taken a completely different path. She would never know; however, she found the whole concept of Samson Powell responding to a teacher with similar looks fascinating. She jotted down the name. Ms Saffron Bolt would be interesting to talk to, if her whereabouts could be established after so long.

The head teacher had then questioned whether Samson's attachment to this teacher could be replicated with other teachers but the query appeared to have been answered by his reaction on hearing Ms Bolt was to go on a period of maternity leave. He'd gone on a rampage of destruction in the classroom, overturning desks, stamping on furniture and smashing up the blackboard with the leg of a chair as well as beating up a fellow pupil with the same chair leg. For that he was arrested and spent time in juvenile detention, never setting foot in the school again. His education, or any attempts at education was over.

His next few years in the care system seemed to Charlie to be like a roller coaster. One month he appeared to settle, before the next brought fresh upheaval with new staff bringing new battles and new residents bringing intimidation and recrimination. Samson lurched from one crisis to the next, one home to another. It was no wonder his life had turned out as it had.

The only thing that appeared to calm his outbursts a little was the arrival of a girl, Lisa Forrester, to whom he grew close. She arrived at the same care home as he, soon after he'd finished at the special school and remained with him, on and off, until his death. She was almost as damaged as he, by all accounts, but the social services reports again acknowledged that she could sometimes be a good influence on his moods. However, the opposite could also be the case, and so their relationship was stormy. It was one of only a handful of known relationships that Samson Powell had ever managed to maintain and Lisa had been a presence throughout his life.

Once Samson Powell reached eighteen, the children's services of the local council effectively washed their hands of their troubled ward and he arrived on the doorstep of the DSS and Housing. They needn't have worried though; Powell spent as much time in prison as out. Sometimes he was allowed to keep possession of his council property, sometimes he had to hand it back. Sometimes Lisa kept it running, paying the rent while he was gone, sometimes she was forced to sofa-surf until he was released. Their list of hostels, flats and bedsits could have made up a geographia of South London, with addresses in Lambeth, Wandsworth, Merton and Peckham, whichever borough took their fancy.

His life went into free fall, the money required to fund his alcohol abuse, Lisa and her habits forcing him to steal and rob. Lisa was pimped out to assist the cash flow. He didn't care what she did and neither did she. She was there to be used... and she was there to be abused. So was he, and the assaults were usually two-way. Lisa demanded his attention, and if she didn't get it, her quick temper then ensured he attended A & E... just as often as she. The list of convictions and referrals grew as every year passed, with Powell arrested for the vast majority of the allegations made by Lisa, while refusing to substantiate anything against her.

The printouts of his offending history swelled, filling a folder to itself: GBH, ABH, rape, sexual assault, burglary, robbery, pick-pocketing, theft of cars and from cars, shoplifting and criminal damage. It was all there catalogued, some with charges and convictions, some NFA'd, some cautioned. He'd done time in many of Her Majesty's Prisons in London: Wandsworth, Brixton, Belmarsh and Wormwood Scrubs, as well as a few in Surrey.

Prison and punishment did not discourage his criminality, however; they cemented it. He was locked into a vicious cycle of discipline and defiance. As a child his antisocial behaviour had been noted; as an adult, it had been diagnosed as being more synonymous with those of a psychopath or sociopath. In other words, Samson Powell was unable to understand the social norms, with low or no capacity for remorse. What he did, he did without emotion, each assault on Lisa inflicted without mercy, the scalding incident being the culmination of his cruelty. The judge presiding over the case had deemed it preferable to submit him to a term in hospital rather than prison. He needed to be cured, not punished… but there was no cure, only a slow treatment that tried to change the symptoms, without being able to fix the cause. Powell was unfixable, maybe he always had been, and as he graduated to the murder of three police officers, each one was carried out meticulously and without remorse. In his mind, for whatever reason, they deserved to die and he seemed quite happy to be the one to assist them into the next life.

What Charlie was trying to establish, as she read through the plethora of information on him, was *why* he believed that each of them deserved to die. What links could there be between Samson Powell and his three victims and how did he choose the methods he used? His history was so extensive he could have come across each one, or heard about them from associates, inmates, or fellow patients, but in her mind it wasn't good enough just to be able to prove that he had killed all three police officers; she had to be able to prove why. She also had to understand more of what made a psychopath tick. What had started Powell off on his murderous rampage? Could it have been Lisa's removal from his life to go into detox? Could it just be his nature, his body enacting what his imagination had visualised for so long... but what drove him? What controlled him?

Or, as it seemed with his teacher, was it possible for someone to control him?

Chapter 24

Tuesday 4th July 2017

'You fucking killed him, you bastards. I want to speak to the person responsible for murdering my Samson and I'm not leaving until I do.'

Charlie didn't wait for the tannoy. She'd seen the woman staggering towards the glass-fronted facade of Lambeth HQ on her way in and recognised her from her photos on custody imaging. Now as she peered down from their fourth-floor office, she watched as Samson Powell's partner lurched away from the revolving doors on to the pavement, turning round and aiming her vitriol at the faceless receptionist. Lisa Forrester was not going to go away. Hunter came out from his office and joined her, the sound waves from the initial shouting having travelled up the lift shafts and spread across the whole building.

'I wondered how long it would take for us to get the blame.' Hunter sighed heavily.

Charlie watched the woman, her face screwed up, her eyes blazing, screaming out her demands. She was propped against the same lamp post as Ben had often leant against and Charlie felt a wave of nostalgia roll over her at the memory. She would go to visit Ben after work and drag him out for a run. A muffled scream broke through her thoughts as Lisa Forrester pitched forward towards the entrance again.

'Come on, let's get this over with,' Hunter turned towards the door. 'She's not going to leave us alone until we at least try to explain what happened.'

'I get the feeling she's not going to listen to a single word we say,' Charlie swung round to follow him. 'But I guess we might be interested in some of the things she has to say.'

By the time they got to the reception, Lisa Forrester's screams were magnified. She had taken the middle seat of a set of three, her arms spread out across the length of them and her feet planted firmly in front of her to maintain her balance. Clumps of auburn hair stuck out at all angles in a mass of tangles, an elastic band stretched thin, holding the remnants of a long, straw-like ponytail askew at the side of her head. Grey roots slashed her scalp in criss-cross lines and black rings of smudged mascara scarred her cheeks.

She wore tight grey leggings that hugged every inch of the loose skin on her belly, whilst bagging out, stained and dirty at the knees; one leg pulled up and caught over the top of knee-length scuffed black boots. A thin, pink T-shirt struggled to meet the overstretched waistband of her leggings, leaving a jagged expanse of flesh hanging out from between.

If she had ever been on the wagon, she had now very clearly tumbled from the uppermost seats to the stony surface below. Her breath reeked of booze and her pupils were tiny pinpricks, her body having succumbed to the combination of drugs and alcohol.

Hunter held out his hand towards her. 'Lisa Forrester?'

The woman stared up towards him. 'Yeah, why? Who the fuck are you?'

'My name is DI Geoffrey Hunter and this is DC Charlotte Stafford. I am the officer in charge of the case your partner was involved in.'

'Oh, are you now?' She leant forward, revealing a glimpse of grubby cleavage from the top of her T-shirt, her eyes wide and blazing. 'Well, before we start, I can tell you that he weren't involved in nuffin'. And he didn't top himself neither. You bastards killed him. You pushed 'im to it. In fact, you may as well 'ave pushed him off the side of that hole yourselves.'

She turned her head and spat on the tiles in front of Hunter's feet. Hunter didn't move. Keeping his voice low and serious, he stared straight into Lisa Forrester's face.

'I was going to explain what we know, Lisa, but I'm not going to speak to you if you carry on like that. Come on, DC Stafford, let's go. If you wish to make a complaint, Ms Forrester I suggest you speak to our colleagues at the desk, but I can tell you now, I will instruct them not to listen to you unless you treat them civilly.' He turned and took a few paces towards the security door into the police area of the reception. Charlie followed behind, watching as he pressed in the code to open the lock. As he did so, Charlie heard a wail from behind.

'Don't go. I need to know what 'appened.'

She turned to see Lisa Forrester rock forward on to her knees, bending down to wipe the spit up from the tiles with her T-shirt. 'He's gone and killed 'imself and I weren't even there to try and stop 'im. How do you fink that makes me feel? Him and me 'ave been togever all our lives and I weren't wiv 'im when 'e needed me.'

The woman started to sob, rubbing at her cheeks and smudging the make-up still further around her face. Charlie pulled a tissue from her pocket and handed it to her. Underneath the thin, outwardly tough veneer, the woman in front of her was broken and vulnerable. She probably always had been. She put an arm around Lisa and ushered her into an interview room and sat down opposite, waiting for the tears to subside. Hunter came in too, his expression soft. Gone were the harsh words. Lisa Forrester, like the majority of the women that they dealt with, needed support and sympathy. It was what made them seek help. It was also what might help Charlie fill in the pieces of the jigsaw.

Charlie started. 'Lisa, firstly, we are sorry for your loss.'

Lisa Forrester sniffed hard and raised tired eyes. 'I doubt you are. I doubt anyone is, 'cept me.'

'You were with him a long time.'

'We was together since I was thirteen, almost our whole lives.' She paused and stuck out her bottom lip. 'Give or take a few years 'ere and there, but if 'e weren't inside the nick or the nuthouse, 'e was wiv me.'

Charlie smiled encouragingly towards the middle-aged woman in front of her. 'There're not many people who can stay together that long. What was he like?'

Lisa shook her head and exhaled through her nose. 'Well, 'e weren't no angel. I fink you can probably see that for yourself. Didn't care about 'imself; in fact 'e didn't care for much at all, 'cept me. Whatever 'appened, he always looked after me… in 'is own way.' Her expression softened as she spoke. 'We was bad for each other, but we was also good for each other. We would fight like cat and dog, but we would always end up together again. We couldn't live wiv, or wivout each other.' Her face crumpled. 'I don't know what I'm gonna do without 'im. I should never 'ave told 'im I weren't coming back from detox.' She rolled the tissue up and screwed it into her eyes. 'Whatever 'e's done, he's done because I weren't there.'

'Lisa, do you know what he's alleged to have done?'

'They told me 'e'd killed three coppers and then topped 'imself.' She nodded towards Hunter. 'He always hated you lot. Right from the start 'e said you lot knew who had killed his parents but you never nicked 'em. It made him mad. 'E was only little when they was burned to death but 'e remembered it as if it was yesterday. Still carries 'is own scars... and still carried round a picture of 'is mum to this day.'

'I know, Lisa. I saw it. She was very pretty.'

'That's what 'e always said. An' he used to say that I was pretty too, like 'is mother. As dainty as Delilah. That was 'er name. He always said he weren't good enough for me. That one day I would see sense and leave 'im. And if that 'appened, his life wouldn't be worth livin'. He said that everybody important always left 'im.'

'Who else left him?' Charlie remembered the teacher.

Lisa pursed her lips, her forehead creased in thought. 'Well, his parents for a start, though I suppose they didn't really 'ave a choice. There was a few others 'ere and there; the odd guy from prison that 'e got matey wiv for a while, though probably more for business, if ya know what I mean' Then there was this teacher he told me about when we first met. He really liked 'er, tried to do everything she asked of 'im but she left to 'ave a baby.'

'Ms Saffron Bolt?'

'Yeah that was her. I remember 'er name 'cause Saffron sounds posh and Bolt is like Usain Bolt. Shame Samson couldn't run as fast as 'im. You lot would never 'ave caught him then.' She chuckled at the thought. 'And a few others, some shrink 'e got friendly wiv that 'e mentioned. Then there was me, I suppose. He must 'ave thought I really 'ad left him.'

Charlie watched as the tears restarted.

'Maybe that's why he really lost it this time. 'E must 'ave blamed you lot for helping me to get detox. For taking me away from 'im. He always went mad when I weren't there. Maybe it's all my fault.'

Hunter chipped in. 'It's not your fault, Lisa. You're not responsible for his actions. You know the evidence is pretty conclusive. DNA, forensics, that sort of thing'

She nodded. 'Yeah, I heard you'd got 'im bang to rights for murdering the three cops'

Charlie pulled out her phone and scrolled to the albums. She had the official warrant card photos of each of their victims.

'Take a look at these pictures. Do you know any of the three officers? Or do you know if Samson might have.' She passed the phone across the table and watched as Lisa stared at all three, squinting towards the pictures of Brian Ashton and Philippa McGovern, before returning to the photo of DS Leonard Cookson.

'The others look familiar, like. Maybe I've seen them around, but Samson definitely knew 'im.' She held the phone up towards them. 'Samson hated 'im. I remember his name too, Leonard Cookson. Samson swore that one day 'e'd get his just deserts and someone would do 'im in.'

Charlie leant forward across the table and took the phone.

'How did Samson know him, Lisa?' she asked.

'He was responsible for banging up one of our neighbours' boys. When we was living on the Angell Town estate in Brixton.' She stopped and held out her hand, counting out four fingers. 'It must 'ave been about four years ago. Shirley, the woman next door 'ad three boys. They was good lads really but they got 'emselves involved in all the gang stuff that was 'appening on the streets.' She pointed at the photo again. ''Im, Leonard Cookson, was in charge of one of those fucking Trident teams that persecute the black kids. They kicked in her door at five o'clock in the morning. Made a right noise, as I remember, shoutin' and bangin'. Anyway, they nicked one of 'er boys, Troy, with a burner, just a small one, but he swore down that cop, Cookson, had planted it and framed 'im with it. Well Shirley believed 'er boy. Wouldn't 'ave it any other way. Butter wouldn't melt in 'is mouth, as it were.' She chuckled to herself again. 'I don't know though. Boys will be boys, especially round there, and it weren't the first time he'd bin nicked. You lot charged 'im with possession of a firearm and 'e got found guilty too. Got banged up in Brixton prison just up the Hill. But Shirley wouldn't let it drop. She still goes to visit Troy every week. Still swears that 'e was set up.'

Charlie nodded. She'd read all about it. It was the ongoing perjury complaint that they'd discovered just after Cookson's body and the Bible had been found.

'Ah, yes. Shirley and Troy Sangster. I've read about them. She made a formal complaint against Leonard Cookson. It's still ongoing after all these years. She alleged that Cookson committed perjury and that Troy was unlawfully arrested and unlawfully detained. Why did Samson feel so aggrieved though?'

'Because of Shirley. She got everyone all whipped up about it. Saying Troy was only arrested 'cause he was black, even though 'e's mixed race. That police are racists, all that stuff. There was lots in the community that believed 'er, including Samson. I think it brought back memories of when his mum died and 'e was told it was racists who done it then. 'E would go on marches that Shirley arranged, demonstrations outside the nick in Brixton. He even helped 'er make placards an' stuff. That's why I remember 'is face so well. Shirley is still fightin' for Troy an' all the black kids in the area. She wants to get 'is conviction overturned. Blames Cookson for it all and almost stalks 'im. She knows everything about him. What car 'e drives, where 'e works, she's even found out how many wives 'e's had. I don't know where she gets it all from.'

A vague recollection of a bleached-blonde ball of fiery rage came to Charlie.

'So, did Samson still see Shirley often? Would he class her as a friend, do you think?' Charlie was intrigued. Could this be the same Shirley that had come to the assistance of the knifeman she and Paul had chased in Brixton the previous week?

Lisa Forrester tilted her head to one side and reached up, attempting to run her hands through her hair. She quickly gave up.

'I'm not sure, to be honest. 'E certainly used to bump into 'er fairly regular, like, and I think 'e had 'er number. He'd probably class 'er as a friend. Well, as much of a friend as Samson ever had.'

'Lisa, would you be prepared to make a statement about Samson's associates and his friendship with Shirley?'

Hunter was looking slightly bemused.

'You've got to be kiddin' ain't you?' Lisa stood up suddenly, swaying slightly. 'I ain't prepared to put nuffin' down on paper, nor would I swear to nuffin' in court. I ain't no grass and never will be. I've lost Samson and now I 'ave to get on. An' I won't, if people like Shirley Sangster find out I'm snitchin' on who's wiv who and that sort of thing. I'll see ya around.' She grabbed hold of the door frame, pulling the door open and with a wave of her hand was gone.

Charlie leant back, her mind processing the information. She remembered the teacher's report from all those years ago. Samson Powell was capable of being attentive and following instructions. He also considered Shirley to be a friend. He would very likely try to please her, as he had Ms Saffron Bolt.

Charlie felt herself warming to the idea. As well as the physical evidence, they now had a definite link between Powell and Leonard Cookson, and a motivation for his murder, even if Lisa was not prepared to put it in writing. Could Shirley Sangster have wished harm on Leonard Cookson during her ongoing campaign against him? It was certainly possible, especially if she truly believed her son had been framed... and Samson Powell was a friend of hers, with antisocial traits and no moral compass.

So... if that was the case, could Samson Powell have exacted revenge on Cookson in the way he had, out of misplaced loyalty to Shirley? Or... could Shirley Sangster have actively encouraged him to kill the man she so hated?

Chapter 25

The photo of Shirley Sangster was old but it was definitely the same woman who had screamed at her and Paul in the street a few days previously. She appeared to have become the self-appointed spokeswoman for the youth of Lambeth, particularly since the arrest and conviction of her son Troy, and her complaint against Cookson.

She refused to believe her son was guilty, even though a jury had seen fit to convict him. To Charlie, reading the details of the case against Troy Sangster, it seemed cut and dried. Most complaints died on conviction, many having been made in the hopes of instilling uncertainty in the minds of jurors at court... but Shirley Sangster had not given up.

Charlie was still reading through the details when DCI O'Connor walked in.

'Ah Charlie, just the person. DS Boyle from DPS will be in again this afternoon to see you and Hunter.' He peered at the file Charlie had out in front of her. 'I recognise that one. I read it recently when Hunter told me about its link to the method used to kill Cookson. It's a load of rubbish, but it's like so many complaints.' He adjusted his trousers and sighed heavily. 'If they don't get knocked on the head swiftly, they go on and on forever and become a bloody nightmare. That's why I want you both at my office later.'

Charlie nodded. 'I found out earlier that Powell was good friends with Shirley Sangster. Just looking at the complaint again now, I see DS Boyle is shown as the investigating officer. Do you think, when she's finished interviewing me I could ask her a few questions? I'd be interested in her thoughts on Sangster.'

'I'm sure that would be fine. Hayley's very professional. I spoke briefly to the Chief Superintendent at DPS about all the officers dealing with the individual complaints and he rates her very highly. There's no evidence to support this particular allegation, but Sangster won't let it drop. She keeps writing to her MP and various members of the Equality and Human Rights Commission... and then they in turn take it up with the IPCC and the local commander. It's like a bad smell. They can't get rid of it, but I'm sure DS Boyle can fill you in more later on.' He turned to go, before swinging back round to face her. 'Two p.m. sharp in my office. And no excuses this time.'

*

Hayley Boyle was seated with the DCI when Charlie arrived ten minutes late and with a smudge of ketchup from a hastily eaten bacon sandwich down the front of her shirt. The DCI's eyes flicked from his watch to the smudge and then straight to DS Boyle.

'You've met DC Stafford before, I believe, Hayley. Maybe when you've finished today you can have a talk with her about professional standards and the importance of punctuality and a smart appearance.'

Charlie moved her arm in front of the smudge and dipped her head. 'Sorry, sir. I didn't have the chance to get breakfast this morning so I…' She stopped speaking, suddenly aware of how scruffy the DCI's shoes were and whether it was worth trying to compare appearances but decided against it. It was always better to keep on the right side of senior officers. 'I won't let it happen again,' she said instead.

DS Boyle stood up and offered Charlie her hand, an expression of mild amusement flicking on her face at the reappearance of the ketchup stain as Charlie stretched out towards her.

'Shall we get on with the questions I've been asked to go over again. It won't take long, I promise.' She smiled through thin lips and started to move towards the door of an adjoining office, her heels clicking against the lino. Charlie fell in behind her, wishing she could look as effortlessly smart as the woman she was following. DS Boyle wore a pale pink shirt underneath a tailored grey trouser suit, the cut fitting the swing of her slim body perfectly. Gleaming black patent, two-inch heeled shoes and black-framed oblong glasses completed the professional appearance acclaimed by the DCI.

The sergeant was everything her department, the Directorate of Professional Standards, required. Smart, business-like and hard-working; her appearance matched her work, faultless. She had been in the police service for twenty-two years, having previously worked at West End Central Police Station, before transferring to Hackney as a DS. She'd met and married an inspector involved in training, but they had chosen not to have children, preferring to plough their efforts into their careers. He had risen through the ranks to superintendent while she had gone to the DPS to get evidence for the next rank. However, she had developed such a penchant for rooting out crooked cops that she'd returned to the unit several times. She'd now been wedded to the same department on and off for as long as she'd been wedded to her husband, both liaisons having lasted fifteen years.

Charlie followed her through to a smaller office and took a seat, realising as she made herself comfortable that Hayley Boyle was almost an exact replica of her opposite number, Ms Brenda Leach at the IPCC. Both had worn similar outfits and were quintessentially corporate; grey personalities, dressed in grey clothing. Like a dog and its owner, they had morphed to look like one another. The only difference between the two was that underneath the fur and feathers, Hayley Boyle was a copper too.

DS Boyle pulled out a file and opened it, fingering a small silver crucifix that hung around her neck as she read out the first of a short list of questions. She listened intently as Charlie answered, jotting down notes.

Most of the questions were based on the exact orders given in the previous operation and concluded with Charlie's opinion of Hunter and whether she would have done anything differently. She felt a sense of déjà vu as she answered, realising that they were almost identical to what she'd been asked previously by Ms Leach. Maybe they were hoping to catch her out by asking the same questions again.

'How many more times am I going to be asked the same questions?' she said finally, exasperated.

'I know and I'm sorry, but last time it wasn't written down.' Hayley Boyle looked embarrassed, her face reddening slightly. 'I believe it was off the record?'

Charlie shook her head. 'You can ask me as many times as you want. I said exactly the same last time. DI Hunter did a great job. In the circumstances there was nothing else we could have done. He made the right decisions.' She crossed her arms in front of her and leant back. 'I've said everything I'm going to say on the case, but I need to speak to you about another matter.'

Hayley Boyle cocked her head, questioningly before closing the file.

'Go on,' she instructed.

Charlie leant forwards. 'Shirley Sangster. She made the complaint against DS Leonard Cookson for perjury. I'm assisting with the investigation into his murder. I believe you know her?'

Hayley Boyle looked away, frowning. 'Yes, I do. She's an extremely strong woman.'

'Do you believe her claim that Cookson planted the firearm that was found in Troy's bedroom?'

'Troy was heavily connected to the local gangs and there was regular intelligence coming in from informants stating that he had a gun. Would a police officer with less than five years to go before retirement really put his pension on the line to get one kid sent down? And where would he have got the gun from to plant? The whole thing would have been far too risky… and for what? You tell me; Cookson had never had any dealings with the family before. Much more likely that it was Troy's or he knew all about it but just couldn't, or wouldn't, admit it to his mum. She'd probably kill him.'

Charlie looked directly at Hayley Boyle. 'But could she kill anyone else? She swore she would never give up until she got justice for Troy, and now Leonard Cookson is dead, with his tongue cut out, his trousers set on fire and a page of the Bible containing the words "Thou shalt not bare false witness" left alongside his body. Do you think she could have had something to do with Cookson's murder?'

The DS reached for her crucifix and spun it round in her fingers. 'I don't know. She did despise Leonard Cookson. I tried for several years to get her to accept the evidence and the court decision, but if anything, she got worse, she hated him with a vengeance. She does have contacts with all the right people in all the right places.'

'But do you think she could also have contacts with all the "wrong" people, if you know what I mean; people like Samson Powell and his partner, Lisa Forrester. People who could do her dirty work for her?'

DS Boyle chewed on her bottom lip, her eyes darting about anxiously.

'Shirley Sangster virtually runs her estate. She knows everybody and everything that moves on it, and the whole of Brixton for that matter. She's a very powerful woman these days. I've got no doubt there are enough people around that she could use; people that love her and hate the police as much as she does.'

Charlie stared at the DS in front of her, her face now creased in anguish as she continued.

'If somebody had a grudge against a copper for whatever reason and wanted her help, then Shirley Sangster would certainly be capable of mobilising the right… or the wrong people. But whether or not we could ever prove it…'

Chapter 26

Two hours later Charlie watched as a large A4 envelope was dropped on to her desk. She ripped open the envelope before pulling out the contents. There were several original statements from officers in the underwater search teams who had scoured the bottom of the well shaft, and an exhibits record. One exhibit immediately grabbed her attention from the list of junk and rubbish dredged from the silt. It was simply labelled 'One (1) Nokia mobile phone', but a comment from the exhibiting officer stated that due to its relatively clean appearance he believed it to have only recently been discarded. There were no other items recovered that weren't rusted, broken or obviously ancient.

As she read the statement, Charlie knew, without doubt, that it must have belonged to Samson Powell. His personal phone, containing his list of contacts, photos and messages had been found at his home address, striking Charlie as strange, until it transpired that it had been left at his address each time he went out to kill. But why would he have another phone? Especially one of this nature; small, cheap and unregistered – a 'burner phone' that couldn't be traced, was difficult to be linked to anybody and was easily disposable. Charlie's curiosity was in overdrive after her conversation with Hayley Boyle. There had to be more of a reason for Powell's actions. Maybe this would hold the key.

The question was, after lying in water, would the phone technicians be able to extract anything useful from it… but they had to try.

She knocked on Hunter's door and entered with the envelope, to find him seated with his head in his hands, squinting at the computer screen, having only recently returned to his office. He looked tired, grey rings circling his eyes, casting dark shadows across his cheeks.

'How did your interview with Hayley Boyle go?' she asked.

'It didn't. I'm far too busy to waste my time on that again, and anyway, I've said as much as I'm going to say. Is that your interim report?' he barely looked up.

'No, not yet. I just need your authorisation to get a phone interrogated.' She placed the statement on the desk in front of him excitedly. It was a great lead. 'It's a new disposable Nokia found in the well shaft. The police diver who found it believes that it had only recently been thrown in. It must be Samson Powell's. After Lisa explained how Powell knew Shirley Sangster, I did some more digging and DS Boyle is investigating her complaint. She knows

Sangster well. According to her, Sangster has a lot of contacts in the community, both good and bad. I think Powell could have killed Cookson for her.'

'And just how are you going to prove this?' Hunter's head shot up angrily. 'Suspicion is not enough. You need good hard evidence, like Sabira, Naz and Nick have against Powell for the murders. Drop it, Charlie. We need to move on. We've got the right man, bang to rights. It doesn't matter why he's done it. The fact is that he has, and then he's topped himself when he knew we were on to him.'

'But, boss, there's nothing to suggest he even knew Brian Ashton or Philippa McGovern. It doesn't make sense.'

Hunter sighed heavily and rubbed his eyes with his fist. 'It doesn't have to. I need your report on Powell's suicide. The others have completed their interim reports and I intend sending them off shortly. I need yours ASAP, but I need facts, not speculation.'

Charlie stared at Hunter. He wasn't normally like this. He was usually interested in any new theories, especially if it involved other possible arrests and convictions. Maybe he'd been under more pressure with the speed of the three murders than any of them had realised? Maybe he wasn't bothered now Powell was dead? Or maybe the stress of the ongoing investigation against him was weighing more heavily than she'd thought? Still, she needed the phone examined.

'OK, guv, I understand,' she conceded, her mind whirring. 'But I still think we should have the phone looked at. Powell may have sent a suicide message on it, or contacted someone that could assist with his frame of mind at the time of his death. I'm sure the Coroner would want that covered.'

Hunter closed his eyes briefly, before smiling weakly at her. 'OK, you win. You have my authority… but I want you to concentrate on the evidence we have, not wild, improbable theories. I want this case done and dusted as soon as we can. It hasn't exactly cloaked us in glory.'

Charlie nodded, feeling her earlier excitement draining away. 'Cheers, guv,' she said flatly. 'I'll get the paperwork emailed to you immediately, for your authority. Oh, and boss, for your information, I told the DPS sergeant that I totally trusted your judgement in everything you did.'

Hunter shook his head and smiled again, but this time his smile was tinged with an edge of despondency. 'Thanks, Charlie. After missing my interview, I'll be top of the DCI's hit list, but I appreciate your support. I just wish I could say that everybody thought the same.'

*

'What's the matter with the boss?' Charlie sidled up to Bet and Paul who were having a break from their computers to watch the agitated ramblings of an ageing down-and-out on the pavement below. 'He's just given me a right dressing-down for mentioning my thoughts on Shirley Sangster.'

Bet shrugged and passed her a packet of Minstrels. They had all heard her theory when she'd returned from the interview with DS Boyle. 'I think he's still smarting because he got it in the neck for missing Powell. He disappeared after the DCI came in to speak to him while you were being interviewed. Before he left he was mumbling something about the powers-that-be criticising him for not having had anyone watching Powell's address before we all hit it with the warrant.'

'We didn't exactly have time.' Charlie poured half a dozen Minstrels into her hand. 'It was all hands on deck when we got the DNA hit. Anyway, even if someone had gone straight to his flat we'd probably have been none the wiser. Powell could have been sleeping inside, or he could have been out. He could even have been getting ready for his next murder or disposing of evidence from the last. We couldn't afford to sit back and wait and let him do another. We were just unlucky.'

'Like with Carl Hookham,' Nick chipped in sarcastically.

Charlie swung round, angrily. 'Yes. Like with Carl Hookham. Why? Have you got a point to make?'

'Just saying.' Nick snorted and stretched back in his chair. He had returned to his scruffy dress code; the effort of dressing smartly having been expended several days before. Hunter had either ignored his appearance or had been too preoccupied to care.

'Well, you can piss off, if that's what you think.' Charlie was suddenly outraged. 'I didn't see you helping us for the whole weekend when everything was going off. We all came in but you obviously couldn't give a toss.'

'I do my hours.' Nick grinned lazily.

'You do nothing more than you have to. So don't think you can lecture us on what we should, or shouldn't have done, when we're all prepared to put in the extra time for our colleagues.'

'At least *I've* done what was requested. I didn't see you taking your completed interim report into the boss.'

Charlie frowned defensively. 'That's because I've had far more to do than you. I had to look at Powell's full history as well as trying to establish his state of mind. The Coroner will need to be satisfied that he *intended* to kill himself.'

Nick laughed out loud. 'Oh yes, rather than by chance coming across a bloody deep hole in the ground and just randomly happening to have a length of cable on him, which he then decided on the spur of the moment to tie around his neck, before accidently slipping and falling over the side?'

'You're a total knob, Nick Arrowsmith.' She took a deep breath, feeling the angry heat rushing to her face.

Bet aimed the bag of chocolates towards her again. 'Ignore him, he's just a twat,' she said loudly, while Paul clapped a hand on Charlie's shoulder.

'Yes, Nick. I think you've said enough,' Naz agreed, while Sabira completed the team solidarity, standing up and firing an icy glare towards him.

Nick got to his feet, tucking his T-shirt back into the waistband of his jeans and shrugged. 'OK have it your way, Charlie. You keep on chasing imaginary suspects. We've all had to listen to your trumped-up theories. Samson Powell was just a fucking psycho. He didn't need anyone telling him what to do. He did it all by himself. For once, and possibly the only time so far, I agree with the boss.' He moved towards the door, before turning around towards Charlie and the team and grinned. 'And don't worry, you lot. She loves me really.'

*

Charlie was still seething when she arrived at Ben's flat. Nick was a useless, lazy waster, who thought he was God's gift. He might look hot, but he acted like an arrogant prick.

There was no answer, so she let herself in to find Ben lying asleep across the sofa, the TV, as always, blaring in the background. Charlie shook him gently, but when at last he came to properly, he was almost as despondent as Hunter.

Nothing seemed to be working for him. He still wasn't sleeping well and the tablets he'd been prescribed to calm him at night were worse than useless. She sat down next to him, hoping that the heat from her body might stir him into positivity, but nothing she said or did changed his mood. He didn't want to run. He didn't want to do anything. He was due to see Anna Christophe the day after next and she was supposed to be going with him. Hopefully, both of them would be in a better frame of mind by then, but perhaps they wouldn't. Maybe they were destined to remain like this for a lifetime; locked into a needy friendship, neither of them willing or able to commit fully, or sever the ties.

In the end she could hide her anger no longer. She had to go. 'I'll see you on Thursday, if you can be bothered.'

She slammed the door as she left, regretting her words instantly but not able to stop her rage at his lethargy increasing with every footstep. Pulling her phone from her pocket, she dialled her mother, cancelling her usual Tuesday evening outing to her family. There was no way she would be able to control her emotions there tonight.

She *needed* to be on her own, but at the same time she didn't *want* to be on her own.

There was only one place that had always offered solace and companionship but she hadn't stayed there alone for a long while. It was time to fight her own fears. The evening was warm and dry and the night was predicted to stay the same. Tonight she would sleep under the light of the moon and allow the negativity to drain away. Tonight she would rest close to her brother. Tomorrow would be a new day.

Chapter 27

It was a movement in the alleyway that led out from a notorious crack house on the Stockwell Park Gardens Estate that first caught Charlie's eye, as she drove towards the office the next morning. Emerging from the shadows were two people she recognised in an instant. Lisa Forrester, her hair even more matted than the previous day, stumbled across the pavement and slumped hard against a lamp post, a bottle clasped firmly in one hand. Her head was tilted back and her mouth open wide as she laughed raucously at her male companion.

The man followed on, a smirk plastered across his face as he grasped Lisa's sleeve and hauled her upright. There was no mistaking the bushy black and grey-tinged hair and beard of Dennis Walters. His pockmarked face was screwed up in an expression of delight, the antics of Forrester clearly causing him amusement.

Charlie felt her heartbeat quicken. Why hadn't she thought of this yesterday when Lisa was at the station? Why hadn't she had the sense to show the woman a photo of their two suspects as well as their victims? Samson Powell was dead; there could be no mishandling of identification procedures for a court case. Both people now in her view had lived and breathed in the same few square miles as each other. Both had drug habits and criminal records that meant they shared the same circle of acquaintances, and if Lisa knew Walters, Samson Powell would almost certainly have done too. They could well have served time together in prison.

She pulled over at the next set of lights and turned into the side road, looking for a place to park where she could see, without being seen. Walters and Forrester were walking in her direction. Sliding down in the driver's seat, she watched as they lurched across the road in front of her, Dennis Walters still with his hand under Lisa's arm. There was no way it was a chance meeting, a quick purchase of drugs from one hand to another. They were together; friends, or friends with benefits. In the world they inhabited, there was no time to waste. With Samson dead, Lisa needed to find a new provider, a symbiotic host whose presence could benefit them both. She had dropped out of the detox programme and had nowhere to go. She needed to trace old friends, call in a favour or two… and Dennis Walters was evidently a name from the past, or present.

They were heading in the direction of Walters' flat. It wouldn't take too long for them to reach it.

Charlie knew the way, the shortcuts they might take on foot, but it was now imperative she got them both housed, preferably at his address. Slowly she edged towards the junction, turning in the same direction as they were travelling, leapfrogging the pair until they entered the stairwell and eventually emerged on the balcony outside his flat. They still had the drugs warrant for Walters' address and it was still within its expiry date. Maybe she could persuade Hunter to think about its execution now she had seen the pair together.

The reason for Powell's murderous spree was taking root now. Shirley Sangster hated Leonard Cookson. Dennis Walters hated Brian Ashton and Philippa McGovern. Lisa Forrester was linked to Dennis Walters, Shirley Sangster and Samson Powell and it appeared that, by association, Samson Powell would also be linked to them all. They all lived and swirled together in the same smouldering cauldron of hate and criminality.

Samson Powell was the killer, now the question she needed answered was whether he had acted on his own? As she made her way into the office, Charlie knew, with or without Hunter's approval, she wouldn't rest until she had that answer.

*

A jam doughnut sat on a plate in pride of place on Charlie's desk when she got in. Next to it, scrawled flamboyantly on a piece of paper, was the word 'Sorry', accompanied by a note to 'PTO'. She turned the paper over and saw the word 'Dinner?'

Glancing around the office, her sight came to rest on Nick, sitting at his desk peering sheepishly across at her over the computer monitor. He mouthed his apology again and she felt her cheeks colouring immediately. He was still a knob, but he was a charming knob and one that she couldn't, yet, fully make up her mind about. For now, she'd accept his apology, but as for dinner… that could wait until he demonstrated he meant it, but she had to admit to a sense of pleasure at the thought. It had been a long time since she'd been wined and dined. Ben was certainly not making the effort, although, judging by the cards laid out within his sight the other night, she was clearly still in his thoughts.

She shook her head but smiled at Nick, before picking up the doughnut and sinking her teeth into it. After her night in the open air, the shower was calling, but before she made herself presentable she'd check for any new emails.

Her eyes were immediately drawn to a reply from the laboratory technicians entitled, 'Samson Powell – Phone download.' They didn't usually respond so quickly; maybe the phone had been too badly damaged for any data to be retrieved.

She opened it apprehensively and scanned the message. The tech guy who had sent it was well known to her, they often spoke at length if Charlie needed anything explained. It was because of this friendship that he had taken the time to examine the exhibit before he left work the previous evening. The phone was still being dried out and the SIM card was damaged but careful examination had revealed the contact list was intact. It showed only one number, one number that was saved into its memory under the name 'ICE', a word that she recognised as the acronym for an emergency contact, 'In case of emergency'.

Quickly she opened the interim report on Powell's suicide and flicked to the phone data file from the personal phone found at his flat. She copied the number into the search machine and waited while the record was scanned, before reading the result she was expecting. The number was not known. The name was not known.

Charlie could hardly contain her excitement. It was the type of phone a drug dealer, like Samson might use... but why would it have just the one number? Could he have had the burner phone because he was planning to go out on another kill? To make or receive one call, before then disposing of it. She read through the message several more times, noting that an update would come if the phone itself wasn't too badly damaged. With any luck this would confirm the details they had from the SIM and any further call data to link Powell definitively with the phone.

Until then she would get some checks completed on the number herself, obtain a registered keeper, if there was one, and any instances where it was known on police systems.

She logged in to complete a subscriber's check immediately, her pulse quickening at the thought. Could the number belong to the one person who was always there for him, in case of emergency? Whom Powell was keen to please, who he listened to? Could that number hold the key to what, or who was behind Powell's murderous spree?

The answer was in identifying its owner.

*

It was Paul who gave Charlie the warning.

'Hunter expects your interim report in today and he's not in a good mood.'

Bet edged up behind Paul. 'And you look like you've been dragged through a hedge backwards. Could I suggest you smarten yourself up?' She shot a glance over to the calendar on Charlie's desk. 'Ah, it's Wednesday. I forgot. Is everything OK?'

'It couldn't be better actually,' Charlie grinned up at their mirrored expressions. 'Though I doubt Hunter will think so, but I need you two to do me a favour.'

Quickly she brought them both up to speed on what she needed, before disappearing into the steamy recess of the shower. Within fifteen minutes she returned, her cheeks glowing red from the heat and her eyes alive with expectation. Whether it was the offer of dinner, she didn't know, but she had taken a little extra care with her appearance, tying her usually unruly hair neatly off her face to reveal a beautiful complexion and stunningly bright green eyes. Even she had been pleasantly surprised at the transformation.

Bet nodded approvingly. 'Looking and smelling good! We're already making headway on your enquiry. Get on with finishing your report for the boss and we'll have an answer for you by this afternoon.'

Charlie thanked her and sat down at her desk. She knew better than to argue against Bet's wisdom, and anyway, Bet and Paul were right. The interim report had to be done.

As if on cue, Hunter came through, his face serious, the vein on his forehead at full stretch.

'Is your report done yet?' he snapped.

'It'll be on your desk by lunchtime, guv.' Charlie tried to keep her voice business-like but it was difficult to keep the edge of concern from it. He looked so stressed. In the end she blurted out what she'd been asked herself earlier. 'Are you OK?' Hunter rounded on her angrily. 'I would be if you'd done your work, like I asked.' He turned away, his shoulders slumping immediately, and sighed heavily. 'Sorry, guys. You know what I'm like when the management are on my case. I just want to get on with the job.' Without facing them, he straightened. 'The DCI is threatening to discipline me for insubordination because I missed the interview with DS Boyle yesterday, but I'll be buggered if I'm going to keep going over and over the same details. I made one error but I more than compensated for it afterwards and I'm not going to be strung up for it. It seems to have become a bit of a crusade for them, but I'm not backing down. They can do what they want.'

'I thought they'd have had everything they needed after I spoke with her.' Charlie was about to offer to speak to DS Boyle again but thought better of it. Hunter was more than capable of fighting his own battles. He didn't need, and more to the point, wouldn't appreciate his subordinate sticking her oar in. 'Well you know we're all behind you. I'll have Powell's report ready for you ASAP,' she said instead.

Hunter walked wordlessly back to his office before pausing briefly. 'Thanks,' he said, before pulling the door to. 'Make sure you do.'

*

Charlie was as good as her word. The interim report into Samson Louis Powell's death was on his desk by midday, all the various files from his earlier life précised and attached. The facts were clearly laid out. In the absence of a suicide note though, it would be for the Coroner to decide whether the act was deliberately planned or the spontaneous act of a drunken murderer who knew his time was up.

That done, she had the afternoon to dwell on her earlier findings.

Naz and Sabira were continuing with their honour-based acid case. Another morning spent in the specialised burns unit at Roehampton hospital with the young female victim, Preet Bakshi, had convinced them both to keep up the pressure for information.

Preet had now agreed to make a statement, but as her attacker had been standing in a group of men immediately before the acid was thrown, she wasn't able to say conclusively which man was guilty. The

Punjabi community, as was the way with many other minority groups, had closed ranks; none of the other male witnesses being prepared, at this point, to assist, so Naz and Sabira were left trying to establish which man had the greatest motivation. Most of the group had now been eliminated, leaving only a couple of credible suspects, but they needed more… and that required one single man in the group being persuaded to step forward and talk. They were working on a plan of action to do this when Paul beckoned Charlie over to where he and Bet were sitting.

'I think I've got what you're after, so to speak.' He winked at her before ripping off the corner of a piece of paper from a pile on his desk. 'Here you go. Saffron Bolt, now retired but living in the same area.' He scribbled down the contact details. 'There can't be many ladies of a similar age with that name around. Do you want me to come with you?'

Charlie clapped him on the back. 'You're a star, Paul and yes please. I'm not quite ready to spend too much time alone with Nick yet, or let him in on anymore of my theories.'

*

It was good to get away from the cool sterile environment of the office; it was much warmer outside than she realised. Very soon the car windows were wide open and the hot air was flowing across Charlie's face. She breathed in sharply as a fly caught her on the cheek, before flicking it away and watching as it was sucked back out of the window in a jet stream of dust and pollen spores, barrel-rolling several times before regaining its flight wings.

Bromley Borough was as far removed from the boroughs of Lambeth and Peckham as was possible. Gone were the bleak, grey tower blocks and estates, replaced instead by long avenues of emerald- and olive-green trees, shielding the well-heeled inhabitants of the mainly privately owned detached suburban houses from prying eyes.

Ms Saffron Bolt lived in a smart bungalow at the end of a leafy cul-de-sac. Each window was draped with swathes of colourful fabric, framing glass that sparkled in the bright sunlight, spotlessly clean. Brilliant-white net curtains undulated their way horizontally across each expanse of opening, bringing privacy and shade to its interior. The front garden was immaculate and two pots of bright pink petunias stood sentry on the doorstep, their cornet-shaped flowers trumpeting out a welcome to any callers.

Paul parked against the kerb outside and together they headed towards the bungalow. Charlie pressed the bell and the door was answered by the tall, slender figure of an elderly lady. Her gait was upright and her expression serious but her skin and pupils glowed with such honey-beige intensity that she exuded warmth.

'Ms Saffron Bolt?' Charlie held up her warrant card. 'I'm DC Charlotte Stafford and this is my colleague DC Paul Parker. Could we speak to you about a former pupil of yours, Samson Powell? We're hoping you remember him.'

Saffron Bolt's expression darkened. 'How could I forget Samson?' She stood to one side and opened the door. 'I've been watching the news. You'd better come through.'

She showed them through to a paved area at the rear. A dark green parasol filled the space, shielding a large patio table and chairs from the strongest of the sun's rays. The garden exuded colour and life.

'You have a beautiful garden,' Charlie started.

'Thank you,' Saffron Bolt chose a seat and indicated with a movement of her hand for them all to sit, like she would a class of unruly children. 'I work hard at it.' She turned towards them and stared directly at Charlie. 'I'll come straight to the point. I count myself lucky. I had an extremely happy childhood and I have been gifted a beautiful life. Not every child is that fortunate.'

'You mean Samson?'

Ms Bolt nodded. 'Yes, I mean Samson, and other boys and girls like him. He lost so much at such a young age. Is it any wonder that he turned out like he did?'

Charlie returned the teacher's gaze, their eyes locking in mutual understanding. 'I've read about his background. He did have a terrible start to life… he was lucky to survive.'

'Maybe there are those that wish he hadn't now?' Ms Bolt looked away, fixing her sight instead on a spider weaving an intricate web through the air.

'Maybe there are. But he didn't have to end up like he did. Many children lose loved ones and experience loss.' The teacher swung back around and their eyes locked again. 'Many have horrific upbringings but thankfully don't turn to murder. What do you think made Samson turn the way he did?'

'Everybody gave up on him. Plain and simple. He didn't care for himself and he didn't care about anyone or anything else. He was never able to form any sort of bond… with anybody.'

'Except you?'

'Yes, perhaps.' Ms Bolt bit on her bottom lip. 'For some reason, Samson grew very attached to me. I don't know why. Possibly because I gave him time, or because he said I looked like his mother, but I would find Samson hanging about outside my classroom at the end of school most days. I would let him in and he would help me sort out the room ready for the next day, stacking books, clearing away, that sort of thing. He didn't say much; in fact he hardly spoke at all. I did all the talking, but I think he just liked to be with someone that accepted him and enjoyed his company, you could see it in his eyes; a sort of wretched adulation. It was pitiable really. It's a shame others couldn't see through his bad behaviour. He was damaged, but he was a sweet kid really.'

Charlie raised her eyebrows and she saw Paul do the same. She couldn't imagine the man who had committed such brutal murders ever being described as 'sweet', but just as quickly, she recalled her inexplicable feeling of pathos at the scene of his suicide.

'I gather he would do anything for you.'

'Yes, he would, even the smallest things. He worked harder for me than any other person probably in his life and it was beginning to reap rewards. It was a shame when I had to leave so quickly.' She turned away from them both again. 'You see, I got pregnant, which wouldn't normally be an issue, but I had health problems. There was no way I could continue teaching. It was badly timed, certainly as far as Samson was concerned. Such a shame too, just when it seemed as if my work with him was yielding results.'

'He took it badly then?'

'Yes extremely. I only had a short time to try to explain, but it was if he'd been waiting for that moment to come. Everybody in his young life had gone and I was no different. He smashed up the classroom the next day.'

'And beat up another boy.'

'Yes. Ashley Pitcorn was his name.'

'So, Samson was prone to violence then, even at that age?' Charlie tilted her head towards the retired teacher.

'Maybe he was, like a lot of young boys from damaged backgrounds trying to find their place in a world from which they already felt isolated and alienated. But this was different; Samson beat Ashley up mercilessly. I was told he could have killed him if he hadn't been stopped. He had no concept of what his actions could lead to and no conscience to stop himself.'

'Did he give any reason for it?'

Saffron Bolt stood up and looked down the garden, her gaze far away from the flowering shrubs and colourful stems in her eyeline.

'No, he said nothing; apparently just shrugged when he was arrested and smiled when he was told he was being expelled.' She paused briefly. 'But I know why he did it, though I've never told anyone else.'

Charlie waited, not wanting to break into the silence.

'It was because I gave him the idea; inadvertently of course.' She dropped her gaze to the floor. 'When I was in the process of telling Samson that I was leaving, Ashley kept interrupting us, popping in and out of the room and laughing at Samson. All the other kids knew that he had a soft spot for me. I snapped on the last occasion. I just wanted to give Samson my full attention. I said that I wished somebody would just sort the boy out properly; meaning of course to come and get him and deal with what he needed. Samson must have taken my words literally and in his mind decided that he should be the one to "sort" Ashley out.' She paused again and sighed heavily. 'I should have been more careful how I'd phrased my frustration about the boy. I knew Samson always followed my every word.'

'Even as far as beating up this boy?' Charlie was intrigued.

'Yes I believe so. He would have done anything for me that I asked.'

'Anything?'

Saffron Bolt nodded, before turning her gaze towards them, flicking between her and Paul, before coming to rest on Charlie again. Her expression was etched with pain.

'When I read the news about what he'd done, I didn't want to acknowledge it could be Samson. I didn't think he'd be capable of such brutality, but then I remembered this incident… and how he would do everything I asked, down to the last detail. I might be wrong, but I'm not sure he would be capable of planning the killings himself, to the degree that appears apparent.'

'But if there was someone else that he'd grown close to, who was suggesting what to do; someone who was planning his exact actions, pulling his strings, so to speak…?' Charlie held her breath.

'Then yes. I think he would be capable of anything.'

Chapter 28

The volume of squabbling was getting louder as each party box was served. A long table set out for a birthday party was crammed on both sides with nine-year-old boys, each vying for the attention of the waitress. The poor woman had a thankless task, trying to keep the recipients of each 'Happy meal' happy. He watched as one of the bigger boys with bright red hair, climbed on to the table, drumming his fist against his chest and squealing with laughter, much to the consternation of the frazzled mother in charge. A smaller, younger boy, with the same distinctive red hair tugged on his sleeve, urging him to climb down. With a jerk of the material and a kick to the younger boy's arm, the older one dismissed his plea with barely a thought. He was clearly used to calling the shots.

The man continued to watch the two boys. They looked like brothers and they acted like brothers. It reminded him of his own.

The minutes ticked by as he waited for the call. Thursday afternoon was dragging and he wanted to get it over with. He chewed slowly on the burger he'd ordered, too nervous even to taste the ketchup in which it was smothered. His cheap Nokia mobile phone pinged into life and he jumped, squeezing a globule of blood-red sauce around his mouth. He licked it away quickly, wiping the last of the redness on his sleeve.

Pressing the phone to his ear, he strained to hear the voice over the background noise. It was calm, almost hypnotic, the intonations of its pitch those that he'd known for so long. The instructions were spoken clearly, repeated several times. He was to walk from the restaurant, through the underpass and into the centre of Wandsworth roundabout, dropping down into its bowels, unseen through the high walls that shielded its view from the five lanes of traffic. He knew the area well. Only the odd person traversed its hidden depths, most preferring the busier, more public crossings above.

Once there he must go past the sculpture of white entwined rings that stood at its centre, to an area of grass and shrubs, next to which he'd see the hollow remains of a dead chestnut tree. It was the only one there. Inside he would find a black plastic carrier bag with its contents wrapped in brown paper. He was to don the gloves he'd bought earlier and lift the bag out, taking it intact and unopened, to his room. Only then could he unwrap the package and only with the face mask and gloves on. There would be a new phone and SIM card which he must make ready. The one he now used must be destroyed. There could be no slip-ups. He had done well so far, but now he should prepare to kill. His fingerprints and DNA must not be left on anything in the bag. No risks were to be taken. His identity must remain unknown.

At 22.00 hours he would receive further instructions on the new phone, but until then he must get prepared and wait. Wait and be ready to act when instructed.

'Do you understand?' the voice said calmly at the end of the conversation.

'Yes,' he said. 'I understand.'

'You know you must follow all my instructions? Every single one, exactly. You won't let me down, will you?'

'No, I won't,' he said.

'You'd better not,' the voice soothed. 'I can't work with failures.'

*

Charlie watched Ben as he shuffled across the common towards her. Nothing had changed since Tuesday evening; even her harsh words having failed to provoke a reaction. Today everything about him screamed defeat.

She glanced at her watch. He was here at least and punctual, but this was clearly yet another bad day. She swallowed her disappointment and kissed him lightly on the cheek, ignoring the waft of cigarettes and body odour that clung to his clothing.

'Right, let's get you in to see what Anna can do with you this week.' She tried to sound cheerful.

He smiled, but his face remained static, frozen within the current nightmare that his PTSD had thrown at him during the hours of darkness. Once again, she longed for the Ben that had been her saviour such a short time ago, but once again, she watched as the door shut behind him, knowing that she might never get him back.

After he'd gone, Charlie lay on the grass and closed her eyes, waiting for the hour to be over. Saffron Bolt's words had provoked further ambiguities, which hopefully Anna could answer. After a while she jumped up, jogged to the nearby shop and bought some bottled water, returning just as Ben emerged from the psychologist's door, blinking in the bright sunshine.

'I'm gonna beat this, Charlie,' he grinned optimistically, as he did at the end of every session. 'I'll show you I can be bothered.'

'OK soldier,' she said just as optimistically. She threw a bottle of water towards him and he caught it with one hand, laughing with delight. 'Wait here. I'm just going to have a quick word with Anna.'

She sprinted away into the gloom of Anna Christophe's consulting room, turning as she did so to check that Ben was staying put. He was; his head tilted backwards, letting the sun shine across his face. For a second she stopped to take in the sight, her heart leaping at the momentary glow of optimism across his handsome features. He deserved so much more.

Anna was standing at the top of the stairs as Charlie mounted them two at a time.

'Woah there,' she laughed. 'To what do I owe this pleasure? I take it you're not here to talk about yourself?'

Charlie frowned mischievously. 'Of course not but… I was hoping you could clear up something I've been wondering about.'

'You'd better come in then and I'll try to help.'

She followed the psychologist through to the treatment room and pulled up a seat, careful to skirt right around the couch. Even the sight of it made her shudder. 'In a minute I'm going to be testing your knowledge of all things psychological, but before I do can I just ask how's Ben doing?' She held her hands up. 'And before you tell me you can't discuss individual cases, all I need to know is if there is anything I, personally, can do to help him.'

Anna rubbed a finger across her lips and concentrated. 'He needs something, or someone, to keep him motivated throughout the whole week. I know you try, but you have your work, and, as you well know, you're half the problem.' She paused and smiled sympathetically at Charlie. 'He's very lucky to have you though Charlie, we all know that, but he needs a routine. So… if you want to help, try to think of something to keep him busy, a hobby, an interest, even if it's temporary, something he has to get up for in the morning. He needs something new.'

Charlie nodded enthusiastically. 'I've got a few ideas, Anna. I'll come back to you when I've worked them out.' She looked up and grinned. 'Right, my question. I'll get straight to the point. Could someone diagnosed as a psychopath be controlled by another person?'

'Wow, just a little query then!' Anna Christophe tilted her head to one side. 'It would be unusual but not impossible. A psychopath doesn't usually like following orders. They like to live by their own rules and they don't care about what anyone else thinks. However, if they actually enjoyed doing what's been asked of them, they might let the person *think* they have control.'

'What about if that other person is also a psychopath?'

'OK, interesting. Let me think.' She paused for a minute before starting. 'Again, it would be hard to imagine that they could be completely controlled, but they could make it appear so, particularly if a course of action appealed to them both. It's fairly rare though, thankfully; psychopaths don't tend to like each other. If two did get together, however, they might enjoy trying to manipulate the other, to pit themselves against their adversary, see who wins. If they were truly to work together in a criminal partnership, well, it could be catastrophic, both pushing the other to commit worse and worse offences, both seeking the ultimate thrill.'

Charlie knew exactly what Anna meant. She'd witnessed the crime scenes. 'So a psychopath could theoretically have their strings pulled by another, but they would have to want to do it too?'

'Yes, they could.' She paused briefly. 'Do you want me to explain the make-up of psychopaths? Their personalities can be split up into four distinctive personality traits.'

Charlie nodded. She found this sort of information intriguing.

Anna Christophe pulled a chair out from under her desk and sat down. 'Well there are four main traits associated with psychopathy and sociopathy. They are antisocial traits, interpersonal traits, affective traits and lifestyle traits.' She pulled a book out from a shelf above her desk but laid it on the table unopened, before continuing. 'Antisocial traits include childhood behavioural disturbance, pre-teen and teenage delinquency and, very often, involvement in criminality. Research has shown that psychopaths are born with a predisposition to antisocial behaviour or psychopathy but this doesn't usually come to fruition unless the person also grows up in an unhealthy environment. A full-blown psychopath almost always comes from an abusive or disturbed background, with harsh or inconsistent parenting.'

Charlie concentrated on Anna's words carefully. The psychologist could almost be describing Samson's early years, watching his parents burn to death and then having no stability or consistency, with continual medical issues and schooling challenges; certainly, his criminal behaviour had started young. Maybe it was already too late for him by the time he met Saffron Bolt. She had to ask. 'Could a teacher stop a thirteen-year-old child from becoming a psychopath? Get them to obey rules and do what they asked?'

'It's probably too late by then. By that age it's more likely that the young psychopath would be testing their own capacity to play the teacher. It's the second sign, what are called interpersonal traits, or the ability to manipulate and deceive. The child might want to get extra status or enhanced privileges, so they could try to start a particular friendship with a teacher in order to get these. It might look to the teacher like they are being successful, but really the child is learning how to behave in a certain way to get what they want.'

'And if that teacher made a comment by accident that might suggest an action, would the child be likely to do it, even if it was inherently wrong?'

'Yes, the young psychopath could well do it, believing that they would benefit from executing what the teacher suggested.'

'Even if it meant beating up another child?'

'Possibly even more so. So-called affective traits are also a symptom of psychopathic behaviour. They include callousness towards others, limited emotional responsiveness, avoiding personal responsibility and an absence of guilt or regret. In other words, a psychopath would know the action is wrong but they don't care.'

Charlie shook her head in disbelief. So Samson Powell had happily beaten Ashley Pitcorn to a pulp not only because he'd hoped to please his teacher but also because he'd enjoy the chance to demonstrate his violence; and if it didn't work he didn't really care. The assault and damage was just a chance to show off his power. Maybe he'd got Ms Bolt fooled, but then… she'd been adamant that he was vulnerable. Who knew? 'And the fourth trait?' she said finally.

'Lifestyle traits,' Anna replied. 'Such as impulsive behaviour and the pursuit of stimulating experiences. Psychopaths often indulge in risky or deviant sexual practices or the pursuit of more and more violent and exhilarating experiences.'

'Like murder?'

'At the furthest extreme, but yes it could include killing. Basically they can't handle the fact that life is sometimes dull and they crave more and more stimuli. If they are unemployed they often commit crime. If they are able to get irregular jobs, they will often move around, changing from one to another, but psychopaths vary greatly. Some have successfully held down jobs and marriages. For example, a man called Gary Ridgeway, better known as the Green River Killer, was married and stayed in his job for twenty-three years, as well as being a regular attendee at church. He killed forty-eight women over twenty years and no one ever suspected him.' She paused, flicking the book open, before shutting it again.

'Others are academics or charmers and can be very successful at hiding their lack of regard for anyone or anything. Ted Bundy was handsome and charismatic but was one of the most notorious serial killers in America in the 1970s. He killed at least thirty young women, seducing his victims into trusting him. Whether they work or don't work, psychopaths think they are the most important beings on the planet. Everything revolves around them, and that includes their associates. They are excellent at spotting the weak and vulnerable and will positively thrive on making them bend to their will, getting them to provide everything they need, financially, physically or materially.'

Charlie thought immediately of Lisa Forrester used and abused by Samson for years, a victim of his lusts… but also able to extract what she needed from the relationship. Maybe she too had psychopathic tendencies? Maybe she recognised in him a kindred spirit, able to move on if necessary but remaining teamed up with him in a toxic combination while it suited them both. Maybe though, just like Ms Saffron Bolt, she may have believed there was some good in the man, that Samson Powell was, after all, capable of loving her.

'So, if two psychopaths come together is one likely to be more dominant?'

'It depends on each pairing. You've only got to read the papers, especially with Ian Brady dying recently. He and Myra Hindley are a good example. Brady was a psychopath who revelled in fetishes. Hindley was initially thought to be a naive teenager, totally taken in by him, but research has now suggested she too had psychopathic traits. She certainly wasn't a submissive accomplice. Brady might have called the shots initially but we'll never know who ended up enjoying their twisted pleasures more.'

'I was born after they were locked up but I still remember my mum talking about them and what they did. I'm glad they're both dead now. They even looked evil.' Charlie shuddered involuntarily at the memory, thinking of Samson Powell's sinister custody image. 'What about suicide? Are psychopaths likely to take their own lives?'

Anna turned and looked at Charlie thoughtfully. 'This isn't about anybody you know personally is it?'

Charlie smiled. She might have unresolved issues from her childhood but she'd never turned her problems inwards. She was all about fighting. 'No, no, don't worry. Just someone I've come across recently, in a professional capacity.'

'Ah, OK,' Anna nodded. 'I don't like talking about suicide unless I know why.'

'I understand,' Charlie urged. 'Go on.'

'Well in that case, no, they don't usually take their own lives. Psychopaths are devoid of emotion so they don't tend to worry about life issues as most of us do. Many of those locked up for murder will spend their whole lives behind bars rather than kill themselves, because it suits them better to live. That said, some might try as a means of manipulation; Ian Brady again, for example, tried to kill himself by going on a hunger strike. The courts ruled that he should be kept alive by force-feeding so he couldn't win. Why he chose this particular method is interesting though, possibly to get publicity, but more likely as a way of testing his manipulative skills and relieving the boredom. He'd have had perfect control until the time when he'd lapse into a coma. A bit of game-playing to while away the time.'

'Very interesting.' Charlie was genuinely intrigued, but Samson Powell's suicide didn't really fit this bill. Nobody knew what he was about to do, except perhaps the one person on the other end of the phone. 'Any other reasons?'

'Well, they might choose to commit suicide if it suits the situation. Harold Shipman hanged himself in his cell, partly because he thought it might financially benefit his wife Primrose, but also because it meant he had total control over the authorities who wanted him to attend courses aimed at making him confess. It was planned and carried out as meticulously as his murders. He had a reason to die and therefore it suited him.'

'Like, if they were about to be arrested and put away for life? Or to taunt the authorities? "You can't punish me because I'm dead." That sort of thing?'

'Yes, either of those reasons. As a means of rationally controlling what happened to them, or game-playing. They win because they take away the opportunity to get even.'

'What about,' Charlie's mind was racing, 'if they had lost somebody important in their life?'

'Hmm. Well on an emotional level, the majority of psychopaths wouldn't care if they ever saw that person again, but there are the odd exceptions. Fred and Rosemary West, for example, were a particularly interesting couple. They murdered twelve people including Fred's pregnant lover, his daughter and the daughter they had together. Fred had a low IQ and a high drive for sexual deviancy. Rose was his perfect partner, more than competing with his needs.'

Anna reached across for the book and flicked through it until she reached a page showing a photo of the Wests. Charlie leant across and stared at the innocuous-looking faces of the two serial killers. Rosemary stared out from the page, prim and proper with a dark fringe and large square glasses framing startlingly dead eyes. Fred sat curly-haired and grinning, his gap-toothed expression somehow exhibiting a glimpse of pathos, a doe-eyed acceptance that maybe he needed Rose more than she needed him.

She was reminded again, as she looked at Fred West, of the face of the dead Samson Powell, sad and pathetic, a man predisposed to antisocial tendencies but moulded by the horrific deaths of his parents and his ensuing upbringing. He had died with a photo of his mother in his pocket, a tiny hint at the depths of his psyche, that perhaps he had a vulnerability and wasn't all evil. Perhaps Saffron Bolt, the woman who looked like his mother, had recognised this, after all. Perhaps another psychopath had recognised this too.

Anna pointed at the photo and continued. 'Fred was charged with murder, but when Rose was arrested, she rebuffed his attempt to touch her at a remand hearing and then ignored a love letter he wrote from his prison cell. In Fred's warped mind the rejection was more powerful than any revulsion or remorse he had for his actions. He committed suicide in prison on New Year's Day, before he could face trial. We'll never know whether he did it because he was upset at her rejection, or so outraged that he exacted his revenge by leaving her to deal with their convictions alone. So… it's certainly possible that being left could be the trigger for suicide.'

Charlie reached across and shut the book. The image of Rose West's dark, cold eyes disturbed her.

'One last question then. Might a psychopath commit suicide if somebody told them to?'

Anna frowned. 'Well… I suppose it's a possibility. Psychopaths are prone to risk-taking and impulsive behaviour but it would have to suit them too. If the other person is a psychopath, it could be part of their power games. "See what happens to you now if I do kill myself." "You need me as much as I need you." That sort of thing.' Anna stood up, her frown even deeper. 'But if there is someone else out there calling the shots, someone that your person was working with, why would they tell your person to kill themselves?'

Charlie glanced towards the closed book as a thought surfaced that until now she hadn't wanted to entertain. As the thought solidified in her head she stared at the woman opposite her, comprehending Anna's concern and said aloud the words that they were both thinking.

'Unless they have someone else lined up to take their place!'

Chapter 29

PC Jason Lloyd checked himself in the rear-view mirror of his car and liked what he saw. Clean-cut charm, with a hint of mischief; or at least that's how he'd described his looks on his dating profiles. 'If you want a touch of romance, a touch of class or just a touch – I'm the one for you,' he'd typed into his personal summary, adding three winking emojis.

Subtlety was not Jason's strong point, but then subtlety was outdated and overrated these days, as was patience, honour and respect. Women wanted to know what they were getting, and with him, they were getting the lot; brawn, brains and a body that would keep the Incredible Hulk green with envy.

He ran his tongue over his lips and popped another mint into his mouth, grinning into the mirror again, his teeth held firmly together and his eyes scanning across each pearly white for any sign of discolouration. He'd recently paid a fortune to have them whitened, but the money had been well-spent. Women were transfixed by their perfection. One lopsided smile and they were putty in his hands. He'd practised that too. It was no use having a strong forehead, piercingly dark irises and a masculine smattering of stubble across his angular jaw, if he didn't have cuteness. Excessive testosterone was daunting to most females. A wonky grin, a suggestion of vulnerability and a single dimple provided the rebalance, even though it had taken many years perfecting the art. He checked in the mirror again and winked. Matt Damon eat your heart out.

Pulling a comb out, he ran it across his scalp. A tuft of dark hair had broken free at the front of his hairline and was sticking out at an angle. It was making a habit of doing its own thing these days, but he liked its rebelliousness, the way it challenged the path that was set... it reminded him of himself: defiant, disobedient, a risk-taker.

No, he was after fun, with a capital F. All the F's in fact: fun, freedom and fucking with no ties, no commitment and no waiting. It didn't usually take too long for the girl to see his point of view, but if it did, well, he'd either persuade her into letting him have his way... or send her on hers. A well-timed photo in police uniform was usually enough to provide all the ammunition he required; every girl liked a man in uniform, didn't they, and recently he'd become so adept at recognising vulnerability that he rarely even had to fall back on his charm. They were willing participants... or too weak to say they weren't.

He pulled out his phone and scrolled down to check the arrangements. This particular woman had pretty much offered him everything on a plate; a Tinder conquest who had suggested a quiet, unobtrusive country lane in which to put their words into practice. The photos of her looked hot and they had been sexting for a couple of weeks. He couldn't wait; in fact, he could feel himself getting aroused just at the thought. He glanced down at the two wineglasses, set next to a bottle of Chardonnay in the centre consul. If he was really in the mood for acting out a few fantasies, then a little crushed Rohypnol slipped into one of these would make the night even more memorable… for him at least. His fingers moved to the small packet of white powder burning a hole in his pocket. She wouldn't complain, she was clearly gagging for it anyway.

He shifted in his seat gazing out from the lane in which he was parked. The area was one that he had never previously visited, having only recently moved into this part of West London. It was a few miles from Heathrow Airport, sandwiched between the suburban sprawl of Slough and Hayes, where the rivers Fray and Colne joined up with the Grand Union Canal. A sprinkling of lakes and brooks signalled the abundance of waterways, the area being described as an oasis of greens and blues in an otherwise dull grey landscape. By night, however, it was bathed in darkness, the lingering shimmer from the capital's street lights, the only thing serving to lessen the blackness of the sky to a warm grey.

The few houses that stood in the lane were situated in tight knots of humanity; the remainder of the road, where he now was, given over to nature. A rabbit lolloped to the edge of the road, turning its head in the direction of the car, its whiskers twitching in time with the wings of a moth fluttering haphazardly across the car windscreen. Even within the centre of the country's population hub, birdlife, insect life and animal life still prospered. It was an area of natural beauty, hidden within a city of concrete, one of London's forgotten treasures.

Jason Lloyd, however, was not interested in the landscape. He was interested in only one thing, from one person… and that one person was due to arrive at any time. No doubt a set of headlights would soon be travelling towards where he waited at the designated spot, at the end of the deserted cul-de-sac.

He straightened, peering out into the darkness, and opened the window, allowing the sounds of the woodland to enter. Even though it was almost midnight, the air outside was warmer than the air-conditioned interior and the smell of the landscape earthy and fragranced. An owl hooted in the distance, its distinctive call fading into the background drone of traffic from the M25, London's

Orbital road, that thundered overhead. A breath of wind stirred the leaves of the bushes in the nearest hedgerow. He couldn't wait. A twig snapped in the undergrowth. Sweat seeped into the indentation at the base of his back. Only a few more minutes.

He swung his head towards the mirror again, flicking the switch to turn the light on, plunging the interior into a momentarily blinding radiance. He blinked, feeling a shudder of anticipation running up his spine as he grinned towards his reflection. He was so busy checking on his appearance that he didn't notice the figure step out from the cover of the trees and the glint of the knife as it was thrust towards his neck.

*

Two hours later the man picked up the phone and pressed the only number saved on it. The fingers of his gloves glistened bright red in the subdued lighting under the motorway bridge, the policeman's blood still wet on his clothing. He pulled the balaclava from his head and sucked in the night air, wiping the blade of the knife unsteadily on a clean towel, before placing them both in his bag. His hands shook violently as he waited for the phone to be answered.

The call clicked in, and recognising Ice's greeting, he started to speak immediately, his voice loud and excited, pumped up. Each word was garbled, each sentence rushed, the nervous tension of the last few hours expended in a jumble of victorious ramblings. He had done it, and he had done it well, unlike the last miserable sucker who had committed suicide, rather than face up to his failure. It had been all over the news, much to Ice's annoyance. Samson Powell had failed to follow instructions, but *he* had done everything right. Ice would be proud. His brother would have been proud. After a few minutes, the man stopped talking, panicking slightly.

'I did everything as you instructed, Ice. I hope I've done OK?' he asked, suddenly nervous.

The voice that answered him was also excited at hearing the news but the tone remained calm, sing-song even.

'You've done well. You've done very well. In a few minutes I'll tell you exactly what you must do to get rid of the evidence. I have already planned out our next piece of work. Now, calm down,' Ice sighed, breathing slowly. 'And tell me again exactly what you did to that bastard. I want to hear every single thing, in detail.'

Chapter 30

Friday 7th July 2017

'Poets Day today,' Nick winked at Charlie as he sauntered past. 'Fancy a drink later?'

'I thought Poets Day meant pissing off early, not turning up late.' She shook her head in amused disbelief. 'Do you realise it's also twelve years to the day since the 7/7 London bombings in 2005. I joined the police on the 6th July 2007, but my mum still quoted what happened that day as a reason for not joining. Obviously I ignored her. Maybe, we should all go for a drink to celebrate my ten years and a day in the job? It's been a long, frustrating week for everyone and I could use a pint of ice-cold lager.'

'That's a date then, at least for you and me. I'm not sure about the others.' Nick flashed her a mischievous smile before strolling out of the office. 'You know I'm an expert at dealing with frustrated women.'

Paul lifted his head up from behind his workstation and pushed his chair back. 'Charlie, you lucky cow. I wish he'd deal with frustrated men too.' He stood up and stretched, before tucking his shirt back into his trousers. 'I am one extremely frustrated man at the moment!'

Bet pulled a face, as the phone rang. 'TMI,' she said, as Charlie laughed. She picked up the receiver and Charlie watched as her expression became serious.

'Shit!' Charlie shook her head. 'By the look on Bet's face I think Poets Day has just been cancelled.'

Bet put the receiver down. 'You're dead right, I'm afraid. You'll all have to stay frustrated for the time being. That was Hunter. He's had a call from DCI O'Connor. A body has turned up over at Hillingdon, not far from Heathrow. I know it's not our borough, but they want us to assist. It's another police officer. Named as Jason Lloyd. Cut and mutilated, like ours were. Hunter thinks we might have a copycat killer. He's on his way back with Naz and Sab. They've also just had some information that their acid burns suspect is going to try to flee the country tomorrow so their weekend is messed up too. He'll be here in a few minutes and he wants you ready to go with him to the scene, Charlie. The rest of us have to start looking into Lloyd's background.'

Charlie felt her pulse quicken as her conversation with Anna Christophe came into sharp focus. It was what she had been dreading.

*

The journey to Hillingdon went quickly and silently, neither Hunter nor Charlie wanting to put their thoughts into words. Charlie guessed that Hunter would know what she was thinking, but if he had guessed, he certainly wasn't saying; so much easier to think of a copycat killer than a continuation to the first series.

The crime scene cordons were already in place, as they had expected, forming a boundary around the area where Jason Lloyd's car had been found abandoned, to where his body lay. After kitting up, they were escorted along the forensic pathway to the body.

The forensic route took them parallel to the usual well-trodden footpath, towards a large lake, before skirting away through a more densely forested area towards several secluded spots on the banks. In these places the trees hung low over small fishing pitches, the grass having been trampled down and the branches giving shelter to any individuals whose purchase of a permit allowed them a day of tranquillity away from the stresses of the city. Pushing through a number of branches at the side of one of these sites, they reached the place where another of their colleagues had met his death.

Charlie stared at the figure, lying on its back, partially stripped, legs and arms splayed out at angles, facing skywards, on a patch of mud at the edge of the lake. His body was half naked, his trousers and underwear having been pulled down and his T-shirt torn open across his chest. His lower limbs and groin were covered in blood that had drained out from what appeared to be two deep slits across his torso running from the bottom right-hand side of his chest to his left shoulder. A large, sharpened fish hook was firmly implanted in both lips, from which a nylon line looped around a tree branch, holding his head up off the ground, his face grotesque and stretched as the skin of his lips and cheeks held the weight of his upper body.

A single red rose, devoid of thorns, lay on the grass next to the body.

Charlie turned away at the sight, her mind not able to fully comprehend what her eyes were seeing.

'What the fuck!' she muttered, picking up her mobile and dialling Paul's number. She turned the speaker on and held it out so Hunter could hear the conversation. 'Paul it's me. Please tell me Jason Lloyd doesn't have a complaint outstanding?'

'Hi, Charlie. That was the first thing we checked… and he has.'

She turned her head back towards where Hunter stood, staring mutely at the body. He looked as perplexed as she.

'What was the complaint for?'

'It was for sexual assault and malfeasance in office. I've read the details. Basically it alleges that he was using the fact that he was a police officer for his own personal gain; to get sexual favours, sometimes from victims of crime and sometimes to exert pressure on girls he met on dating websites. There are four known victims that have come forward to make complaints so far; two who used one website, one who used another and one burglary victim, but it is believed there could be more.'

'Shit.' Her mind was in overdrive as her eyes focussed on the injuries, the way he had been strung up deliberately from the hook, caught and skewered. 'Was one of the dating websites "Plenty of Fish"?' she said eventually.

'Yes, it was. How on earth did you know that?'

'I'll explain later, Paul. And the other?'

'Tinder. Two of the complainants met him on there.'

She looked towards Jason Lloyd with the two deep gauges into his flesh from left to right, trying to recall the conversations she'd had with Naz who regularly used the site. 'Boss, look. On the dating app Tinder, you swipe right, if you match with someone. Two of the complainants had obviously met him so they must have swiped right. And he has two slits upwards from left to right as you look at him.'

'And he's strung up like a fish; hence "Plenty of Fish",' Hunter joined in. 'And partially stripped because of the sexual nature of the complaint.'

'Shit,' Paul echoed Charlie's sentiment. 'I heard that and it sounds disgusting. Oh, also while you're there, it's suggested that he may have drugged his victims in some way. A couple of them can't remember exactly what happened or how they got to where they eventually woke up.'

'That might explain how our killer got him here then' Charlie pursed her lips.

Hunter nodded. 'They've taken a sample of blood already for just that reason, but it doesn't explain how this one links in to the three we've already solved. Samson Powell did ours and he's dead… and anyway, it's too far from our patch to be connected. I know there's a rose here but it must be a copycat killer who's read the publicity and has decided to do the same thing in West London.'

'Boss,' Paul interrupted, 'Jason Lloyd might've lived and worked over on Hillingdon's ground but he hasn't always. The one complainant who was a burglary victim lives just off our patch in Balham and, for about six months, Jason Lloyd worked in Wandsworth borough. He's suspended from work at the moment, but it was the reason he got moved to Hillingdon. If what is being suggested is right and there are other victims, it's very possible that either the burglary victim or one of them might have passed on Lloyd's details to someone on our ground.'

*

The journey back to the office was equally quiet. Charlie was bursting to do something, anything, while Hunter sat in stony silence. As they pulled into Lambeth HQ she could hold her frustration no longer.

'Guv, we've got to do something. It's Friday night and we've got the whole weekend ahead of us. We can't just sit back and wait for the next killing.'

'Who said there'll be another one?' Hunter almost exploded. 'I know you think it's all part of a sinister plot and Samson Powell was just a poor man who was exploited by some evil genius… but he was not. He's been shown to be a violent psychopath who did exactly what he wanted, when he wanted and to whoever he wanted.'

Charlie opened her mouth to speak but closed it abruptly.

Hunter's expression was dark. 'This latest murder may just be the work of another psycho needing a bit of a thrill, who has somehow got hold of the information about Jason Lloyd's complaint and has decided to copy Powell's "punishment to fit the crime" methods. We need to wait for any forensics and his phone data to come back before rushing into anything and making ourselves look even more foolish than we have already. This time, Charlie, we need some actual evidence.'

'Boss,' she spoke quietly. 'I'm not aware that the fact the previous roses all had the barbs removed was ever released publicly, yet this one has been prepared in the same way. Nor do I think Powell was a poor man. You're quite right. He was a violent psychopath and I think he knew exactly what he was doing and chose that course of action himself.' She took a deep breath. 'What I do think, though, is that someone told him, or suggested, who to kill. He didn't know all his victims, so why would he target them in the way he did. But he did know Dennis Walters and Lisa Forrester and Shirley Sangster, and from what DS Boyle says, Shirley knows everyone who is anyone. If Jason Lloyd worked nearby and was doing what's been alleged, it's quite possible that word would have got around and I'm convinced Sangster and the others might be involved.'

'But where's your evidence, Charlie?'

'I haven't much at the moment but let me at least try to get some, guv.' She railed. 'We've still got the drugs warrant on Dennis Walters' address, haven't we? And it's still in date. It's the weekend; he's bound to have a stash of gear in his place to sell on. Why not go in tonight and see what we can find. If there're drugs, we can at least keep him in custody out the way for as long as possible. Who knows what else we might find if he is involved. He might even be the next foot soldier. He's similar in profile to Samson and hates police. At the end of the day, we can't do nothing… and we can't be seen to do nothing!'

Hunter sighed heavily and frowned. 'OK, you win, again. We left with our tails between our legs last time and Walters does need putting straight. But it's the last time I'm going to pander to your ideas. Get things started and I'll join you when I've updated the DCI.'

She squeezed the car into a space and jumped out. 'Thanks, guv, you won't be sorry.'

'I'm not so sure about that,' Hunter replied. 'I may well live to regret it.'

Chapter 31

A light rain was falling as they lined up at the side of the apartment block. The clouds were low over the towers around the Elephant and Castle, making Dennis Walters' building seem even greyer and more dull than usual. Lethargy had set in around the estate and only a few locals could be bothered to frequent the bars and cafes of the shopping centre; even its amusement arcades were silent and lifeless. Charlie had cobbled together a team of twelve uniformed officers as well as her, Hunter, Paul, Nick, Naz and Sabira. Nick had begrudgingly agreed to stay on for the warrant, but his reticence had been noted by them all. Bet was manning the radio, ready to do any intelligence checks or liaise with the control room if required.

Charlie had briefed them all on what was known and they were ready to go. They were looking primarily for drugs, but they were also to look for anything that might be relevant to the murders and let her or Hunter know immediately. Sweat glistened on their faces, the humidity of the evening and extra layers of protective uniform making them clammy and uncomfortable. Above them the scaffolding and tarpaulins still creaked in the breeze. Charlie peered up towards the fourth floor, noting that many of the balcony doors and windows were flung open. Walters' flat remained firmly closed; good for the element of surprise but bad for the extra heat they would be encountering on entry. Whatever the climate outside, crossing the threshold of a crackhead's property always seemed to be like entering the inner caverns of a volcano: hot, smoky and foul-smelling. The first job was always to throw open as many windows as possible to allow in some fresh air.

She beckoned the team onwards and they climbed the four flights of stairs, stopping to catch their breath at the top briefly before treading silently along the landing. The padlock was still in place, hanging open on its catch, signifying the presence of people within. At least on this occasion it looked as if they might be lucky. This time there would be no softly-softly approach, it would be Dennis Walters on the back foot.

'Go, go, go,' the word was given and within seconds the door lay in a heap of splintered wood and their subjects were in sight. Dennis Walters sprang forward in surprise from his armchair, his hands shooting towards his groin, before being forcibly placed in handcuffs. He continued to struggle, kicking out at anyone close enough, until he was lifted up and dumped unceremoniously on the dirty carpet, his mouth against the filth.

Lisa Forrester was spread out lazily along the sofa, her skinny legs propped up over the armrest, her pupils dilated in the half-light. She made no attempt to move, smiling languidly in obvious amusement as Walters struggled and spat, before she too was placed in handcuffs.

On a coffee table in front of Walters lay the remnants of his evening's labours. A cutting block with a dusting of white powder, scales, cling film and razor blades, along with a pile of empty snap-bags and the remains of some herbal cannabis plants. It was clear he liked to offer his customers a choice.

Charlie and Hunter stepped forward when the situation was calm and Charlie put a copy of the warrant down.

'Nice to see you again, Lisa,' she said, before turning towards Walters. 'Dennis, I have a warrant to search you and your flat for drugs, under s23 Misuse of Drugs Act.' She nodded towards the coffee table. 'I see you and Lisa know exactly what I'm talking about.'

Dennis Walters strained towards her. 'Well, if it's not the same two arrogant pigs as before. I remember the last time you visited me. In fact I remember everything about you. I had a feeling I would be seeing the pair of you again after I fucked you off, squealing with fright. You lot can never leave me alone, can you?'

'Actually, it looks like we need to keep an even closer eye on you.' Charlie ignored the jibe.

'You silly bitch. You might think you can pin me down, but you can't.' Walters laughed, his mouth contorted in a sneer, before turning towards Hunter and starting to grunt and squeal.

Hunter took a step towards Walters and bent down, staring straight into his face. 'You might think you're a big man, in front of your new woman, but you're not.' He stood back up, still looking straight into his face as Walters continued to grunt like a pig.

'Dennis, leave it,' Lisa Forrester piped up. 'It ain't worth it.'

Walters turned towards her angrily but stopped the noise abruptly before facing his guards. 'All right, all right, but look at them, your Samson was right doing the things what he did. All cops are filthy pigs. They all deserve what he was handing out.'

Hunter bent towards him again. 'And you're just a piece-of-shit drug dealer, who likes to take his orders from a woman. Now shut up, Dennis, like Lisa here has told you.' Hunter straightened, before turning towards Paul, Nick and two other officers holding Walters. 'Get him up and take him into the bathroom. Strip-search him… and make sure you do it thoroughly.'

With that, Dennis Walters was lifted to his feet and frogmarched from the room.

Lisa's eyes followed him out as he left before turning towards Charlie. 'Stupid bastard, 'e'll never learn to keep his mouth shut. None of 'em do.' She slumped back against the sofa.

'You need to be searched too.' Charlie took hold of her arm and helped her to stand, before walking her through to the bedroom with Naz.

'Well you won't find nuffin' on me. I smoked it all earlier.' She laughed. 'By the way, you didn't look surprised to see me here.'

'I saw you and him together the other morning. And when we last spoke you said you were looking for somewhere to stay. It didn't take too much to put two and two together. Were you with him last night, Lisa?'

'I was for a bit, but then I weren't. He 'ad something 'e needed to do.'

'Do you know what?'

'Nah, I wouldn't ask, an' 'e didn't say. 'E was out most of the night. Never heard 'im come in at all. Probably out there doin' what he was gonna be doin' tonight.'

'And what's that?'

'Nuffin'. I mean I ain't saying nuffin' more.'

'Could he have been doing what Samson did?'

'What d'ya mean?'

'There was another police officer killed last night.'

'I know. I saw it flash up on the news on my phone,' Lisa Forrester sat up straight and blinked hard. 'I told Dennis when he woke up; 'e's been in bed most of the day. 'E just laughed and made a comment about someone obviously carrying on the good work. Shit! 'E couldn't 'ave done it.' She paused. 'Could he?'

Charlie shook her head. 'That's what we need to find out.'

There was nothing of note on Lisa, as she'd forecast; though, as they searched her, Charlie couldn't help noticing the needle tracks running up her arms and groin, and the scars all over her body, the result of years of drug abuse and physical assaults at the hands of Samson Powell. She'd transferred her affections from one violent man to another, her vulnerability forcing her life choices.

'Lisa, if we could help you get detox again, would you let me know if you hear anything about who's doing these killings? You've lost your partner and now, four families have lost their loved ones. We really need to stop it happening and I think there might be more than one person involved.'

'You mean Samson might not 'ave bin doing what 'e did on 'is own? Even though you said all the evidence was that 'e had.'

'All the physical evidence does show him as the perpetrator, but we need to find out whether there was anyone else working with him, giving him specific information or co-ordinating things.'

Lisa paused before putting her T-shirt back on, rubbing her hand across a large bruise on her shoulder blade. 'I know what it's like 'aving someone telling you what to do all the time.' She smiled wistfully and they moved back into the front room which had now been searched.

Hunter was waiting, looking out from the dirty windows of the flat towards the city of London. He turned around and faced them as they returned.

'Paul says they've found a load of gear down Dennis's pants,' he explained. 'What a surprise, eh? Eleven wraps of crack cocaine and ten snap-bags of skunk cannabis. He's been arrested and will be leaving shortly.'

'Lisa had nothing on her, guv. She's agreed to keep her ears open for anything that might help us with our enquiries.'

'In that case, I think we'll put the last remnants of drugs on the coffee table down to Dennis too. It is his flat, after all, and you haven't been here for long, have you Lisa?' His speech was interrupted by several loud shouts from the direction of the bathroom.

Dennis Walters was bundled out, still struggling and swearing loudly, his clothing in disarray and his arms held behind his back. Paul was grinning broadly, while Nick walked a few paces behind, his cheeks flushed red, letting the uniformed officers do all the restraining.

'Mr Walters, it seems we have at least pinned you down for something; possession of drugs with intent to supply.' Hunter turned towards him. 'I shall look forward to hearing what you have to say later, at the station.'

'You bastards. It's for my personal fucking use, as well you know it. You'll never prove supply.' His mouth curled up in a sneer. 'Everyone knows you have to bulk-buy if you're a user and check what you're given to make sure you're not ripped off. That's all I'm fucking doing.'

'Yes, well, you can tell the court why you choose to secrete your precious drugs down your pants, rather than smoking it, or hiding it safely here.' He turned towards Lisa. 'Miss Forrester will be staying here. She'll look after your place while you're with us. I'm sure she'll do whatever's needed.'

Charlie smiled. It was the best arrangement Lisa could have hoped for; a roof over her head, with no fear of violence. A few hours or days to relax without fear.

Dennis Walters swivelled round towards Lisa, spitting saliva as he spoke. 'Lisa, in that case I need you to contact Shirley Sangster. Tell her that DI

Geoffrey Hunter and DC Charlotte Stafford have arrested me.' He pronounced each name carefully. 'Tell her it's an emergency and they've been harassing me and have used excessive force. She'll know what to do.'

Chapter 32

On a whim, Charlie drove Paul through the Angell Town Estate where Shirley Sangster lived, navigating the narrow streets, between rows of identically proportioned houses and larger blocks.

The search of Walters' flat had just been concluded and nothing of note found relating to the murders. Like Powell's residence, the flat appeared to be clean. They had only the stash of drugs to keep Walters in custody, but hopefully that would be enough to get him locked up out of the way, at least for a while. Hunter had been called back to speak to the DCI, taking Nick with him.

'So… what happened in there with Nick?' Charlie couldn't wait to ask.

Paul laughed. 'Walters took an instant dislike to him. Kept calling him a pretty boy and asking if he was my boyfriend, that sort of thing. It doesn't bother me. I'm used to it, but Nick didn't know what to say, especially when they found the drugs strapped to his bollocks and Walters grabbed Nick's hand and asked if he wanted to have a feel. He turned beetroot red and just shrunk into the corner.'

Charlie shook her head. 'I don't think he's cut out for this job.'

'And I'm damn sure that Hunter thinks the same,' Paul agreed. 'It's just a matter of time before he loses his last life. If he hasn't already, judging by Hunter's face when he found out what had happened. I'll miss his cute little arse, though, if he goes.'

'So will Naz. She thinks he's hot.'

'And you will. Don't pretend you don't like him. I've seen you peeking.'

She wound the window down, wondering if Paul was right. 'Well let's just wait and see,' she said as they passed a basketball court, watching as a team of lads jumped and twisted, their shouts gaining the attention of a group of women stood chatting on the corner. The sound of their gossip brought her thoughts back into sharp focus.

'Paul, you heard what Walters said. Do you think Shirley Sangster could be our missing link?'

'I think, if there is a missing link, she would fit the bill perfectly, but you need to go careful, Charlie. I did some digging when you first mentioned her name and Sangster does hold an awful lot of clout. One wrong word and that could be the end of your career as you know it.'

Charlie grimaced. 'I'm well aware of that, but she is ideally placed and would naturally have followers who she could influence.'

'Like Samson Powell and Dennis Walters.' Paul wound his own window down. 'What's been worrying me since Powell's suicide, and I heard your ideas, was why were Brian Ashton and Philippa McGovern killed in the way they were. If Sangster was organising the deaths and the methods to be used, why choose those? It's fair enough to select the method she did for Leonard Cookson, she knows that case personally… but Walters had a grudge against Brian Ashton for harassment and unlawful arrest, not theft. And he hated Philippa McGovern because he thought she'd deliberately targeted him for domestic violence issues… not laziness and incompetence. Surely Sangster would have chosen methods to fit Walters' gripes, not the official complaints.'

'You're right, Paul. And Jason Lloyd's murder is the same. Sangster might have heard talk on the streets from the one burglary victim who lived nearby, but how would she have known about the other sexual harassment complaints against him or the details of which websites and apps were used by the other victims?'

'By having access to our official complaints system?'

'But each complaint is being investigated by a different DPS officer, I checked.' She swallowed hard as the final piece to her jigsaw appeared to fall into place. 'But if Shirley Sangster is involved… Shit, Paul.'

Paul stayed silent.

'DS Hayley Boyle. She's in regular contact with Sangster because she's still dealing with Shirley's complaint against Leonard Cookson for framing her son. It would also explain why both Powell's and Walters' flats were pretty much devoid of anything to link them with the crimes. Boyle could advise them on being forensically aware. Thinking about it, she did seem nervous when I first asked her about Sangster… as if she was hiding something.'

'And she's been in the DPS for years.' Paul shrugged his shoulders. 'None of us want corrupt coppers in our ranks. We know that more than most… but a fair few of the complaints are made to muddy the waters at court, or are mischief-making or just plain malicious.'

Charlie swung the car out of the estate and pressed down on the accelerator, her pulse racing. They needed to get back to the office quickly. Her mind flew to the smartly suited DPS officer intent on asking both her and Hunter about the details of their previous case. 'Who in their right minds would want to spend their career dealing with complaints against their own hard-working colleagues?'

'Someone who is very driven to get any officer she considers to be a bad apple off the streets.'

A chill ran up Charlie's spine as Paul spoke. 'Or crush them completely.'

*

Hunter was still holed up in DCI O'Connor's office when Charlie and Paul returned, desperate to share their suspicions. The others had booked off-duty, Nick having disappeared immediately on his return, all thoughts of waiting for Charlie to join him for a drink being firmly put on hold.

After knocking smartly on his door, impatience got the better of her and Charlie opened it to see both men staring frostily at one another.

'What do you want?' Declan O'Connor was clearly in no mood for pleasantries.

'Boss, we need to speak to you both urgently… about the latest murder.' She turned towards Hunter. 'You know you thought it could be the work of a copycat killer, who has somehow got hold of the information about Jason Lloyd's complaint, well, Paul and I think we might know how.'

'You'd better come in then,' the DCI said, his expression one of interest.

'And you'd better have evidence,' Hunter said at the same time, his expression one of weary annoyance.

*

It took almost half an hour for Charlie to fully explain the whole basis for her theories, during which time Declan O'Connor went from mild interest to deep concentration. Charlie explained everything, from the information that Saffron Bolt had given about Samson Powell's willingness to do everything she'd asked of him, to her discussions with Anna Christophe about the personality traits of a psychopath and their worry that other replacements had been lined up in the event of Powell's culpability being established. The fact that the latest murder could well have proved them right was not lost on the DCI and his frown deepened as Charlie listed the associations between Powell, Lisa Forrester, Dennis Walters and Shirley Sangster. At the mention of Sangster's name, he let out an audible groan.

'Please say she's not involved. That woman is the bane of my life. She must come to the police station ranting and raving at least two or three times every week, and she's usually surrounded by half a dozen of her cronies.'

Charlie rubbed at a patch of dirt on her sleeve. 'Worse than that, boss. We think it might be her who selects which officers she wants to kill from listening to those same cronies, but then chooses her methods from finding out about any official outstanding complaints. There are not many active coppers, in contentious departments like Trident, the CSU or team that don't have at least one outstanding complaint these days.'

'Am I understanding you correctly? Are you saying there is someone passing her this information?' DCI O'Connor stood up and paced around the desk.

'That's exactly what we're suggesting, sir. It's only a suspicion, but the information must be getting leaked from somewhere. The methods used are absolutely specific to the complaints, especially the latest. Research might have provided a few answers, but there's no way anyone could accurately find out every detail, even down to which dating websites Jason Lloyd was using, without some inside information.'

'And now you're going to tell me who?' He stopped pacing and stared directly at Charlie, who coloured immediately.

'Well... again it's only a suspicion at present but,' she looked at Paul for reassurance and he nodded in return. 'We were thinking, maybe DS Hayley Boyle. She is in regular contact with Shirley Sangster and there was something odd in her manner when I asked her about the woman the other day after my interview.'

The DCI looked pointedly at Hunter, before sitting down abruptly, chewing on his bottom lip.

'Shit.' Charlie watched as the DCI's frown deepened, before he continued. 'Do you remember the day you got the DNA result on Samson Powell? You two were supposed to be meeting Hayley for interviews that afternoon, weren't you?'

'And you said the only way you would let us off them was to bring you the name, address and inside leg measurement of your suspect.' Hunter nodded.

'Yes, that's right. Well, when you did, I phoned Hayley straight away to tell her you had to conduct an urgent arrest enquiry and to cancel her.' The DCI shook his head in obvious disgust. 'And she would have known which case you were on. Bloody hell! I thought you just had bad luck on the day, but if you're right in what you suspect, she could have phoned that information on to Sangster... and that's why Powell wasn't in.'

'And why he knew we were on to him,' Hunter added.

Charlie felt the colour drain from her cheeks at the thought of Powell's dead body hanging grotesquely from the electrical cable. 'And why he chose to kill himself rather than spend the rest of his life in prison.'

*

In the silence that followed, the implication of Declan O'Connor's words was not lost on any of them.

'Our conversation goes absolutely no further than these four walls.' The DCI stood up again and pulled at his already loose tie, looking round at each of them individually. 'We will be investigating the investigators.'

'I know Ray Hooper, the Chief Superintendent at DPS, and I trust him implicitly,' he continued. 'I've got the work phone numbers of both women already in my contacts, but let me know if you find any others they use. I'll speak to Ray and get everything we can on Hayley Boyle and I'll ask him to arrange for downloads on both their phone records ASAP. Go home now, but be back in early tomorrow morning... and remember.' He pulled his phone out of his pocket and tapped in a number. 'This will have to be *the* most confidential operation you are ever likely to be involved in. I can't have any hint of what we're about to do getting out. A senior police officer in Lambeth authorising covert work on a leading member of the community is pretty bloody politically explosive. A senior DPS officer investigating another ranked DPS officer is even worse; it's like pressing the button on a nuclear warhead. If the public found out that the officers investigating bent police officers are corrupt themselves, the fallout would be worse than anything even Donald Trump could leave in his wake.'

He smiled weakly at his attempt to lighten the situation, but they all knew that he was deadly serious. Police officers' lives depended on it.

Chapter 33

Shirley Sangster was very well known to all the officers at Lambeth but not for the usual reasons. Her criminal record showed nothing of note; a couple of arrests as a young woman for shoplifting, along with several public order offences while demonstrating for the rights of others, was pretty much the sum total.

She was a middle-aged, white woman with small piercing eyes that were almost lost in between rounded rosy cheeks and a low forehead. Her eyebrows were thick lines of black pencil and her lips were a slightly brighter shade of red than her cheeks. She habitually wore large hooped earrings and her hair was dyed blonde, cropped over both ears and longer at the top, swept into a small tight ponytail. She was apple-shaped with a larger than average midriff, scrawny legs and sloping shoulders.

Her three boys were her life. All were mixed-race, the product of Shirley and a long-standing Rastafarian partner who liked to share his love around half a dozen local women. Looking at their history of offending, they probably also took up most of her life. Involved in the gang scene from their primary years, they clearly had always done their own thing, freed by the lack of a live-in father and a mother who worshipped their every move. She had spent many hours in the custody office at Brixton police station with her boys and almost as many with social services and whichever correctional facility was dealing with juveniles at the time. Her bark, when it came to her boys, may have been loud, but her bite was clearly toothless.

When they weren't in prison, the boys spent most of their time on the streets, involved in low-level drug dealing, tit-for-tat fights with other postcode gangs and trying to obtain any firearm or weapon that would bolster their respect. Every arrest ending up with a charge led to an obligatory not-guilty plea at court. Her beautiful boys could never be guilty of wrongdoing and would therefore never admit to a thing.

Shirley had defended them as far as was possible and it was this that had brought her into contact with the lengthy list of people with whom she was now associated, including many of the good, the great and the downright dangerous. Charlie's job was to try to work out which of the dangerous she might now be grooming.

Hunter, grim-faced and aloof, stayed mainly in his office, as if the weight of the world was pressing on his shoulders again. He wasn't his usual self and Charlie didn't know what was wrong, or how to fix it. Every now and again he would emerge to shuttle between her, Paul and DCI O'Connor, who had come in to better supervise the investigation, but little was said between them.

By mid-morning Sangster's phone records had been returned and Charlie was scrolling through them. It read like a who's who of politics, policing and the public; as expected she had numbers for hundreds of people, including Dennis Walters, Samson Powell, DS Hayley Boyle, DCI O'Connor, and many other senior police officers; leaders of community groups, solicitors, MP's, and members of staff from the IPCC and the Equality and Human Rights Commission.

It wasn't really anything more than they didn't already know, or couldn't have guessed. Shirley Sangster had connections, but it was not who was of interest, so much as what was said when they did connect… and there were literally thousands of calls and texts logged. The woman must have been on the phone constantly. Texts could be retrieved, but the contents of phone calls would never be known.

Paul was starting the process, noting down any calls made to the associates they were interested in, along with times and dates. There were sporadic calls to each of their suspects and regular ones to Hayley

Boyle. To Charlie though, her earlier enthusiasm was melting away because just looking at the reams of paper was filling her with dread. Samson Powell had used a throwaway phone with just one number and that was not shown on Sangster's list. Nor was there a call made from Shirley's usual number to Samson's on the day of his death. It had been the first thing they had checked. But if the woman was switched on, like their murderer appeared to be, she too would have a different phone to the one she used to speak with politicians.

*

At midday DCI O'Connor summoned Paul, Hunter and Charlie to his office to go through any new developments. Hunter's phone started to ring as they entered, so he switched it to silent. The DCI pulled the door shut, checking the corridor as he did so, as if he expected to see small camera lenses planted in hidden places.

'What have you found so far?' he asked, sitting down at his desk.

'We can prove regular contact between Shirley Sangster and Hayley Boyle, but then we knew that anyway,' Paul spoke out, referring to the beginnings of his list. 'Obviously I don't know what was said in the calls but some are quite lengthy.'

'I'm still waiting for the call data back on DS Boyle's phone. It should be arriving shortly.' DCI O'Connor cleared his throat, before continuing. 'Ray Hooper is working with us as a matter of priority and he's called in a trusted inspector as a witness. They're experts on the technical stuff and IT systems. They have accessed Hayley Boyle's computer and have discovered that she has created her own spreadsheet detailing all the complaints that have come into her department in South London. There's absolutely no need for her to do this as every complaint is automatically logged by the admin officer when it arrives. Boyle colour-codes each complaint depending on how serious it is and who is dealing with it and has been making notes on how each investigation is progressing.

'As you know, she is dealing with Shirley Sangster's complaint against Leonard Cookson, but she also has access to the complaints against Brian Ashton, Philippa McGovern and Jason Lloyd and these are on her personal spreadsheet too.

'When the complaints are concluded she colour-codes them green.' The DCI glanced towards Paul and Charlie. 'The most worrying issue, though, is that she prints the spreadsheet off about once a fortnight and we don't know what for. There's no sign of any of the copies on her desk or in her drawers, so we don't know what she does with them.'

'Bloody hell,' Charlie blurted out. 'And you think that might be how she is passing on the information?'

'We don't know as yet, but needless to say, this sort of thing is contrary to all Data Protection guidelines and is strictly forbidden. Nothing of that nature should be printed out, and it certainly shouldn't be leaving the office.'

He paused, running his hands through his hair before shoving them deep into the pockets of his trousers and staring round at them all. 'And, worse still, you are all well aware that DPS have access to all our duties on CARMS, when we book on and off and take leave, etc. Well, Ray did a check on Hayley Boyle's search history and in the last month, amongst others, she has checked the records of all of our victims.'

Charlie shook her head. It was unbelievable that this could be happening.

'So she would have known what duties they were supposed to be on… and the fact that Philippa McGovern had annual leave booked?'

DCI O'Connor nodded. 'Yes she would, and DPS have access to every officer's personal details. In fact, they pretty much have access to everything in this job and they can use the same methods as we use in our criminal investigations to catch us out. It's worth remembering that.'

He glanced around at the three of them before logging into his computer and clicking on the list of recent emails.

'Here you go. Hayley Boyle's download has just come through,' he said, pressing print and getting up. 'Do you want to take a look, while it's printing?'

Charlie and Paul shot up from their chairs and made their way round while the printer whirred into action. A quick search of the contacts showed that Shirley Sangster's personal phone number came up a great many times, corroborating the fact that they spoke regularly to each other.

Charlie turned towards Paul. 'Take a look at the calls made the morning of Samson Powell's suicide. There should be communication between her and Sangster if Boyle passed on the fact that we'd identified Powell.'

Paul typed in the date, Monday 26/06/2017 and they watched the list of calls appear on the screen. At exactly 09.09 Shirley Sangster's number appeared in an incoming call to Hayley Boyle. The call lasted for eight minutes finishing at 09.17. A list of data then appeared, some numbers had no names, some names she recognised as officers, some had notes of who they were and where they worked. Charlie could feel her frustration growing again. The call would have been before Powell had been identified, and needed to have been outgoing.

Paul kept scrolling slowly down the list until 11.50 when Charlie watched an incoming unnamed number pop up on the screen... a number that was fixed indelibly in her memory... a number that had been attached to a three-lettered word.

'That's the same number as Samson Powell had on the phone he threw away, just before he killed himself,' she exclaimed excitedly, pointing at the screen. 'The only number on the SIM card.'

'Did you ever get anything else on it?' Hunter asked.

'No, in the end all we got was the name "ICE" on the SIM. There was no trace on any of our systems of the same number and it was unregistered, as I'd expected.' She turned to the DCI. 'And the actual phone was too badly water-damaged to get anything more. It was a "burner" phone, probably just to be used during one murder and thrown away. Whoever was using this number probably did the same.' She paused, still staring at the computer screen. 'So... both he and DS Hayley Boyle spoke to the same number, "ICE", whoever he or she is?'

The room went quiet, each person processing the information.

'Isn't that the name for next of kin to be contacted "in case of emergency"?' Declan O'Connor picked up the printout. 'My teenage daughter has it on her phone.'

'Yes, that's right, sir.' Charlie suddenly thought back to the previous evening. 'And isn't that what Dennis Walters instructed Lisa Forrester to specifically say. "Contact Shirley Sangster and tell her it's an emergency. She'll know what to do."'

*

Today was to be a day to remember. Storm clouds were already gathering and the air smouldered with pent-up rage. The wind had dropped. Everything was still; even time had stopped; every single second waiting for the next chapter to be put into motion.

Tonight would be another night when all the years of careful planning would come to fruition. It had been a long process of selection, grooming, training, watching as the choices were whittled away. The executioners were almost as flawed as the bastards chosen to die; weak, pathetic specimens who didn't deserve the accolade of being chosen.

The vision of Samson falling through the darkness swam into Ice's mind, the moment when the cable tightened around his neck playing and replaying. It would have been good to watch him die… but now there was another.

Number Two was primed and ready. The parcel had been delivered; the instructions given, the chase about to commence. Ice shuddered with pleasure at the thought, but a note of caution resonated; care would be required. Number Two wasn't like Samson. Samson had been strong-willed while this one was fragile; strong in body but delicate in mind, chosen and moulded for exactly this reason. This one was desperate to please, but this one needed closer supervision.

A noise broke through the silence; the thud of footsteps as the neighbours returned, slamming through the door, pounding and pounding across the flooring, dragging Ice back to her childhood, hiding behind the armchair. She watched, trembling, as her father meted out his violence, the black boots, uniform trousers, epaulettes, symbols of his dominance and infallibility. She saw her mother's body lying broken at the foot of the stairs again. She heard his voice singing, each word mocking their frailty, sweating with pleasure as he hunted her out. But this time he couldn't find her. He wouldn't find her.

This time the power would be hers.

Tonight, she would be there watching, waiting, taking part. This one had been specially selected. This one used violence, just as her father had; and this one had also got away with the crime. She wanted to watch this one die. It would be a fitting epitaph.

A cat yowled in a nearby yard breaking her reverie. Anticipation crackled all around in the hot, balmy air. She bent down, picking up the single red rose that lay on the cabinet, feeling the thorns, sharp on its stem. Carefully, she snapped one off, before pushing it into the soft skin of her hand, trembling momentarily at the prick of pain as the blood rushed to the surface. With pain came pleasure. She lifted her hand, sucking on the tiny wound, licking away the small globule of sweet-tasting blood as it appeared. The pain receded as she concentrated on the hours to come.

If everything went to plan the pleasure would be intense.

Chapter 34

The call from Lisa Forrester took Charlie by surprise. She pressed the phone to her ear as Hunter, Paul and the DCI hushed. She could barely make out the whispered words, but the meaning was clear.

'Dennis has just come in. 'E's busy in the other room, so I thought I'd catch you quick. I weren't expecting 'im back this soon, but Shirley must 'ave sprung 'im. I only got round to speaking to 'er this morning. Wanted a quiet night to meself last night, see. You said for me to tell yer if there was something 'appening, right?' She paused.

'Yes that's right, what's happened, Lisa?'

'Well, Shirley weren't happy when I said 'e was in the nick. Not happy at all; started swearing and cursing. Said I 'ad to be bleedin' jokin', she 'as something arranged for 'im to do this evening but didn't say what, an' I didn't ask. I know better than that. When I left, she said she would get straight on to it. Seems like she 'as. She's a bloody miracle worker. I know who to call next time I'm in bother meself now.'

The phone went dead before Charlie could say anything more, ringing off to the sound of laughter. Once again it appeared that Shirley Sangster was making a mockery of the system. She tapped in the number to Brixton custody office and confirmed the news, shaking her head at the custody sergeant's words.

When she rang off, the others were all staring at her open-mouthed.

Charlie shoved her phone in her pocket. 'They've released Dennis Walters,' she said flatly. 'Shirley Sangster turned up at the front office with Justin Latchmere kicking off and they've managed to get him bailed out.'

'On what grounds?' Hunter was fuming.

'On the grounds that we know who he is and where he lives… and we haven't been able to get the drugs analysed yet, or the phone downloaded. The custody sergeant didn't think that would be possible within the twenty-four hours that we have, particularly with it being the weekend. Apparently, he's been trying to contact you for the last hour or so, guv,' she looked towards Hunter. 'But he couldn't get through, so in the end he made the decision to bail him for six weeks. Oh, and he kept Walters' phone obviously, so it can be downloaded, so now we don't even have a number for him.'

Hunter pulled his phone out and swore. She could see from where she stood that the screen was showing seven missed calls. 'Damn it. He could have waited until we did make contact.'

'I think he thought he was doing us a favour. He didn't know the background to Walters' arrest, just that he was in for possession with intent... which is two a penny in Lambeth.'

'Maybe if you'd answered your phone,' DCI O'Connor commented, raising his eyebrows at Hunter. 'This wouldn't have happened.'

Hunter shot to his feet, frowning angrily. 'Maybe, with respect sir, you'd like to take over. I'll be going with Naz and Sabira to Heathrow, as planned, to assist them in arresting their suspect. I was going to arrange a replacement to stand in for me, but I can see I'm obviously more of a hindrance here. I'd be better use with them.'

With that, Hunter turned tail and disappeared out through the door. Charlie watched as he stormed away, she'd never seen him react in that way before. She made her excuses and went after him, but by the time she'd caught up, he was talking to Naz and Sabira in the office.

Perhaps realising why she'd followed him, he turned towards her, his voice formal. 'I'll see you later when I've finished helping Naz and Sabira. They've come in especially after receiving information yesterday that the Punjabi suspect has booked flights and is scheduled to try to leave the country this evening. I'll be heading towards Heathrow with them, to liaise with the airport police to get the suspect apprehended before he leaves. If you need me I'll be on the phone.' He made a point of emphasising his last words as if blaming her for mentioning the missed calls a few minutes earlier. 'DCI O'Connor and I are not exactly on the same wavelength at the moment. You can work out your next course of action with him.'

Charlie stood, her cheeks burning red, while Naz and Sabira looked on clearly confused at the scene playing out in front of them. There was nothing she could say or do, and as he turned his back on her to speak further with her two colleagues; she felt the sting of disapproval as hard as if he'd slapped her around the face.

*

DCI O'Connor was certainly taking charge. By the time Charlie returned, Paul had started the paperwork to get directed surveillance targeting both Shirley Sangster and Dennis Walters up and running. The DCI himself, was making calls to get the right people teed up ready to go as soon as possible. They needed more evidence of what exactly Shirley Sangster had in mind for Dennis Walters to do this evening but, more importantly, they needed to prevent another murder taking place. Forensics, phone downloads, CCTV evidence all took time and

Samson Powell had killed three officers within a very short spell.

With the killings looking to have restarted with a new perpetrator, there was every likelihood that the suspect, or suspects, organising things in the background could work just as fast again... and they had to consider Hayley Boyle to be part of the conspiracy now too. Whether she was the one co-ordinating the whole killing spree; a fully participating partner; or just a loose tongue, they didn't know. Either way, it appeared that she was the conduit for the methodology.

Charlie set to work on a full briefing, returning to the office to do so. She knew the ins and outs of the case better than anyone and could put life to the faces she spoke about. Hunter, Naz and Sabira were leaving as she walked in; it was clear the two girls still didn't know what was going on, any more than she did. Sadly, she watched them go; it didn't feel right with the team split.

The room became quiet. Charlie copied the faces of Sangster and Walters on to the briefing. The role of Hayley Boyle was not yet to be mentioned. DCI O'Connor was still liaising with Ray Hooper at DPS, to discuss the best way forward in dealing with her.

Paul came in with the paperwork, printed and authorised, and walked across to where she sat. Within minutes Bet pushed the door open and came bustling through too. Charlie looked up, and the sight of her friend and confidante lifted her spirits immediately.

'Nothing like a Saturday afternoon call-out,' Bet said cheerily. 'Not that I mind. There was nothing on the box apart from the usual weekend sport and Dave, bless him, had already fallen asleep, snoring lustily after drinking a few beers and shouting at the horse racing.' She paused for a few seconds before chortling out loud. 'It's the only thing he does lustily these days, before you ask, Paul.'

Charlie grinned. It was good to have the pair of them with her.

A text message pinged on to her phone. Looking down, she read Sabira's words, promising to help out just as soon as she and Naz could. She smiled and typed her thanks, ignoring the question at the end of Sabira's message asking what was up with Hunter. She didn't know the answer.

'Is Nick coming in?' she asked instead, guessing the reply before Paul confirmed it.

'Nah. Not answering his phone. Definitely not a team player.'

'No. He's just a player,' Bet gave Charlie a nudge. 'You'd be better off waiting for Ben to get his act together than falling for Nick's charms.'

Before she could answer, the door opened again and a slow trickle of officers began to appear, conjured up from the weekend list of on-call surveillance staff.

When the room was full to bursting DCI O'Connor appeared. His hair looked to have been recently brushed, his tie was fixed in place and he appeared to have changed into a crease-free matching cream suit.

'Thank you all for coming at such short notice, ladies and gents. DC Stafford here will brief you on the job and our subjects and then you will be split into four; two surveillance teams with an arrest squad attached to each, and a skipper on each taking the lead. If you need any checks or information, come straight through to our intel cell, which will be staffed by Bet.' He pointed towards her and she lifted her hand in acknowledgement. 'I will be co-ordinating the operation with the help of two inspectors. If I get called away for any reason, then please defer to them. Right, without further ado.'

He nodded towards Charlie who ran through the slides, explaining the associations and the main subjects, before finishing on a slide with a split screen showing the two faces of Dennis Walters and Shirley Sangster.'

'Those are your two main subjects,' DCI O'Connor concluded, as Charlie sat down. 'Do not attempt to detain them without prior authority and do not, whatever you do, let them out of your sight.

I'm not being overdramatic when I say the safety of every officer in the Met could be in your hands and… more to the point, the press will be all over us if we fail. If they get a sniff that we've screwed up, there'll be a few more officers whose heads will roll.'

*

It didn't take long before everyone was deployed. One surveillance team and an arrest squad were watching Walters' block in the Elephant and Castle, code named OP1, and the other team was holed up near Sangster's house, on the Angell Town Estate, OP2. It would be a difficult operation; the locals on both estates were notoriously wary of strangers, but Walters and Sangster needed to be monitored for as long as it took. They couldn't risk leaving them to their own devices.

Charlie was driving an unmarked car with Paul as her radio operator and the DCI maintaining overall control from the rear. They parked up in a quiet street between the two addresses to monitor the three radio channels in use.

Declan O'Connor was in his element. It had obviously been a while since he'd got out of the office and done 'proper' police work, as Hunter always called it. He had been liaising almost constantly with Ray Hooper and was providing updates as he got them. They now had a small team of trusted tech guys continually cell-siting the mobiles of Shirley Sangster and Hayley Boyle to monitor their up-to-date locations. The DCI had also ordered an immediate download of Jason Lloyd's phone as a matter of urgency, while they waited for any possible forensics from the crime scene. Now they had a live operation running they needed to research any phone contacts he might have inadvertently made with his killer and to track back to dating websites used in the hours, days and weeks leading up to his murder. If they could find details of relevant conversations, they may then be able to establish the email details of the contacts and IP addresses for the computers used. The chances of identifying Lloyd's murderer were slim but they had to try; they couldn't afford not to.

'All units standby, there's movement at OP1. Door opened and male out, out, out. Positive ID on Subject 1, Dennis Walters, wearing black T-shirt and black trousers with a brown belt, carrying a dark-coloured rucksack. He's walking along the landing and now into the lift. Standby.'

'Here we go,' Charlie felt her pulse rate increase.

'Out of the lift now and on foot towards the shopping centre.'

'All units standby, there's movement at OP2.' The other radio channel sparked up into life. 'Subject 2 out of venue, Positive ID on Shirley Sangster, wearing dark leggings, long red top and heels. Turning right, right, right.'

Charlie listened as both subjects were tracked on foot. Walters disappeared straight into the underground station, closely followed by an undercover officer, the wait nerve-wracking until he finally appeared out on to the streets of Stockwell. Sangster was no less easy, walking through a maze of alleyways, into the middle of Brixton and the hustle and bustle of Saturday-evening revellers.

'They're heading towards each other,' Paul commented as the follows continued.

'Walters is now on Acre Lane, heading east towards Brixton, just crossed over on to the South footway.'

'Sangster is now on Acre Lane, heading west towards Stockwell, crossing over on to the South footway.'

'They are literally going to bump into each other in a minute.' Charlie held her breath.

'Standby, Walters has stopped, eyes about and in, in, in to "Hair Today" hairdressers at junction with Holborn Street.'

'Standby, Sangster crossing Holborn Street and in, in, in to hairdressers called "Hair Today".

Both radio channels went quiet. Charlie could almost hear her own heartbeat thumping within the interior of the car.

Bet called up on the third channel, her voice serious. 'Boss, I've done some immediate checks and "Hair Today" is flagged with a firearms warning marker. It's shown as a front for a busy bar, used by many of the high-ranking Acre Lane gang members in Brixton. Entry is either through the hairdressers and down into a large basement or through a side entrance from a small car park. The bar is unlicensed at present and the licensing department at Lambeth are in the process of taking steps to get it closed. A firearm was discharged at the venue last weekend.'

'Damn it,' DCI O'Connor muttered. 'That's all I need. We have no idea what our subjects are doing and there's no way I can risk sending any surveillance guys in, they'd stand out a mile... and it would take a full scale armed op for any uniform to enter.'

'Standby. Subject 1, Walters out, out. Eyes about. Crossing Acre Lane and east towards Brixton town centre. On, on, on.' There was a pause. 'Stopped now, talking with a group of males on the corner outside KFC. I'm walking past. I need someone else to take over the eye.'

There was another pause.

'Subject in sight,' another voice came on to the channel. 'But I'm a long way off. Subject moving away now, heading north in Brixton Road, he's jogging across the main road, through traffic towards Brixton underground station. Standby, loss, loss, between moving buses. Any other units nearby?' The radio became a hive of activity, various units calling up to assist. Mobile and foot units converged and there was a general melee of voices and movements.

'Come on, come on,' DCI O'Connor growled. 'Find him, for fuck's sake. We can't afford to lose him now.'

Charlie held her breath. The heat in the car was reaching boiling point. She opened the window and a waft of air brought with it the statement that Dennis Walters was confirmed as lost by the surveillance team. Cars were being despatched to the nearest underground stations on the line and other units were crawling all over the town centre trying to re-establish sight of their subject but there wasn't much hope. The railway station lay behind the underground station and a whole array of buses passed through the centre of town. Walters could have slipped on to any one of these, or he could have just passed across the road right in front of them, secreted within a group of revellers and into one of the numerous passages that led to a labyrinth of alleyways criss-crossing the main shopping area.

'Fucking hell,' DCI O'Connor exploded. 'Both our subjects are lost to us now and we haven't a clue what they're up to. Sangster could be in that bar all night co-ordinating things and we don't have a mobile number to track Walters.' He picked up his phone and keyed in a number, speaking urgently to Ray Hooper.

Charlie waited, thinking through what she would do if she had to make the decision. In her book there was only one option left and it meant showing their hand earlier than they would have liked… but they had no choice.

'Head towards Kew and get shifting,' the DCI commanded, as if reading her mind. 'We're going to have to see what Hayley Boyle knows.'

Chapter 35

Hayley Boyle lived on the first floor of a converted house, almost opposite Kew Gardens, home to one of the largest living botanical plant collections in the world. Paul gave a low whistle as they got closer; the houses seemed to get larger and more spacious with every mile they travelled.

As they pulled up outside, Charlie peered up at the windows, willing her to be in. Paul was to remain in the car, overseeing any liaison with Ray Hooper, Bet or the surveillance units, allowing her and DCI O'Connor to speak with Boyle. The mobile phone number they had for her was sited to the address but they all knew that, in this investigation, that meant nothing. The curtains were open and a light was on.

DCI O'Connor climbed out of the car and strode up the path towards the house, pushing the doorbell several times. A face appeared at the window, squinting down at the visitors with a frown. It was Hayley Boyle.

Charlie jumped out of their car and joined the DCI, relief washing over her. At least they might get some answers now.

The door was opened and the detective sergeant stood in front of them, flanked by her husband, who

Charlie recalled was a superintendent. He was older than she, grey-haired and heavy-jawed, with glasses that perched on the end of his nose.

'Can we come in, Hayley?' DCI O'Connor said, taking a step forward.

'It's Saturday evening and this looks official. Can't it wait?' her husband stayed firmly planted in front of them.

'No, it can't wait,' the DCI drew his other foot level so that he was standing directly in the husband's space. Their eyes locked, neither wanting to back down first.

Charlie turned to Hayley Boyle.

'Please, Hayley. It is actually very important. Otherwise we wouldn't have come.' Charlie looked directly at the sergeant, who gave the slightest of nods in return, before placing one hand on her husband's arm. The other hand flew to the same crucifix necklace she always wore, fingering each angle of the cross.

'It's alright Andrew, I'll deal with this.'

Andrew Boyle turned and looked at her questioningly, before stepping to one side. DCI O'Connor walked forward immediately, starting towards the stairs, with the rest of them scampering upwards in his wake.

The flat was shabbier than Charlie had expected, piles of books and files of correspondence stacked haphazardly on a range of bookshelves along one wall of the lounge. A large fan circulated air from one corner of the room; the breeze expelled blowing the edges of loose paperwork up and down as it oscillated slowly from one side to the other. An arrangement of slightly dusty dried flowers swayed in time to the fan at the base of an ornate black Victorian fireplace.

DCI O'Connor positioned himself in front of the fireplace, standing with arms folded in centre stage. The rest of them sat stony-faced around a cluttered dining room table.

'It's come to our notice that confidential information may be getting leaked to members of the public,' he started. 'And we've got reason to think it might be coming from your office.' He was like a bull in a china shop and Charlie could see, by the looks on both their faces, that their guards had gone up. Neither spoke.

'Hayley, I've spoken with your Chief Superintendent, Ray Hooper, and he's found some irregularities in your paperwork,' he tried again.

Andrew Boyle stood up and shook his head. 'And you've chosen a Saturday evening to come and tell Hayley this!' He turned to his wife. 'Hayley, you know the proper procedures for doing this, as do I. And it isn't in your own house at the weekend. May I advise you not to say a word until you've been properly briefed by a federation representative and have been served with the appropriate paperwork?'

'In that case I might have to think about arresting you.' The DCI was making things worse.

Hayley Boyle gasped audibly and her hand flew to her mouth. If she was the brains behind the killing spree, her lips would now be sealed.

Her husband turned towards her and then spun around, squaring up to the DCI.

'I don't know what this is about, but I think you should either arrest my wife and allow her to seek proper legal advice or get out. This conversation is now concluded.'

Charlie stared at both men. If Hayley Boyle was indeed implicated with Sangster and Walters they desperately needed to know. Either option was untenable. Walking out would leave them with nothing. Arrest would lead to a silent impasse.

'DS Boyle,' she turned to the woman, hoping that neither the DCI nor Andrew Boyle would cut her down. 'Do you remember when we last spoke, I asked you about Shirley Sangster?'

The mention of her name seemed to send a shock wave across the room, silencing them all. Hayley Boyle nodded mutely, her face visibly paling. She put her hand out on her husband's arm again, staying him from speaking further.

Charlie ploughed on, 'You said she surrounded herself with the wrong sort of people, and we wondered whether she could have influenced one of them to kill Leonard Cookson.' The DS was staring at her, with the same look of anxiety as she'd seen before, her hands twisting the crucifix around her neck manically.

Charlie continued. 'We think she might be in the process of doing that again tonight, but we need your help. She seems to know exactly which complaints each officer had against them. You know her well. Could you have inadvertently let slip any information?'

She needed to give the DS an escape route.

'Chief Superintendent Hooper has found a spreadsheet on your computer…' DCI O'Connor interrupted.

Andrew Boyle broke his silence. 'Hayley, you don't have to say a thing.'

Charlie put her hand up towards both men. Neither was helping.

'Hayley, please. You know what could be at stake. We've looked at your phone data and you received a phone call on Monday 26th June, from the same person Samuel Powell had as a contact on the phone we found near him, when he committed suicide. It was the only number Samson had on his cheap Nokia and it wasn't assigned to a contact on your phone. Could that number have belonged to Shirley Sangster, Hayley? You spoke to her earlier that day on her usual number; maybe there was something wrong with her phone, maybe she phoned back on a different number to ask you something else? Do you remember speaking to her again? It would have been after DCI O'Connor here cancelled your meeting with Hunter and me. Could you have accidentally passed on any snippet of information that could have alerted her to the fact that we knew that Samuel Powell was Cookson's killer?'

Hayley Boyle looked from Charlie to her husband, before sitting down suddenly. When she next looked up, her eyes were filled with apprehension.

'Shirley Sangster phones every Monday morning to check on my progress in her case. I spoke to her for a while about how Leonard Cookson's death might affect it. But I remember that later call, I remember it well... but it wasn't from Shirley Sangster.'

Chapter 36

The storm was getting closer. Rain fell sporadically. Clouds formed dark and livid, one minute rolling angrily in the sky above, the next swept away impatiently by a gust of wind. The sun looked diminished in the gathering squall; a small ball of flame skulking out intermittently from behind the storm clouds to paint a red hue across the evening sky. In a few hours, it would disappear behind the horizon completely, leaving the city shrouded in darkness.

A murmuration of starlings swirled in a maelstrom of wings, soaring up and down in the foreground, appearing and disappearing behind the flat roofs of an estate of commercial buildings. They seemed out of place in the setting, but their flight was in sync, never settling in one place, rising and falling as if in one body heaving and gasping in its death throes.

He watched the birds' antics, their swell matching the movement of his chest. He could feel his heart beating hard and fast as the time pushed onwards. The blade of the knife burnt hot in his pocket, the metallic cold of the handcuffs a dead weight in his other.

A low rumble built to a crescendo as a jet roared overhead, a bright arrow of lights across the sky. He watched as it disappeared into the blur of clouds, its presence replaced within minutes by the next, its noise ebbing and flowing around the nearby buildings.

A gate opened between the walls in his immediate view and a van emerged, heavy on its axles, laden down with boxes for delivery to the nearby warehouses. The vehicle stopped in front of the gates and the driver put a phone to his ear, his head nodding with the movement of his lips.

He watched for a while, before pulling out his new Nokia throwaway mobile phone and checking the screen. It was nearly six thirty.

Very soon he would be collecting Ice and together they would despatch their next victim.

*

'Well, if it wasn't Shirley Sangster, who the hell was it?' Charlie frowned.

Hayley Boyle's face was white as she stared back at her. 'It was Brenda Leach, from the IPCC. She phoned to ask if the meeting with you and DI Hunter had been arranged, as she wanted to conclude her recommendations finally.'

'On an unknown number?'

'Yes, she does have a regular number, but she often phoned on different numbers. I asked her about it once and she said she uses a new SIM card when dealing with each separate case. She had to phone some fairly unsavoury people and she didn't like them having a number they could hassle her on at all hours of the day or night. I didn't think anything more about it after that. It seemed to make good sense at the time. I didn't bother to save any of her random numbers but I remember the call.'

'You said you remembered it well. Any particular reason?'

'Because, by the end of the call she seemed so interested! Even more so than usual. We work on many cases together and liaise a lot. She keeps me on my toes, checking on the progress of investigations and pushing to get interviews arranged and jobs concluded. She will oversee our investigations but she doesn't have day-to-day access to them like I do. She'll sometimes phone me and ask when she can get hold of an officer and I'll help her out with details of what shifts they're on.' She looked round from one to the other. 'I don't know what's going on here or why that number was on Samson Powell's phone. What on Earth would he be speaking to her about?'

Charlie stared at the woman, trying to work out whether she was knowingly giving out information or naively being used. As if to elaborate, Hayley Boyle pulled a file from one of the shelves and opened it, flipping through several copies of spreadsheets.

'I know I shouldn't really do this,' she glanced at DCI O'Connor. 'But it's just so I can see more easily which jobs we're all working on. I work bloody hard. I always have. My caseload is greater than any other officer working on my unit.' She pointed to where her name was shown highlighted in yellow against case after case. 'The police service is a great place to work. The vast majority of officers are good, moral, hard-working men and women, but there are a few corrupt ones who give us all a bad name. I want to root them out; always have, and that's why I've stayed in this unit for so long. Brenda Leach wants the same. We work very well together.'

'So why were you so nervous when we spoke about Shirley Sangster?'

Hayley Boyle pulled at the crucifix hard, twisting it round and round between her fingers. She looked between her husband and the DCI.

'I was always so careful when I met Shirley, or spoke to her. She does, like I say, have so many connections within the community and a deeply rooted hatred of the police because of what happened to Troy and other stuff previously. She's a very powerful woman… and she knows Brenda Leach well. Brenda was overseeing Troy's complaint.' She stared down at the floor.

'That doesn't explain why you were so cagey about Shirley Sangster with me.'

Hayley Boyle continued to stare at the floor. 'Well, I met Shirley a couple of months ago. It was the last meeting of the day and I had printed off one of my spreadsheets. When I got home I couldn't find it, even though I looked everywhere. I thought I might have mislaid it and that perhaps Shirley had picked it up. Obviously there are confidential details about the actual complaints on it that she should never be privy to... and I knew I'd get in trouble if anyone found out I'd been doing this. When these murders started I was worried that somehow the paperwork had fallen into the wrong hands.'

'You're right to be worried too,' the DCI warned. 'It is totally inappropriate what you've been doing.'

Andrew Boyle shook his head at his wife and sighed heavily, as if in disbelief.

'And you didn't think to tell me that, when I was talking to you about Shirley Sangster and the murders?' Charlie asked, ignoring the DCI's comment.

'Well, by that time you had your man and the other idea about Sangster being involved sounded a bit fanciful. I didn't really think it would matter... and I didn't want to get into trouble after all the work I've done.'

'DS Boyle, your work could be the reason why these police officers have met their deaths in the way they have,' Declan O'Connor almost shouted. 'And believe me, they're not the ways you or I would choose to go.'

The atmosphere was getting heated again. Hayley Boyle had voiced what Hunter had thought.

Charlie dropped her voice. She wished she had Hunter with her now to run through everything with. 'Are you aware another police officer was found murdered yesterday?' she said eventually. 'And there'll almost certainly be more to follow.'

DS Boyle was silent.

'What exactly did you tell Brenda Leach when you spoke to her that morning?'

'I told her that a meeting with you and DI Hunter had been arranged for two o'clock that day, but that it had just been postponed as you had a named suspect for the case you were working on.' She stopped talking and looked at the DCI. 'You didn't tell me who you had, though, so I didn't give any names away.'

'You might not have had to.' Charlie was thinking fast. 'Not if she already knew.'

*

The time had come. He had his instructions clearly and concisely from Ice. He closed his eyes momentarily and his mind focussed on what he had to do.

'Come to the location I instructed earlier and be prepared. This is the one that you've been waiting for, the one I promised you. This one is for you. I will instruct you in detail on your arrival. Come now.'

He could feel his heart beating hard in his chest as the memories crowded into his brain, a jumble of emotions, fear, hatred, longing. He turned the switch and the engine growled into life, its pitch rising and falling with the movement of his foot. He needed to get this right. He had waited half his life for this opportunity.

*

Charlie stared at the fireplace in Hayley Boyle's flat trying to process the information. Her head was swimming. They still didn't know what Boyle's involvement was, but Brenda Leach had now been added to the list of suspects, and Boyle had just confirmed that Sangster was well known to Leach. So even if Brenda Leach was Ice, they still couldn't rule out Shirley Sangster or Dennis Walters. With them all knowing each other, it was possible that Ice might not even be a single person; it could be a code name they all used together. The waters were even muddier than before.

Paul had been briefed on what had been said and had spoken in confidence to Bet who was now in the process of rechecking any possible texts or conversations between the group of suspects, as well as getting as much information on Brenda Leach as possible. They needed to know where she lived and everything about her. Why was she the only contact on Samson's burner phone and what knowledge did they have of each other prior to his suicide?

DCI O'Connor had also apprised Ray Hooper, who was getting his team to work on the regular phone number Brenda Leach normally used. Progress had been made on the download of Jason Lloyd's mobile and they had found several text conversations that appeared to have followed on from contacts with three possible women from the Tinder dating app. Could one of these women be Brenda Leach or Shirley Sangster, or could it be another foot soldier purporting to be a woman?

Charlie felt her frustration building again. They had no idea at this point where Brenda Leach lived or where she was. Shirley Sangster was still in the bar in Brixton as far as they knew; and Dennis Walters was still missing. Every step forward seemed to lead to several steps back.

'For fuck's sake,' she said, moving across to the table and gazing down at Hayley Boyle's spreadsheet. 'Where are we supposed to go from here? We don't know where all our suspects are and, worse still, any one of these officers could be the next target.'

Hayley Boyle walked up behind her and stared at the front page.

'Oh my God,' she said suddenly, taking Charlie by the arm and gripping it tightly. 'I bet I can guess. If Brenda Leach is involved, she has a real thing about this officer.' With her other hand, she pointed towards the page, her finger wavering over a name that Charlie knew only too well.

DCI O'Connor stepped forward and stared at where the detective sergeant's finger was pointing.

'Shit,' he swore out loud. 'I gave Brenda Leach his work mobile number yesterday and mentioned he was due at Heathrow today to assist with a job and to contact him direct if she wanted a meet. I was fed up of trying and I know you hadn't had much luck either. She said she would ring. She wanted to get it sorted before she went on holiday this weekend.'

'Holiday? She's not going on holiday,' Hayley Boyle said quietly. 'She was trying to tie up all her loose ends because she's actually retiring.'

The comment was met with silence. Charlie ran her hands through her hair, panic threatening to overwhelm her. She knew the exact nature of the complaint. She took a deep breath before opening her mouth. 'If Brenda Leach really is retiring and you're right in your assumption Hayley, … my guess is that she'll want her last job to go with a bang.'

*

Hunter wasn't picking up. They had all tried, on both his phones and there was no response.

In one way it was a good thing. If he wasn't answering the phone to them, he was probably not answering the phone to anyone, but on the other hand, it might just be them he was ignoring because of their spat. Charlie was still upset by the events of earlier and this discomfiture was being exacerbated by his silence. It wasn't like him at all.

She called Naz, who quickly agreed to try to find him. She and Sabira were both busy dealing with their prisoner at Heathrow, the suspect having been apprehended as he waited in line to board the jet to India. Hunter had been on hand to assist with the arrangements and the actual arrest, but after their arrival back to custody had made his excuses and disappeared. They would return the call if they located him.

On a whim, she dialled his home number, putting the call on speakerphone so the DCI could hear the conversation. Perhaps Mrs H, his wife, could shed some light on where he was. The phone was answered immediately and a voice came on the line.

'Charlie, is that you?'

'Hi, Mrs H, yes it is,' she said, trying to keep the worry out of her tone. What she was doing was almost the metaphorical knock on the door all partners feared and, if Hunter was right, then Mrs H would know straight away that something was wrong. 'I was just trying to track Hunter down. You know what he's like with his phones.' She tried to make light of the comment but knew straight away that she'd been unsuccessful.

'He's disappeared, hasn't he?'

She hesitated and the momentary silence emphasised her failure to hide her worry.

'Oh Charlie, he has, hasn't he? He's been acting so strangely the last few weeks. I almost phoned you to find out what was going on, but I knew if he found out, he'd be cross and I didn't want to make matters worse.'

'I'm sure he's fine, Mrs H. He's probably out of phone range or just doesn't want to speak to us.'

'Charlie, that's the trouble. It's as if he's cut himself off from you guys in the office... especially you... and that's just not like him. He thinks he let you down badly on that last job and that he's losing it. He's wandering around with a continual frown on his face. His blood pressure has rocketed sky-high and his tablets don't seem to be working like they should. He can't seem to focus on anything and he keeps saying that you'd all be better off without him.'

'You know that's not true,' Charlie spluttered, her voice catching. 'Hunter did absolutely nothing wrong. I would have done exactly the same. He saved my life with his quick thinking and I told him that… and I've told the people investigating the case that too.' She looked pointedly towards Hayley Boyle who had stopped gathering together some things to listen.

'I know that, Charlie. He told me what you'd said. He was actually very touched by your comments, not that he would ever tell you. You've hit the nail on the head, though. It's the ongoing investigation that has really rattled him. You know what he's like. He just wants to get on with the job and it just seems to be dragging on and on. He thinks they're gunning for him. Every time he's interviewed he gets more convinced that he failed you.'

'Which is probably why he keeps avoiding yet another interview." She didn't mention her desperate hope that he had avoided it again this time. 'OK then, Mrs H. Let me know if he does get in touch and I'll do the same. I'm sure it's Hunter just being Hunter.'

'That's exactly the trouble though, Charlie,' she hesitated. 'At the moment, Hunter is not being Hunter.'

Hayley Boyle stepped out into the muggy heat of the evening behind DCI O'Connor and took a deep breath. All her life she had tried to do the right thing but now her career was in ruins and she would have to fight to avoid being branded as crooked as the cops she'd fought so hard to get punished. Even her own husband seemed disappointed with her. She thought back to when she'd first started working with Brenda Leach. Everything had seemed so perfect; another woman as focussed on ridding the service of bad apples as she was. As time had progressed and their work together had continued she had allowed Brenda more and more information. They had spoken regularly; met for coffee even. Now it had all backfired spectacularly.

Had Brenda been passing on the information to Shirley Sangster or had Shirley found the spreadsheet she'd mislaid… and why was Brenda in direct contact with Samson Powell? Whatever the answers, she was deep in the shit.

She climbed into the back of the police car; her promise to do whatever she could, seemingly of little use. With any luck she could try and repair some of the damage to her career, and marriage even. Leaning back, her head against the seat, she let her mind run through the last few conversations and meetings she'd had with Brenda Leach, the woman that up until now she had trusted so much. Had she said anything that she shouldn't? Had she disclosed any documents that were confidential? Had she shown her any exhibits that could give rise to controversy?

Her mind focussed on the last case they had discussed, over a sea of exhibits each taken and examined, one by one from boxes packed and stored in the property office at Brixton police station. It was the case in which Leonard Cookson had attracted his perjury complaint, one that was close to the heart of both women of whom they had just spoken. Hayley strained to remember the meeting, how she had been called to one side to answer the phone, how when she had turned back, the boxes had been repacked. She closed her eyes to recall the moment. How careful had she been at ensuring all the exhibits had been replaced?

Her warrant card lay on her lap, along with her house keys and mobile phone. She opened the wallet, glancing down at her image alongside the words 'Police Officer' and the crest of the Metropolitan Police Service. As Charlie climbed in beside her, Hayley Boyle remembered the words her backseat colleague had so recently uttered about Leach's last job going with a bang. She thought of Hunter and how they hadn't been able to contact him. His actions had been exemplary. He had done nothing wrong. She knew that... but had she kept him believing that he had. She recalled the words of worry Mrs Hunter had so recently spoken about her husband, feeling they were out to get him, gunning for him.

She stared at her own photograph, so young and enthusiastic to do the right thing, and thought back to the scene in the property office, as a wave of pure dread ran up her spine.

Chapter 37

'I don't care what time it is on a Saturday evening, constable. You get your supervisor to find the keys and go and check the property store now. And I mean now.' The DCI's expression was thunderous. Paul was now driving, while Charlie and Hayley Boyle huddled in the rear, all three silently listening as he vented his anger on the recipient of each call. Charlie could see Hayley's hands visibly shaking as she turned the crucifix round and round with her fingers.

The surveillance teams were next.

'Any more sightings of Subject 1, Walters?' he shouted down the radio.

'No, sir, nothing at present. We've got units situated at his home address and where he was last seen and others on mobile patrol at places where he's been stopped in the past. Hopefully we'll pick him up again at some point and I'll come straight back to you.'

'Hopefully is not good enough!' DCI O'Connor bellowed, abruptly finishing the transmission.

'Any sightings of subject 2, Sangster,' he called up the other team.

'Not yet, sir,' the sergeant sounded sheepish. 'Or at least not on foot. We believe she is still within the hairdressers or bar, but there is vehicular access to a small, fenced-off car park at the rear and there have been some cars coming and going. We've got an OP fairly close to the rear and have been checking the vehicles as they leave as best we can. So far we haven't seen any females dressed in a red shirt in any of the vehicles.'

'Are you telling me that your IDs are based on what colour shirt the occupants are wearing?!'

'It's all we have to go on, sir. We can't get close enough to see them facially and some of the cars have tinted glass. It's going to get even harder with the light starting to fade.'

'So, you're saying that if she happened to have changed her shirt, or put a jacket over the top, or is sitting behind tints, you might have missed her?'

There was a long pause, during which time the DCI's face turned crimson with rage.

'We're doing our best, sir. Checks are being run on every car that leaves and, so far, none are connected directly to her or any of her family members.'

'That bloody woman knows everyone in the area. She probably knows everyone in the building. From what you say she could have disappeared in any one of the vehicles and she could be anywhere by now.'

'Not all of them, sir. We can definitely discount some.' The voice sounded desperate.

'She only bloody well needs one!' the DCI roared. He threw the radio down into the foot well in front of him and stared out of the side window at the changing landscape as it sped by. They were on their way to an address that Bet had tracked down for Brenda Leach, by contacting the 24-hour security officer at her office and getting the registration number of the vehicle, she was authorised to use. This information had furnished them with her usual car and its registered address.

Bet had a way of separating the wheat from the chaff; the evidence from the inconsequential. She was invaluable in any crisis and was competent and composed, as was Hunter. They were certainly missing him and his calm authority now.

Charlie picked up her phone and dialled his number once more, listening to the dialling tone as it rang out again. At least the phone was still switched on and that would make cell-siting possible. Ray Hooper was on to it already.

Her thoughts were interrupted by the DCI's mobile ringtone. He pressed the speaker and a voice boomed out across the interior of the car.

'There's no trace of those two exhibits you asked for, in any of the boxes that are shown for the Troy

Sangster case. I've checked through them thoroughly several times.'

Hayley Boyle shrank down into her seat, burrowing even further into the upholstery than she had previously. Her voice was barely more than a whisper as she said the words that Charlie had feared more than anything since hearing her admission.

'So the handgun and the ammunition *are* missing.'

*

Charlie's mind was racing almost as fast as the car when Bet phoned.

'Hi, Charlie,' she started. 'I thought you'd be interested in this background info I've found so far on Brenda Leach. She's a very interesting character, all over the pages of Google. She's been working for the IPCC since 2010, but before then she seems to have made quite a habit of getting herself involved in a variety of other institutions, including churches, prisons and psychiatric hospitals, both as a paid employee but also doing voluntary work.'

'Go on,' Charlie prompted, remembering Anna's words about Ted Bundy – successful, academically astute, charismatic, charming… and excellent at spotting the weak and vulnerable.

'Anyway, between 2004 and 2009 she worked at Bethlem Royal Hospital in Beckenham.'

'Isn't that where Samson Powell was sectioned after the boiling water incident with Lisa?'

'Yes it is, and he would have been there at the same time.'

'And Dennis Walters?'

'I'm working on it. They could have met through Samson or Shirley Sangster, but it's also quite possible he met Leach at one of the prisons at some point.'

'Shit! If that is the link with Samson and she recruited him all these years later… how many others could she have lined up ready to use?'

She thanked Bet and leant back in her seat, listening to DCI O'Connor updating Ray Hooper from DPS. They were running out of time fast.

'As well as continuing to try to locate DI Hunter, we need up-to-date tracking on the mobile phone numbers I have for Brenda Leach, and still on Shirley Sangster please, guv,' the DCI was saying. 'And I need them ASAP. If we're going on the premise that the punishment is designed to fit the crime, then now we know that the firearm is missing, it's odds on that Hunter *is* the intended target.'

'I'll get my guys on to it straight away, Declan. It won't take long. In the meantime, we have an IP address for the computer that was used to make contact with Jason Lloyd.' Charlie pulled out a notebook. 'There were three possibles but two come back to reputable, young women, if a little lonely, so we've ruled them out for the time being. Our priority has to be the third, which is an internet cafe.' He read out the address which Charlie noted down.

'I'll phone Naz and Sabira in a second,' she called out. 'They're nearby.'

'Excellent. It's going to be difficult, but my guys have got dates and times of when the computer was used for each contact with Jason Lloyd. Most of these cafes have CCTV and most will take the basic details of who is using them and for how long. So get a unit to view it and if you can match someone using the computer with the times and dates we have established, then bingo, you could have your new recruit, or the one you think is organising it, or both.'

Charlie snapped her notebook shut. If only it were that easy.

*

The blue railings and dark brown brickwork of Heathrow police station were in sight as Hunter checked his watch. He'd been gone for over an hour while Naz and Sab got on with the process of booking their prisoner in, taking the chance to leave the claustrophobic atmosphere of the custody area in favour of views across the perimeter fence towards the runways and terminals of the UK's largest airport. Both his work and personal mobiles had been ringing constantly; calls from the DCI and Paul coming through on his work mobile and calls from Mrs H and Charlie coming in on his personal one. Both had been switched to silent. He needed time out.

He'd walked slowly, sipping on a coffee purchased from the nearby deli before standing for what seemed like hours watching the jumbos and double-decker airbuses thundering down the tarmac before lifting, as if by magic, gracefully into the air. All his life he had been in awe of aeroplanes; fascinated by their structure and the way five hundred tons of metal had the ability to transform into the intricate machinery required to take millions of passengers across the world to their holiday destinations of choice. As a boy, he'd run out into his garden every afternoon to watch the sleek, streamlined contours of Concorde as it passed overhead, the roar of its supersonic engine sending a shudder of pure delight through his young body. He still couldn't quite believe it was finally gone after watching footage of its last flight in 2003... until he'd stood on Westminster Bridge the following year, staring down at the wingless carcass encased inside the bowels of a barge, steaming slowly along the River Thames to be transferred to a larger vessel and taken to its final resting place in East Lothian, Scotland. Even now fourteen years on, he still missed the spectacle.

He turned one last time to watch a Virgin Atlantic aeroplane soar into the air just above him, its bright red tail colour easily recognisable, and smiled for the first time in days. The hour spent watching the aircraft had done him good.

As he neared the station, the weight shifted back on to his shoulders as his eyes alighted on the blue police lamp that graced the wall to the side of the entrance; the same old-fashioned style as was outside almost every police station in the Met. It too brought back memories of bygone years, thoughts of *Dixon of Dock Green*, *Z-cars*, *The Sweeney*, the era when the uniform was respected and no child would dare to be rude to a policeman.

He took his work mobile from his pocket and set it back to ring, wondering how long it would take before the DCI was hassling him again. It was a shame they had fallen out… but no doubt they'd resume working relations when the issue was sorted, if it could be. As if on cue, his personal mobile started to vibrate in his trouser pocket. He sighed heavily. Why couldn't they all leave him alone for just a few minutes? It was Charlie. He pulled out his handkerchief and wrapped it around the phone, shoving it deep into his trouser pocket. The sound was switched off, now he wanted to dull even the vibration against his leg. He'd let her down badly and just hearing her voice would be enough to awaken the realisation that his time in the career he loved was coming to an end, while hers was just beginning. If only he could have his time all over; be her age again, in action on the streets, catching the criminals instead of being bogged down with bureaucracy.

He pulled his warrant card out ready to show the civilian staff on the door and was just climbing the steps when he heard a call from behind.

'Are you a police officer?' a man shouted. 'I need help.'

He swung round, his warrant card held out towards the man as he noted immediately the shrunken cheeks and look of bewilderment in the man's eyes.

'Yes I am,' he responded automatically, feeling the familiar adrenalin surge course through his body. It was what he'd always lived for. 'What's happened?'

The man beckoned towards him and started to walk away. 'It's my brother. He's threatening to kill himself. Please can you help me! Come quickly.'

Hunter turned back towards the police station, his mind immediately racing through the risks. Common sense dictated it would be more sensible to go in and summon extra help from those who knew the area better… but by then it might be too late… and he could always use his phone to get more assistance if required. The man needed action, not inaction. He'd show the DCI he wasn't a spent force.

The man was a few steps further away now, the urgency in the waving of his hands cementing Hunter's plan in his head. He was heading towards a dark-coloured Audi. Hunter pulled his work mobile out and started after the man, the burst of speed making him momentarily breathless. The man opened the rear door of the car and nodded towards him.

'Quick, get in and I'll take you to where my brother is.' He left the door open, disappearing around the back of the car to the other side.

Hunter took a deep breath and bent his head, climbing into the rear. As he pulled the door shut, the realisation that he had been a fool slammed forcefully into his head. The man was climbing into the rear seat next to him. He had a large knife and a set of metal handcuffs in his hand. Hunter turned to pull on the door handle, just as he heard the child-locks clunk into place. The phone in his hand started to ring. He stared down at it, not recognising the number that was showing, his confusion growing.

There was a movement in the front of the car and he looked up to see a figure sitting in the driver's seat holding a mobile to their ear. He watched the driver move the phone to one side and end the call. As the button was pressed, Hunter's phone stopped ringing. The driver turned around and smiled, victory radiating out from cold, unblinking eyes.

'Ah, Detective Inspector Hunter. How nice to see you. Let me introduce myself to you properly. My name is Ice; in case of emergency, as cold as, however you'd like to describe me. I think Samson may have inadvertently let you know my name a while ago. Not that he is of consequence any more. He failed in the task he was set. He thought he knew better than me, but no matter... my new man, sitting next to you there has even more reason to get acquainted with you than Samson did. You lot destroyed his life and he really, really hates police, don't you?'

The man nodded wordlessly.

'Right, before we go any further. We'll have your phone.' The man next to him leant across, the knife extended towards his torso, and tore the phone from his hands.

'We wouldn't want you to escape the perfect punishment I've dreamed up for you now, would we?'

Chapter 38

Harmondsworth was a small, sleepless village, populated by nothing much more than a primary school, a short high street and a couple of pubs. Most of the inhabitants worked shifts at the airport and the few that didn't felt as if they did, so caught up were they in the day-to-day roar of the aircraft and rumble of the freight deliveries that blighted their peace and quiet.

Paul stopped at the beginning of the cul-de-sac in which Leach lived and switched the engine off. As the only person there not known to Brenda Leach, he would be the one going to reconnoitre her address. DCI O'Connor was in the process of arranging a hostage negotiator and armed back-up, should it look as if she was in. With a gun and ammunition adrift, they couldn't afford to take any chances.

Charlie climbed out of the car and joined Paul, clapping him on the back as he got himself prepared. He pulled some typed leaflets from his bag, offering his services as a gardener, carefully folded them and put them in his back pocket. She smiled; Paul always had a strategy prepared for just this sort of mission. A woman watering her flowers in a nearby garden stopped what she was doing and stared towards them curiously. They both started to walk along the path towards the target venue, about halfway down on the right, before Charlie peeled away and positioned herself opposite, watching her colleague from behind a garden wall.

The address was a tired-looking ground-floor converted maisonette, not nearly as smartly turned-out as its occupant. Checks had shown that both the ground- and first-floor properties were currently rented, which accounted for its lack of overall well-being. The driveway was paved, with weeds pushing up between the slabs, and a couple of uneven steps led to an entrance porch. Parked on the drive, tucked up close to a peeling garage door, was the car that was registered to Brenda Leach. It too looked shabby, as if it had served a purpose and had now somehow been put out to pasture.

The front door to the lower maisonette was closed but a porch door hung open on its hinges, kept from swinging by a large rock. The main window next to the porch was closed, with no lights on, making the interior look even gloomier in the fading light.

Paul walked straight past the front of the house initially, glancing up at the windows surreptitiously as he did so. A few minutes later he walked back and along the driveway, straight to the front door where he stood listening, his ear down towards the letter box. Charlie watched him from behind the wall as he peered through the letter box, a leaflet ready should the door be opened. After a moment he stepped away, pausing to give her a thumbs-up before disappearing through a side gate and around to the rear. She held her breath while he was out of sight, letting out a sigh of relief as he reappeared a few minutes later and walked back towards the car.

'Doesn't look as if there's anyone in,' he was updating the DCI as she joined him. 'More to the point, it looks like she's actually moved out. There are very few personal items that I can see, just old furniture and some cabinets with paperwork and other shit scattered about the floor.'

'Dammit,' Declan O'Connor shook his head. 'Not just retiring then! Relocating! I'll get in touch with the airport authorities and get them to check the flight manifests, see if she's booked on any flights out. We'll just have to hope we're not too late.'

'And we still don't have a bloody clue where she… or Hunter is.' Charlie chewed on her lip, trying to steady her mounting concern. 'Although there might be something in there that could help us.'

'But we need a warrant to enter and that takes time,' Hayley Boyle chipped in, frowning. 'Which is exactly what we don't have.'

*

'The phones belonging to Hunter and Brenda Leach were cell-sited together half an hour ago, Declan,' Ray Hooper's voice was clear through the speakers.

'Together? They're definitely together!' Charlie heard the message, swallowing hard. At last! Everything was falling into place, though it wasn't the news she'd wanted confirmed.

'But they've both been switched off now.'

'Where was the last location you placed the two of them together?' the DCI asked.

'It was on the Bath Road, close to Heathrow police station.'

'Which is also very close to where we are now,' Charlie stared back towards Leach's closed front door.

'Paul, were there any rooms you couldn't see into?'

Paul looked curious. 'Yes, the bathroom and toilet.'

'Excellent, then as far as I'm concerned we don't need a warrant.' Her eyes lit up. 'We believe Hunter might have been abducted and now we have evidence that he and Leach were together, in this vicinity. He could be lying injured or tied up in the bathroom and section 17 of PACE says…'

'Police can enter premises for the purpose of saving life or limb,' Hayley Boyle smiled. 'Ways and means eh! It's been a long time since I used them.'

The door crashed open within seconds. One kick from Paul's size 10s was all it took. Charlie ran through the doorway and had soon checked in every room, but there was no sign of Hunter. As Paul had said, it looked as if it had been vacated speedily and with little care. An assortment of furniture was spread about, some with their contents spewed out across the carpet. The wardrobes were empty, but there was a pile of clothing stacked in one corner of the bedroom, abandoned. Brenda Leach had moved on and had clearly taken only what she really needed, the rest had been discarded.

Charlie walked into a small kitchen-diner at the rear. Everything left looked like junk. They were at another dead end. Glancing out of the window, she realised despondently that it would soon be dark and their task in finding Hunter would be made even harder. Her gaze was broken by the sight of a rose bush in the back garden, partially torn by the wind from the arch to which it was connected. There were few flowers left on the bush, those remaining being high up at the top, blood red and in full bloom. They had to be in the right place.

Looking around the room, she saw a small pair of secateurs lying on a work surface, next to several green leaves and a single red petal. To their side lay half a dozen tiny triangular thorns; preparations for the next murder. She shouted out and the others came through, looking towards where she was pointing at the remainders of the rose.

Her eyes fell to the floor, searching for any other discarded thorns, before coming to rest on a patch of stained carpet. Lying across the stain was a length of electrical cable poking out from the interior of an old teak cabinet.

'Look at that.' She bent down over it.

'Is that the same cable as Samson Powell used to hang himself?' Paul was staring at it too.

'Yes, and to tie up Leonard Cookson and Philippa McGovern.' She nodded enthusiastically and opened the doors to the cabinet carefully, her eyes not quite believing what she was seeing. The cabinet was split into four compartments. The electrical cable was partially coiled into one of the sections, along with a stack of empty Nokia phone boxes and a pile of SIM cards. A half-empty glass bottle labelled sulphuric acid stood to one side, next to a black container with the words Kimbolton Fireworks stamped on the lid. It was the toolkit Brenda Leach had used to organise Samson Powell's murders.

In the second compartment lay a pack of rubber gloves, several balaclavas, a quantity of black plastic carrier bags and several rolls of brown paper, all carefully squeezed into place. A length of fishing line, several hooks and two empty police exhibit bags were folded to the side. Without reading the wording on the exhibit labels, Charlie knew exactly what they had contained.

In the third compartment was a pile of paperwork. She donned a pair of forensic gloves and carefully pulled out one of the files, staring into the face of Philippa McGovern as she opened it. Underneath her photo was a comprehensive résumé of her personal and work details, along with particulars of the complaint against her that was outstanding. A large red tick had been drawn on the top corner of the page. On other pages were an assortment of other names and faces, some whose dead features were well known to Charlie; some ticked off, others clearly having been of interest to Leach. They were in no obvious order, but Charlie knew she had to confirm what they already suspected. She took a deep breath and flicked through the file until she came to Hunter's image, gasping out loud at the sight of it.

'Shit,' Paul said, watching as Hayley Boyle stumbled across to a chair and sat down. None of them went to her assistance. It was as much as they could do to keep their thoughts to themselves.

The DCI spoke first, pointing at another file in the fourth compartment. 'What's in that one?'

Charlie took it out and opened it. The format inside was similar to the last; page after page of photos, along with personal details and lifestyle data. There were at least thirty profiles. Some had large crosses scored across the front page with the words 'dead' on them; others had detachable notes with the words 'in prison' or 'sectioned' along with release dates, no doubt ready to become active again should those dates allow. She turned a page and saw Samson Powell's dark eyes staring out at her, as evil and vulnerable as when she'd last seen him swinging from the cable. Scrawled across the front of his profile was the word 'FAILED'.

'She's sick,' Charlie turned towards the DCI. 'She wanted us to find this when she'd disappeared. It's her way of game-playing; boasting about how clever she is, a proper psychopath, just like Anna Christophe described. She probably loved it when I told her how much I rated Hunter, especially when she knew she had the means to kill him. How fitting to finish by killing the senior officer that led the investigation into her own murders.'

Hayley Boyle stood up and came across to them, taking Charlie by the arm. 'But she hasn't gone… yet. Yes, she's evil… and sick… and manipulative but she's fucked up. Perhaps she phoned me on purpose from the burner phone, meant just for her and Powell because she thought I wouldn't remember another unregistered number. Or to taunt us after she'd disappeared, like all of this. Maybe she thought Powell would dispose of his phone better before killing himself and their private number would never come to light. She couldn't have known that you would be checking my phone records after all. Or it could be she was just plain careless. After all, she would soon be gone. But it doesn't matter why. The point is… she won't yet know that we're on to her… or that we've found all this.' Hayley Boyle swept her hand over the book of suspect profiles, before taking a deep breath and speaking out clearly.

'One of these faces will be the person she has chosen to kill DI Hunter. She hasn't got the guts to do it herself. We've just got to find the right one.'

Chapter 39

Ice was tiring of the game now. There were only so many things you could say to a tired old man who was past it and knew that he'd lost. He wasn't so arrogant now he'd had to talk to save his life; in fact he'd said very little. It had been disappointing, she'd expected better, but then, there was very little he could say to justify his excessive use of force and the way he'd put guns before diplomacy.

She put the car into gear and pulled out of the quiet spot in which they'd been sat talking, now heading instead towards the final destination. It had been fun to start with, telling their captive how useless and corrupt he and the whole Metropolitan police were, detailing how she'd beaten them at their own game. The gleam in Number Two's eyes showed that he agreed and that he was ready. He might be a pathetic waste of space, a useless weak sap, but for the moment he was primed and ready to do her bidding, the blade of the knife twitching in anticipation. It was perfect.

Very soon the weapon would be swapped, the gun delivered to the marksman. Soon, they would hear the thud of bullets hitting bone, the sight of skin exploding on impact, blood and brains spattered.

This time though it wouldn't be DI Geoffrey Hunter giving the orders. This time it would be her.

*

Blue lights flashed across the windows of The Crown pub in Harmondsworth and sirens cut through the air as they sped through the streets. All around them the ranges of black clouds were still assembling and the wind was increasing steadily. Brenda Leach's address was now a crime scene, but they were still no further forward identifying where she and Hunter were.

There had been no trace of Brenda Leach's name on any of the flight manifests for that day or several days to come, which at least confirmed that they hadn't already missed her… but it did nothing to help in finding her. A reserved ticket would have at least given them a time to which she might be working or proved a useful tool to pinpoint her movements.

They had no clue as to where they were going, helplessly racing against a lack of time and knowledge. Charlie replayed the events of the last hour over and over in her head. There had to be something they had missed.

'Both!' she shouted out loud suddenly, as a single word pricked her memory. 'When Chief

Superintendent Ray Hooper told us about Leach and Hunter being together, he said *both* phones had been switched off.' Charlie pulled her mobile out and scrolled to her contacts. 'Leach has one number, but Hunter has two; work and personal... that would make three.'

'Fuck it.' DCI O'Connor grimaced. 'I only had his work number, the one I gave to Leach. Quick Charlie, what's his personal number. I'll get Ray on to it straight away. Let's hope Hunter is a sly bugger and has it hidden away.'

Within a few minutes Ray Hooper's voice came back on the line. 'The phone is still on. It's just passed a mast on the Northern Perimeter Road. They must be in a vehicle, heading towards the tunnel into the main airport site, but with this storm threatening, the atmospherics will get worse.'

'And when they're through the tunnel,' DCI O'Connor added, 'it'll get even harder. Any signal will bounce off the buildings and won't be specific enough to trace.'

'And if they go inside the thick walls of a terminal building, we'll lose it completely,' Paul muttered, braking sharply and swinging the car round.

Charlie looked up at the sky glumly. 'Not to mention the fact we have no idea what vehicle they're in.' Bad luck was dogging them again. She stared down at Brenda Leach's file of suspects encased in an exhibit bag on her lap. Somewhere within that file was the key. Bet was researching the names already but there were too many. They had to have answers quickly. It was essential to find Leach's new foot soldier. He might be the only thing now that would lead them to her and Hunter.

She rang Naz, her foot tapping impatiently in time with every ring. The enquiry at the internet cafe had taken on a fresh urgency. They now had names and faces to put with any image Naz and Sabira might locate on the CCTV. If only there was CCTV.

The button was pressed on the phone before Naz answered. Charlie could hear her friend shouting in the background. She put the phone on loudspeaker.

'Naz, how are you getting on? It's urgent. We need a name or an image of the person who set up Jason Lloyd's murder.'

The interior of the car fell silent, each person realising the relevance of the question.

'Hi, Charlie. Well we're here but it's busy. We checked the register of customers for a name first and got the one that was written down; John Smith, which is obviously fake. Of course no one here bothered to question it.'

'OK,' Charlie had expected nothing more. 'How about CCTV?'

They could hear the hubbub in the background. After a few seconds Naz shouted down the phone again. 'Well, the owner's here and we've established which computer the IP address comes back to, so we've seized that. There is CCTV operating, but this guy is being a pain in the arse. It's an old system which uses 48-hour tapes which are stored for three months before being used again. We've got the tape for the last date and time when the computer was used to make contact with Jason Lloyd, but he is saying that he can't remember how the system works to play it back. Our only option is to take it to be viewed at a station?'

'Naz, we haven't got time. We need it now.'

They listened as Naz tried again and they heard the man at the cafe make his excuses, his speech lazy and peppered with long gaps. He was clearly being obstructive.

'Pass him over to me,' DCI O'Connor growled.

The man came on the line, his tone belligerent. 'Yes, boss,' he scoffed.

'I don't know what your name is, but mine is Detective Chief Inspector Declan O'Connor. Remember that name because it is the one that will be responsible for shutting down your business and impounding every single one of your computers. I am dealing with a murder investigation and you are obstructing my officers in the execution of their duty. So I suggest you recall how to play back that tape quickly, because I swear if I have to come to your location you will be arrested, and next time it'll be your voice on one of our tapes at the police station explaining to the magistrates why you were not willing to assist in a murder investigation. Do I make myself clear?'

'Yes, boss,' he said again, but this time they could hear he meant it.

The wait seemed to take forever. Paul slowed the car and they could hear the noise of machinery clunking on and off and tapes being played and rewound. Charlie felt sick with anticipation.

'Bingo,' Naz shouted at last. 'It's not a great image but it's clear enough. It's a male, white, aged late thirties, slim build. He has short dark hair and looks scruffy and unkempt. There's quite a good shot of him as he is talking to the manager and paying him on the way out.'

'Can you take a screenshot and send it to me,' Charlie could feel her pulse racing as she waited, carefully scrolling through the suspect profiles to narrow the search down to the ethnicity and age of the man Naz had described. The description had already reduced their suspects to a possible five. Her phone pinged with the notification of an image. Everything was hinging on the image matching one of their suspects.

She opened the inbox with trembling fingers and stared at two images of the man who had facilitated the murder of Jason Lloyd. Hayley Boyle leant across as she turned the five pages of suspect profiles to compare them, letting out an audible sigh of relief as she did so. There was no mistaking the angle of the man's jaw and the hook of his nose as they matched the image with their last profile.

Chapter 40

'Ross Naylor, 28/02/1980, male, white, born in Glasgow,' Charlie read the details out to Bet as they sped towards the main airport buildings. 'According to Leach's profile of him, he was born in Scotland but came to London at the age of twelve when his father left home. His relationship with his mother also broke down, but he had an older brother called Ricky that he idolised. They were inseparable and Ross would do anything Ricky told him to, including crime. In 1999 both boys got arrested for a vicious robbery on a cash-in-transit guard, leaving him with multiple fractures. Ricky got twelve years in prison and Ross four but after two years Ross was released and was instead sectioned under the Mental Health Act to the St Bernard wing of Ealing Hospital, where he met Brenda Leach.'

'Ah yes. She worked there from 2000 to 2004. She must have recognised he was easy pickings on his own.'

'Exactly. Anyway, Leach's notes state that she kept in contact with him. She effectively took Ricky's place, until Ricky was released in 2005 and the brothers paired up again. She then took a background role, but she never let Ross go... and of course she was waiting for him when he went into self-destruct mode, after Ricky was shot dead by police in a bungled robbery two years later.'

'And the evil bitch has kept him on the sideline until now?' Bet swore loudly. 'No wonder she's groomed him though. He sounds pretty vulnerable and he must hate police.'

'She's highlighted that in her notes, calls him a "Stupid lowlife". In his mind, though, she's always been there for him and he'll do anything to keep her.'

'And now she has the means to allow Ross to do to Hunter exactly what police did to his brother…'

'That's where you come in, Bet. We need to know as much as you can find out about the circumstances of Ricky's death. Where, when and why. There must be a link with why she's chosen here.'

The call fell through as they went into the tunnel that led towards terminals one to three and the main hub of the airport, but she'd said what was needed. Hunter was somewhere in here but they couldn't pinpoint his exact whereabouts.

The light had almost gone as they reappeared out of the tunnel, the sky being tightly packed with rainclouds rolling over and over malevolently, but the air remained warm and the atmosphere heavy with moisture. Charlie pressed her face to the window, scanning every person, every vehicle, for the two faces she'd committed to memory and the one that she knew so well.

Every police officer on duty at Heathrow and the whole Metropolitan area had been passed photos of Brenda Leach, Ross Naylor and Hunter, but so far there had been nothing. It was if they had entered the tunnel and disappeared into thin air.

*

Ice wound the car slowly up the ramps towards the top, each level growing quieter as they ascended. She looked out across the airport, watching the workers and the passengers scurry about, their movements appearing to speed up with distance. Like ants, they needed to be squashed; their lives ended like the useless creatures they were.

Above them the sky opened up, the dark forces at play in the clouds sending out waves of wrathful ire. A few spots of rain hit the windscreen, each heavy droplet transmitting shock waves across the glass. She pulled over and pressed the boot release. Inside, carefully wrapped, was the rose, the perfection of its blood-red petals in total contrast to the imperfection of her childhood. Nobody would ever know the treachery of what it symbolised to her; the simple notes of the nursery rhyme striking fear into every part of her being, its words synonymous with the rash on the faces of Plague victims. The beauty of the rose forever intertwined with the horror of the Black Death. This time it would be her that would leave the reminder next to the body; Detective Inspector Hunter would be the recipient of the death flower, but nobody would ever know why.

She glanced around at her captive, handcuffed and subdued, resigned to his fate. Her eyes were drawn to the blade of the knife, the metal dull but devastatingly sharp. It had accomplished what had been required initially but now it needed to be exchanged. The gun was on hand, its beautiful lines and exquisite power concealed within the usual wrapping of brown paper.

She got out and walked slowly to the boot, stooping to retrieve the red rose, and the weapon, marvelling at its weight. A dozen little girls started to sing the words of the nursery rhyme in her head as she unwrapped the paper reverently, running her hands over the smoothness of the grip and down the barrel to its end, from where the bullet would explode, its sharp, deadly force shattering the bastard's skull. *Ring a ring o' roses, a pocket full of posies.* She didn't care that her fingerprints and DNA would be all over it. Soon she would be gone and they would be left astounded at the ineptitude of their chase.

She put the barrel of the gun to her mouth and kissed it, savouring the icy coldness of the metal against her lips. *Atishoo, Atishoo.* In just a few more minutes the sights and sounds of death would be all around them and another arrogant police officer would fall down dead.

*

There were only so many roads within the airport complex that could be accessed and Paul had circulated each route several times. All about them people were going about their business totally unaware of the unfolding drama. It was impossible. If only they had a vehicle for their suspects, but they didn't; just three faces to search for amongst the throngs of people.

The tension inside the car was unbearable. Naz and Sabira were on their way, anxious to assist too, but so far there had been no sightings. Charlie said nothing; all her concentration taken up staring out of the window, her eyes scanning every corner, every profile. If they were there she would see them… or so she'd thought initially. In frustration she pulled out her phone and dialled Bet's number.

'Anything yet, Bet? It's like looking for a needle in a haystack here.'

She heard the DCI's phone start to ring but concentrated on Bet's voice.

'I've got people running to several addresses I've found for Ross Naylor but nothing so far and I can't find anything at all about airports. As far as I can see, he and Ricky never left the country. They'd never even applied for passports.'

'What about Ricky's death?'

'Again, nothing to do with aeroplanes or airports or the area you're in. He and Ross were involved in a robbery on a country post office in Burghfield Common, just outside Reading. Ricky did the robbery, with what turned out to be a replica firearm. Ross was driving the getaway car, but they were spotted leaving and the number was circulated. Armed police picked them up heading into Reading and after a short chase Ross crashed the car just outside The Oracle. He was quickly detained, but Ricky made a run for it and was chased on foot through the shopping centre and up into the car park. He was given a shouted warning to stop and drop the gun, but instead of complying he turned and aimed it towards officers. He was shot three times, twice in the chest and once in the head.'

'That's brilliant,' Charlie shouted, as Bet's words sunk in.

'What's brilliant?' Bet sounded perplexed. 'That he was shot?'

'You said he ran *up* into a car park, so it sounds like a multi-storey. Well, there're a few multi-storey car parks here. We've just got to work out which one.' She turned towards the DCI who had just finished his conversation and was listening intently. His face lit up and he banged his fists against the dashboard.

'Yes!' he shouted. 'That's it. I've just been told the signal for Hunter's phone has pinged up strongly again, as if he's come out into the open. It's on the west side of the airport complex, close to Terminal 3.'

*

Hunter peered over the edge of the parapet at the world below and wondered if he stood any chance of remaining part of it. The handcuffs put on at his capture were biting into the flesh of his wrists and the gag that had just been tied around his head was so tight that the skin around his mouth was already chafed and sore. Everything the woman did was designed to draw out this moment in as painful and humiliating a way as possible.

He hated her. He had always hated her, from the moment he had heard her name. Brenda Leach was evil, pure evil, and listening to her boast about how she'd teased and tantalised Samson Powell into doing her will, then used her position to monitor the investigation and play the police in her warped games had made him sick to the stomach. How could she have got to where she had without anybody realising? Worse still, how could his preoccupation with her investigation into his own actions have blinded him to Charlie's hunch?

Now it was too late. He had run off into the night with his executioner and without a second thought, his mind fogged by self-doubt, letting no one know where he was. He had broken a cardinal rule and had only himself to blame.

Next to him, his captors were preparing the weapon they would use. After dismissing Powell as a failure, she had spent time telling her new man how important he was, how she needed him as much as he needed her... and the man had nodded and smiled his gratitude. He was a simpleton but he clearly knew about guns. Hunter watched, morbidly fascinated, as the man spun the cylinder expertly, slotting in three bullets to the chambers, the delight on his face shining hideously in the hazy lighting of the car park. The rain had stopped. Everything stopped, as the barrel of the gun clicked shut. An image of his wife and son crying over his dead body flashed into his mind.

Brenda Leach held a smooth red rose in her hand, the knowledge of where it would shortly be placed not lost on him. He turned away from them and stared back over the edge, his eyes coming to rest on a vehicle that had pulled to a standstill on the double yellow lines at the approach to the entry barriers. A figure climbed out from it and stood staring up towards where he stood on the roof, it was a figure that looked familiar, that ran its hands through its hair and pointed.

A glimmer of hope rippled through him, weak at first but gaining in strength as the figure was joined by another and both looked upwards. The two figures ran towards the entrance and disappeared from view and the car reversed out of sight. He remained staring downwards as a flash of sheet lightning lit up the sky, fleetingly emphasising the loneliness of the spot where he now stood. Had it been his imagination or had he really seen Charlie. He didn't know and he didn't dare hope.

The sound of a low guttural laugh drew him from his thoughts as the man stepped towards him, raising his arm as he did so. He couldn't believe anything his brain was telling him at that moment, but as he felt the barrel of the gun pressed hard against his temple, he was surprised to realise that the coolness of the metal against his skin, in the oppressive heat of the night, felt vaguely welcome.

*

Charlie sprinted up the steps, the DCI's orders ringing in her ears.

'Do not, on any account, show yourself. You are to stay out of sight until I have armed units and a hostage negotiator with us. Call me directly with a situation report when you have them in view.'

Several flights of stairs behind her was DS Hayley Boyle, labouring slowly up the stairwell. The DPS sergeant was anxious to assist in any way she could and Declan O'Connor had taken the decision to allow her to help Charlie. As the senior officer he would be required to co-ordinate the armed operation and he needed Paul, as a trained driver, to be on hand. It was a risk, but somehow they all knew that the sergeant had been stupid, not murderous. Plus, Hayley Boyle knew the rules and, even though she'd broken some, the DCI clearly wanted this done by the book.

Sweat was prickling on Charlie's temples when she reached the top floor. She crouched behind the door that led out into the parking lot and peered through a laminated glass panel. The view was slightly blurred but she could make out the outlines and movements of the three individuals… and there was no time to spare. Hunter was standing with his back to the outer wall, facing his captors in the car park. The tall slender figure of Brenda Leach stood immediately in front and the man in the photos,

Ross Naylor, to his side, holding a revolver to his head.

She could hear their voices, low and urgent, but couldn't make out what words were being spoken.

Pushing the door carefully, she wedged it open with a discarded tin can and knelt down, taking in the proximity of the three figures. Above them the sky crackled and fizzed, a million electrical currents doing battle with each other within the clouds.

Brenda Leach was laughing now, her eyes flicking from one man to the other, the mole on her cheek dancing a dramatic tango in time with each cackle, a red rose flailing about in the air with every movement. Leach raised her wrist and squinted at her watch before turning towards Hunter.

'What does it feel like being on the other end of the barrel, Detective Inspector Hunter? Not so blasé now are you.' She pressed a button on the side of her watch. 'You have exactly two minutes to tell me why I shouldn't order Ross here to kill you, so start grovelling. Not that either of us will listen.' She chuckled spitefully, leaning forward to undo the gag. 'I want to savour every second of this moment as it happens. My decision has not been made on the *spur of the moment*, like you lot always give as your justification. I have been planning this all my life…'

She pulled the gag away and laughed as Hunter remained silently staring at her, his eyes disdainful.

She returned the stare.

Charlie held her breath, counting down the seconds. She couldn't just watch it happen, yet she had her orders.

'Arrogant even to your dying breath,' Leach said finally, checking her watch again. 'One minute and then I'll give the order, in just the manner you do.'

Charlie watched in horror, feeling Hayley Boyle kneel down beside her, her breath coming in short gasps.

'Sarge,' she whispered, her head and voice suddenly calm. 'Hunter has one minute before Ross pulls the trigger. I can't let that happen.'

Hayley Boyle gripped her arm. 'You can't go out there. She'll kill you too. You don't know what she's like when she's focussed on something.'

'Hunter saved my life…' her voice petered out. 'When I go through the door, make sure it doesn't close properly. Use the can. You'll need to be able to hear what's happening. Keep the DCI briefed for me.'

She pulled her arm away and stood up, taking a deep breath before raising her arms above her head and stepping forward.

Brenda Leach swung around towards the noise of the door, blinking in obvious delight at the sight of Charlie. 'Ah, another witness, excellent. But you're too late! Time's up.' She turned to Ross Naylor. 'Go, go…'

'No, Ross. Don't shoot. Please. Not until we've had a chance to speak.' Charlie's voice was strong.

'Go!' Leach screamed.

The man's head turned from one to the other, panicked.

'Do it for Ricky,' Leach screamed again, blinking wildly.

'That won't bring him justice,' Charlie spoke clearly. 'And it won't bring him back. I should know. I lost my brother too.'

The man swung round towards her, his expression desperate, lowering the gun from where it was aimed but still holding it firmly.

'How?' he paused, unsure. 'How did you lose your brother? Was he shot by police, like my brother was?' He raised his arm again so that the gun pointed at Hunter's chest but his eyes were curious.

'No, he wasn't shot, like Ricky was.' She had to be careful. He was watching her closely. 'But I never got justice for him. I had to watch my only brother Jamie's dead body pulled from the sea because of the criminal recklessness of a boat owner who took us out ill-equipped during a storm.' She glanced up at the sky. 'It was a night like this. We should never have been out at sea.' She remembered the description of Ross and Ricky's relationship on Leach's profile. 'Jamie and I used to do everything together. He was always there for me, just like Ricky was always there for you. I still miss him.'

'I miss my brother too.' His voice caught.

'Don't listen to her,' Leach had regained some of her composure. Her voice was icy. 'She's a police officer, just like the rest. She doesn't care about her brother and she doesn't care about you, or Ricky. You have three bullets; enough to kill them both.'

'Please, stop. DI Hunter is a good police officer. He saved my life, Ross. I would be dead without him. My mother would have lost two children.'

'There's no such thing as a good police officer. They are all murdering bastards, every single one of them, like my father, sticking together against innocent people exactly like they always have done. Do as I say, Ross. Don't fuck this up. You can't fail me now.'

'Like Samson Powell did,' Hunter wiped his hand carefully around his mouth, speaking softly. 'Because otherwise she will have no use for you, just like she had no use for Samson.'

'Samson was a fool,' Leach sneered. 'He thought he knew better than me.'

'You heard what she said in the car, Ross, didn't you?' Hunter was looking towards the man, nodding to him encouragingly, his previous disconsolate look replaced now by steely determination. 'She might be nice to you now but she'll turn against you. She took the piss out of Samson. She hated him. Remember how she laughed? She said that Samson was weak and had a fatal flaw. That he would do anything for her just because he thought she looked like his mother.'

'Delilah Powell.' Charlie said the name out loud. She remembered the photo in the dead man's wallet, the way his teacher Saffron Bolt had said he'd do everything she asked because he thought she too had looked like his mother. So that was why. She stared at Brenda Leach, her coffee-coloured skin, her age and build, her sleek black hair, the way she could change her expression to give the impression of softness, to manipulate and charm… and suddenly she realised why the woman's face had seemed so familiar, how much all three women resembled each other.

'Ross,' she joined in. 'She is just using you, like she used Samson Powell. When she's finished with you she will get rid of you too, just like she did Samson. She probably told him to kill himself!'

Ross Naylor looked towards Leach, his face suddenly anxious.

'You know that's not true, Ross. I have always been there for you, haven't I? Ever since we first met in the hospital.' She was smiling towards him now, her tone sugary. 'Remember how you always used to follow me around and how we laughed because you'd say you were stuck to me, like my surname, Leach. You remember that, don't you Ross. We stayed together through thick and thin. I was there for you when Ricky was in prison, and when he was out… and I was there for you after the murdering police scum killed him, wasn't I?'

The man's face creased as he stood stock-still for what seemed like an age, his expression changing, as if going through every detail of his childhood and the death of his brother. Eventually, when his memories were spent, his face softened.

'I remember you with me, Brenda. Brenda Leach… Ice; always there, in case of emergency.' Ross Naylor smiled back at Leach gratefully.

'And I always will be. So… don't listen to these two liars. Do as I say and kill them both. Now, for Ricky's sake. Then we can get out of here together.'

She placed a hand on his shoulder and the man straightened, pulling himself upright and standing tall, as if a bolt of lightning had sprung from the sky through her fingers, mobilising him into action. Pulling the gun up, he cocked the trigger and held it towards Hunter's head.

'Stop! Don't shoot.'

Charlie swung round to see Hayley Boyle take several paces towards them, holding both arms in the air, her phone lit up in one hand. Her face was pale and her hands shook.

Leach let out a cry, swinging round, her eyes blinking manically. 'Well, well, well. What have we here? DS Hayley Boyle.' She laughed derisively. 'Another useless, snivelling, lying copper. It's lucky we have three bullets, Ross. One for each of them. Shoot them all, now.'

'She's the liar.' Hayley Boyle held out the phone towards Ross Naylor. 'Look at the image on the screen. She was going to leave you to take the flack on your own, Ross. She had no intention of taking you with her. Look, it's a picture of the one-way ticket to Brazil she's bought for herself, so she can disappear straight after this. She was going to get you to do her dirty work, like she did with Samson Powell and then get straight on a plane.'

Ross Naylor was wavering. Still pointing the gun towards Hunter, he took a few steps towards Hayley Boyle and peered at where she was pointing, reading out the print.

'Delilah Powell, Flight LATAM 362 flying to Galeao International Airport, Rio de Janeiro, Brazil. Leaving on Saturday 08/07/2017 at 22.10. Terminal 3.'

'That's not my name. Ignore her,' Leach screamed.

'That's Samson Powell's mother, Ross. Delilah Powell. The woman Samson thought she looked like.' Charlie wanted to laugh. It was brilliant. That was why she'd packed her things, why she had chosen the airport and why they hadn't found any tickets booked under her real name.

'That's not me, Ross. You know my name, Brenda Leach. Remember? I wouldn't leave you. They're lying again.'

Charlie was thinking fast. They had to make him believe she was leaving him, just like Ricky and everyone else in his world had; that he would be all alone.

'She's the one who is lying. I bet if you check in her pockets, Ross, you will find a passport and tickets in the name Delilah Powell.'

His face creased in alarm as Charlie recited her thoughts. Wordlessly he motioned Hunter, Charlie and Hayley to move together and stepped towards Leach, pointing the gun towards her as he did so.

'Don't do this, Ross. I'm telling you the truth. I wouldn't leave you. You know I wouldn't leave you,' she repeated the words, her voice trembling, the mole on her cheek vibrating gently.

'Shut up, Ice.'

He thrust his spare hand into her jacket pocket, pulling out a wad of printed flight information. Tucked into the middle of the paperwork was a maroon EU passport with a boarding pass slipped in between the pages. He opened it slowly staring at the details, comparing the photograph against the name, with the woman standing opposite, and then, as if in slow motion, Charlie watched helplessly as he grabbed hold of Leach around the neck, squeezing her until she screamed in pain, her voice echoed in his own cry of anguish as he picked her up and hurled her bodily over the wall into the livid night sky.

*

Brenda Leach gripped the rose tightly as she fell through the air. A vision of her father's face flashed before her, his eyes glinting malevolently with glee, his mouth turned up in a vicious grin. She remembered his rabid delight, as he swore that she could never truly hide from him; that he would always find her. As the sky swallowed up her scream, she smiled inwardly. Maybe it was meant to end this way. Maybe it had always been an illusion that she could win.

As the pain shot through her whole body, the last things she recalled, before blacking out, were the petals of the rose, battered and torn at her side and the hatred in her father's voice as he sang the last line of the nursery rhyme slowly in her ears.

*

Charlie heard the thud as Brenda Leach's body hit the surface below. At the same time, she saw Ross Naylor aim the gun towards his own head.

With a shout of her own, she launched herself into the air towards the man, hitting him straight in the chest as the firearm exploded in his hand. For an instant, everything was noise; the gunshot reverberating against the walls, the shouts of warning, the rumble of thunder, the clatter as the firearm hit the concrete and spun off across the painted bays.

After a few seconds, the commotion died away and all was still. She opened her eyes and stared down at a small pool of blood forming on the ground beneath them and then through the silence came a noise that took her breath away. It was the sound of a man crying, a sound that she hoped never to hear again. She turned her head to see Ross Naylor sobbing, as if he was the only person left alive in the world.

Chapter 41

The scene turned blue within seconds. All around, squad cars and ambulances were arriving, their tyres squealing and strobe lights flashing as they navigated the ramps of the multi-storey. Ross Naylor lay on the concrete curled into a ball, his hands tightly clasped across his face as he continued to sob. Charlie lay across his body, holding him down, but he wasn't struggling. If he'd ever had any fight within him it had disappeared, washed away with the rain that had started to fall; all will to carry on living gone.

Armed officers with guns and flashlights were running towards them now, taking possession of the firearm, making it safe, unzipping first aid kits, detaining Ross Naylor, securing the scene, taking control of the situation. Charlie rolled away from him on to her back, her arms held high. The rain falling on her face was cool and welcome. She closed her eyes momentarily and inhaled its freshness, letting the tension drain from her body, as it was from the sky. A shadow passed across her eyes and she opened them to see Hunter looming large above her, his face creased with concern. The handcuffs were off him and he held a hand towards her.

'You OK?' he asked, as if it was the most normal question in the world.

'Yeah, I'm OK, I think,' she said, remembering the small pool of blood from a minute previously and the way it was now splashing pink with the raindrops. She spun around to see Hayley Boyle sitting against the wall, her arm red with blood and several paramedics in attendance.

'She'll live,' Hunter smiled, pulling Charlie to her feet. 'It's only a surface graze from the bullet Ross Naylor fired before you took him down. Luckily it missed any vital organs and just caught her arm.'

'I'm getting a bit slow in my old age. I should have realised what he was about to do a lot quicker.' She bent down and brushed at her trousers, knocking some of the dirt from her knees.

Hunter turned away at her words, looking skywards as a large jet lifted into the air above them. The rain so quick to fall was already starting to ease.

'I should have realised what was going on a lot sooner too. I was too busy with my own worries to listen to your concerns.'

'You had a lot going on, guv... and anyway, you know me, always getting carried away on wild goose chases, or mad hunches, with my head in the clouds.' She didn't mention the conversation she'd had with Mrs H. Hopefully no one else ever would. Following the direction Hunter was still staring, she watched as the aeroplane disappeared from view into the stormy sky.

He turned back towards her, suddenly serious. 'You've got a good head on those shoulders of yours, Charlie. You should think about promotion. You'd make a good guvnor.' He paused, his voice catching. 'And perhaps I'm getting too old for this job.'

His last sentence was nearly drowned out by the sound waves of the jet but she could read them on his lips. She pretended not to have heard. They were words she didn't want to hear... and anyway, he'd regret saying them when he got his teeth into the next job.

'We've already got a good guvnor and I'm quite happy to keep it that way,' she bobbed her head from side to side and grinned. 'Though I suppose it wouldn't hurt to get you to write me up for my sergeants'.'

'Of course. It would be my pleasure. I owe you one.'

'I owe you for last time, so let's call it quits.'

'No, Charlie, I do owe you.' His voice was still serious.

She was about to open her mouth to argue but thought better of it. Hunter didn't often speak from the heart and it seemed wrong to disregard the earnestness of his opinion now, however much she disagreed. As far as she was concerned, that's what teamwork was all about; Paul, Naz, Bet and Sabira all understood it too, only Nick didn't. He probably never would. The thought brought her back to earth and she moved towards the parapet, leaning over to see what was happening. She saw Paul immediately, five floors below, marshalling a couple of uniformed officers in the process of setting up a cordon. Naz and Sabira were standing to one side, clipboards in hands. As if sensing he was being watched, Paul looked up, waving towards her, Naz and Sabira quickly joining in too. She waved back, grinning. It was good to know they were close by.

A queue of police cars, fire engines and ambulances were lined up in the road, their blue lights combining with the red and white of brake and headlights to give the impression of a long thin union flag scarf wrapping itself around the car park.

A bridge stretched across from the third floor of the car park to the terminal, constructed of grey metalwork, with beams zig-zagging across its roof and railings at each end. A rectangular foyer jutted out between the walls of the car park and the bridge, its concrete roof directly under where she stood. In the centre of this was the figure of Brenda Leach, stretched out, her legs splayed at abnormal angles, her hair matted down in a pool of her own blood. Lying in her outstretched hand was the red rose, its stem still caught between her fingers, the flower broken and torn, with individual petals stained darker in the blood and rain. Her eyes were closed and a plastic tube protruded from her mouth, held in place by one of three paramedics who were gathered around trying to save her life. From where she stood, Charlie could see they were still working on her.

Hunter came up beside her and peered down.

'What about Leach?' she asked him.

'Alive, just. Luckily for her, she only fell two floors. It looks to me like she's fractured both her legs and could well have spinal injuries. Hopefully, if she survives, she'll never again be able to wreak the sort of havoc that she has.'

'Thank God,' Charlie agreed truthfully, thinking back to her recent fears for Hunter. 'By the way, you need to check that personal phone of yours, wherever you have it hidden. You might find a few more missed calls on it.' She grinned at the comment, watching as Hunter rummaged deep in his pocket and pulled out his phone, unwrapping it from inside his handkerchief and squinting down at the display. 'Oops, eight missed calls from Mrs H.'

'I had to phone her when you were missing,' Charlie admitted, saying nothing further about his wife's concerns. 'I said I'd ring when we located you. She'll be worried sick.'

'I'm going to be well and truly in her bad books then. I'm not sure what it's going to take to sweet-talk her back, especially after the last few weeks'

Charlie looked up as a jet roared over them. 'If it was me, nothing short of being taken on holiday to somewhere with sun, sea and…'

'No senior officers,' Hunter butted in, laughing.

A loud wail came from behind them and they turned to see Ross Naylor being led to a police van, his arms handcuffed behind his back. Tears still seeped from his eyes and his nose ran constantly as he climbed up into the rear cage.

Charlie left Hunter to make his call and walked across to see the man, broken by the one person he'd completely trusted. He sniffed hard and pushed his face against the bars of the cage.

'Officer,' his eyes bored into hers. 'Were you lying to me when you said about losing your brother?'

She shook her head. 'No, I wasn't. Everything I told you was the truth. My brother drowned in front of my eyes and there was nothing I could do. He was an innocent victim who should never have died. That's why I do this job, to try to get the justice for other victims that I never had. I do miss him though, every day.' She stopped talking. Even after all the years she still found it hard.

Naylor looked away from her, his eyes searching the ground. 'I still miss Ricky too. He wasn't innocent, but he was a victim.'

She could see the vulnerability in his face. 'Just like you are, Ross. Brenda Leach used you to do her dirty work and then she betrayed you. She was going to leave you all on your own. She had no intention of staying with you any longer.'

'I know that now… but I still killed a policeman and I'll get sent to prison for the rest of my life.'

'Not necessarily. You did commit a serious crime and you will have to be punished, but Brenda Leach is the real murderer. What did she tell you, Ross?'

'She told me that the policeman at the lake was an armed officer who had killed a defenceless man. She said that he was bad and I believed her.' He started to cry again. 'She told me what to do and I did it. I had to say and do exactly what she told me or else she said she would leave me on my own. She said that Ricky didn't need to have died but the police wanted him dead so they shot him, not once but three times, just because they could and because they knew they would get away with it. They killed my brother. He was all that I had.'

'Apart from Brenda?'

'Yes, apart from her. She promised to be the mother I never really had and said that if I did what she instructed she would look after me forever. She gave me my orders and, when it was time, she provided me with what I needed.'

Charlie thought back to the cabinet of physical evidence in Leach's address. If they were to get convictions for all the murders they would have to prove it was Brenda Leach calling the shots and not Samson Powell or Ross Naylor forcing her to follow their commands. They would need Ross's testimony, explaining her exact methodology. If Leach survived, Charlie wanted her convicted of every single murder she'd instigated, not just the one that Ross Naylor had committed and the conspiracy to murder Hunter. Every friend or family member of Powell's three victims deserved no less. Even Lisa Forrester deserved it. Without Ross's testimony they might struggle to even convict her of Jason Lloyd's murder. She was an evil psychopathic killer but she was also a credible and convincing liar. She would be more than capable of sweet-talking reasonable doubt into the minds of twelve well-meaning jurors.

'Do you believe I'm telling you the truth, Ross, about my brother dying and about Brenda leaving you?'

She took hold of the bars between them and stared deeply into Ross Naylor's eyes, connecting with the man who had, so recently, held a gun to Hunter's head. For a few seconds she was lost in the same black void that was forever present in her own life, the despair, the emptiness, the grief… before forcing herself to blink.

'I do believe you,' he answered flatly.

'In that case I promise to do everything I can to help you to deal with losing Ricky and to get you back on your feet again. There are people and organisations out there who can really assist.'

Ross Naylor was still staring at her as she spoke.

'But I'll be straight with you, Ross,' she said gently. 'I can't promise I can keep you out of prison, but I assure you I will do everything in my power to make sure the courts understand the circumstances of the case and they treat you fairly. To do that, though, I need your help, if you're willing to trust me.'

She nodded towards him and he nodded back. 'I do trust you.'

'In that case, I need you to tell police everything you know about Brenda Leach. How long you've known her, where you first met and how she works. I need to know every little detail of what she's said to you and every single thing she told you to say and do. Do you understand?'

*

It was gone midnight by the time they started the journey back to Lambeth. Everything was in place that could be and the events of the evening were starting to take their toll. The atmosphere in the car was pensive, each person considering the part they had played in the run-up to the night's operation. Paul was still in the driving seat with the DCI next to him. Charlie sat quietly on the backseat next to Hunter, now replacing Hayley Boyle, who had been whisked away to the local hospital for treatment on her arm. They were all deep in their own thoughts when, halfway down the M4, the radio sparked into life.

'All units, standby. Shirley Sangster out, out, out of bar at the rear of "Hair Today". Still wearing red shirt and dark leggings. Talking to a group of males.'

'Bloody hell,' DCI O'Connor said. 'I didn't realise this was still going. I would have thought they'd have stood down a long while ago.'

'I wouldn't have stood down without your express permission,' Charlie laughed suddenly. 'Not after the bollocking you gave both teams earlier.'

'Nor would I, sir,' Hunter grinned. 'Having been on the receiving end of one of them too.'

'Don't "sir" me, Hunter. The only time you do that is when you're just about to totally ignore what I say and disobey a lawful order.'

Charlie sniggered.

'And you can stop laughing, DC Stafford. You're just as bad. What was the last thing I said to you?' He shrugged his shoulders and turned to Paul. 'I don't know which one of them is worse, the older one who should know better, or the younger one who chooses not to.'

Paul shrugged back and grinned. 'They're both as bad as each other, boss. The guys in the office all say they're like two PC's in a pod.'

The tension was broken and the atmosphere lightened, all now interested in what exactly Shirley Sangster was up to, now she wasn't trying to kill them. Paul slipped the blue lights on and they shot along the quiet streets in an effort to get back to assist. Both surveillance teams were in full shout, Dennis Walters too, having mysteriously popped up in the town centre.

As Paul steered the car closer, they listened as their two subjects started moving towards each other again. Sangster, apparently, appeared slightly drunk, her gait relaxed and her high-heeled shoes not helping her attempts at walking straight. She was heading through the town centre in the direction of home.

The teams were converging. Walters was standing by the police station as Sangster passed, nodding in his direction before crossing over the side street towards her estate. Walters fell in behind, catching up as she took her first few steps into the nearby Max Roach Park. They walked together for a few paces before Walters took a rucksack from his shoulder, delved deeply into it and pulled out a black plastic bag, handing it to Sangster, who shoved it straight up under her shirt.

'Wait for them to split and then get them both stopped,' DCI O'Connor instructed down the radio. 'Let's see what they've been up to.'

They were just around the corner now. Paul switched the blue lights off and coasted up the main road towards them as the stops were put in. On one side of the park Charlie could hear shouting as Walters protested his innocence. They turned instead to where Shirley Sangster stood, at the passageway that led into her estate. Several plain-clothed male officers stood with her, holding her by the arms, having just radioed for a female officer to assist with searching. They pulled up alongside and Charlie climbed out, coming face to face with the woman whose image and reputation was so familiar. Shirley Sangster was smaller than she'd remembered and far quieter. Charlie expected the same raging ball of spitting, fiery resentment, but instead the woman stood silently, resigned to what was about to happen.

'It's Spice,' Shirley Sangster said wearily, as Charlie identified herself and pointed towards the bulge in her shirt. 'Take it. It was for Troy, to keep him going.'

Charlie donned her gloves and carefully took the bag from under her shirt, peering into it to see the herbal substance that was the current, most popular, drug of choice.

'It's Sunday,' Sangster added. 'Visiting day.'

Charlie handed the bag to one of the team and opened the car door. 'I'll do a statement and let you have it later,' she said in hushed tones. 'Nick her for possession with intent to supply… and make sure Walters gets nicked for supply too. He's already on bail for a drug offence from Friday night. This should ensure he's kept in custody for a good long time.'

She climbed in and leant her head against the upholstery. It had been a long day, but despite all the drama, in a strange way, it was good to know that some things would never change.

Chapter 42

The motorcycle outrider was the first to show, riding slowly under the stone archway at the entrance to Streatham cemetery. The rider came to a standstill just inside the gates, waiting for the procession to form up behind.

Charlie, Hunter and the team stood upright, in full ceremonial uniform, Hunter's adorned with a clutch of medals pinned to his chest, bright against the dark blue serge of the jacket. The strain had lifted from his shoulders and he stood straight and tall but his cheeks were still ruddy and he had clearly not regained all his previous health. Perhaps the pride in his uniform would be enough to banish the last of the demons that still lurked behind his eyes. She hoped so. Maybe when this day was done they would finally disappear.

Monday morning had dawned warm and bright; far too warm and bright for a funeral. Charlie had been up early to prepare but had still ended up borrowing white gloves and a clean hat from Sabira's ample supply. Nick had arrived at work dead on time, smartly dressed in a pristine uniform, saying

456

little about his absence over the weekend. He had spent fifteen minutes alone with Hunter, exiting the office tight-lipped, leaving the whole team curious as to what had been said. Charlie in particular had been keen to know the content of the conversation but soon put it to the back of her mind, concentrating instead on the forthcoming funeral.

This was the first church service of the four she would be attending as part of the investigation team, but this was also the one in which she was, by far, the most emotionally invested. She had been there for Tina Ashton, helping her through the first days of her bereavement and the birth of baby Bryony and updating her the previous morning on the outcome of her case. As the wife of a serving police officer, Tina would remain supported by the service, but on a personal level Charlie had made several promises to her, one of which was to stay in touch as long as her new friend needed.

A car door slammed by the entrance gate and she looked up to see Tina, Bobby, Emily and Brian's wider family members emerge from several funeral limousines and take up their position behind the hearse carrying Brian's body. His mother, two sisters and four nephews were there, along with his ex-wife, Lorna, and Max, his son from their marriage. There had been no rancour or recriminations, nor would there be. All were present to pay their respects, regardless of what had happened in the previous years.

Charlie looked to her side and shuffled slightly into position. Along each edge of the driveway leading to the old stone cemetery chapel stood a line of policemen and women shoulder to shoulder, some in plain clothes but most dressed in freshly pressed uniforms with shoes gleaming, badges polished and white gloves. Some were older, well used to attending police funerals; others were young, the shock of a colleague and friend's murder still raw. Most knew Brian Ashton and had worked with him, Sabira included, but some were there to show solidarity, the death of a fellow officer almost as distressing as the death of a family member.

As she waited, Brian's coffin was lifted on to the shoulders of six of his closest colleagues, to be carried slowly and reverently into the chapel. Charlie straightened at the spectacle. This wasn't her first job funeral but the sight of the coffin, decorated with a dark blue cloth embroidered with the Metropolitan Police emblem and the dead officer's helmet lying pride of place atop, always brought a lump to her throat.

The procession started to move towards them and the guard of honour stood to attention. A lone man hovered by the gates to the cemetery and she recognised the figure of Carl Hookham. He wouldn't be coming in, but Tina had explained that a mediation session, arranged as a condition of dropping the burglary case had given him the opportunity to explain in a calm, unbiased setting exactly what steps he had taken to better care for his children. Tina in turn now understood how important it was to him for his children to keep his surname. That sorted, their relationship had improved significantly and, as a result, he would be nearby during the service in case it all got too much for Bobby and Emily.

She watched as the funeral procession wound its way closer, a large bouquet of pale blue blooms and white lilies in the shape of 'Dad' lying adjacent to the helmet, a poignant reminder of the short amount of time Brian Ashton had played the role. Tina had their baby strapped tightly to her bosom in a sling, and held the hands of Bobby and Emily as they made their way slowly behind. Whether the allegation against him was true or false was now of no consequence. His death had put an end to that. Whatever the truth, he hadn't deserved to die, and as she watched his coffin slowly transported towards the chapel, the fragility of life was forcefully brought home to every person there. While she still hoped Brian Ashton hadn't fallen prey to temptation, Charlie understood that anything he had done was for the family that now followed on behind. Some police officers went astray, some weakened, some used their position for their own gain but, like her, the majority stood firm, their desire to do what was right and serve their communities the force that drove them onwards.

Tina was dressed in black, tears running silently down her cheeks but she walked tall, her pride in her husband unflinching. Bryony, the baby Brian had never seen, slept soundly in the sling, while Emily cried quietly, constantly looking towards her mother for reassurance. Tina unclasped her hand and pulled her daughter towards her body, her fingers gently stroking the little girl's shoulder. Only Bobby remained dry-eyed, his eyes alight as he looked from one officer to another.

Charlie watched as police officers in the line started to weep, remaining to attention but allowing the tears to flow, unashamed and unwilling to break ranks to wipe them away. As the solid oak door was pulled shut behind the last mourner, the commitment of each and every officer to Brian Ashton's memory was already taking effect. Tina, Lorna, Bobby, Emily, Max and Bryony had been accepted into the police family; the thin blue line might have lost one member, but it had gained another six.

*

'So, what did Brenda Leach say when she had you trapped in the car?' Charlie held a glass of wine in one hand and a plate containing an assortment of cocktail sausages, vol-au-vents and sandwiches in her other. The service and burial over, friends, family and colleagues had reassembled in the back room of The Bedford public house in Balham to toast Brian's memory. With alcohol flowing, the team had found themselves bunched together in a quiet corner of the room, taking the opportunity to talk through the dramatic events of Hunter's escape in hushed tones. Overhead, the trains rumbled along the same railway line as had shielded Samson Powell while he killed Brian Ashton at the start of the spree, a fact not lost on any of them.

Every member of the team was there, Nick having been brought up to speed briefly with the events of the weekend. If he'd been disappointed at not having played his part, he wasn't showing it.

'She said that she was looking forward to watching me die and that I was an arrogant bastard who reminded her of her father.' Hunter shrugged nonchalantly. 'She hated her father. She would have liked to have killed him too, but he drank himself to death a good few years ago.'

'Any particular reason why she wanted to kill him?' Naz shook her head.

'Because he was a policeman who used to beat her and her mother up regularly. She claimed he used to delight in making their lives hell. He would lock them in the house so they couldn't escape and taunt her mother with stories of his affairs with other women. If her mother argued, he would knock her to the floor and kick her until she was black and blue; and if Leach tried to help, he would do the same to her. In the end, she found her mother dead at the bottom of the stairs and her father looking down from the top, laughing. He claimed the death was accidental and got his mates in the force to cover for him but Leach never believed his story. She believes he literally got away with murder.'

'So, what's the significance of the rose at each scene? It certainly wasn't to symbolise romance.' Charlie had been mulling this question over all of the previous day.

'I don't know and I don't think we ever will. She never mentioned it once in the car, but seeing as she clung on to it even when she fell, it's obviously hugely important to her. She'll talk about the violence, but the significance of the rose is a secret that is buried too deep even for her to share.'

'Why didn't she and her mother get help?' Naz was still incensed by the talk of domestic violence.

'Probably because in those days police didn't take domestic abuse seriously,' Bet answered. 'I should know. I had similar problems when I was young. What happened behind closed doors stayed behind closed doors!'

'Even more so when the guilty party was a police officer.' Hunter shook his head. 'By the sound of it he got away with the lot; had carte blanche to do exactly as he wanted because no other police officer wanted to nick one of their own. She grew to hate all police. She said that she has spent all her life planning her revenge. It was chilling listening to her talk. She was so calm; speaking about how she'd deliberately worked in churches, hospitals and prisons in order to select her followers.'

'And so the young girl who was born with a predisposition to antisocial traits became a full-blown psychopath because of her violent and controlling father.' The others were staring at Charlie. 'I wondered why such an outwardly well-educated and successful woman could do the things she has, but you're right, she was calm and seemed almost friendly when she interviewed me. Anna Christophe, Ben's shrink, told me a bit about what makes serial killers tick. Leach must be a high-functioning psychopath, able to recognise weaknesses and vulnerabilities in others and use them. She chose Samson Powell because he was strong, like her, but had the one fatal flaw she could use to exert control: his weakness towards his mother, Delilah, or anyone that looked like her. And she chose Ross Naylor because he was the opposite; so weak and petrified that he could be easily manipulated and deserted.'

'Which was why she kept repeating how clever and loyal he was and how perfectly they worked together.' Hunter took a swig of ale. 'She had no intention of letting him know she was about to fly to the other side of the world, to a country with no extradition treaties, where she would disappear forever.'

'Until Hayley Boyle put two and two together.' Charlie put her wine down and took a bite of a sandwich. 'That was perfect timing. What's going to happen to her?'

'She'll be moved to a different department and probably disciplined for a few minor offences under the Data Protection Act. She's been stupid and naive rather than malicious. Leach, as a member of the IPCC already had access to the complaints, so Boyle, in her efforts to be helpful, only really assisted with the most recent updates and the officers' day-to-day activities. I'm sure Leach could have found out their movements herself, given the way officers leave themselves open on social media these days and never change their regular routines, but there's no doubt Boyle made it easier.'

'But she ended up taking a bullet and saving our lives.'

'And she'll be recognised for that. Oh, and by the way, her husband found the spreadsheet that she thought she'd lost; it turned up in a different file, so she needn't have worried about Shirley Sangster having access to the details… but it'll teach her to be more careful in future.'

'And her arm will be OK?' Bet asked.

'Yes. She's been discharged already.' Hunter smiled. 'She will make a full recovery, unlike Leach. The medical update on her is that her injuries are not going to be life-threatening, but thanks to Charlie's ability to appeal to down-and-outs, she'll hopefully spend what's left of her life locked up. Ross Naylor has already started talking.' He stopped and raised his pint of ale. 'And he's taught me a valuable lesson too. Don't bottle things up. It's good to talk.' He raised his glass. 'Enough said. Cheers! Here's to talking more.'

They all raised their glasses, taking a gulp of their favourite tipple before Paul lunged forward, grabbed a sausage from Charlie's plate and popped it straight into his mouth. He grinned mischievously.

'Talking about gossip, Sabira. What's going on with you and that acid attack victim? Naz says you've got a bit of a soft spot for her.'

They all swung around towards Sabira, Charlie slapping Paul on the hand. Sabira sunk down in her seat mortified at the spotlight, but brightened within seconds as Naz elbowed her.

'Preet and I just get on well,' she smiled. 'Nothing's happened, or is going to happen, until her case is concluded, but it was the reason she didn't want to get married. She always liked girls, but as we all know, our culture doesn't allow relationships between two women.'

Charlie raised her glass again. 'Here's to a time when it does then.'

They all took another sip before Nick piped up. 'And she's not too badly scarred by the acid, I presume?' They all knew exactly what he was getting at.

Sabira shook her head. 'You're sad, Nick Arrowsmith. Most of the acid hit her neck and shoulder, so her face is not too badly affected, but even if it was, she'd still be a beautiful person.'

'Looks aren't everything,' Charlie agreed.

'They are in my book,' Nick grinned. 'Which is why today I've handed in my papers and am taking up the offer of working as a car salesman in a Porsche showroom, near to where I live.'

'Nothing to do with not being able to handle the banter of an ageing crack addict then?' Paul chuckled.

'Or not coming in on time?' Naz joined in.

'Or not coming in at all?' Bet huffed. They had all been sickened by his refusal to answer his phone and join the team when the crunch came.

'Or using up your last life,' Sabira looked towards Hunter for confirmation but got none. What had been said in the privacy of Hunter's office before the funeral was clearly going to remain confidential and discreet, although they could all imagine the gist of the conversation. Hunter had bided his time, but Nick's had run out. It was obvious to them all, Nick had either chosen to jump before he was pushed, or to claim that he had, but Hunter was remaining professionally tight-lipped.

Nick shrugged. 'You'll never know,' he grinned again before heading for the bar. Any criticism would go straight over his head. Keeping up appearances was all that mattered to him.

Charlie watched him as he leant towards the young barmaid, his shoulders square, his shirtsleeves tight against his biceps. His behaviour had subconsciously helped to confirm a decision that, until now, she'd been putting off.

'In my book, giving a shit about the job you do and the people around you is what counts.' She glanced round at each of her friends in turn before stopping at Hunter. 'Tell me you've made it up with Mrs H?'

Hunter chewed on his lip and looked down, before tilting his head to one side and winking mischievously. 'She's only gone and booked two weeks in Spain for us, flying into Barcelona from Heathrow, Terminal 3.' He feigned a frightened face. 'We won't be using that car park though when we go. I don't ever want to be reminded of Ms Brenda Leach or the IPCC again.'

'And you won't have to be,' DCI Declan O'Connor clapped a hand on Hunter's shoulder, before raising a half-empty pint glass in a toast. 'It was confirmed to me this morning that the investigation into your complaint is officially closed. Ms Leach was only keeping it going for her own malicious reasons. You have been exonerated of any misconduct and your decision-making has been praised. You did nothing wrong and everything right.'

Charlie raised her glass as the team celebrated with muted good cheer. They were all still painfully aware of the reason they were there.

'Told you so,' she touched glasses with her boss, noticing immediately the Hunter of old had returned.

'I'll let you have that one for free,' he smiled back. 'But don't expect to be telling me what to do when I get back from holiday.'

She put her glass down and stepped away, smiling. Nick was watching the group from where he stood, oblivious to the barmaid's chatter. She thought she read a hint of sadness, envy even, before he turned away on catching her eye. Checking her watch, she looked up and saw Tina Ashton standing on her own by the window. There had been one thing missing from the funeral that had to be put right.

'Guys, please excuse me,' she said, backing away. 'I have one last thing I need to do.'

*

It wasn't long before she recognised the tall, lean figure of Ben. She watched him fondly as he loped towards where she sat on a fallen tree trunk on the common. He looked fresher than he had been more recently, but that still couldn't disguise the lack of life in his eyes.

She got up and went towards him, pulling gently on the lead in her hand.

'Come on, old boy,' she bent down, stroking Casper softly on the head. 'Meet your new master.'

Ben stared at Charlie for an instant before dropping to his knees and running his hands over the black Labrador's body, nuzzling his head carefully, before looking up questioningly at the large patch of short fur on his belly that still hadn't quite grown back.

'I'll explain everything on our way. Come on. This is Casper, but there's somewhere we need to take him first.'

She passed the lead to Ben and they started to walk, slowly and steadily, immersed in conversation, Ben stopping to encourage Casper onwards every now and again, his joy at the dog's progress palpable. When eventually they passed through the stone arch of the cemetery and got to their destination, they lapsed into silence. The hole had been filled and the family's flowers arranged thoughtfully around the edge. A small wooden cross with a name engraved on a gold plaque was the only thing that denoted whose body lay beneath the mound of freshly dug earth.

Charlie bent down and unclipped the lead and they watched as the old dog moved closer to the grave, his muzzle nudging at the soil, sniffing and whimpering quietly. It was as if he instantly knew the significance of the mound and recognised the familiar scent of his beloved master. After a few minutes, he pawed a small hole in the soil and laid down, his head resting against the fresh earth.

Charlie and Ben watched as he closed his eyes, his breath slowing as his body relaxed. They sat down on a nearby bench, neither needing or wanting to break the silence, and gave their own thoughts free rein.

Understanding came at a price. For Charlie it had meant choosing a career that helped others achieve their own justice. For Brenda Leach it had meant a lifetime of hatred, plotting her own revenge. She didn't yet know whether Ben would make the positive choice, or the negative.

They sat for over an hour before Ben eventually stood and whispered Casper's name. The dog lifted his snout and heaved himself up on to his feet, leaving the soil still clinging to his head and body. He shuffled across and sat in front of Ben, who bent towards him, clipping the lead to his collar but leaving the dusting of earth on his fur.

'It's important you take your memories with you, Casper, but gradually as you move forward they'll fall away.' He took Charlie by the hand and pulled her to her feet, slinging his free arm around her shoulder, before bending down towards the dog again. 'You'll still need to come and revisit your past regularly and I promise to bring you back every day at first, then weekly, then monthly, until you're ready to move on. We'll do this together, old boy.'

Ben started to walk, Charlie and Casper keeping in step with him. As they passed through the graveyard and out under the heavy stone arch he gave Charlie's shoulder a squeeze. 'And one day, sooner rather than later, I guarantee, we'll both be ready.'

Charlie lifted her hand and placed it on top of his, feeling the slight quiver of his fingers against her palm. She squeezed his hand gently in return. That was all she needed to know.

We hope you enjoyed this book!

Sarah Flint's next book is coming in summer 2018

More addictive fiction from Aria:

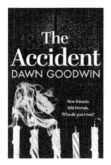 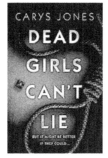 

Find out more
http://headofzeus.com/books/isbn/9781786699633

Find out more
http://headofzeus.com/books/isbn/9781786692504

Find out more
http://headofzeus.com/books/isbn/9781786699015

Acknowledgements

Sometimes in times of adversity comes a seed. The seed for this particular book came to me whilst walking through the fields next to the Kennet and Avon canal in the summer of 2016. It was around the date I decided to retire from the Metropolitan Police Service and was a particularly emotional period for lots of reasons, no less because I had dedicated 35 years of my life to the job I loved and the last few months had taken a toll.

It is a decision that I have not regretted. Sometimes you have to take a leap of faith, to turn something bad, into something good, and adapting to new challenges can be both frightening and exhilarating. I have to say that becoming a *retired* police officer and a full-time author has been inspiring and I now look forward to the years ahead. My heartfelt thanks go to the small group of friends from work that were with me at that time and have remained close. Although we do not see each other so often, you know who you are, and you will always remain important to me. I promise to keep in contact and be there for you too.

I also have to say that I'm sure I was not an easy person to live with or even be around at that time, so special thanks go to my partner Trish and my daughters, Suzie, Jen and Jackie for their continued support and calming influences. You have been my constants in a tumultuous year. Hopefully now domestic tranquillity has been restored.

Extra special thanks also to my great agent Judith Murdoch and inspirational editor and publisher Caroline Ridding and the exceptionally close, enthusiastic team at Aria and Head of Zeus.

Judith, with Nick Walters and Rebecca Winfield have launched my first DC Charlie Stafford novel 'Mummy's Favourite' in Europe, with copies sold to Germany, Poland and the Czech Republic and they continue to spread the word. It's unbelievable to me that other countries would be interested in my writing and I would like to express my sincere thanks to Judith and her team for their faith in me and continued hard work on my behalf.

Caroline Ridding, my superb editor and publisher has endless enthusiasm and sound judgement as well as a loyal, caring and friendly attitude. She, and her team at Aria are a joy to work with and many thanks go to co-workers Sarah Ritherdon, Melanie Price, Nikky Ward, Jade Craddock and Sue Lamprell for all their work on my behalf, as well as Nia Beynon and Yasemin Turan who have moved on to pastures new. Good luck in your new jobs. Thank you so much

Caroline for your continued support – I will try to deliver what you ask for.

Also my appreciation goes to the small group of trusted readers who looked through 'Liar Liar' at its inception and whose feedback helped to mould it towards its final version – your comments and criticisms were greatly appreciated.

Finally, huge thanks to everyone who has bought and read my previous books, 'Mummy's Favourite' and 'The Trophy Taker' and who email, message or leave reviews. I always read your comments with interest and I hope you enjoy following the exploits of Charlie and Hunter, as much as I enjoy writing them. With your endorsement I hope to take them through the next phase of their lives, both professionally and personally and I hope you will share their journey with me.

Thank you so much.

Sarah xx

About Sarah Flint

With a Metropolitan Police career spanning 35 years Sarah Flint has spent her adulthood surrounded by victims, criminals and police officers. She continues to work and lives in London with her partner and has three older daughters.

Find me on Twitter
https://twitter.com/SarahFlint19

Find me on Facebook
https://www.facebook.com/SarahFlintBooks

A Letter from the Author

Hi Everybody,

You've got to the end! Thank you so much for reading my novel and I hope you enjoyed the journey.

As the writer, once my last words are written, edited, re-written, re-edited, proof-read and edited a little more; all I can do is sit back and hope that you have loved reading it, as much as I have enjoyed writing it. If you have a few minutes, please could you post a review of your thoughts on social media – I would really love to read them.

have dealt with crime and criminals all my life and have a fascination for what makes both the law-breakers and the law-makers tick. Sometimes the lines become blurred and justice is a hard thing to achieve; sometimes it is unachievable and victim's lives are blighted by that failing. We can never properly understand but it never stops us wondering.

If you would like to chat further or find out more, feel free to message me on my Facebook page or on Twitter. Just follow the links below.

With love and thanks

Sarah

Find me on Twitter
https://twitter.com/SarahFlint19

Find me on Facebook
https://www.facebook.com/SarahFlintBooks

About the DC Charlotte Stafford Series

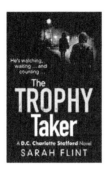

Find out more
http://headofzeus.com/books/isbn/9781786690692

Find out more
http://headofzeus.com/books/isbn/9781786690708

Find out more
http://headofzeus.com/books/isbn/9781786690715

Visit Aria now
http://www.ariafiction.com

Become an Aria Addict

Aria is the new digital-first fiction imprint from Head of Zeus.

It's Aria's ambition to discover and publish tomorrow's superstars, targeting fiction addicts and readers keen to discover new and exciting authors.

Aria will publish a variety of genres under the commercial fiction umbrella such as women's fiction, crime, thrillers, historical fiction, saga and erotica.

So, whether you're a budding writer looking for a publisher or an avid reader looking for something to escape with – Aria will have something for you.

Get in touch: aria@headofzeus.com

Become an Aria Addict
http://ariafiction.com/newsletter/subscribe

Find us on Twitter
https://twitter.com/Aria_Fiction

Find us on Facebook
http://www.facebook.com/ariafiction

Find us on BookGrail
http://www.bookgrail.com/store/aria/

Addictive Fiction

Aria
c/o Head of Zeus
First Floor East
5–8 Hardwick Street
London EC1R 4RG

www.ariafiction.com

Printed in Great Britain
by Amazon

60605539R10281